C000212828

BRUTAL
ARRANGEMENT

BRUTAL
ARRANGEMENT

NEW YORK TIMES BESTSELLING AUTHOR
LAURELIN PAIGE

ALSO BY LAURELIN PAIGE

WONDERING WHAT TO READ NEXT? I CAN HELP!

Visit www.laurelinpaige.com for content warnings and a more detailed reading order.

Brutal Billionaires

Brutal Billionaire - a standalone (Holt Sebastian)

Dirty Filthy Billionaire - a novella (Steele Sebastian)

Brutal Secret - a standalone (Reid Sebastian)

Brutal Arrangement - a standalone (Alex Sebastian)

The Dirty Universe

Dirty Duet (Donovan Kincaid)

Dirty Filthy Rich Men | Dirty Filthy Rich Love

Kincaid

Dirty Games Duet (Weston King)

Dirty Sexy Player | Dirty Sexy Games

Dirty Sweet Duet (Dylan Locke)

Sweet Liar | Sweet Fate

(Nate Sinclair) Dirty Filthy Fix (a spinoff novella)

Dirty Wild Trilogy (Cade Warren)

Wild Rebel | Wild War | Wild Heart

Sex Symbol

Star Struck

Dating Season

Spring Fling | Summer Rebound | Fall Hard

Winter Bloom | Spring Fever | Summer Lovin

Also written with Kayti McGee under the name Laurelin McGee

Miss Match | Love Struck | MisTaken | Holiday for Hire

Written with Sierra Simone

Porn Star | Hot Cop

Be sure to **sign up for my newsletter** where you'll receive **a FREE book every month** from bestselling authors, only available to my subscribers, as well as up-to-date information on my latest releases.

PRO TIP: Add laurelin@laurelinpaige.com to your contacts before signing up to be sure the list comes right to your inbox.

DID YOU KNOW...
This book is available in both paperback and audiobook editions at all major online retailers! Links are on my website.
If you'd like to order a signed paperback, my online store is open several times a year here.

I am an only child, but my mother came from a big family like the Sebastians. All those members can be confusing.

To help sort that out, you can find a family tree on my website.

For every Good Girl who would rather be Bad.

CHAPTER
ONE
RIAH

The only thing worse than having bad style is having no style.

At least that's what my manager, Claude, seems to think. And my boyfriend, apparently, since he decided it was important enough to warrant flying from New York to his Malibu house for an emergency meeting to discuss it.

Though, he can't think it's *that* important since he disappeared to take a phone call ten minutes after we arrived. He didn't stay long enough to see the rebrand options that Claude had his team draw up.

Not like he's missing anything. They're a real snoozefest.

Or maybe I'm out of touch because Claude seems really excited about them. "I like this look, personally." He points to an AI-rendered version of me looking like I stepped out of an episode of the *Gilmore Girls*. "Girl next door. Real down to earth. Kind of a brunette Madilyn Bailey. We could try to set up a duet with her, even."

I glance over at my sister, Whitney, who doesn't look up from her phone, but her eyebrows raise, and I'm sure she has capital T—Thoughts.

"I'm not sure." I wish I had a better instinct for branding. "Does Madilyn Bailey really match the vibe of my latest material? You do realize 'Finger Painting' is about alone time."

Claude isn't fazed. "Colbie Caillat's *Bubbly* song is about a full-body orgasm. You can have a good girl image and sing the dirty songs just fine."

"Really? That's what that song's about?" I mentally skim through the lyrics that talk about feeling good from head to toe. *Huh. Who knew?* "Regardless, I don't really think that's my sound."

"So we rough the look up." Pushing the image aside, he reveals another version of me, this one with a blunter haircut and vampy makeup. "We'll get you on a song with Olivia Rodrigo instead. She's higher profile, too. Better for your career."

I bite back a laugh. "Olivia Rodrigo isn't going to do a duet with me."

When I was coming off a hit record in my teens, maybe she would have, but not now. Turns out you can't take four years off in this business to raise your sister and expect to find an audience waiting. The comeback album I released two years ago was practically a flop, and I'm pretty sure my label would have dropped me from my contract if Hunter hadn't come onto the scene.

"Sure, she will. You have influence now."

first time I looked at them. "Can I have some time to think about these?"

"Of course." He stands and buttons his sports jacket. "It's late, anyway. I'll leave these, so you can look them over more and see if something jibes."

We say our goodbyes, and only after he's left do I notice he's left the folder with the rejected images. I push aside the punk version and pick up the other. In it, I'm wearing thigh-high spike-heeled boots, dark eye shadow, see-through panties, and pasties. I don't even know if I would have the guts to wear something so revealing in public, but maybe if I classed it up just a tad…

"Don't waste your time. They're all shit."

I look up to find Alex headed toward me. I haven't forgotten he's been here, working at the kitchen table all night. After nine months of dating his brother, I should be used to him being around. He's a shadow dressed in a suit, often traveling with Hunter for who knows what reason—because they're used to each other? Because it's what they've always done? Because Hunter expects an entourage?

Whatever the reason, his presence often gets under my skin. Particularly because it's led to more than one unasked-for opinion. I usually try to be nice—girl-next-door nice, even—because it's not like I can afford to alienate my boyfriend by telling his brother to shove it.

He's right, but his unwanted feedback prickles. "How can you say that? You haven't even seen them."

Unless Claude sent the images to him as well, which frankly, at this point, wouldn't surprise me.

"Didn't need to. Brunette Madilyn Bailey? I'm bored already."

"They aren't *all* shit. Some of them have potential."

He grabs a Coke from the beverage refrigerator and brings it with him to the counter, opposite me. Then he pours some into my wineglass.

I take a swallow of the concoction. Finally, it's drinkable.

He's annoying as fuck, but at least he can remember I prefer my wine diluted when his brother can't. Not that I'm with Hunter for the details. And Alex strikes me as someone who is just more observant in general.

"What, like this one?" He picks up the image I had just been looking at. It almost seems like his eyes darken, but then he lets out a laugh. "You couldn't pull it off."

So it's one thing to not have confidence in myself about something, but it's an entirely different thing to have some asshat decide my limits for me. "Thanks for the faith. You haven't seen me try."

"Some things you just know." He takes a swallow from the Coke can.

"No. No. You don't know that." *I* don't know it. How the hell can he? "It might be different from what I was doing before, but that's the whole idea behind a rebrand. Mr. VP of Commercial Strategy, you should know all about that, shouldn't you? Isn't image creation what you're all about? It's all smoke and mirrors. Makeup and costume."

He tilts his head and appears to weigh whether or not I'm worth the time it will take him to explain. "Selling industrial tech isn't quite the same as selling popular music, but in all marketing, there has to be at least a kernel of truth, or you'll lose customers. And this isn't you."

CHAPTER
TWO
RIAH

The next morning, I spot Hunter on the deck post-morning workout, with his cup of coffee and tablet, catching up on SNC's latest news feed, if I know him.

His side of the bed wasn't slept in, which isn't anything new. As charismatic as he is, he's also fond of his solitude, and it isn't unusual for him to spend nights in the guest room.

It probably says something about our relationship that I'm not bothered by sleeping alone. Maybe it just means I like my solitude too. In that case, we're the perfect match.

But there's a knot in my stomach as I open the glass door and go out to join him. The phone call that took him away last night might not bother me so much if I didn't feel bloated and PMS-y this morning. The very epitome of unsexy in my T-shirt and baggy sweatpants pajamas. Alex's words are a haunting refrain running through my head. *You couldn't pull it off.*

So of course, I'm convinced Hunter spent the night in someone else's panties. I've summoned up the courage to call him out on it, but when I reach him, he's the one who speaks first. "I got Jake Dunham."

"What?" Admittedly, I haven't had my morning dose of caffeine, but I can't for the life of me figure out why my boyfriend is bringing up the ten-time Grammy winner producer and star maker of dozens.

He takes off his sunglasses, and his eyes are lit with triumph. "Jake fucking Dunham, Zy. He wants to produce."

Just like that, my pulse goes soaring. "Jake Dunham?" I drop into the deck chair, my knees unable to support myself. "He wants to produce...*me*?"

It's unfathomable. Even when I was at the height of my career, I didn't have what it takes to interest the likes of Jake. He's picky about who he works with, and for good reason. Everything he's touched has turned to gold. He wouldn't want to break his track record with someone who doesn't have the chops.

Which is why I still can't comprehend what Hunter is telling me. "Are you sure?"

He laughs. "Yes, I'm fucking sure. Do you think I would tease you with something as serious as this? He's going to turn your life around, Zyah."

He says it like it's fact because it's pretty much impossible to work with Jake and not have a hit. Even if the material is mediocre, the man commands attention, so yeah. Working with Jake means things could definitely change.

But Jake wouldn't even know who I am if not for Hunter.

"Holy shit, Hunter." Gratitude is such a one-eighty from what I was feeling when I first stepped out onto the deck. "How on earth did you get him?"

He tosses his tablet on the table and gives me his infamous self-confident smirk. "I knew how to speak his language."

Money. It has to be money. Or what money can buy. That's Hunter's not-at-all-secret weapon. Does Jake even like my music? Has he even heard it?

As if he can read my mind, Hunter leans forward to reassure me. "Stop, Zy. He's heard your latest demo reel, and he's into it. He wants to work with you."

"For real? I don't want to be some pity—"

"Like Jake Dunham is going to take on someone he doesn't believe in. You think he's going to fuck up his whole reputation to make a pity record? Not happening. But before it's a done deal, you can meet him and audition him."

"*Me* audition *him*." I can't help but laugh.

"He's hosting a big party tonight. He invited us over, so you can meet and play around a bit in his studio."

I've seen pictures of Jake's private studio. It's the real deal. Lady Gaga laid down tracks for her latest there. Nikki Minaj did her whole album in his B studio.

I honestly don't know what to say. Which is why my mind goes to the most unimportant details first. "Will he come out to New York to record?" We're technically only supposed to be here through the weekend, and since Hunter is gearing up to get the CEO job at his family's media corporation, I know he won't want to extend our stay on the West Coast so I can knock out an entire record.

But Hunter waves his hand like it's no biggie. "He only records in his space. You'll be okay if I head back to Manhattan? There's a board meeting next week, and I need to be there in person."

"Yeah, yeah. Of course." It's understandable, but it feels disappointing. Like a hand-off.

It doesn't help that Hunter adds, "It will be like the old days."

The *old days* when I was only his West Coast Girlfriend. He put me up in this house, and whenever he was in town, he poured all his focus on me. I didn't ask questions about when he was gone, but Hunter Sebastian's harem of women has always been a favorite topic of the paparazzi, so it wasn't like I didn't know.

I knew before I even started dating him. It was clear from our very first night that that would be the arrangement, and since my eyes were open going in, I was okay with it.

It was actually a pretty good deal for me. I was fresh off a recording disaster. I had no college degree and no alternate plans for a career. My experience with men was limited, having spent my early twenties raising Whit, and I was eager for something new and exciting. Having someone take care of me, for once—a hot as fuck billionaire, no less—was enticing. I didn't even mind sharing. He's always been adamant about using condoms, and the time he spent with his other women meant more time for Whitney and my music.

As an added bonus, as soon as I began appearing in

public with Hunter, my sales began to pick up. It was an arrangement that worked well for both of us.

Then, five months into our relationship, he came to me with a new proposal.

He wanted the CEO job at his family's news corp, and after some scandal involving his cousin who previously held the position, he thought his image might be improved if he cleaned up his playboy ways. No more girlfriends on every coast—he picked me to be exclusive.

Maybe I was fooling myself when I thought I didn't mind sharing because the past four months have been really good. Not swept-off-my-feet, head-over-heels-in-love good, but it turns out that monogamy is for me.

At risk of souring the conversation, I tip-toe toward clarification. "But not *exactly* like the old days."

He looks out over the ocean and takes a swallow of his coffee before he answers. "I think we'd both prefer our reputations remain free from scandal."

It's not the most romantic answer, but I suppose romance isn't in Hunter's repertoire, so I try to be encouraged.

Of course, that's when Alex decides to walk out onto the lower deck for his morning swim. My entire body tenses at the sight of him. Rationally, I know that he isn't entirely the source of my irritation, but he's an easy target since I've decided he's a class-A dick. "Is Alex going back to New York, too?"

"Why wouldn't he?" Hunter sounds distracted, and without looking over at him, I can tell he's gone back to his tablet.

Below us, Alex steps out on the diving board and dives in headfirst, barely making any splash.

It's annoying how expertly he moves his body through the water. He obviously has no problem owning his sexuality. White, rich, man—attractive to boot—he probably thinks he's a god.

I bring my feet up so they're on the edge of the chair and rest my chin on my knees. "Why did he even come with us in the first place?"

"He likes to be around me. He has since he was a kid." There's a shrug in Hunter's voice.

"Isn't that weird? He's like...what? Thirty-six? Thirty-seven?"

"Thirty-five."

I twist my head to look at Hunter. It takes him a second, but he finally feels the pressure of my eyes.

With a sigh, he sets the tablet down again. "I don't know. He's a month away from inheriting his trust fund, which will be good for him because he won't have to keep working with Dad at the Industrial Corp. But getting money in a lump sum can be overwhelming."

"Oh. I'm sure it's the worst."

"When you haven't seen your mother since you were eight because she accepted a paycheck to never see you again?"

His delivery is casual, but it drops a bomb on my chest. "Fuck. That happened to you?"

Hunter so rarely talks about his upbringing. I've always suspected it was bad, but not mother-abandoned-him bad.

"To *him*. We have different mothers."

"Oh." My gaze returns to Alex, and I'm feeling some

sort of way I can't explain. Compassionate, I suppose, but also fuck that. He's still a dick. "That's terrible. It is. But he's had money his whole life. Is it really traumatizing to be given more? And I don't get why he hangs around you all the time because of it."

"I don't know, Zyah. It's not like we have heart-to-hearts over a bottle of wine about it. I'm guessing here. He started tailing after me when she left, and he's been tailing me more recently, so I did the math. I make him feel grounded or something."

And I'm sure Hunter hasn't ever complained because he's the kind of guy who likes an entourage.

"Anyway, fuck about Alex. Are you going to be cool with Jake if I'm not here?"

"Believe it or not, I made albums before you came around."

"I'm trying to help."

God, he is. And he's delivered the best gift an artist could ask for. So why do I feel so prickly about it?

Again, I hear Alex's voice in my head. *You of all people seem to understand transactional relationships.*

Hunter must see something in my expression or sense something from my energy because he pushes his chair back so there's room between him and the table. "Come here."

Without hesitation, I crawl onto his lap.

"You know I have every faith in you," he says, wrapping his arms around me. "I wouldn't have set you up with the best in the biz if I didn't think you were up for it."

"I know. I appreciate it. I'm just in a mood today, I guess."

"You're going to kill this."

"Thank you."

It strikes me, though, that he assumes what's bothering me most is a crisis of confidence in my work—which is part of it—and not our relationship.

Would it really hurt for him to say he'll miss me? That he'll call? That he'll fly back a few times while I'm recording to visit?

Next thing I know, I'm back to thinking about his phone call last night. There's a good chance it was Jake he was talking to then. Hunter's nothing if not honest. If I ask; he'll tell me.

I'm just not sure I want to know.

So I settle for a passive-aggressive remark instead. "We could have used your input last night. We didn't settle on any of the looks."

"Yeah, Claude told me." I'm tilted to the side as he shifts to grab his phone out of the pocket of his lounge pants. He swipes and types with one hand then shows me a pic. "I told him we should go with this."

I cup my hand, so I can see the screen without the sun's glare. It's not the girl next door image, thankfully. It's probably the classiest of the looks that Claude's team worked up, actually. Mature, responsible. Wife and mother material. It's a wise move to follow my angsty teen era.

But I'm stuck on fucking Alex Sebastian and all the shit things he said to me last night.

Taking the phone from Hunter's hand, I scroll forward a few pics, assuming he's downloaded all that were sent.

Sure enough, four images later is the dirtied-up version. "You didn't consider this one?"

He chuckles. "For the bedroom, sure."

"It would attract attention, though. That's what we want, right?"

"The wrong kind of attention."

It's strange to think he's the same man I started dating nine months ago. He was the dirtiest of boyfriends when I met him, and fuck if he cared what the media thought.

Logically, I know he has different priorities now, but can a man really change that much? Is that really the only reason he's pushing me away from this option? Or is he worried I'll embarrass him if I go this route? "Is it because you don't think I can pull it off?"

"What do you mean, pull it off?"

"Like, do you think I'm not sexy enough to present myself like this?"

He twists so he's facing me. "What are you talking about? This is easy. Anyone can do this. It's a gimmick. You're above it. You don't need the tricks. You have the talent. Let your music sell you. You don't need this shit."

He never actually answered the question, but I know he's trying to make me feel better. It's a traditional sentiment. Be the woman a man marries, not the woman that he dicks around with. That's supposed to be the dream, isn't it?

It *is* the dream.

It's safe, and safe is stable, and that's what I need right now. Not big-time risks. Grown-up, classy, mature—that's a solid vibe. Hell, I should be honored that Hunter thinks I can pull *that* off. What anyone else thinks shouldn't fucking matter.

Again, my eyes drift down to Alex in the pool below. At

the end of his lap, he pauses at the edge and wipes the water from his face with his palm.

Despite the self-pep talk and Hunter's arms around me, I'm still irritated. At the things he hasn't said as much as the things that his brother has said, so when Alex looks up and catches my eye, I can't help myself—I flip him off.

In response, the fucker lifts his chin and grins.

CHAPTER
THREE
RIAH

J ake Dunham, it turns out, isn't into people.

At least, that's the word amongst his guests as Hunter and I make our way through the packed crowd to get to Jake's pool-house-turned-studio, our destined meeting spot. Apparently, he's been holed up there all night. This huge party is raging on his premises, and he's insulated with drywall and soundproof paneling because though he's "inspired by chaos, he prefers to be *near* it, not part of it."

I haven't even officially met him, and I already know he's my kind of guy.

As eager as I am to get to our meeting, it takes us the better part of an hour to get from the front door to the studio door because Hunter has to stop to charm everyone he knows, and he knows anyone who's anyone, and anyone who's anyone and currently in L.A. appears to be at this party.

It's Hunter's type of scene—not mine. I prefer smaller gatherings. It's why I'm not much of a concertgoer unless I'm the one performing. I'd much rather watch a show on my couch where my personal space is respected, and I can actually hear more than the bass line.

So despite how nervous I am to meet *the* Jake Dunham, it's a relief when we finally leave behind the clamor and step into the quiet of his studio, especially when I have a feeling I'm about to meet a man after my own introverted heart.

"You can call me Riah, though," I say after Hunter intros me as Zyah. "Sorry, we weren't here sooner. There's a...lot going on out there." I wonder if he's aware that there's a full-on orgy happening in his hot tub.

"Yeah, yeah. Sure." Jake's attitude is as mellow as his attire. Like, I saw guests dressed in outfits fit for a red carpet, and he's in faded jeans and a plain blue T-shirt. The man is seriously chill. "Did you get a chance to enjoy yourselves first? Visit the caviar bar or the toke room?"

Not only is he one of the foremost geniuses in the biz, he's apparently also the perfect host.

"Uh...I'm good. Thanks." There's nowhere else I'd rather be, in fact, especially when I realize it's my tune that's coming from the cans around his neck. "Is that...?"

"I was messing with the chords on "Tasted." Here, I'll put it over the speakers." He bends over the soundboard, flicks a button, and suddenly my song fills the room.

My song, but different.

My song, but *better*. "Oh, fuck...did you sub F# minor there?"

He nods. "It adds flavor, right?"

The beat takes over my body as excitement floods through me. "It adds everything."

I've already practically forgotten Hunter's in the room, so it's more distracting than considerate when he excuses himself. "Looks like you're set. I'm going to check out that caviar bar. Text me if you need anything."

"Thanks for the hook-up, H.S.," Jake says.

"Zyah?"

"Good. It's good. Good." I'm too focused on the music to give him anything more, which I know is shitty because Hunter's the reason I'm about to have the best night of my career. I'll owe him a blowjob. Or anal. Whatever. There's no doubt he deserves it.

But right now, he's the last thing on my mind. I don't even hear the door shut behind him. "What do you think if we layered an electronic bass to that?" I ask. "Like a boom, boom, boom, boom—just on the verses."

"Sort of hip-hop inspired." It's not a question. He nods in agreement.

"With a Lana Del Rey vibe."

He uses his mouse to select earlier in the track, and the next time the verse comes around, he plays something into the sampler. Not quite what I'd been imagining, but it's close and maybe even better. "Pull the tempo back. Do you think?"

He slows the song and starts back at the beginning. "Yeah, that's something."

This time, the transition to the chorus gives me chills. I start singing over the accompaniment.

"I wanted the boy to love me...

The candy that I can't put in my mouth,
out of reach, and wasted.
Never been tasted."

When the song comes to an end, Jake's looking at me with intent eyes. Not the kind of eyes that want to get me naked—thank God, because I'm met with those eyes way too often in this biz—but the kind that says we have a connection.

I feel it too. The magic collaboration vibe that only comes once in a lifetime if ever at all.

After a beat, he scans his eyes down my body—still not in a creepy way—as though it's the first time he's really looked at me. "No one's going to believe that sound comes out of that package."

I glance down at my sleeveless cream pantsuit. It's an upscale look. Something I'd wear to the theater or to a fancy job interview, which was what I considered this. An outfit that matches the persona Hunter chose for me just this morning.

I try to see myself through Jake's eyes—my long brown beach waves hair, my nude lip color, my low-heeled sandal —he's looking at the epitome of tame when the sound we just heard has a bit of grit. It's definitely a mismatch.

It's only now that I realize that I have to let the music decide what my look needs to be. "I'm reworking my brand. Haven't landed yet, but this helps."

"I'm into it. I think we've got something sublime. Glad to be on board." He offers his hand.

I take it, and with a simple handshake, I'm working with a music god.

The five-foot-eleven blonde is the epitome of perfection. Nothing on her jiggles. Her impeccably arched brows grow that way. She has beauty and fashion sense and self-esteem for days, from what I've gleaned from those who know her.

She's the absolute last person on earth I want to see right now. My already frail ego can't handle giving her an opportunity to compare us side by side. Sure, I should feel secure since he dumped her in order to be exclusive with me, but I can come up with plenty of excuses for that, which I'm sure are just as obvious to her. Supermodel girlfriends, for one, don't scream cleaned-up image. Especially when the bi-curious Kelsey has indulged in two high-profile threesomes, and those are just the ones the media knows about.

She's a woman who is not only comfortable with her sexuality but owns it, and if I didn't feel so envious and threatened by her existence, I might get on my knees and worship her.

What the hell is she even doing in the States? Isn't Fashion Week coming up?

Needless to say, I continue to watch her through the crack while she applies her bright purple lipstick—who on earth can even pull that off besides her?—and fluffs her already perfect hair.

When she's done and gone, I count to ten before venturing out.

Then I make a mad beeline to the front driveway, where I hide from both Alex and Kelsey while I text Hunter where I am, and that I'm ready to go.

Thankfully, he only takes ten minutes to extricate himself from whatever social interaction he was engaged in, and since he called for the car as soon as I texted, the limo shows up at the same time he does.

"Was it good?" he asks, opening the door for me before the driver has a chance to get out.

I step toward him. "Absolutely amaz—" My words stop short just as I'm about to get in the car.

Because this close to him, it's impossible to miss the very obvious smudge on his collar of bright purple lipstick.

CHAPTER
FOUR
RIAH

wait until the car is moving before I address him. Unless he wants to tell the driver to pull over on Mulholland, he's stuck for this conversation. "Is Kelsey the reason we had to rush out to the coast?"

He looks up from his phone. Probably texting her as we speak. If he's surprised by my accusation, his face doesn't show it. "She's the one who introduced me to Dunham. Don't get your panties twisted."

So he's gaslighting now.

It's unusual since he's the direct type, which maybe is a sign that this relationship actually means something to him.

Unfortunately for him, it's not enough. "Yeah, because you don't have other people who could make an intro with him. And I suspect that she's the one who had her panties twisted." I nod to his lipstick stain. "If there's any chance the ring around your cock matches your collar, I'd think carefully before responding."

His jaw is tense as he pockets his phone. It's nice, I suppose, to have his full attention, but it's a whole lot of too little too late. "Look. It's fine as long as no one knows."

"Excuse me?" I'd braced for a confession, but not a dismissal.

He clarifies. "It's only a problem if the media finds out."

"Uh…no. It's a problem if your girlfriend finds out, and in case it isn't clear, she just did."

"Honestly?" He has the nerve to face me full-on. "I thought you already knew."

Uh…what?

That trip he took to Germany last month pops into my mind. The weeks he spent in London right after the holidays, too. All the times he's been callous and distracted. He was fucking her the whole time.

What's that Maya Angelou phrase? *When someone shows you who they are, believe them.*

How could I ever think he would be faithful? I knew he liked to dick around. Why would he have changed for me?

I thought I was mostly mad, but there's a helluva lot of other emotions warring inside me, not the least of which is humiliation. "I'm such an idiot."

"You know monogamy isn't in my bones. I've been straightforward about that from the beginning."

"And then you said let's be exclusive, and I'm the giant ass fool for thinking you meant it."

"I did mean it. Fuck." He wipes his long hand over his beard. "I tried, Zyah. I did."

"It must have been a torturous four months. It's a wonder you survived."

"Don't be glib."

"I'm not being glib, you prick. I'm being hurt."

He swears again. Under his breath, so I can't make out exactly which curse word it is, but I expect it's another F-bomb. His eyes meet mine.

Surprisingly, my eyes prick. I'm not usually one to cry. Pain is better channeled into songs. Part of my mind is writing even as we sit here. My current work in progress is titled *All Right, Asshole.*

I'm also taking notes for a follow-up called, *Who's the Dummy Here?*

It probably doesn't need saying, but the answer is me.

I turn my head from him and swipe at a stray tear.

"Zyah…" It's so strange to have an intimate discussion with a name that doesn't belong to me, but it's what Hunter's always called me. "You can't tell me you're in love."

I almost want to say it just to prove him wrong.

But he's right. I'm not in love with him.

He's fun—I won't deny that. He's taken me all around the world, brought me into situations I would never have been able to experience on my own. I had dinner at the White House because of him. I met the queen of Denmark.

The sex is great, too, when he's not too tortured to give me the time of day.

But no, I don't love him.

It doesn't mean I don't feel utterly betrayed. We had a partnership. He was my guaranteed plus-one. I trusted him, and he's made me a fool.

I can just see the headlines on the gossip sites. *Girl, Should Have Known.*

An even more distressing thought pops into my head.

"Is Jake even going to want to work with me now?" Claude is going to kill me for losing this connection.

"Why wouldn't he want to work with you? This has nothing to do with…" Hunter's sharp, so it's surprising that it takes him a beat to realize what I thought was obvious. "Come on, Zyah. You aren't suggesting we break up over this."

"How can you possibly think I'd stay with you? You cheated on me."

"It wasn't ch—" He cuts himself off with a laugh. "This was never a traditional relationship. Or actually, that's exactly what this was. Traditional relationships were never about feelings. They were about security and dowries. They were transactional."

Transactional.

There's already a knife in my chest, and with that one word, he twists it. Leave it to Alex to have better insight into my own relationship than I've had. "So that's what this was for you. You give me connections and media attention, and I turn my head while you fuck whoever you feel like fucking."

"You can have side relationships of your own, if that's what you need."

It's my turn to huff. "Uh, thank you so very much for your permission."

"It wasn't permission. It was advice."

"Advice." My hands are balled up so tight that my nails are cutting into my palms. "I don't know how that serves you to have me fucking around. Aren't I supposed to clean up your image? Don't you need me to be a *good girl*?"

"Yes, I'd expect you to be discreet, but—"

"Oh my God, Hunter. No. I'm not interested."

"Zyah. Come on." His tone is laser-focused, determined to win me over. "I've been good to you. You can't say that I haven't."

I throw my hands in the air. "Well, you fucking cheated on me, so…"

He cringes at my choice of words. "Besides this."

"That's not fair. Any awful situation could be framed that way. 'He was amazing except when he beat me.' 'He was the best except that time he stuck me with the knife.'"

"Tell me you aren't comparing cheating with violence. And it's not even cheating, really, because…"

"It's cheating, Hunter. You put your dick in someone else's hole while in an exclusive relationship. It's the very definition of cheating."

"You knew who I was when we started this. I've done everything I've promised. I've taken care of you. I've treated you well—very well—in the bedroom. I've helped with your career. I've opened the door to opportunities. I'm on your side, and you know there are benefits for both of us to keep this relationship going."

I don't know why it hurts so much for him to fight for me like this, but it does. Maybe because it feels like he's declaring this is all I'm worth—transactions and good sex. And not even *that* good sex, otherwise he wouldn't need to get it elsewhere.

No wonder no one thinks I can pull off sexy on stage. I can't even keep my boyfriend interested. How am I supposed to seduce an entire audience?

I'm shame-spiraling, I know, so I force myself to try to be reasonable about his suggestion. Even if I manage to keep Jake as a producer without Hunter, there are other things I'll lose if we break up. The spotlight, for one. It's possible my label will even cancel my album.

But a transactional relationship is the last thing I need for my mental health. I'm already struggling with feeling like an imposter. The worst thing I could do is purposely take on the role of fraud.

It's my ego and my bruised heart that ultimately make the decision. "I can't be in any sort of relationship with you, Hunter. I can't even fucking look at you."

I normally tend to have lousy timing, but the universe must feel I've had it bad enough tonight because the limo pulls up in the driveway right when I can't stomach being in the car a minute longer. "We're going to have to deal with the details of separating over text. I can't be in your presence right now, and I don't want to see you again before you leave for New York."

Pushing open the door before the driver has a chance to get to it, I climb out of the car and rush toward the house, the tears streaming now.

Unfortunately, I don't make it inside before Alex pulls up—there's my usual bad timing at play—and I have to duck my head, so he doesn't see that my face is a mess.

He must see something, though, because he calls after me. "Hey, Riah, what's wrong?"

The asshole almost sounds like he cares.

It's ironic, actually, that he accused me of being the cheater at the very moment his brother was likely balls-deep in Kelsey Kline. I'd point that out if I wasn't on the verge of a gigantic breakdown.

Instead, I ignore him. Behind me, I hear him pose the question to his brother.

"It's nothing," Hunter says, dismissively, which feels about right. "Jet's taking off at seven. You'll be ready?"

I slam the front door behind me before hearing Alex's response, but his answer better be yes. As far as I'm concerned, one Sebastian is the same as another, and I've decided I hate them all.

———

I PAD out to the kitchen the next morning—closer to noon, actually—with a headache and swollen eyes to find Whitney waiting for me.

"Finally! I thought you'd never wake up. I've been dying to hear about Jake Dunham. I can't believe you didn't come to tell me about him last—" She cuts off when she sees my face. "Oh, shit. Did it not go well?"

"Jake went...fine." I'm trying to remember she's an adult, and that I should foster our sisterhood after so many years playing guardian. That means telling her both the highs and lows of the previous evening, and I will.

Right now, I don't have the energy. "Can I fill you in later?" I ask, dropping my phone on the counter. "I need caffeine."

"Uh, sure." It's hard to miss the note of concern in her voice. "There's Coke."

Simultaneously, I open the fridge to discover there's also a bunch of other groceries that weren't there the day before.

"Alex had stuff delivered."

"Huh. That's…" Nice, I guess. I can't bother to give him

that much credit, and I leave the sentence unfinished. I swipe a can and crack it open, too eager to wait for coffee to brew. "The guys are gone?"

"Left before I woke up. Alex left a note."

It's there on the fridge when I close the door. Simple, to the point.

Groceries on the way at ten. -A

"I put them away," she explains.

"Thanks." I stare at Alex's note, wondering what the whole shopping gesture is supposed to mean. Probably, Hunter put him up to it. Another attempt to prove he takes care of me.

"I'm going to miss him," Whit says.

"Hunter?"

"Alex." That makes more sense, considering she has yet to know about my breakup. "He's a decent hang."

"You must know a different Alex than I do," I say as my phone starts vibrating. I glance at the screen and see Claude's name.

Dammit. I'm not ready for this.

But if I don't answer, he'll call Hunter—if he hasn't already—so I pick up. "Hey, can I—?"

Before I can suggest putting off a talk until later in the day, he jumps in. "You got the cover of *Rolling Stone*."

"What? Oh my God. Really?"

"*What?*" mouths Whit.

"*Rolling Stone*," I mouth back. Then into my phone. "How did that happen?"

"Pics hit social media this morning with you and

Hunter at Jake Dunham's place last night and fans are going crazy speculating about a collaboration. Preorders for the album have jumped too. I just got off the phone with the execs at your label, and they're talking about expanding the marketing budget and giving you a real tour. Everything you're doing right now is exactly what you need to be doing."

I let out a half-laugh, half-cry sound. "So not a good time to tell you Hunter and I broke up?"

"What?"

I ignore Whit to focus on Claude. "You're kidding, right? You better be fucking kidding. If you're not kidding, then I don't want to know. You just do what you need to do. Get on your knees. Have a threesome. Whatever it takes to win him back."

I love how he thinks it's me who needs to win him back.

With that thought, I'm hit with morning—afternoon—clarity: Why should I have to pay for Hunter's flaws?

He's not the key to my success. I've succeeded without him before, and I could again, but there's no denying it will be easier with him. I shouldn't have to take the harder path just because he fucked up. Breaking up doesn't make me noble. It makes me stupid.

And yeah, I'm thinking about agreeing to a relationship that is one hundred percent transactional. The only problem with quid pro quo is if I'm holding out hope that we'll turn into something more, and that's not the case. My eyes are wide fucking open. I get to make the decision.

So I make the choice with pride. "Yeah, I'm kidding," I tell Claude. "Definitely kidding."

"Thank God. You had me going for a minute."

You and me, both.

Good thing I pulled my head out of my ass in the nick of time.

"*Rolling* fucking *Stone*," Whit says when I hang up.

"*Rolling* Fucking *Stone*," I say, already texting Hunter.

> I have terms, but I'll do it.

Thankfully, I have several weeks before I have to see him again. Hopefully, by then, I won't be too bitter to play the part. In the meantime, I can focus on my career without his brooding and overbooked social calendar distracting me.

Boyfriend-free is always more productive for my creative process, anyway. Maybe Hunter's wandering dick is a blessing in disguise.

When the message is sent, I turn off notifications. "How about we get out of here and celebrate? I can tell you all about last night."

"About how you and Jake Dunham are going to take over the music world with your combined genius?"

"Yeah. That."

The cool thing? For the first time possibly ever, I actually might believe it.

CHAPTER
FIVE
RIAH

I walk into Spice feeling naked. It's strange to be anywhere without a phone these days, and the rules of the club require all digital devices to be checked in at the door.

On top of that, my outfit is on the skimpy side. The colorful geometric shapes and the material help downplay the fact that I'm basically wearing a short skirt and a bra. It's nothing that will raise eyebrows in this environment—though the early April New York weather has me rethinking my choice—but I'm pretty sure Hunter won't be a fan.

It's probably why I chose it.

Six weeks later, and I swear I'm over him, but I'm not about to give up my grudge.

First thing I notice when I scan the dance floor and tables for a familiar face is that there is a hell of a lot of people here. Technically, Spice is closed for a private event

—Alex's birthday—and Hunter had assured me it would be an intimate gathering. So I thought it would be the perfect place to try out our new relationship arrangement on a small scale before having to put on a face for the masses.

But there are at least two hundred people in the joint. Lots of them famous.

Welp.

Hunter had made arrangements with his brother, the club owner, to soft debut one of my new songs tonight. Now I'm not so sure it was a good idea.

I'm still getting my bearings when I'm literally pounced on by one of Hunter's cousins.

"You made it!" She hugs me like we're close, when in reality we've never spoken.

In fact, I'm not even sure I know her name. "Uh...hi!"

"Adly," she says when she lets go. Her lips are full, her light brown hair is streaked with blonde, and she has brows that most women would kill for. I would kill for them, anyway. Worst part is that I think they're natural. "Do you go by Zyah or...?"

"Riah," I say, pleased to be given the choice. "But I'll answer to whatever."

"Riah. Cool. I'll remember that."

Then she's pulling me toward a group of tables filled with familiar faces. "Everyone's over here. I'll introduce you. I'm Adly, if I didn't say. Did I say? You probably don't remember, but we almost met at Christmas, and I apologize because I'm already terribly drunk, and I don't usually do this, but I have to tell you I'm a fan, and I'd love to feature you on my network."

Despite claiming to be intoxicated, she's poised and none of her words are slurred.

"Oh. Thank you. I didn't realize you had a network."

"She doesn't," someone says. A man who I think is another one of Hunter's cousins.

"Right," Adly confirms. "I don't. But if I did. I'd feature you. Everyone, this is Riah or Zyah. Preferably Riah. Who haven't you met?"

She's confusing, but I instantly like her, even when she asks a question and then skips giving me a chance to respond. "That was Holt, by the way. He's my brother, and so is Steele. That's his girlfriend, Simone."

"I'm here for the open bar," Simone declares proudly.

"I'm here for her," says Steele.

I greet them both while Adly looks for someone in particular. "I'm not sure where Holt's girlfriend is."

A blonde pokes her head up on the other side of me. "Right here. I'm Brystin."

"Brystin Shaw," I say, at the same time, recognizing her from TV.

"That's me."

Before I can talk more with the news anchor—or with anyone I've been intro'd to—Adly's pushing me toward the other side of the table. "You probably know Hunter's brother, Reid. My cousin. He owns this place."

The dark-haired man stands to talk to me. We've met but most of our conversation has been over email in preparation for tonight. "I have the tracks you sent over. You still interested in performing something?"

Like a truly scorned woman, I had fantasies of coming in here tonight, performing the shit out of my song, and making Hunter eat his heart out. At the moment, my stomach is so twisted with anxiety, I'm not sure I could get a single note out. "We'll see how the night goes."

He winks as if he understands the pressure of his family. "Just let me know."

Of course, I'm not given any time to thank him before Adly points out someone new. "And this is my stepsister, Lina."

The redhead turns in her seat to give me her full attention. "I'm also Reid's girlfriend, which is complicated on some levels since his family and Adly's family don't get along. My family, I mean. I guess it's my family now? Since my mother married her dad. So, yeah, my family. Just not by blood. Because that would be really weird if I was dating my actual cousin. But I'm not. He's just my stepcousin, and that's a lot of shit you didn't ask for, so I'm going to stop talking now. Also, I really love your music." For the first time since she started talking, she takes a breath. "And your nails."

Whit manicured them for me on the flight from L.A. this morning, each nail is a different color, matching my multicolored outfit. "Thank you."

It's only now that I realize an important member of the party is missing.

As if reading my mind, Adly points to a group of women circled around the bar. "The birthday boy is doing shots with his Unrequited Love Club."

"Unrequited Love Club?" I have a hard time imagining any Sebastian not getting what he wants, let alone being capable of loving anyone.

"I think it's some scam to get in their panties. He probably thinks it gives him some sort of edge. Maybe it works. They seem to flock around him."

On cue, one of the women steps away, and there's Alex, throwing back a drink, and for some reason, my heart rate speeds up.

Probably because I'm still irked by his belief that I can't pull off a raunchier brand. It was a stupid passing comment for him, I'm sure, but I think about it every day. It's been my motivation for the last month and a half for long dance classes and extra crunches, which I would be too embarrassed to admit to anyone besides myself.

Finally, Adly's attention lands on my ex/not-ex. "And you know Hunter." With that, she plops onto a chair next to Holt. "God, that was exhausting. I need another drink."

"Zyah," Hunter says, not bothering to stand up or make a place for me at the table.

"Hi." There aren't any butterflies, I notice. Not a single flutter over him, and it earns me a point on my mental tally sheet. This situation would be unbearable if I were secretly still pining. "I thought you said it was just a family affair."

"This is family," Ax says.

"Oh, fuck off, Ax. You are not family." Adly had skipped over him in her introductions, and now I realize it was purposeful.

I share her apparent sentiment. Axel Morgan is Hunter's best friend, and therefore is part of the Hunter entourage, which means I know him well. Unfortunately.

"Lookin' hot, Z," he says. "Did you start doing ab work? Oh, no, I guess that's just a shadow."

He's a typical privileged male douchebag. The kind who

still acts like a frat boy at the age of thirty-eight, despite his very grown-up job as President of Programming at SNC.

I'm pretty sure sparring is Ax's love language. In the past, I've ignored his jabs and played nice.

But now that I don't have to try so hard to keep Hunter happy, I poke right on back. "Funny, I thought you'd grown a dick, but I guess it's just a crease in your pants. My bad."

Adly's mouth drops with delight. "Oh, my God, I love you. Can we be best friends?"

"Could be arranged. The spot is currently open." I stare at Hunter when I say it, hoping he takes it pointedly, even though I never considered us friends.

He doesn't bat an eye, but he does—finally—stand up to greet me. Fortunately, he's never been big on PDA, so the kiss he lands on my cheek is enough to stake his claim.

"By the way," Adly says, "and I hope this isn't a barrier in our new friendship or anything, but most of us hate your boyfriend. No judgment on you."

"Fuck all of you." Hunter's arm comes around my waist. "Reid, can you get my girl some wine?"

Internally, I cringe at the *my girl* comment. It's over the top, considering I've never heard him use the endearment before. So now that we're faking this, he's going to double down?

I'm going to need to be drunk to get through this. "Actually, can you make it a sea breeze?"

Reid passes on my order to someone, and Hunter directs me away from the group, summoning the event photographer as he does. It's the one and only camera allowed in the club. Any image that gets posted in the media from tonight will be taken by her, so of course Hunter wants one of us together.

It's all about the image after all.

We pose, the bulb flashes, the photographer walks away, and Hunter's hand drops from my waist.

It was subtle contact, but I feel a liberated rush when he's no longer touching me. Hopefully, this is all the private interaction he'll require from me tonight. If I can spend the rest of the evening drinking and dancing with the group, this faking shit will be a whole lot easier.

But as soon as we're alone, he says, "It's good to see you."

I recognize that tone. "I'm not fucking you."

"Whoa, how did we get to fucking? I was just saying hello."

"Hello with you usually leads to your bed. Except for when it leads to someone else's bed." I give myself a point then double it when I realize how pissed Hunter is about it.

"Are you sure you can pull this off? This isn't going to work if you're constantly holding that over my head."

"But it's so fun." His hard stare says he doesn't agree, and I force myself to remember that I'm getting something out of this alliance too, so I should at least try to play nice. "Yes. Yes. Sorry. Truce. I can do this. Anyone here know the truth?"

"No. Definitely not. The board I'm trying to impress is all made up of family members, so these are the people who need to think we're still hot and heavy and exclusive."

"I got it. I got it. I'll make sure we leave together." I'm still staying in his apartment building, anyway. One floor down. "But I'm not fucking you. Like, at all."

"I was seeing other women when we first got together, and it wasn't a problem for you then."

"It's not a problem for me now, either, because we're not fucking." I've accepted the nature of our relationship as being one of convenience, but adding sex to the mix makes me feel like a whore.

Keeping this strictly a business relationship preserves some of my dignity. Not to mention that I've lost all interest.

"We can discuss it more later." He steers me back toward the tables. "They're getting ready to do birthday shit."

There's nothing to discuss, but I return with him to the group with a smile. Hunter wants something I don't have to give, and that feels empowering as hell.

I'd still prefer to get through this night with a buzz, so I slam down my sea breeze as soon as it's handed to me and am immediately given another, which I nurse as I listen to the banter amongst the family, perfectly content to be a silent observer.

But after a while, I feel a column of heat coming from behind me, and when I turn around to see who's there, I come face-to-face with Alex.

"So you're here. You look…" His eyes scan down my body, and if I didn't already know him, I would almost say they do so with interest. But then he changes direction. "This persona wasn't one of the choices I saw."

Yeah, that's more what I'd expect from the asshole.

Once again, I feel no obligation to play nice. "Because I'm a three-dimensional person, not a program put together by a media team. Also, not your business."

"I didn't mean it to be a combative statement."

"Oh. I didn't realize you had a non-combative mode."

He places his hand on my elbow, demanding my full attention. "I'm a three-dimensional person, Riah Watson."

He's drunk. He has to be.

Or I'm drunk because the warmth of his touch is distracting, and his retort almost comes off as charming.

I hide my smile with a swallow of my sea breeze and use the opportunity to take him in. He's wearing his typical suit, as though he came straight from the office. Even on his last day, he probably worked until the last possible minute. At least he's lost his jacket to the back of a chair, and his sleeves are rolled up. His tie is still in place, but loose, and I wonder for a moment which one of the women who have been fawning over him will have it around their neck before the night is over.

I start to reach out with the impulse to tug on it but stop myself and bring both palms around my glass instead.

His eyes narrow as he nods at my hands, and I tense up, thinking he must sense my urge to touch him. "You're drinking the hard stuff," he says, apparently not reading my mind after all. "As opposed to Coked-down wine."

Just like that, I'm irritated all over again with the proof that he still remembers my usual drinking tastes, unlike the man I dated for nine months. "I thought it might be a hard night."

He raises a brow.

Thank God sense hits me, and I realize I need to take this conversation back to safe ground. "So what are you doing now that you're done with work?"

"Taking some time off. I'm looking at making some investments. Have a big deal already lined up."

"Congrats. And happy birthday, I guess."

He shifts to the side, making room for someone to walk past him, and when he does, I catch Hunter staring at us with narrowed eyes. As if he's bothered.

Him. Bothered about me. Talking to his brother, no less.

His jealousy is juvenile and unwarranted. *Payback's a bitch, isn't it?*

It stirs something equally petty in me. Makes me want to show him more of what he can no longer have. "Actually, Alex. I have a present."

Before my nerves can get the better of me, I catch Reid's eye.

"You ready?" he asks.

"Third track," I tell him. "I'll begin a cappella. Start the music as soon as I get to the last word of the song?"

He nods. "Yep."

With a snap of his fingers, his staff is on it. Someone brings me a mic. Someone else brings down the lights so they're focused on the dance floor. Adly gets everyone to turn their chairs and puts Alex front and center. Reid announces me, and then I'm standing in the spotlight.

It's not until all eyes are on me that I realize I should probably have prepared something to say. Since I'm not great at improv, it's too late now.

Here goes nothing.

With confidence I don't really possess, I start singing "Happy Birthday." All by myself, with no accompaniment, in the famous breathy style that Marilyn Monroe used on Kennedy. I play demure and innocent, which probably comes off as a cliché attempt at sexy, but that's what I'm going for right now. This is only the prologue.

The real show starts when I get to the last line.

"Happy Birthday to you."

The music track plays right on cue. A down and dirty groove, the most provocative of the songs Jack and I worked on this last month and a half. It's completely new. The sound is nothing I've done before; the lyrics are pure filth. Part of me wants to keep one eye on Hunter the whole time to watch him flip out, but his probable reaction is only a bonus.

This performance is meant for Alex. So I keep my gaze pinned on him. He pretty much inspired the song in the first place since he always rubs me the wrong way. I just flipped the meaning to make it fit the point I want to prove.

"Rub me wrong.
Make it nasty.
Make it bad.
Rub me wrong, and I'm yours yours yours."

And as I sing, I put to use all the time I've spent in the studio recently, learning how to pole dance. Though I'm still a beginner at the form, it's helped strengthen my thighs and given me enough of a basis to know how to grind my booty in front of Alex's face.

And over his lap.

By the end, I'm straddling him. The cheers and hollers from everyone else fade away, and it's suddenly just me and him. I've never noticed how striking his features are. How his sharp cheekbones contrast perfectly with his full lips. How cut his jaw is under the scruff of beard. How he smells like pepper and amber wood, and how his hair flops into a perfect mess. His eyes are black liquid, and his mouth parts when I writhe just above his pelvis. So close that I'm dead positive it isn't just a pants crease rubbing against the crotch of my panties.

The man is packing a fully loaded gun.

Can't pull sexy off?

Then go ahead and explain to me, Alex Sebastian, how I just got you so hard.

CHAPTER
SIX
RIAH

As soon as the music ends, Alex shoves me off his lap and takes off into the crowd. I only barely manage not to land on my ass. Blinking, I stare after him, trying to understand why my stomach is doing flip-flops and why I have goosebumps when I was just doing what amounts to aerobic exercise.

Thankfully there's enough commotion that it seems no one notices either his antagonistic behavior or my dazed reaction. Good commotion. People telling me how much they liked the song. Telling me how much they liked the performance. Asking about the album and the tour. It's not just people I already know paying the compliments, but strangers. Musicians and others in the biz.

Honestly, I staged the whole routine for my own personal satisfaction. Because I wanted to prove something to Alex, no one else. The overwhelmingly positive reactions from the crowd are a surprising bonus, and they boost my confidence much more than I had imagined.

But I also feel strangely let down as well. Like the payoff didn't quite pay out.

Maybe because I didn't get a chance to throw it in Alex's face, but I hadn't really planned on that anyway. Pointing out that I've been harboring a grudge over his stupid-ass comment doesn't seem like the best way to earn a win.

More likely, my problem is that I got worked up too. My panties feel damp, and I'm certain it's not just from sweat. Probably just because I've never done anything like that before. I'm sure more experienced lap dancers can separate their emotions from the performance.

I do my best not to let it distract me, instead giving my attention to every single person who wants to talk to me about my song and dance routine.

"I'd love to book you on my show," Brystin says, approaching me when the throng starts to clear. "Unlike Adly, I actually do have a show. SHE network is all about women and female empowerment. My viewers would really relate to the direction you've taken your music."

Brystin is the media personality who's dating Hunter's cousin, Holt. I'm not aware of all the ins and outs of the Sebastian politics and rivalries, but I know they exist. While I hate to have to clear my appearances with Hunter first, I have a feeling it's the wise thing to do in this case, especially since he's likely already feeling blindsided. He knew I was potentially performing tonight but had no idea what sort of performance I'd be giving.

Considering the fact that I haven't seen hide nor hair

from him since the spotlight went out, I suspect I'm in a fair amount of trouble as it is.

Thankfully, it's easy to dodge making a commitment by pushing her onto Claude. "I'd love to discuss it more. Can I get you in touch with my manager? He's in charge of my schedule."

Along with Hunter, but that doesn't need mentioning.

Without phones to swap numbers, Brystin says she'll have Holt reach out to Hunter for my info. Then she thinks about it for a beat. "Or maybe I'll reach out through Alex."

Ah, so there is beef between Hunter and Holt. There goes any opportunity with SHE. "Sounds good."

I don't tell her that I doubt Alex will be any more helpful. Partly because I'm not sure I can say his name yet without a flush rising up my cheeks.

It isn't until I make my way to the bar, almost half an hour later, that Hunter appears at my side. "Are you sure you should be ordering more alcohol?"

It's the first time he's ever tried to curtail my drinking. Usually, he's handing me glass after glass of cocktails I don't like. "Why? Are you worried I'm drunk?"

"It's the only excuse I can come up with for whatever that performance of yours was." His anger is restrained, but just barely.

Prepared for it as I am, it still strikes a nerve.

Fortunately, that's exactly the moment the bartender delivers the tootsie roll shot I ordered, and I throw it back before answering. "Not drunk yet, but now I'm definitely planning on it."

"What the fuck was that, Zy? That was not anything I've ever seen from you before."

"No, it wasn't. I was trying something new. And I had people's attention."

"Because you were practically dry humping Alex in front of them like one of his paid sluts."

Oh, the irony.

"I was not dry humping him." I mean, I kinda really was, but he can't know that unless he talked to Alex.

Which he might have since I haven't seen Alex since he pushed me off him either.

I'm going to need more shots.

I signal the bartender to give me two more of the same then turn to face Hunter head-on. "Just to be clear—are you upset because my performance was too sexy or because my performance was for Alex?"

Hunter, who never hesitates, hesitates.

"There's no way you're jealous of Alex."

"I'm not jealous. I didn't say—" He steps closer and lowers his voice. "It doesn't matter who the performance was for. It was flagrant filth. How would you feel if Whitney saw that?"

"Good thing it's a video-free environment."

"That's not the point. This is the shit you've been working on?"

I take a deep breath before I do something stupid like slap him or cry. All my hard work with Jake, and Hunter has reduced it to "shit" at his first listen.

To his credit, he must realize he's crossed a line because his tone is suddenly softer. "Look, it was good. Okay? The music was really good. The whole album is. I've listened to the raw tracks, and I'm really impressed. I just didn't see the need for you to gimmick it up with sex. It's strong enough on its own."

It's his version of an apology. One where the words *I'm sorry* are never uttered by him and couched in a backhanded compliment. He might as well say he loves my music but only if I interpret it his way because that's what he means. Doesn't he realize that half of the artistry is in the expression?

The worst part is that I understand where he's coming from, even if he doesn't seem to understand me. This arrangement only works for him if I deliver what he needs.

It doesn't make the conversation any less painful.

"Chill out, okay?" I shoot the next two shots as fast as the first, wiping my mouth with the back of my hand. "Tonight was fun among friends and family. "Rub Me Wrong" isn't even going to be released as a single. I'll probably never perform it again. No one captured it on film. I'm still exactly the girl you need me to be."

I slam the empty shot glass on the counter and stomp off, so he knows that, even though I'm cooperating, I'm pissed.

It's petty, but I'm officially drunk now, and that means I feel justified. Only tomorrow's version of me will know if my justification holds when sober.

Half afraid he'll follow me; I head to the bathroom until I see that the line extends outside the door. Changing direction, I end up in an employee's only hall where a door to the outside is propped open, letting fresh air in.

On the verge of exploding, I push through the door, into a private courtyard, and as soon as I've escaped, I lift my head up to the sky and scream.

It's not low and guttural. Not shrill enough to be heard over the thump of the bass inside the club, but it is loud, and by the time I'm finished, I feel a hell of a lot better.

Until I realize that I'm not alone.

"What was that?"

I recognize Alex's voice without looking at him. My entire face goes hot, which is saying something since I was already feeling warm from the alcohol.

Turning my head, I find him sitting on a bench, his legs stretched out in front of him.

"Post-performance adrenaline?" It's an easier answer than trying to explain. I'm not even sure anything I could say would make sense when Hunter has explicitly said that his family should be kept in the dark about our personal arrangement.

He stands. It's not very many steps with his long stride before he's standing right in front of me. "That's not what I was asking."

For fuck's sake.

"Not you, too. It was supposed to be something fun. Sorry, I'm not up to your lap dance standards."

It's bad enough having to justify myself to Hunter. I didn't escape him only to have to be berated by Alex instead.

I take a step back toward the club, but he reaches out to grab my wrist, then easily tugs me back to him. "I haven't heard that edge in your sound before. It was compelling."

My voice catches momentarily in my throat. There's awe in his tone. The kind I would never hear from Hunter.

I shake away the surprise with a toss of my head. "I didn't realize you listened to my stuff."

"Usually, your tone is smooth. Butter. This had grit."

His dark and hooded eyes meet mine, and with the heat of his touch on my skin, all thoughts of Hunter disappear. Suddenly, I remember that, just a little bit ago, I had this man turned on.

Really turned on.

Okay, that shouldn't be something I ever forgot, but I have had several shots, and with the memory now front and center, I also remember that he wasn't the only one affected.

I swallow and find myself taking another step closer. "By grit, do you mean…it was sexy?"

Instead of answering, his attention goes to my hair. "This is new, too."

It's a subtle change. Blunt staggered steps and caramel highlights. It's styled on the tamer side tonight, but the cut lends to teasing. With a little time with a comb, I could go from pop princess to grunge rocker.

He's the first one tonight to notice.

"It's more mature." Without removing his hand from my wrist, he takes his other and wraps it in my hair. Then he tugs on it in a way that can't help but elicit an array of filthy thoughts.

The same thoughts flicker across his expression. I'm not always the best at reading the cues of men, but there's no mistaking that Alex is looking at me like I'm something he wants to eat.

Something flashes in his eyes, and his brows crease. "Oh…is this all about…? Don't tell me you're trying to pull off the bad girl bit after all."

"*Trying* to pull it off? I think I did more than try."

He tilts his face, a smirk playing on his lips.

"Are you trying to pretend it didn't work?" I prod.

"You think it worked?"

Is it a dare? An invitation? I can see the outline in his pants. He's as turned on now as he was when I was on his lap.

My head is buzzing, but so are other parts of me. My skin. My thighs. The space between.

"I think I've had too much to drink," I say. With that declaration, a good girl would step away. Excuse herself and go inside.

I don't move to leave.

Almost of its own volition, my free hand reaches out to cup the shape tenting in his pants. He hisses when I touch him.

Or I do.

Electricity sparks through my body like he's a conduit in a lightning storm, and instead of letting go, I grip him tighter. Rub my palm down his length. His cock grows in my hand, thick and firm, and I'm desperate to feel him for real. Feel his hot skin against my flesh.

I look up at him—for permission? For courage? For him to knock some sense into the both of us?

His expression is strained, his jaw tense. He shakes his head once, quickly.

Then all of a sudden, he has me backed against the wall, and his mouth collides against mine. With the focus and fervor of a starving man, he eats me up. First just with desperate lips, kissing along my jawline and my neck, while his hand holds me in place at my throat.

Then more urgently, his tongue slides into my mouth.

He tastes like scotch and cinnamon and pure physical need. His breaths are ragged, and somewhere in the haze of lust, I'm aware of my own sighs and gasps and moans, each one singing a variation of the word *more*.

Fuck. Just… *More*.

The intensity of his kiss is magnified by the wandering of his hands. Firmly, he strokes up and down my arms, then his fingers explore across the exposed skin of my belly. Soon he's cupping my breasts over my bra.

Then under.

His thumb grazes my nipple, and I'm still gasping when he bends down to take it in his mouth. My knees give way, and if I weren't pressed against a wall, there's no way I'd still be standing. I feel like I've never been touched before. Never been touched like this. That I'll never be touched again with such astute awareness. As though only Alex knows where each of my nerve endings meets my skin. As though only he knows how to set each one on fire.

My own hands are aimless as they roam over his chest and back and ass and thighs. There's too much to know about the contours of his body. Too much to learn, and I want to learn it all at the same time. Want him to learn all of me.

Impatiently, my pelvis rocks against the firm ridge of his cock, trying to soothe the ache that has taken residence inside me. When it's not enough, I return to stroking him— outside of his pants until his kisses are as full of need as I am. Then, too eager to deal with unfastening his pants, I manage to slip my hand past his belt inside his underwear. The sensation of his skin against my palm is so vivid, I can feel it before my hand makes contact—the silky head of his cock, the drop of moisture at the tip, the heat radiating through my fingertips.

When the touch finally happens, my entire body jolts with sensation.

As if he can feel it too, Alex jerks.

Then, abruptly, he pushes away from me, leaving me molten and gasping for breath.

Staring at me, he shakes his head as he gulps for air, his expression hard. And confused. And mean.

"He's my brother," he says, finally. With so much disgust I feel like I've been slapped.

"But we…." I cut myself off just in time.

He doesn't know.

I don't know why I thought he would. Hunter said it's his family who need to believe he's cleaned up his image, but for some reason, I assumed Alex wasn't part of that. They're so close. I thought they shared everything, and maybe Hunter intends to tell him that we aren't really together, but if Alex doesn't know now, I can't be the one to tell him.

I bring my hands to my face.

He must think I'm a monster. All the shitty things he's ever thought about me have just been validated. And even if he knew, would it make it any better? Who ends a relationship with one brother just to jump into bed with another? Rich brothers, no less.

"Guess you proved you can play the role of slut," he says. "Gold star to you."

I drop my hands from my face. "Hey, I wasn't making out with myself here."

But I'm too late. He's already gone.

CHAPTER
SEVEN
ALEX

When I step into the elevator to Hunter's penthouse the day after my birthday, I'm still not sure what I'm going to say about last night, but I'm definitely telling him.

It was a shitty move to make out with his girlfriend. I admit it. And he'll probably have some choice words for me. But we're brothers. Our blood is thick. We'll get through this.

Riah Watson, however, is a problem.

Imagine if it was someone else she'd drunkenly mouth-fucked in the courtyard of the Sebastian Center. Someone who blabbed to the press. Made Hunter and the Sebastian name a joke.

She isn't what the family needs. She isn't what Hunter needs, and if he can't see that after I tell him about last night, he's delusional. Honestly, I'm not even sure he'd miss her that much. The clipped way he talks to her sometimes doesn't suggest he's head over heels. He almost comes off more as a manager than a boyfriend. If he's only about the pussy, he can easily find a replacement.

I mean, I get what he sees in her.

Now more than ever. Not that I hadn't thought about it before. A lot of times, if I'm honest, though I never planned to do anything about it. Sometimes when I was drunk, I may have even wished I met her first.

But it was all just physical attraction. Who doesn't want to do nasty things to those full bowed lips of hers? Her tight body and soft curves would get any guy hard, even though she's reserved with her sexuality. For some men, that's maybe even part of the turn-on.

Personally, I prefer my women to be less inhibited.

Which Riah was last night, to my surprise. I didn't think she had it in her, and the way that she showed me she did…

I swallow back a groan at the memory of her hand squeezing my cock. It was so nasty and wrong, and she was committed.

That's got to be the reason I fell under her spell last night. Because she owned that body of hers. She was fully in control of herself as she writhed on my lap. Why wouldn't my cock perk up? I'm only human. Hunter won't like it, but he'll understand why I reacted the way I did.

He might not understand why I whacked off to thoughts of her for twenty minutes in the shower last night —and again this morning—but he doesn't need to know that.

What he does need to know is that she isn't the girl he thinks she is. She's trouble and a distraction. A temptation that I don't need. Hunter needs to kick her to the curb before she ruins everything he's been working for.

Are you sure that's what you want?

The thought catches me off guard as I arrive at Hunter's floor. I'm so completely thrown by it that the elevator doors start to close again before I shake the notion off and get moving.

Of course, I want her gone.

Without hesitation.

Though the gallery and living room are empty, I find Ax in the library playing darts. Like me, he has free reign of the house, so his presence doesn't mean Hunter's here. It's almost eleven in the morning, but it's possible he isn't even awake yet since the hours he keeps wildly fluctuate.

"Hey. What up?" Ax asks when he sees me.

It crosses my mind to tell him about Riah. He's been Hunter's best friend since we were kids, and even though I've always been the tagalong little brother, in some ways, we understand each other more than either of us understands Hunt.

But I'm afraid Ax will tell me to keep the whole thing to myself. It's our unspoken job to keep Hunter looking good. We're the entourage. Axel and Alex, the supporting cast. We look out for his best interests, and a breakup drenched in scandal doesn't exactly make for the best press.

Still. Bad press or not, it's my opinion that Hunter needs to know who he's dating. Rather than have to plead my case to Ax, I keep my mouth shut and just shrug.

"I feel you." He pauses his game to check me over. "You look like shit, by the way. Guessing that means last night was a good time."

He assumes I got lucky since I rarely go home alone. I'd planned on it when the night began. After Riah got me worked up, I should have walked back into the club and found the first thing hot and willing to erase her from my mind.

I have no idea why I didn't.

But I have no intention of letting Ax think I slept in a cold bed, so I answer with another shrug.

"Fuck you," he says. "You never share the deets."

"People who need to brag are usually bluffing." It's pointed since Ax tends to brag about his conquests.

"Like I said—fuck you."

I perch on the edge of Hunter's desk, out of the way of flying darts, and watch him throw a few in silence. "You crash here last night?"

"Nah. Got here first thing." His last throw hits a bull's-eye, which means he has to do a stupid victory dance like he's a football player in the end zone before he slumps down on the couch. "I had some insight yesterday on the direction your Uncle Sam is trying to take SNC. He's trying to shut Hunter out of the running. We had to regroup before the announcement on Monday."

Sebastian News Corp is one of the two businesses owned by our Grandpa Irving. In an attempt to prevent his five sons from fighting about who would work where, he made the assignments himself. My father and his line are at the Industrial Corp—and to be fair, Hunter put in his time until he got his trust fund—but since then, with the backing of Dad, Hunter has his eyes on taking over the News Corp.

The thing is, the company does need a new figurehead. SNC is a mess. There have been a series of interim CEOs since Uncle Samuel stepped down from his full-time position after a heart attack. The board—composed almost entirely of family members—is as divided as Congress. All rivals. All with their own agendas.

Currently, they're gearing up to find a new permanent company head, and after the last CEO broke up the marriage of one of their media stars, they're looking for someone with more traditional values. Hunter has never been traditional, but he's doing a hell of a job trying to play the part.

Besides our father, Ax is probably Hunt's number one supporter. Though the Morgans are family friends, Ax was named President of Programming at SNC on merit. It's one of the highest positions in the company, and anytime he has insider info, he passes it on to Hunter.

He's not even committing corporate espionage since Hunter is on the board and technically privy to all that happens at SNC. It's just unlikely that we'd know all the ins and outs in a timely manner without Ax's eyes and ears. If Sam has found a way to shut out prospects for the CEO position, Ax would be the one to know.

"That's got to have Hunter in a tailspin," I say, reassessing whether or not this is the best time to tell him about his cheating woman.

"He's working off his mood as we speak." Ax nods toward the wall that the library shares with the master bedroom.

I tilt my head in question, but now that I'm paying attention, I hear it—a rhythmic thumping intermingled with soft moans and grunts. The distinct sounds of fucking.

It's not the first time I've overheard my brother having

sex. It's the nature of spending so much time together. We hear things. We see things. Sometimes, we've even shared.

But then he started dating Riah, and I have so little interest in their bedroom antics that I've made an effort to not be around for any of it. Usually, it's easy because the two of them tend to be bedtime sexers, and like I said before, I don't sleep alone. Any woman I'm with is sure to make more than enough noise to drown out whatever is happening in Hunter's room.

Hearing Hunter and Riah together now is unexpected.

But the most unexpected part is how much it pisses me off.

She was kissing *me* last night.

Stroking my cock like I matter, and now she's on her back again for my brother, not twelve hours later, like what happened between us was no big deal.

Not that I thought there'd be anything more between us, but for reasons I can't explain, it feels…bad.

I shouldn't be surprised. I don't know what else I expected from her. That she'd tell on herself? That she'd feel remorse? That she'd be suddenly hung up on me?

Nope. She's tangled in bedsheets with him in the middle of a Saturday morning like they're newlyweds, and I'm so ticked off, I can't think straight. "Why is he even with her?"

"I don't know." Ax doesn't seem bothered by the contempt in my tone. Though I've never vocally objected to her presence in Hunter's life, I've never shown support either. "Maybe he loves her."

I give him a dubious stare. "You actually think that's possible?"

"He thinks he needs her. For him, I think that's as close to love as you get."

Sad, but Ax is probably right. Some men are raised to find wives and have families. My brothers and I were raised to make money. We were taught that women are for fun, not commitment. Fuck them, don't love them. Give them your cock, not your balls. Never ever give them your heart.

Hunter is more like our father than any of us, so I doubt the L word has ever crossed his lips, but he might still think that whatever he has with Riah is as special as it gets.

He might even think she's the one he should settle down with. All the more reason to let him know about last night.

Another moan comes from the bedroom, and I want to claw my ears out.

I stand, needing to get farther away from the noise, but when I turn, I notice a stack of papers on the desk.

More specifically, I catch sight of a name—HotHouse Enterprise. "What's this?"

"That's part of the regrouping we had to do. Hunter invested in that HotHouse PR firm that's taken off recently. You know them?"

Yeah, I know them. The only reason Hunter knows about them is because I've been in talks with them for months, preparing to buy in as soon as I had access to my trust fund. This is what I planned to focus on next. This is supposed to be my future.

"He invested?" I must be missing something. Maybe he only bought a few shares.

But a glance through the contract says my brother has assumed controlling interest. "There's no way."

"Finalized the deal last night," Ax says. "Had the notary come out bright and early this morning."

My blood feels cold. Hunter's always been ruthless, but I've never been the one standing on the rug when he decided to pull.

And to think I came here today because I was concerned about *him*.

I'm ten seconds from storming into the bedroom and confronting his ass, never mind what I interrupt, when lo and behold he strolls into the library.

"Yo. Don't need to see your dick," Ax says because, of course, Hunter hasn't bothered to pull on any clothes.

"Don't be in my house then." Hunter passes me as he heads toward the bar. "What's the face for, Alex?"

I answer by holding up the signed contract. "You bought HotHouse out? What the fuck? I had them nearly wrapped up."

At least he has the decency to look sorry. "I know. I swooped in, and on your birthday too. It was a dick move, and I owe you. But I needed a plus on my side since Sam is cutting out any candidates without a history of revenue management above five hundred million annually. This will get me to that."

He's practical with his explanation, as though the facts of his need clear him of any wrongdoing. As though he thinks that's all it will take to mollify me.

Am I usually this easy to walk over? Or is he just that arrogant?

Whichever, I'm not letting it slide. "You're a fucking asshole, Hunter."

"It was time-sensitive. I had to have it in place before

Monday, start of day. There weren't any other investments I could pull in that quickly."

"You wouldn't have even known about HotHouse if not for me."

"You're right, and you fucking saved me since you already had it vetted."

"I had it vetted for *me*."

"Shit happens, okay? That's business. There will be other investments." He swipes two tumblers and a bottle of bourbon, already returning to whatever he was doing before. As if this conversation has already been played out.

When he turns back toward me, he must realize I'm by no means appeased. "Look, I'll funnel you the profits. I don't give a shit about the money. It's about the portfolio."

"I don't give a shit about the money, either, Hunter. It's the fucking principle." It's not even that. It's everything. It's his whole narcissistic, career-motivated attitude. It's his inability to acknowledge that anything matters beyond his own self-centered goals. "We saw each other last night. You had the chance to talk to me."

"It was your birthday party."

"Since when do social events prevent you from talking business?"

"Since you were preoccupied with my girlfriend in your lap."

Most likely, it's a joke, but I'm once again back in that courtyard with Riah's hot body grinding against mine, and I'm not sure I'm in a position to fling accusations at him.

It's a good opening, actually, for me to tell him what happened.

I just can't seem to remember why I cared so much.

Because I was trying to protect him? He seems to be able to take care of himself. At all costs.

He's so materialistic and self-absorbed, in fact, that for half a second, I wonder if it's Riah who should be warned about him.

Then I remember she's currently washing off Hunter's cum and all sympathy evaporates instantly.

God, maybe they're perfect for each other.

"Speaking of Zyah…" Hunter says, apparently deciding all is cool between us. "I need you here for a photo shoot on Monday. I'm meeting with the HotHouse team to make sure the press announcements go without a hitch, and Zy needs some babysitting."

Unbelievable.

Just like that, he thinks he can go back to treating me like the loyal little bro. Yeah, I fucked up last night, and maybe it makes us close to even, but it doesn't count since he doesn't know.

Unless he does.

There's the chance, I guess, that Riah already told him, her excusing it as a drunken lapse of judgment. Both having a good chuckle because I was so into it. Because I was so nobly guilt-stricken when I pushed away.

I swipe the bourbon from Hunter's hand and take a gulp before I open my mouth to tell him to fuck off.

But what comes out instead is, "Babysitting?"

"She's in her head about the rollout of this album. I need someone to keep her focused and within the lines."

My eye twitches. Spending time with Riah is the last thing I want to do. "It's my first official day free, and you're already trying to dictate my time?"

"I'm not trying to dictate your time; I'm asking for a favor."

"I don't even know what I'd—"

He cuts me off. "Just fucking be here, okay? You have an eye for this shit. You know brands. And I trust you."

He trusts me.

Wish I could say the same about him.

Wonder how much he'd want me to be here on Monday if I told him that I can't promise not to keep my hands off his girl. Would he still trust me then?

I wonder if he'd even care.

Fuck them both. They deserve each other.

CHAPTER
EIGHT
RIAH

Everything is wrong.

My clothes, my hair, my makeup. Justin, the photographer, has great ideas—for someone else. For me and my brand, everything he suggests feels disconnected.

It's possible it's me. That I'm too in my head and insecure, or maybe I'm just a terrible model. But I've done many photo shoots by this time in my career and never acted like such a newbie. There's something different this time, something not right. Justin keeps on shouting out directions, correcting the slightest tilts of my head, sighing under his breath, and I feel like a big fat failure.

"Let's cut for a minute," he says when I can't seem to nail the shot in front of the fireplace. My makeup artist, Zully, runs over to powder the sweat off my forehead and tuck flyaways into my ponytail, and I have to peer around her to watch Justin's face as he flips through the shots so far.

If his expression means anything, he hasn't captured anything particularly exciting.

"Can I take a peek?"

"Sure."

He hands me the camera, and I study the shots. They actually aren't as bad as I'd imagined. Some are quite spectacular, but the standout is the architecture behind me. My cream suit blends right into Hunter's colorless living room. Even though my jacket is open over a corset, there's nothing sexy about me. I look like I'm selling real estate.

I kick myself for not seeing it would be a problem in the planning stages.

The vision proposed for my album cover is *teenage pop star grows up and is now a strong woman on top of the world.* Hunter's apartment seemed like the perfect background. Nothing says success like a thirty-million-dollar penthouse. In theory, it was perfect.

Maybe it still can be. We just have to adjust a few things.

"What if we take this to the terrace?" My outfit might stand out more against the greenery outside, and what's more on top of the world than a balcony looking seventy floors down to the ground?

"It wasn't on the shot list."

I have to bite my tongue and take a breath before responding. "Can we add it now?" I don't give him a chance to say no. "Thank you!"

He's been a pain in my ass all morning, and I can't decide whether I'm more upset at him for not assuming that a woman could have any authority or at Hunter for not informing him that I was in charge when he set the whole thing up.

It might not have been an issue if Hunter were here to oversee things, but I was actually relieved when he said he couldn't make it. With all that I appreciate that he does for my career, I want to feel like it is still *my* career.

On the other hand, it would be nice to not be floundering alone.

While Justin and his crew of two move the lights to the new location, I get my phone and link it to Hunter's sound system. Maybe playing the raw tracks from the album in the background will help with the vibe. Help tune me in to what my music is about.

I close my eyes and let my body groove. Within minutes, I feel looser already.

When Justin's ready to shoot again, I notice I move differently. I'm more comfortable in my skin. He's no longer cursing under his breath at my awkward poses, and it finally feels like we're onto something.

Except, now that the music is playing, some of the disconnects are even more apparent. Would a woman sing about messy relationships and primal emotions while dressed like she's supposed to give a TED talk?

"You're overthinking," Justin says, pulling me from my thoughts. "These latest shots are primo. Can you lift your chin? Try not to smile."

"That's new. A man telling me not to smile."

He stares at me as if I've interrupted his very important work, which is patronizing since it's as much my work as it is his, and maybe I work better with a little bit of levity.

I'm about to say as much when there's suddenly an extra person standing behind Justin watching.

Alex.

My stomach flips at the sight of him, and my hands are instantly clammy. Hunter had said Alex might be here—for who knows what reason—but I was hoping he wouldn't show. After what happened on Friday night...the way he left me with that stricken look on his face...I've been in knots all weekend.

I thought about reaching out.

For one thing, though, it would have been a process to get his number. I couldn't think of an excuse to ask for it. It might have been less glaring if I had seen Hunter since the party, but I haven't because I've been staying with Whitney in an apartment one floor down. Today's the first day I've been back to the penthouse since we left for L.A. weeks ago.

And if I'd had Alex's number, what would I have said?

That I liked it? That I would have gone farther? That I wanted to? None of that would sit right without him knowing that Hunter and I aren't a real thing anymore, and even if I could tell him that, Alex still might regret it. Lots of people don't want to hook up with their siblings' exes, for good reason. It's messy and awkward.

Hunter would probably hate it. He gave me "permission" to fool around with whoever as long as it was on the down-low, but I'm sure that didn't mean he wanted me messing around with his little brother. Not that he should have a say in my love life—he certainly didn't give me a say in his.

But I can't think about all of that right now because I have to shut my mouth, try not to smile, and look powerful and iconic all while ignoring the hot man staring at me like I'm the devil incarnate.

Justin notes my distraction and follows my sightline.

When he notices Alex, he gives him a welcoming grin and crosses over to him. "Hey. You just get here?"

"I was watching inside for a bit."

"We had a bumpy start, but I think we have it now. You good with what you've seen?"

Oh, that little fucker.

"He is not the one in charge," I say, but not loud enough to catch anyone's attention.

Except Alex. He looks straight at me when he replies. "It's exactly what Hunter wants."

But what about what I want?

It's not the way the music world works, I know. Most artists are at the bottom of the hierarchy, unless they're already a big deal, with dozens of hits behind them. Then they can write their own rules, but that's not me. I have people to answer to. There's the label and the execs and my tour sponsors. Claude didn't come up with these ideas in a vacuum. He spent hours getting everyone on the same page, including Hunter, who was, yes, very on board.

To be fair, I was too. The ideas seemed okay on paper, but I'm not the most visionary person. I have to see things to know if they're right. I have to try things on and try things out, and after trying today, I feel like we've missed the mark.

As nervous as I feel about talking to Alex again, I approach the two men. "I really think the vibe is wrong."

"These last ones are really strong," Justin protests.

Alex stares at me for a beat before reaching for the camera. "Let me see."

"Have at it. Mind if I smoke out here?" The asshole points the question to Alex instead of me.

"It's actually not—" I start.

Alex cuts me off as if I haven't spoken. "Use the ashtray."

Great. I have zero say here. Love how this whole shoot is supposed to focus on the empowerment of a woman who literally isn't allowed to finish sentences in her own apartment.

I mean, not my apartment, really, but since everyone thinks I'm living with Hunter, it might as well be.

My only hope is that Alex sees sense. I study him as he flips through the images, going back even to the ones taken before he arrived. He's wearing a black suit, tailored to his shape, but no tie. His hair is flopped, as usual, with little styling. His jaw is tense, his mouth set in a serious line. There's so much animosity rolling off him. The tension is suffocating.

It doesn't help that he's standing so close that I can smell him. His cinnamon and musk scent makes my blood start to thrum as if I need to be reminded that he had me turned all the way on just a few days ago. My pulse beats unevenly, and despite the breeze, my skin feels hot.

Midway through scanning the photos, he mutters to himself. "What is this, Madonna circa 1989?"

I'm so relieved to have support that I pounce. "Right? It's not working. I knew it wasn't."

But instead of saying more, he just glares.

All the tension and fierce stares—it's obvious he has

thoughts about the other night. Of course, he does. I expected he would, and I know I need to say something.

But what? "I should, um." I clear my throat then lower my voice. "We should probably talk."

His gaze returns to the camera before he replies. "Why?"

There's no way he was so drunk he blacked it out. Was it really just so unremarkable to him that he doesn't think there's anything to talk about?

No, that can't be it. He was so upset when he came to his senses and remembered Hunter.

I try again. "Because…the other night…"

His stare returns, and this time it's challenging. As if he's daring me to put our sin into words.

Which is hard to do when I have more information than he does. He sees me as the bad guy. *A slut*, according to his own words, and I want to correct the record so badly. "I don't want you to have the wrong impression about what happened."

"You shouldn't care what I think."

He couldn't make this easy, could he? "We were drinking—"

He cuts me off. "And it was a mistake. You think I need to be told that?"

His sharp tone makes me flinch.

But then I straighten my spine and give him the same sharpness in return. "I don't know what you need because you ran out before we could talk and straighten things out." Even if he'd stayed, I wouldn't have been able to say what could make it better.

I know Hunter said his family has to think we're still

together, but I'm not sure that means Alex. Obviously, I can't say anything, but Hunter could.

Not a perfect solution, but the only one I've got, so I nudge him in that direction. "I'll understand if you need to tell your brother."

This time when Alex looks at me, his stare is mean. "If I told Hunter about every girl of his that ever had their hand around my cock, he wouldn't have time to deliver you your career on a platter. We aren't anything, Riah. There's nothing to straighten out."

It's a knife in my gut. Unexpected and cleanly inserted. He couldn't have been any clearer about how meaningless Friday was to him. How insignificant I am in his world.

Fine, then.

At least I know where he stands.

Thankfully, Justin returns, smelling like menthol and smoke, before I end up saying anything that will make the situation worse. "I have fifty minutes before I have to go. Do you want to try something else, or can we call it a wrap?"

"I think we should try one more setup." I'm not sure what that setup should be, but as fucked up as Alex is acting about Friday, I'm hopeful he has some ideas.

He doesn't acknowledge me when he hands back the camera to Justin. "There's something in there that will work."

I can't help exploding. "Are you kidding me?"

"It's in line with the plan your team sent over." He manages to not sound callous, but I can feel the subtext like he's underscoring it with a big yellow highlighter—*don't ask me to be on your side.*

Fuck his subtext. "It was a bad plan. You know this whole concept is outdated and disconnected. I look like I'm launching a cover of *Architectural Digest*, not a serious work of music."

He just shrugs. "Sounds like a personal problem."

If only it were just a personal problem! I would love to have the power to solve this, but no. The decisions are made by my label and my sponsors and the stupid ex who's slipping stocks in their back pockets.

I'm so mad, I lash out. "Oh, right. I forgot. You're Hunter's lapdog. Sucking up to him is more important than doing the right thing."

To my surprise, the comment seems to hit a nerve.

Alex takes a step toward me, pointing like he has something to say—something cruel, I reckon—but before anything comes out, he drops his hand and walks away.

Only to spin around and return five seconds later. "Scrap all this," he barks to anyone listening. "Set up in the library. We'll use the desk. Someone will need to flip all the books on the shelves, so no titles are seen. Where's hair and makeup? Are you still set up somewhere?"

Zully raises her hand. "In the master bathroom."

"Let's go." He walks inside and disappears down the hall that leads to the bedroom.

I'm pretty sure Zully is supposed to follow, but she crosses to me as everyone hurries to their tasks. It's my first time working with her—a referral I got from Adly—and so far, she's been the only decent part of this day.

"Every time I see one of these Sebastians make a whole room jump to business, I swear I need to change my panties," she says.

"Because you're turned on or because you're scared to death?"

"Yes."

Personally, I feel the same. I should probably be grateful too, but that's going too far. Justin should have listened to me when I said it wasn't working. I shouldn't need a man with deep pockets to get everyone's attention.

But it is excitingly frightening how easily Alex can get people to move.

He returns a moment later, a scowl on his face. "I said, 'Let's go.' Why are you both still standing here?"

We spring to join him.

Alex has his phone in hand, and when we reach him, he sidles next to Zully, so he can point out images to her as we walk. "Rat her hair. Like this...okay? And the makeup should be..." He scrolls through his phone. "This. Like this. Dark, thick liner. Red lip."

"That's perfect," she says. "I love it."

I stretch my neck to see what he showed her, but he pockets his phone before I can see much.

Once we're in the bathroom, he turns his focus on me, and tugs on my suit pants. "What's under here? The panties match the top?"

It feels a little strange to have him asking about my underwear after what he did to the pair I was wearing on Friday—talk about needing a change of panties—but I manage to give a straight answer. "Yes."

He nods. "Keep the corset and panties. Lose the rest." He turns to Zully. "Hair and makeup need to be fast. We're in a time crunch."

Then he disappears into the master closet.

Quickly, I strip down as he asked—no, demanded—then join Zully in front of the mirror. She hands me the short silk robe I wore the first time we did makeup, and after I put it on, I sit in the chair.

"I think we can do the makeup without starting over. Your hair has had a lot of spray, though. Pray that it cooperates."

Originally, my hair had been pulled into a slick ponytail and then hair sprayed to the max. After removing the tie and pins, it takes a minute to convince my hair to do anything but stick back, but Zully must be magic because a short time later, she has it down and ratted.

She's just starting on my makeup changes when Alex returns from the closet with a pair of dark stockings and a cream garter. I guess they're mine, but they're older clothes. I haven't moved anything down to the other apartment yet because I have enough that I brought back from Los Angeles.

He sets the garter on the sink and throws me the stockings. "We have Justin for thirty more minutes. Can we hurry this up?"

"I need five." Zully directs me to look up, and I do.

But I feel the clock ticking, and so I bring my foot up and attempt to put a stocking on at the same time.

Which doesn't really work when Zully needs me to be still so she can put on my eyeliner. "Okay, we're going for smudged, not smeared across your entire face."

With the stocking still rolled up, I drop my hand in my lap and hold still for Zully.

I can feel Alex move closer rather than see him.

"Give them here." He takes the stockings from me without waiting for me to offer them.

Then he kneels in front of me. "Lift your foot."

With only the slightest hesitation, I stretch my leg out toward him.

It's a strange feeling when he starts to work the nylon up my leg. It's somewhat uncomfortable, but I almost think I'm only uneasy because there's a third person here. Though, he wouldn't be dressing me at all if it weren't for the fact that she's working on me as well.

It's also extremely intimate.

His fingers are hot against my skin, and he unrolls the stocking slowly, careful not to ruin them, like someone who is familiar with women's lingerie and how easily they snag.

Or slow like someone who wants to make sure his fingertips touch every inch of the path along the back of my calf, over my knee, up the length of my thigh.

My pulse stutters, and I curse silently when my knees move farther apart, farther than they need to, without making the decision to do so.

I feel his touch so vividly, I don't need to see him to know that his expression is intense as he looks at me. It makes my belly hot. It makes me want to squirm. It takes all my willpower not to give in to the impulse, each silent second that passes infinitely harder than the last.

"Hunter won't be happy with a change in direction," I say, needing conversation to distract from the rapidness of my breathing.

I feel him tense at the mention of his brother's name.

But he continues with his task. "Five minutes ago, you said that his direction was wrong." He's bent so close; I swear I can feel him exhale against my skin. "Which is it?"

"It *is* wrong. I'm just saying Hunter won't be happy."

Finished with the first leg, all he says is, "I need your other foot."

The process begins again. Inching up even slower than before.

Zully finishes my eyes, and when she moves to her bag to find her powder brush, I peer down at Alex and watch him. The dancing of his fingers on my leg is intentional. Goosebumps scatter across my skin.

A pulse starts deep in my pussy, that I try so so hard to ignore. It's inconvenient and inappropriate. It's dangerous. "I don't want you to get caught in the crossfire."

"You probably should have thought about that before."

It hadn't occurred to me before. That there could be tension between Hunter and Alex because of how today's shoot goes. "I'm thinking about it now."

"I can handle my brother." His hands linger at the top of the stocking. Leisurely, they push up higher, under the hem of my robe. Close to the source of my throbbing. "The question is—can you?"

"I don't…" *know.* I trail off, the last word unspoken, when Zully returns to dust my face.

Alex's fingers are still too high on my leg. I wonder if Zully's aware.

I wonder if I care.

Meanwhile, his question rings in my ear. I'm not sure if he's still talking about the photo shoot or if he's talking about something else entirely. Is it about our Friday night tryst, an event in the past that need not ever be brought up, or is he alluding to something that could happen in the future?

"If I were you, I'd stop worrying about the guy who isn't even in the room." His fingers brush against the crotch of my panties as he pushes to his feet so he can whisper in my ear. "And start worrying about the one who is."

He stands straight, and when he speaks again, it's at a normal volume. "I'll see you in the library."

When he leaves, I realize I've been holding my breath, and it returns in quick spurts. My face feels pale and hot all at the same time, and I'm not sure if I should be this eager to follow after him or if I should lock myself in this bathroom until he's long gone.

"Oh, my," Zully says.

And I can hear in her voice that she feels exactly the same way I do—the only person in need of worry right now is myself.

CHAPTER
NINE
RIAH

After my makeup is finished, I remove my robe, put on the garter, and attach it to my stockings. Alex didn't say anything about shoes, but I slip on the black strappy ones I had on earlier. Then I stand in front of the full-length mirror and nearly shit myself.

My ratted hair looks mussed, but not out of control. My makeup is edgy without being sloppy. The cream-colored corset fits me perfectly—my tits have never looked better (or bigger). In combination with the dark thigh-highs and heels, I'm transformed.

Bye-bye, Miss American Pie. The woman in front of me is a long way from innocent girl next door.

Zully takes the words right out of my mouth. "Hot damn."

"It's not too raunchy, is it?"

She screws up her face. "Is there such a thing?"

It's the question I'm struggling with personally. A

morality code ingrained in my head at some point over the course of my lifetime, riddled with shame and guilt concerning women's bodies and what they do with them. Theoretically, I think that I should be able to express myself however I want.

Practically, I fear there are consequences that I haven't yet foreseen.

On top of that, there are the ones I *can* predict. "My boyfriend sure thinks so." It's so weird to call Hunter my boyfriend these days that I almost trip on the word.

"If he didn't approve, I don't think he would have been in here personally dressing you."

"Oh." Heat gathers along my clavicle bone. "Alex isn't my boyfriend."

Zully tosses her thick braids behind her shoulder with a grin. "Well, then. I'll say it again…hot damn."

It occurs to me that whatever she thinks—scandalous ideas that I am not at liberty to correct, even if I did have the time—could cause problems down the line.

I turn to face her. "Would it be terribly disrespectful to this potential new friendship of ours if I asked you to maybe—?"

She puts a finger up to silence me. "Girl, this isn't my first rodeo with a Sebastian. Mum's the word. Now you should probably get out there before Mr. Hands-Under-Your-Robe comes back and gets bossy again." She ponders. "Though, he sure does look good when he's barking orders, doesn't he?"

I press my lips together and force myself not to consider the answer.

Instead, I take a deep breath and head out of the bathroom, only to return a second later for the robe. I might look like I have the confidence of a woman comfortable with her sexual appeal, but I'm still very much an imposter.

"I've got twenty more minutes," Justin is saying when I slip into the library.

The mood is entirely different here from the first part of the photo shoot. While the living room lacks color in its design, the library is done in dark, masculine tones. The desk is a deep mahogany wood that matches the floor. The walls are muted gray. The furniture is all cherry leather.

Justin had relied on natural light in our earlier pictures. Here, the curtains are drawn and softbox lights are pointed toward Hunter's desk. The books have been turned around to prevent any unintentional advertising. It feels much more like a studio shoot, which is already a big improvement. The scene is set up to focus on me, not Hunter's luxury penthouse.

Additionally, my music is still playing, louder now, and finally, there's a connection between the sound and the setting.

This is definitely the right track.

Alex notices my entrance first. His face remains unchanged, but I feel his eyes settle on my robe.

I'm about to tell him that I'll take it off when we shoot—make up some excuse about the temperature rather than my discomfort—but he speaks before I get a chance. "Everyone who isn't necessary to this shoot, get out now."

It's only two fewer people in the room—because of course Alex doesn't leave—but I immediately feel so much better. I mean, not grateful enough to tell him, but I am able to remove the robe without being coaxed.

The appreciative gaze in Alex's eyes as he scans down my body gives me the confidence to keep it off.

Justin, on the other hand…

The way he looks at me is both lewd and demeaning.

Just twenty minutes, I remind myself. Though there will be a whole lot of Justins in the world looking at my picture with the same mindset if we use this for the album cover.

I try not to think about that.

"What are we going for?" Justin asks, his eyes glued to my tits. "Pin-up girl?"

"Stop-at-nothing vixen," Alex says.

"So, woman who sleeps her way to the top," Justin suggests.

I'm pretty sure that's what Alex means, too. It's not *my* definition of stop-at-nothing vixen. It's not what my vision is for this concept, but the interpretation is going to differ from viewer to viewer just like any other work of art, and I think we're on the same page about the actual imagery, so I let the comment go.

But Alex looks like he's going to take Justin's balls off. "Until you're at the top yourself, I wouldn't judge what it takes to get there."

I swallow my laugh and it turns into a snort. Does he think I should be grateful for that backhanded compliment?

"For the record, I didn't sleep my way to the top." It's overly defensive and maybe not exactly true. But I didn't start dating Hunter for his connections, and I'm not sleeping with him now.

Hard to justify when everyone still thinks I am.

Alex's glare seems to validate his misunderstanding of my situation. "I thought your music was about having the right to choose what you do with your body without judgment."

"Well…not just my body…" Honestly, I'm surprised he's paid that much attention to the lyrics.

"If you're doing this, you have to own your sex appeal, Riah. There's no half-ass about empowerment."

Maybe he does understand my vision after all.

And he's right. "I'll try," I say.

He raises his brows.

"I mean…I'll own it."

Easier said than done. Owning it doesn't happen overnight. It's certainly not going to happen in the span of two statements.

But I do try.

I get on Hunter's desk. I conjure Miley Cyrus in her Wrecking Ball years. I slink. I writhe.

Alex taps at his lip with a single finger as he watches. Judging me, I'm sure. Feeling validated about his initial claim that I could never pull this off. All the ingredients are right now. The only thing that can go wrong from here is me, so if it's not working, there's no doubt who the problem is.

Sure enough, not five minutes into it, Alex calls, "Stop."

Then he says, "Not *on* the desk. Behind it."

Suddenly it all clicks. He's exactly right. The image I'm after is the woman who has what it takes to be both the boss and the beauty. Maybe she used every part of herself— her brain, her body, her heart, her soul—to climb the ladder, but now she's the one sitting in the chair.

"We don't even need the desk at all," I say, at the same time he says, "Lose the desk completely."

Yes.

Justin and Alex quickly pull the desk to the side of the room. I take a seat in the oversized leather chair positioned in front of the wall of books. It's strange, but I've never sat in this chair before. In fact, I've never seen anyone in this seat but Hunter. It's one of the few places in the apartment that are unspoken-ly designated as his. This is where he sits when he's conducting any business. This is where he sits when he makes decisions, without a blink of an eye, which will impact hundreds of people. This is his place of power. This is his throne.

The second I sit in it; I feel an indescribable jolt of privilege fire through my veins.

This is it. This is the shot.

Then, right before Justin starts clicking, Alex once again interrupts. "Hold on."

He takes off his jacket and throws it on the sofa then removes his shirt as he crosses to me.

"Uh…" Any protest dissolves from my lips the minute the man is shirtless.

Holy abs.

The man has them for days. Every inch of his torso is lean and defined. And it's not just his abs that are hot as all get out. Like, when did shoulders turn me on? The men who I know who work out usually have more bulk than I appreciate, but Alex's body is unpretentiously ripped, which I didn't even know was a thing until just now.

All to say, I've been rendered speechless by the sight when he takes his shirt and wraps me in it.

"This is what was missing." He turns the collar up, his knuckles grazing my neck.

It smells like him. Cinnamon and musk cling to the fabric, and I'm embarrassed at how badly I want to deeply inhale, so I can permanently implant the scent in my head.

Wearing it feels…right.

For the picture, but also wrong. But wrong in a way that I'm not sure is actually *wrong*. Naughty, more like. Dangerous.

"Hunter's closet is next door." It's an attempt to regain the authority I felt like I had just a minute ago. "You could have grabbed one of his. You didn't have to give me the shirt off your back."

"Yes, I did."

Okay.

I don't think this is about the album cover anymore. Not for Alex. Maybe not entirely for me either.

But minutes are ticking down, and I don't have the time to decipher his motives, and besides, starting down that rabbit hole would mean deciphering my own thoughts and feelings, and I'm not sure that's something I can tackle without several hours and a bottle of dessert wine.

What matters now is that this is definitely the right shot.

Confident. Sexy. Bold. I know that's how I'm coming across as I stretch out my legs in front of me. Then cross them. Then spread them. I'm the bitch and the boss. I'm the predator, not the prey.

But there's another story happening underneath that one. A story that only belongs to me and Alex.

I'm so very aware of his eyes on me as the camera clicks. So very aware that he is half naked himself. So very aware that I'm wearing his shirt—smelling like him, dressed by him—while sitting in his brother's chair, and though I feel like I have power here, I also feel very owned. By two Sebastian men, in very different ways.

And while Hunter's ownership is stifling, Alex's gives me nerve. Makes me feel strong. And provocative. And so fucking hot.

I can still feel his hands on me from earlier. Can feel the places that his fingertips touched, high under my robe. Feel them as though they pressed harder, stayed longer.

Alex is right there in it with me. The sexual tension between us is so thick that Justin's presence is almost uncomfortable. I know he has to have the shot. That there's something in there already that will work, but Alex presses Justin to take picture after picture after picture.

The remaining minutes start to feel like a decade.

My movements are somehow controlled when inside I'm desperate and needy, and finally, a minute before Justin's time is up, Alex shouts, "It's done. Get out."

His voice is raw, his teeth gritted. His arms are folded across his bare chest, his muscles tight. As though he's struggling with his grip.

I knew I was affecting him, but I'm stung by the dismissal. Which is ridiculous because whatever this thing is between us, it needs not to be pursued. Alex is the smart one right now. He's thinking with his right head.

I gather his shirt around me and start to stand, but he shouts again. "Not you. Him."

Justin looks as surprised as I am. "I need to get my men in here to break down the equip—"

Alex cuts him off. "I'll have it sent to you."

"It will just take—"

"Get out!"

Without another argument, Justin goes, shutting the door behind him. I have half a presence of mind to wonder if he needs his light boxes and equipment for his next gig, but one look at Alex reminds me that those are the kinds of things that I don't have to worry about in the presence of Sebastian men.

The only thing I have to worry about is myself.

A shiver rolls through me.

If Alex isn't strong enough to have the presence of mind, it needs to be me. Again, I start to stand.

"Stay," he commands.

Just like that, I stay.

"Spread your legs."

Heart racing, I do. I spread them wide until there's only a thin layer of fabric between his eyes and my most intimate parts. My pussy throbs under the attention of his laser focus.

"I can see the wet spot on your panties from here."

A very different kind of heat spreads through me.

"Oh my God." I'm going to die of embarrassment. That's why he kicked Justin out. How many of the pictures caught it? I will never be able to show my face to Justin again.

I might never be able to show my face to anyone again, period.

For the third time, I start to get up, this time ready to run to the nearest bedroom, so I can hide under the covers.

But the second I move, Alex halts me. "I said stay."

It's as though he has some sort of magical influence over me. The single word stills me. As though there's no other choice. As though I'm stuck here now, committed to Alex's bidding until he releases me from this spell.

He stalks toward me then circles behind the chair. My breaths are heavy when I feel him bend to speak near my ear. "Tell me, Riah...were you so turned on because you were in his chair? Or because I was watching you?"

I shake my head, afraid the truth is the wrong answer, afraid the wrong answer is what he wants to hear.

"Answer me, Riah."

My voice shakes when I respond. "Because I was in his chair. And because you were watching me."

He inhales audibly. Satisfied. "Make yourself come."

I had to have heard him incorrectly. "Um...what?"

"Make yourself come. In my brother's chair. While I watch."

I can say no. I can walk out.

I can still hear the sounds of Justin packing up the rest of his gear from the other room. I'm not in trouble here.

Except, I'm very much in trouble because I don't want to walk out. I don't want to say no. And not saying no means I'm cheating on Hunter.

Well, not really, since we aren't having sex with each other anymore, and he even said I could have other partners—not that I need his permission—but Alex doesn't know that, and it just feels...*wrong*.

So why am I so into it? Why am I glued to this spot, heart tripping with excitement?

Alex's hand strokes down the side of my face. "I can smell your pussy, Riah. It's begging for relief."

I shift to try to look at him, but he puts his hand on my

shoulder, pinning me into place. "You don't need to see me. I'm right here."

It's funny, but not looking at him makes it easier. It's as if he knows that. It's like being on stage, when the lights are on me, and all that surrounds me is a sea of darkness. There could be a hundred thousand people in the audience or there could be no one, and when I can't see them, when I don't know for sure, then the performance becomes about what I want to say rather than what they want to hear.

That's when I'm my most real—singing for my own joy without caring who looks on.

I take in a shaky breath. "What should I…what do you want me to do?"

"Slip those fingers in your panties and rub that fat little clit of yours. Can you do that for me?"

I don't think.

I just close my eyes and do as he says, slip my fingers under the band of my panties and find I'm already slick. At some point, the music had stopped, all the tracks played, so the sound of my hand sliding through my wetness distinctly fills the room.

"That's it. Pet that dirty little kitty for me. Put your cum all over my brother's chair."

My core tightens deep and low. The tension builds. My pussy is on fire. "Oh, God. Why does that make me so hot?"

"Because you're a good girl who's desperate to break free and be bad. Such a good girl that you need permission first, and I'm giving you permission. Rub that pussy like you mean it. Show me how nasty you can be. Make a puddle for me, baby. Soak the fabric. Make a mess."

He strokes my face and neck and shoulders as I work myself toward pleasure. His gentle touch is a strange contrast with his filthy words. Both coax me on, until my fingers are rapidly massaging my clit and my thighs are trembling and my panties have much more than a single wet spot.

Soon—much sooner than I usually climax—I explode. My thighs quiver as my thumb continues to rub, until the whole room flashes white, and I no longer have control of my hands or my body or my voice or my mind. A strangled moan erupts from my lips and my entire frame spasms with ecstasy and release that goes on and on and on and on.

It feels like whole minutes have passed from the time my orgasm began to the time I'm fully spent.

When I open my eyes again, Alex is in front of me. Wordlessly, he helps me out of his shirt then uses it to clean up the liquid that has trailed down my thighs and onto the seat. He brings it up to his nose to sniff when he's done, before putting it on himself.

Oh, God. I could get worked up again just from that.

But the tension between us is different now. The prominent outline of solid cock in his pants reminds me that I'm the only one here that has come.

At the same time, my orgasm has cleared my mind enough to realize that something needs to be said.

"Alex…" And then I'm stuck. I haven't had a chance to process any of this. So many lines crossed, and I'm not sure yet which I regret. If any. If all.

I peer up at him, hoping he can find the words that I can't.

His expression is hard when he speaks. "It's leather, so it will stain."

It takes me a full five seconds to register what he means. I glance down at the chair between my legs, at the pool of moisture I've left behind.

I thought I was going to die of embarrassment before, and that's nothing like what I'm feeling now. This is complete mortification. Hunter will fucking freak.

I jump from the chair to get my robe and start dabbing at the stain, trying to soak it up, even though silk is one of the worst fabrics on the planet to use for sopping things up.

Alex puts on his jacket as he watches on. "Trying to clean it will only make it worse."

"So what am I supposed to do about it?"

He shrugs. "There's a good chance he won't notice. He might not blame you if he does. It's a ten-thousand-dollar chair, though, so…"

"That doesn't inspire a lot of confidence."

"I don't know what to tell you. It's not my cum on his chair."

It's casual and cruel and hits me right where he intends. Making me feel like the slut he's made me, without taking any of the responsibility himself.

I'm instantly ashamed and confused. This whole thing feels like it was a set-up of some kind. A trap.

Why? To humiliate me?

To exert authority over me?

To make sure that no matter what I might mean to his brother—never mind that I'm only a transaction in Hunter's mind—that I know good and well I'm only a whore?

If that's the part he's cast me in, I might as well play it up because there's no way I'm letting him see how deeply he got to me. "Guess me and this chair will have to give another performance then. For Hunter, this time."

With as much casualness as I can muster, I gesture to the disorganized room. "You'll clean all this up on your way out, won't you? I'm sure Hunter expects you'll have things back in order before he comes home. Now if you'll excuse me, I need to go clean up."

Alex draws back. Not a lot—he's very stoic when he wants to be—but just enough for me to know that my comments hit their mark. It was only a guess that he felt like his brother's lackey. The validation that at least some part of him does almost makes me regret saying it.

But only almost because I'm still wounded from his remarks.

So without giving him a chance to respond, I walk out and head directly to Hunter's shower, where I proceed to scrub and scrub and scrub, trying to remove all the bad feelings, as though this kind of shame can be washed off with luxury brand soap and softened water.

CHAPTER
TEN
RIAH

From the Zoom app window at the corner of my screen, Claude furrows his brow and frowns. "I think the biggest problem we're going to have with these is figuring out which one is the best to use."

I click through the images on my shared screen, trying to decide. It took Justin a little over a week to get the edited versions sent over. My stomach was in knots the whole time, waiting, so when the email came in, I asked Claude if he'd go through them with me.

They're both not what I expected and somehow even better. Well, not the ones taken earlier in the day. Those were just terrible. I didn't even have to convince Claude that they were wrong. I saw it all over his face as he barked, "Next," over and over at me so I'd keep on clicking through.

But the later ones, after Alex dolled me up and put me in Hunter's chair...those are gold. They're not just album-cover worthy—they're art. Several times, I've had to remind myself that it's me in the pictures because I swear, I've never looked so strong or formidable. Justin is an ass of a human, but his photography is top-notch.

I'm sure I should be giving Alex credit for the concept too, but I'm trying not to think about him at all. I haven't seen him since the shoot, which makes it somewhat easier. During the day, at least. Nights are a whole different story. I toss and turn and sweat and buzz until eventually, my hand slips down to my pussy, and I give myself some relief.

That's probably the reason I was so afraid I'd see these images and immediately think porn—not that there's anything wrong with porn in the proper place—but surprisingly, they don't come off that way at all.

"The black and white is classic," Claude says when I linger on one particularly striking photo. My elbows are resting on the arms of the chair, my back straight, my legs crossed. My expression is serious as I look straight at the camera. Or rather, at something behind it. Some*one*. I can practically see Alex in the reflection of my eyes.

"I think I like the dark-blue-tinged version best." I arrange the windows so it's side by side with the other for comparison. "Yeah."

"That's the one."

That's the one.

Except getting Claude on board is the easy part. I still have to convince my label and my sponsors. I still have to convince Hunter.

Just thinking of him makes the knots return. "You don't think it's too risqué? I know Jennica wants us to be able to get product placement."

"We might have some pushback if we choose one of the photos where your legs are spread, but even then, I don't think it's going to create too much of an issue. It's sexy, but it's classy. Not slutty."

I cringe at the term slut. I'm tempted to explain how derogatory the comment is and how much harm it does to suggest there is something wrong with a woman having numerous sexual partners. It's no one's business what a woman does with her sexuality, and certain words imply judgment that wouldn't be cast on a man.

Not to mention, how a woman dresses says nothing about their chosen lifestyle. A woman could dress like a Victoria's Secret catalog entry and still have never kissed a man in her life.

Even though I know those things, a part of me worries I'm somehow wrong. Or at least, I worry that there are enough people in the world who believe that a promiscuous outfit equals a promiscuous woman that it might as well be true.

Then there's the fact that I know what happened right after these pictures were taken. I was dressed like a "slut," and I behaved like a "slut," and then Alex treated me like a "slut," and even though I fully consented—and as much as I enjoyed all of it while it was going on—I'm not sure it should have happened.

Especially since Alex thinks I'm still with Hunter.

For all intents and purposes, I am.

So now I'm not just a slut—I'm a *cheating* slut, and the line between wrong or right in this situation is so gray, I can't help but feel ashamed.

Needless to say, I don't think I'm in the right mindset to stand on my soapbox today.

"Let's go ahead and put together five to eight options, including some of the more salacious ones, knowing those will get shot down, and I'll send it over to Jennica to see what the label thinks."

I barely hear Claude, though, because just then, Whitney walks by the living room where I'm working, and somewhat ironically, distracts me with her choice of outfit. "I thought you had your interview this afternoon?"

She's taking a gap year to decide what she wants to do now that she's done with high school, but meanwhile, she wants a job so she can have work experience. Since she's adamant that she doesn't want to work in food service, I suggested a temp agency. Her appointment was supposed to be today.

But she's wearing a short white skirt, yellow knee-high stockings, and a yellow jacket that's open to expose a bikini top, so maybe I'm wrong.

"I do," she says, and now I'm confused. There's no way she thinks what she's wearing is appropriate.

I look at the clock on my computer. "Are you going to have time to change?"

"I planned on wearing this."

"Interview for what?" Claude asks from my laptop screen.

"Claude, can I call you back? I have to deal with something."

Whit rolls her eyes. "You don't have to deal with anything. I've got this."

But I've already clicked End Meeting, and my sister

most definitely doesn't "got this." "I'm not sure that you do."

She cocks her hip and gives me that expression that says she has zero interest in my opinion, but I give it to her anyway. "You can't wear that to an interview."

"Why? I look cute."

She looks like a fetishized schoolgirl, but I just had a mental conversation with myself about not shaming a woman for what she wears, so I don't say that.

Unfortunately, though, the world will still judge. "You look adorable, but it's not quite the right vibe for an interview."

"It's not really an interview. It's just the take-in assessment. This is fine."

"That's basically an interview. They're going to decide what jobs you best match up with based on how you present yourself." Mad at myself for not telling her this earlier, I set the laptop on the couch and stand. "Come on. I'll help you pick something else out."

She doesn't move.

"Come on, Whit. You'll be late."

"I'm not changing."

"Yes, you are."

"I'm not. This is fine. Get over yourself." She heads over to the drop table we have by the front door and rummages through her purse.

For the most part, she and I don't fight. Generally, I stand back and let her *do her*, but every now and then, I have to put my foot down. "That outfit gives the wrong impression. Stop wasting time and find something more business-friendly."

She pulls lip gloss out of her purse and then stares at herself in the hall mirror. "You're not my guardian anymore, Riah." She applies her gloss while she talks. "I'm an adult, remember? I don't have to listen to you."

"For fuck's sake. I'm not trying to boss you around. I'm telling you that, if you go dressed like that, the service is going to hook you up at a strip club. Which you're too young to work at, so don't even suggest that's okay."

"If this place can't respect my clothing choices, then maybe I don't want their job."

Oh my God, where did I go wrong?

"Look, Whit, anywhere you apply is going to have the same expectations. Google it, if you don't believe me. I'm telling you what I know from experience. How you dress matters."

She turns from the mirror to look at me. "Didn't I just walk in on you talking to Claude about how slutty you look on your album cover?"

Internally, I groan at the slut word once again.

I'll definitely have to get on my soapbox about that for her but now isn't the time. More immediately, I hear how hypocritical I must sound to her.

I also know my situation is completely different. "I don't have a traditional job. Apples to oranges in comparison."

"And this is why you could never take the place of Mom. She would have known what she was talking about. She was someone I could look up to."

She's good at hitting me where it hurts when she wants. Usually with that specific line. Often for some reason that has nothing to do with me, which I never discover until later. In the moment, though, it always lands just right to wound.

Unfortunately, I haven't learned how to hide the impact of the hard blows, and I snap back. "Fine. Don't get a job. Then what? How do you plan on paying for your life? You think you're living off me forever?"

"You mean living off Hunter? Because you haven't paid your own rent in…how long?"

It's exactly the wrong thing to hear when I'm already questioning all my moral choices. She's the one person who knows something of the truth about my Hunter arrangement—I told her we were taking space, hence why we were living apart—and somehow, that makes her statement worse. Sure, I'm not sleeping with the guy anymore, but I'm still a kept woman.

That shame from earlier comes flooding back through me like a fire hose turned on at full force.

Whit must see it on my face, and she rushes with her apology. "I'm sorry. I didn't mean it. I shouldn't have said it."

I'm not ready to hear it. My wounds are too raw. "Make your own choices then. Since you're old enough. Just remember Hunter pays for the roof over your head, too."

With that, I snatch the laptop off the couch and dash to my bedroom where I lock my door behind me.

For several minutes, I pace the room, trying to decide if I'm going to cry about this fight or if I want to write about it or maybe just climb in bed and take a nap. Eventually, my wounded feelings give way to guilt.

This whole misunderstanding is my fault.

First and foremost because I was never the best choice

to be her guardian. There was just no one else in our family to do it, and I wasn't letting her go into foster care. It's another area where I have always felt like an imposter. I spent all the years away from the music business pining to be back. I didn't dedicate enough of my attention to her.

The truth of the matter is that I returned to my career before she was ready, too. She hadn't even graduated yet. It wasn't a decision I made on my own, of course. Claude and Jennica put heavy pressure on me, and Whit insisted she was grown up enough to deal with my split focus, but it was my choice in the end, and my decision was selfish.

And so are my current career choices.

It might be the voice of self-pity, but it's the loudest in my head. How am I supposed to exemplify what it means to be a strong, confident, respectable woman to my sister when I'm manipulating my audience with my fake relationship, cheating on my fake boyfriend with his brother, emphasizing the sex in my music, and posing in my underwear on my album cover?

Without thinking it all the way through, I plop on my bed with my laptop and pull up Justin's emails with the photos attached.

I hit REPLY ALL and type a short note.

> We need to reshoot. When is the soonest I can get on your schedule?

It's not the biggest offense on my list, but it's the easiest one to do something about.

Not one minute after I hit SEND, my phone rings from an unknown number. I don't usually accept calls when I don't know who they're from, but the timing makes me think it might possibly be Justin calling to rebook.

It's not Justin's voice that answers when I say hello. "Why are you asking for a reshoot? These pictures are solid."

"Alex?" Instantly, my body perks up. Or at least my nipples do. Two traitorous arms stretched outright to wave hello.

My brain, meanwhile, requires a couple of seconds to remember that he had been copied on Justin's email. So he was also copied when I replied all.

"Is this Hunter's doing?" he asks.

"No, Hunter still hasn't seen them. This is all me."

"Are you out of your fucking mind? You can't get any more on point than these."

I lean against the headboard and swear under my breath. I had not intended to have to explain this to Alex. Remembering his behavior toward me the last time I saw him makes me not want to try.

"You know what? I appreciate your help with everything, but frankly, it's not your—"

"Don't you dare say that it isn't my business. Your boyfriend made it my business when he invited me there. You made it my business when you blinked your big brown pleading eyes. *Help me, Alex. Help me get it right.* You basically begged."

"Fuck you, I didn't beg."

His voice is suddenly low. "But you would have. If I'd asked you to. I wouldn't have even had to ask nice."

His words should make me want to hang up.

Instead, heat spreads through my limbs, which is

embarrassing, but also, he's right, and I'm definitely starting to think that I might have some kinks I've never explored.

And this is exactly what's wrong with me.

I close my eyes and when I inhale, my breath shakes audibly.

"What's wrong, Riah?" His tone is softer now, but just as intense.

It catches me off guard, and maybe that's why I give him an honest answer. "It's a big thing, you know? To be stripped down like that in front of everyone. It shouldn't be an invitation for judgment, but it is. You know it is. People will make assumptions about my sex life. About my career. About what I've done to get where I am. What I'm willing to do. And maybe some of what they think will be true, but that doesn't mean I want to hear their opinion on it. Plus, not only does it open me up for that scrutiny, but everyone else around me too. It's a big thing. Not a small decision to make at all."

He's quiet for so long that I start to regret unloading. "I don't expect you to under—"

"But they'll say that shit anyway," he interrupts.

"What do you mean?"

"You could present yourself as a purity princess, and someone's still going to call you a whore. A lot of some-ones, most likely. Or they'll call you a man-hater. Or a brainwashed feminist. Or they'll question your sexual orientation. It isn't a matter of what you put out there—it's putting yourself out there at all that invites judgment."

"So basically, I'm fucked no matter what. Great. Was that supposed to make me feel better?"

"It was supposed to wake you the fuck up. You can't be in a public-facing career and escape the court of public opinion. You can't be successful without them weighing in. You can't be good at what you do or have money or anything that puts you on the radar. Everyone will always adjust their image of you to fit their narrative. Like it or not, that's the world we live in. Don't be so naïve."

It hits me that he's dealt with the public saying shit about him his whole life. He *does* understand.

"So what do you do about it?"

"Nothing. Live your life. Live it as big as you want. You know what the truth is. The rest is just bullshit. If they're going to call you names anyway, might as well deserve it."

The rest is just bullshit.

He's right, of course. I shouldn't care what people think. What matters is what I know to be true, and the rest is just bullshit. It's stupid how reassuring that notion is. So reassuring that I might get emotional about it if I think about it too hard, so I attempt a bit of levity. "Is that why you're such a manwhore? Because people will accuse you of it anyway?"

"Who said I'm a manwhore?"

It's a deadpan delivery, and it works. I laugh. "Goddammit, Alex. I was set on feeling sorry for myself for at least another few hours."

"I have a habit of disappointing people. Get used to it."

His tone is almost friendly, and even though I'm sitting down, it makes me dizzy. "Careful. I might accuse you of being nice."

"Don't think so highly of yourself. I just can't stand by people making stupid decisions simply because they're cowards. It's pathetic. Besides, what you do reflects on Hunter and that reflects on the Sebastian name."

It's a complete one-eighty the way he goes from pleasant to cold. I should be used to it by now, but it still stuns me every time.

I try my best not to show its effect on me. "So this advice is self-serving."

"It's certainly not for you."

"Of course not." Regardless, it's been helpful. "I appreciate the candor. As always." I hang up before he can respond.

As offended as I am now, he did calm me down enough to think clearly. I haven't been straightforward enough with Whitney. Hunter can't expect me to keep the truth from my sister. Maybe if I explain everything to her about what's going on, she won't be so judgy.

I went into all of this hoping she'd respect me, after all.

Or support me, at least.

If she isn't on my side right now, then who is?

CHAPTER
ELEVEN
ALEX

"What happened?"

Those are Holt's first words to me when I step into his office at SHE. It's actually not his office, but his girlfriend's—fiancée as of a couple of weeks ago—but like me, he's currently trying to decide what to do next, and apparently for him that involves spending as much time as he can with Brystin.

Personally, it makes me nauseous, but apparently, he's in love. It's not an emotion in which I have any interest. Especially not if it means camping out all day in an office with Tiffany-blue walls and decorative throw pillows on the couch like this one has.

I finish my scan of the room, so I can properly judge him before I answer. "Gotta give me a little more context than that, dude."

"HotHouse. You had that clinched up." He nods toward the seating area.

Shit. I guess it's him judging me.

"You heard about that." I cross the room toward the couch, with him following.

He waits for me to sit before he takes the chair across from me. "Everyone heard about it. Hunter's been on a PR tour letting everyone know he's now an investor. Stocks are soaring. Big firms are jumping for a chance to be a client."

He doesn't have to tell me how well HotHouse is doing. Believe me, I've been watching. As soon as the announcement was made, the stocks doubled. Two days later, they nabbed a multi-billion-dollar contract and the stocks doubled again. I stopped calculating how much profit I'd lost at that point. It made me too sick to think about.

Especially when Hunter walked back his offer to send all the profits my way and decided to just share a portion. Since it was "his money and his name" doing all the work, after all. As if I didn't have access to both of those things myself.

To add insult to injury, he pointed out that, if I were to invest in another PR firm, it would make us competitors. Sebastian pitted against Sebastian in the same exact field. In *my* fucking field, not his. Hunter's a snake, too. I don't really want to be his opposition, which means I'm left aimless in my quest to figure out what I do next.

But as strained as my relationship is with my brother, I've never been all that close to Holt. The two of them have had a lifelong feud, and while I don't pretend to understand everything about it, I landed on Hunter's side by default.

My loyalty to him is rote at this point. "Yeah. Hunter's really turning it around. What about it?"

Holt's stare drills into me. "At your party, you told me you were about to be the one investing. It seemed you were really looking forward to it, and so again, I have to ask, what the fuck happened?"

"Seriously?" I run my hand over my beard, really not in the mood to explain myself to him. To anyone. "This better not be why you asked me to come out here today."

"One of the reasons."

If this is what he started with, I'm not sure I want to hear what else is on his list. Mentally, I try to decide what motive Holt has in asking. I can think of a few possible reasons, but none of them are ones I like. "There's not a story here, Holt. Leave it and move on."

Holt's not the type to let go of a bone. "He fucked you over, didn't he?"

"And you're gloating?"

"No, I'm not gloating, you asshole."

"Then why do you care? If you're looking for me to suddenly become your ally as a form of revenge, then you shouldn't have invited me."

Besides, I already got revenge—I fucked around with his girl behind his back. It's done and passed, and he didn't find out so there's no fallout or confrontation, but I still get the smug satisfaction of knowing I've seen what Riah's face looks like when she comes.

I start to stand, but he puts a hand up to stop me. "Look, Alex, we've never been that close. But that's because Hunter never let us be. I didn't call you here to gloat. I didn't expect you to go against him. I just know what it feels like to be fucked over by Hunter. I know what it feels like to stand in his shadow, and I wanted you to realize you have someone who gets it."

He sounds sincere enough, and maybe he is. I let myself view things from his perspective, and okay, maybe there's nothing nefarious in his gesture, but we're Sebastians. The both of us. I'm not even sure either of us knows how to not have an agenda.

So I simply shrug. "Okay."

Disappointment flickers across his face before he masks it. "Okay."

"Is that all, then?"

"Well, no. I figured since you aren't investing in HotHouse, that means you have some cash lying around."

There it is. The agenda. "Right. Of course. Of course, you wanted to be there for me and also ask for my money."

"For fuck's sake, Alex, I'm not—" He cuts himself off, clearly frustrated. He waits a beat to speak again, and when he does, he's composed. "I get it. I get why it's hard to trust me, and because I get it, I'm not going to spend hours trying to convince you. You're either going to have to come to that on your own or not. All I can do is present the opportunity."

Opportunity is the buzzword that big-talking money men use to make their traps look less odious. I can't believe he's trying to use that bullshit on me.

The wise thing to do would be to leave it there and walk out, but there are reasons to stay. Curiosity, for one. And I can't deny the appeal in sticking it to Hunter. Fucking around with Riah does have its downside. It involves another person, and while I still believe she deserves what she gets, it's also complicated in ways I don't want to try to analyze.

Complicated like I shouldn't still be thinking about her two days after hearing her voice on the phone.

Complicated like I shouldn't be looking for a reason to call her again.

Complicated as in that needs to be the end of that method of revenge.

Joining up with Holt to do a deal, though…that's interesting.

"I'm listening." I'm not saying yes. I'm inquiring, is all.

"Bob Peterson is looking to sell SHE network."

Ah, then he isn't just hanging out here because of Brystin after all.

"And you want to buy it." The mere thought of it makes me laugh. One of the reasons Hunter wants the CEO position at SNC so badly is because it's technically Holt's birthright.

And Holt isn't even interested. Instead, he's interested in a rival station. It's so genius, only someone with blood as brutal as the Sebastians' could think of it.

God, if I joined in on that…

I wouldn't want to be Hunter's competitor on my own, but it would be a different story with backup. It would piss Hunter off so much, I'm not sure we could recover from it.

"It's not all that you're thinking," Holt says as if he has any idea what I'm thinking. "The station is dedicated to programming for and by women. It should be run by a woman, not fucking Bob Peterson."

"Uh, last I checked, Holt, you aren't packing the right equipment."

"Which is why Adly would be CEO, and all the chief officers would be women."

I make a show of looking down at my crotch. "For a minute, I thought I must have lost my balls or something because I don't understand why else you'd be pitching this to me. What are you thinking? That we'd be silent partners? Brystin must have some damn fine pussy to turn you into some noble feminist."

He chuckles. "It's not noble. There's money to be made here. But yeah, the truth is that there's a need for women-run corporations, but they often don't get anywhere in this culture without being legitimized by male participation. Bob won't even talk about selling to anyone who doesn't have a dick."

He leans forward and rests his elbows on his thighs. "But also because of culture, there haven't been as many opportunities for women to learn the things we've learned because we've held positions that have been outside their reach. My father only ever let Adly run HR. She has the chops but not the experience, that both of us have. So you and I come on as consultants. I know network strategy and you know branding. We could bring a lot to the table."

I consider it for a minute. He's right—it's not noble. It reeks of opportunism and male savior syndrome, but at the same time, I actually think Holt is trying to do something good.

It's not the Sebastian way at all.

Hunter wouldn't hate me for teaming up on something like this. He'd laugh his fucking ass off.

I don't know what I want to do with my life yet—or my money—but I'm not quite sure I'm interested in being the butt of Hunter's jokes, no matter how many nobility points are earned.

Holt seems to sense a no drawing on my lips, so once again he puts a hand up. "Don't answer now. Think about it. Even with you on board, we're still short some money, so you have time."

"Yeah, sure. Sure. I'll think about it."

He stands when I do and shakes my hand, holding it longer than necessary. "Hey, while you're here, you should let me give you a tour. Give you what you need to make an informed decision."

I laugh. "You're a real pushy motherfucker, you know that, Holt?"

His smirk suggests he considers it a compliment.

I'm not in the fucking mood, but hell. What else do I have going on? "Yeah, while I'm here. Let's do it."

The tour is less of a tour and more of a chance for Holt to give me the financials on the SHE network. He spouts numbers from memory as he walks me through the offices. They're modest and don't reflect the feminine touch that the programming exemplifies, which I'm guessing has to do with Bob Peterson's presence. I can just imagine the place under Adly's thumb. The whole floor would be decked in pink.

I listen half-heartedly to Holt's report. From what I take in, there is definitely a growth opportunity, but none of what he says or shows me is compelling until he takes me to the production control room, and I can see what's happening on one of the studio stages.

And then it's not really the studio stage that catches my interest, but who's on the studio stage. "Is that…?"

"Zyah, yeah." Holt checks his watch. "It must still be sound check. She's debuting a song from her next album on our afternoon news show. There are three different women who rotate hosting—four now, actually, since Brystin's spending more time on her weekly program."

He keeps talking, giving me more info about the operations that I couldn't give a shit about. I can't even pretend like I was earlier. All of my attention is now on Riah as the musicians behind her play her lead-in.

I can't help going into critique mode.

Her hair and makeup are already done, and while it isn't as pretentious as it had been when I first arrived at her photo shoot, it's still too conservative for the sound she's presenting. Her clothing is good, though. The olive-green blouse is ruffled with long sleeves, but it's transparent. The bejeweled net skirt over her shorts and the black sandals that lace all the way up her calves are both edgy and sexy. All in all, it emulates the brand she's striving for without going so far that Hunter will lay into her for it.

If I have to guess, I'd say she's learning the fine art of compromising with a man who refuses to take part in actual compromise.

I wouldn't go so far as to say I'm impressed, but I'm not *not* impressed.

And then she starts to sing, and I'm instantly transported to my birthday night. It's not the same song or the same mood, but there's a rawness to her sound that I've only ever heard a few times. That night, for one. When she sat on my lap and writhed against my dick.

Instantly, I have a semi. The only reason I'm not all the way hard is because Holt is standing right next to me.

How the fuck would I explain getting stiff for my brother's girl to him?

And I'm not stiff for my brother's girl, exactly. It's the memory of her ass grinding against me. That's all. It's the memory that this particular tone of her voice elicits. Nothing more.

Even now she's guarded with it. As though she doesn't know how to relax all the way into it. As though she can't quite access her muse. Like how she knew what she wanted for her cover art but wasn't able to let herself be bold enough to execute it without a little push. Without permission.

I could give her permission.

Wouldn't that piss Hunter off.

And now I'm suddenly back in Holt's office, hearing him tell me that he knows Hunter fucked me over, and I'm thinking about the obscene dollar amount that now lines my brother's pockets instead of mine, and even though I'd told myself we were even, I begin to think that maybe we aren't.

Maybe there's more for me to take.

Not this way, remember? Riah is messy.

But Hunter is the one who creates these messes. He's the one who stands in the way of others' progress. He's the one who fucks everyone over.

He's the one who demands and expects us to always jump when he does.

And if Riah asks for the help, and he isn't here to give it…who can blame me for stepping in?

CHAPTER
TWELVE
RIAH

"Well, it seems to me,
it must be my turn to speak,
But what can I say
when I don't feel anything."

There's a small smattering of applause when I finish the song, about what's expected from a sound check, so I try not to make anything from the lack of enthusiasm.

I'm perfectly capable of judging my performance on my own, anyway.

And it was not there.

Get your head in the game, Riah.

Shielding my eyes from the set lights, I squint toward the box to see if they've gotten what they need from me, but

I can't see any faces through the glass. I hear the door open and can see a couple of figures approaching, but I can't make them out either.

Claude gets to me before they do. "You look good. You sound great. Wish we had a live audience for you to feed off, but it is what it is. How do you feel about it?"

"It was…um…" I'm still struggling to articulate my feelings when the figures step into the light, and I recognize Holt. So I smile.

Then my gaze drifts to his companion. I'd thought I'd gotten the swarm of bees in my stomach under control earlier, but at the sight of Alex, they start buzzing away.

It's just nerves about debuting the song, that's all.

Alex only stirred them up because I'm sure that for whatever reason he's here, it probably falls under the category of babysitter, and being under watch always makes me anxious.

So it's not my fault when I forget to say hello. "Did Hunter ask you to come?"

He was supposed to be here himself. Still might show up, if he finishes up with whatever appointment he had that conflicted with this appearance. It would be just like him to send his brother in his place.

Why do I find myself hoping that's the case?

"Uh, believe it or not, my life does not revolve around you and my brother." His irritation is subtler than usual, maybe because his cousin is here.

I'm not sure I believe him. "Just stopped by on a whim?"

Holt and Alex exchange a glance before Alex answers. "I stopped by to congratulate Holt on his recent engagement."

Holt jumps in after that. "And then I offered to give him a tour of the place."

"Oh." I feel silly for the assumption. Of course, there are a million reasons for Alex to be here that don't involve me. "Congratulations. Zully told me during hair and makeup. How exciting."

He thanks me and says something about the wedding date being a long way off yet.

Then Claude interrupts to say he has some calls to make.

I wave him off then turn my attention back to Holt.

Try to, rather, because my head is in a million places at once. I'm still thinking about the song, and I was distracted anyway, and then there's Alex standing so close that I smell whiffs of cinnamon every time I point my nose in his direction.

And then there's the way he keeps staring at me. Like I'm something he could eat if he wanted to.

There's a low pull in my belly at the thought of what his mouth would feel like on my skin, and I shiver.

"I'm sorry, what were you saying?" I ask when I realize there's a lull in the conversation that signals, I should be speaking. "I'm in my head. Thinking about the show."

"Nothing important," Holt insists. "We shouldn't be intruding on your pre-performance time, anyway. You sounded incredible from the booth."

"Ah. Thank you. It felt like it was missing something, but…" I shake my head. It's a terrible habit to dismiss a compliment. "I don't know. I'm sure it was fine."

"It wasn't fine. You were on fire." Someone calls Holt's name, and he glances over his shoulder in their direction.

"Speaking of fires...I think I have one that needs to be put out; if you'll excuse me."

I expect Alex to follow him, and I start to turn away, but he stops me. "Missing something?"

He sounds deeply interested, and I'm so surprised that it takes me a second to respond. "It just wasn't as dialed in as—"

I'm cut off by a member of the crew shouting for the area to be cleared. There's another performer who needs a sound check, and all non-essential people are banned from the set.

Another crew member informs me they'll come get me when I'm on.

I lose Alex in the hubbub, so I head to my dressing room.

After I push through the door, a hand reaches out to stop it from closing. I turn and once again come face-to-face with Alex.

"Missing...what?" he asks, picking up the conversation where we left off.

I'm instantly aware that it's just the two of us now. The rest of the rooms in this hallway are empty. We're pretty much the definition of alone.

He leans against the doorframe, blocking any escape, and my heart quickens. That low tug in my belly resumes along with a flood of heat.

Missing...this.

Missing this spark. This authenticity. This connection to my femininity.

My music needs the bold confidence of a woman who

owns her sexuality, and I didn't have it out there at sound check.

As quickly as the realization hits, the denials follow—I do not need Alex fucking Sebastian to access my sound. I don't. I can't.

I won't.

"Missing nothing." I turn my back to him, trying to escape his piercing gaze, only to meet it in the mirror.

"You figured it out."

"No." It's too quick. "Figured what out?"

"What you need."

I shake my head, emphatically. "I've been doing this all my life. Years and years. My mother wanted us to be musicians from the minute we were born. Named us after two of her favorite singers—Mariah Carey and Whitney Houston—hoping one of us would want to pursue it, and Whit couldn't care less about music, but I grabbed hold right away. I've been studying performance since I could hold a microphone."

"Okay. Your mother would be proud. Do you have a point?"

Honestly, the speech was meant for me.

I swivel back to face him. "Why are you here?"

"I told you—"

"In my dressing room. Why are you here right now?"

He steps the rest of the way in and kicks the door shut with his foot. "Worried about being alone with me?"

"Why would I be worried about that?"

"I don't know. You tell me."

My tug in my belly spreads down the insides of my thighs.

I'm pretty sure he's just trying to rile me up, like he always does, but there's a slight hint of invitation in his voice, and even though it's wrong...

God, it's so wrong.

He thinks I'm sleeping with his brother. I'm letting him think I'm sleeping with his brother.

I turn back to the mirror. "The point is that I know what I'm doing. I don't need you to come and fix everything for me all the time." I pick up the lip gloss and reapply it to my red-stained lips, hoping he'll take my statement as a dismissal.

Sort of hoping.

Okay, not really hoping.

"Sure. You don't need me." He's intensely casual, which I didn't know was a thing until just now, and it unnerves me. "What is it you need then?"

I'm not sure it's a need, actually. If it is, it's very base. Primitive. Primal.

Again, I meet his gaze in the reflection. His eyes are hooded and dark and brimming with heat.

We can't.

Determined to get this out of my head, I let out a breath. "I'm distracted, is all." I pick up one of Zully's brushes and add powder that I don't need to my forehead and cheeks. "My sister. Not that it's any of your business."

It's not even a lie. When she came back from the temp agency after having only been gone for half an hour, I knew without her telling me that her outfit had made exactly the wrong impression I'd said it would.

It could have been an opportunity for us to have the conversation that I need to have with her about me and

Hunter, as well as a larger conversation about how the world perceives and treats women, but any time I try to talk to her, she runs to her room and slams the door.

It's been two days of silent treatment, and it shouldn't be that big of a deal—it *wouldn't* be that big of a deal if I weren't so unsure about everything else in my life. I'm not good at compartmentalizing and the wrought feelings where she's concerned are bleeding into this debut. If my approach is failing with her, who's to say my approach isn't failing everywhere?

It's a waiting shame spiral of despair that I cannot go down right now, so I shake my head and will the distracting thoughts away. "I just need to meditate, and I'll be fine."

I'm not sure if I'm trying to convince Alex or myself.

He chortles. "Meditation is not going to get you into the frame of mind you need for that song."

My threadbare willpower breaks, and losing any semblance of composure, I twist toward him. "And you think that you're the answer? That being bad with you is what I need?"

In a flash, he crosses the room, wrenches my hands behind my back, and pushes me against the makeup counter until his body is pressed against mine. The powder brush falls from my hand and my heart rate soars. I can feel my pulse everywhere in my body. In my chest, in my ears. In the space between my thighs.

"You aren't thinking about your sister now, are you?"

"I'm not thinking about my song either. I'm thinking about kicking you in the nuts."

He isn't fazed. "That's not what you're thinking about doing to my nuts."

His audacity annoys me, never mind that he's right. "I'm supposed to be thinking about my song."

He shakes his head. "I don't want you thinking about your song. You shouldn't be thinking at all. You need to get in the right headspace and then just be there."

"What headspace is that? The one where I murder you in your sleep?"

He bends low, so I can feel his hot breath skid across my earlobe. "The one where you remember you choose to be used."

Choose to be used.

There's power in that choice. It's the power I took hold of when I chose to go along with this PR arrangement with Hunter. Whether it's because of societal norms and the noise of public opinion or because I'm just not used to recognizing it, it's a power I keep forgetting I have.

It's exactly the power I need to embrace when I walk out on that set today to unveil this gritty new sound of mine.

Alex stares at me. "You have to ask for it. You have to choose it."

My chest is pounding, and he's as cool as a cucumber. Not a single crease of tension on his features. I'd think he was completely unaffected if his very hard dick wasn't jabbing into my belly button.

His hard dick is not my responsibility.

But it can be if I want it to be. If I choose it.

I glance at the clock on the wall. There's roughly ten minutes before I'm supposed to be on stage. My eyes flick to the door. "It's not locked."

"Isn't a problem for me."

My stomach flip-flops with an anticipation that I haven't felt in a long time. A dangerous sort of excitement. Both the thrill of something forbidden and something new.

When I tug lightly against his hold on my wrists, he lets them free, and I reach for his belt buckle.

His cock jerks against me, but he quickly pulls my hand away. "Choose it, Riah. Say it."

My breath shakes as I inhale.

When I exhale again, I make the choice. "Dirty me up, Alex."

As quick as he moved to back me up against the counter, he steps back and undoes his buckle. He's instantly in charge. "On your knees."

I drop to the floor, ignoring the concern about ripping the netting of my skirt that threatens to sidetrack me and open my mouth before he even has his pants down.

When his cock pops out, the familiar shape is accompanied by an unfamiliar scent of musk and soap. Hunter is far from my mind, but also right here with us in the ways I can't disregard. It seems the gene that determined their generous size is one they share. The shape is similar, too, and the length.

It's eerie at first. Cringey, even. To be kneeling in front of a man I shouldn't be kneeling in front of and seeing the dick of a man I don't want to ever kneel in front of again.

It's so much wrong, and guilt twists inside my stomach.

But it's buried under the weight of my desire, and all thoughts of my ex immediately vanish when Alex wraps his hand tightly in my hair and uses it to force my head forward. It's mean and bossy in a way that Hunter never was with me. There's a sense of desperation and passion in Alex as well, and while I'm generally a reluctant BJ giver, I find my tongue eagerly licking off the filmy bead of liquid at the tip of his crown.

Then I take his head into my mouth and swirl my tongue around it, drinking in his salty taste. I peer up, as I do, watching for his reaction. Learning him.

But instead of letting me explore like I want to, he thrusts his entire length into my mouth, making my eyes water. I barely manage to relax my throat so that I don't gag.

"Should have known you could deep throat. I can't imagine my brother likes it any other way. He likes to be sure you feel it when he fucks you."

Apparently, I'm not the only one who can't keep Hunter from joining us.

It should send up alarm bells. It's sick and twisted, and any woman with any sense of self would be turned off and disgusted.

But it does just the opposite. My pussy slickens, and that furnace inside my belly spikes hotter.

He pulls out, only to quickly shove inside me again.

I grab onto his thighs to steady myself. To feel a sense of control.

"You're just a plaything, aren't you?"

I'm not. I'm so much more. But I hum an agreement because that's part of the scene we're playing and because it's somehow true too, and he groans.

"Fucking little tease." He pulls on my hair so hard I have to move forward to lessen the pain. "You like that don't you, you little cock sucker?"

Yeah, yeah. I do. Used and abused kink officially unlocked because I really do.

What the hell is wrong with me?

It's for the song.

That's all. It's method acting. He's using me, and I'm using him. I like it because of what I get out of it. Nothing more.

He continues to thrust his hips into my face, pushing me to my limits and barely allowing me to take a breath as he does. His language is full of filth as he continues his movement in and out of my mouth with force. "You're such a dirty slut. Made to take Sebastian cock. I bet that's what your songs are secretly about." His voice is low and patronizing. "Thinly veiled odes to your desire to be dominated."

It's insulting.

It *should* be insulting.

To have my music diminished to a simple metaphor of me on my knees. It's what I most fear people will think. It's not at all what I'm about or the message I want to give.

But I'm here by choice. Because I want to be, and because it makes my pussy throb, and I have to push my thighs together to ease the ache, and that's what my music *is* about. About the ability to choose this. The ability to be used how I want to be.

A big fat cock thrusting in and out of my mouth, and I've never felt so empowered.

I struggle to take it all in, the strange dichotomy of power and submission, the rapid thrusts of Alex's hips. He mercilessly fucks my throat, and each time I try to pull away for a moment of air, he tightens his grip on my hair and feeds me more filthy words.

The sensation is almost unbearable until he finally pulls out just enough that I manage a few breaths before he pushes back in again. I'm so wet, I can almost smell myself.

It isn't just doing it for me. Alex's thighs tense and his thrusts grow erratic, and I'm sure he's getting close to orgasm when there's a sharp knock on the door. "Getting close to show time," a female voice says through the thick wood.

I try to pull away, horrified, and I swear my heart stops beating.

The door is unlocked. The door is unlocked. The door is unlocked.

But Alex grabs both sides of my head and holds me in place. "Breathe," he says softly. "Breathe. Through your nose." Then he calls out. "She needs five minutes."

"She has three." The sound of heels clicking down the hallway follows, and I practically melt in relief.

"We better hurry then because the only way you're singing that song the way it needs to be sung is with my cum coating your throat."

I think I've surrendered all control, but I also think he's asking me for permission to let everything loose. It's hard to believe he hasn't already, and I'm not sure I can take much more. My knees are numb from the hard floor. My throat is already raw as it is. And I have to sing after this.

But I'm not thinking about the song. I'm here right now, and I want to taste him. I have no ability to speak, and he's holding me so tight that I can barely nod, so I meet his eyes and hope he reads what I'm trying to tell him.

Yes. Do this. Turn me to filth.

Either he gets the message, or he just doesn't care

because he begins ramming deeper than ever before until his whole body shakes with pleasure, letting out a masculine roar like no other as he comes inside my mouth. Watching his body tense feels like watching art. Art that I made. His breath catches as he empties his load into my mouth. The hot splash of him on my tongue is like nothing I've ever tasted before.

"Show me." His voice is ragged and forceful.

I open my mouth and stick out my tongue showing I've swallowed everything, and maybe I'm in a delirious haze, but I'm pretty sure it wrests the last bit of control from him. He unravels.

I watch him as he catches his breath. As he resumes his composure. As he flips the switch from one kind of monster to another. From alpha dominant to alphahole. It's subtle but distinct. The first monster hates to want me. The second wants to hate me. He even might believe that he does.

I know how he feels.

After everything we've just done, witnessing the transformation is more intimate than the rest, and I almost forget that I'm wanted on stage until he's tugging me to my feet and pushing me to the mirror.

My reflection surprises me.

I hadn't thought about how disheveled I'd look. My hair is tangled and my mascara has run and my lipstick is smudged.

Alex pats my hair down so that it seems like there's method to the madness and then peers over my shoulder into the glass. When I reach for the lipstick, he stops me. "It's good like this."

"I look like I just gave head."

"And if you don't try to hide it, it looks like you don't give a fuck that everyone knows."

A zero-fuck attitude? That's power too.

And the more I stare, the more I realize that everyone will think the look is part of the act. No one will think I was actually in the backroom sucking off my "boyfriend's" brother. No one can see the knot of guilt inside me.

But adrenaline and lust are flowing through my veins, fucking real as can be. There's no way it won't show up in my performance.

"Sing a line," he orders.

"Why don't you stop staring at me like you expect me to give you my best."

Alex's smug expression tells me that not only is the raw sound perfect but he thinks he deserves some of the credit.

I can't decide whether I should thank him or slap him.

While I'm considering, he meets my gaze in the reflection and holds it. Holds it so long that my skin starts to itch from the intimacy. From the fear that he'll see something he shouldn't.

And then, as if he's afraid of the same thing, a veil drops, and the look in his eyes clouds. "You know, you're so easy to exploit, I don't even mind the sloppy seconds."

I should have known he couldn't stay nice for long.

Slap him it is, then.

Well, verbally, anyway. Since I do my best damage with words. "Funny how you think I'm the one who's been exploited. After my performance, it will be my name on all the social media sites. I think I got what I needed from this."

He wrinkles his nose as if he thinks my attempt to

offend him is charming. "But everybody already knows my name."

There's another knock on the door. My cue.

I turn to go but stop to deliver my final jab. "And how far down the list of Sebastians do they get before they remember you? Don't worry. I'm sure Hunter's only a few above you."

The hurt settles in his jaw, as obvious as if I'd left a handprint.

It's a shitty game, baiting Alex the way I do. Using his brother's name to poke at his insecurities.

If I hate myself for it, I'm sure it will be fine.

Just one more thing I can put in the music.

CHAPTER
THIRTEEN
RIAH

I killed my performance on SHE.

Twenty-four hours later, the video has over a million plays on YouTube, plus my single is streaming in the top one hundred. Claude has an inbox full of interview offers from all the major networks and music magazines, and the internet is begging for info about the album release date. The overwhelming remark from critics is *Zyah has gone bad and the world is here for it*.

It's everything I could have hoped for and more.

Hunter is less than pleased.

At least this time we don't have to fly to L.A. for the emergency team meeting. Claude was already in New York for the launch, and my tour sponsors are located here as well, so rather than meet at my label's office, which is located on the West Coast, Hunter booked a conference room at the Sebastian Center.

"Thank you for gathering on short notice, and thank

you so much for hosting, Hunter. I wish I could be there in person, but this will have to do." Jennica's the exec at Topaz, my label, and the rightful one to lead this conversation, so I'm glad when she starts the meeting. I'd been half afraid Hunter would take it upon himself.

Now that she's begun, it's unlikely he'll try to take the reins. It doesn't mean he won't be liberal with his opinion, though, and it's possible Jennica and Stew—the rep from my tour sponsor—will not like the sexified turn to my persona, but I'm hoping the response to yesterday's debut will speak for which direction my future performances should skew.

We all focus on the screen as Jennica introduces everyone in attendance—Claude, Hunter, Stew and his assistant, me, and Alex, who walks in just as she's finishing up.

My knees were already bouncing under the table, but the sight of the tall, blue-eyed devil has my heart launching for my throat.

Jennica pauses at the interruption, and Hunter must give him an inquisitive look because Alex points to Claude and says, "He thought I should be here."

Which is news to me.

The two of them might have spoken while I was performing yesterday—Alex was gone by the time I was done—but this meeting wasn't scheduled until later, meaning Claude had to have reached out. What the actual fuck?

Hunter doesn't seem to question it. In fact, he responds with a nod that suggests he not only thinks his brother's presence is a good idea but also that he's not surprised Alex would want to contribute.

It's not enough information for me.

"What are you doing here?" I whisper-ask when he slides into the seat next to me because of course it's the only empty place at the table, and now I'm sandwiched between two Sebastian gods, and I feel very much like a piece of bologna.

"Someone needs to defend that cover," he says. As if it's obvious.

Claude must have told him we'd be discussing it today.

I'm not sure how to take this news. I want to be offended—like, why do they think I can't handle this myself? And why does Claude think Alex has more sway than I do? And can everyone tell that my blood warmed a degree or five as soon as he walked into the room?

Never mind what's going on in my panties.

On the other hand, I'm not sure I have any allies here beyond Claude, and having Alex on my side is definitely a coup.

After a moment of digestion, I whisper a reluctant thanks.

"Oh, baby, it's not for you."

Right. Why would I have thought otherwise? Here to make sure I don't embarrass the precious Sebastian name, most likely.

And no, I didn't just get goosebumps at the term *baby*. The AC is on, and it's cold in here. Duh.

Hunter glares at us, either irritated about being left out of the exchange or irritated that we're interrupting or just irritated because that's how he's been since the performance went live.

Technically, Hunter is also a tour sponsor, since he's been kicking in money and favors left and right to make this new album happen. Meaning, it really isn't in my favor to piss him off.

So I clam up and return my gaze to the screen, and try my hardest not to think about the fact that I know what his brother's cock looks like—and tastes like—when I very much shouldn't.

Really taking the bad girl a bit far, aren't you?

God, how did I get into this mess?

"To be clear," Jennica says, with a tone that suggests she also thinks this situation is a mess, "though we were blindsided by Zyah's performance choices, we're quite happy about the numbers coming off the launch."

Claude takes the complimentary words as an opportunity to redirect the conversation. "If everyone's happy, I think we should be discussing how to lean into these performance choices and make sure we replicate them going forward."

"Well, obviously we want to ensure continued success." Jennica speaks carefully, as though afraid she'll put her stamp on something unintentionally.

"Then it's settled. We do more of the same." Claude acts as if the case is closed. "Anything else we need to discuss?"

Sometimes I forget that he really is a good manager. He might not be in touch with what it is I want to do on stage, but he knows how to handle people on my behalf.

Jennica, on the other hand, represents more than just

me. "It's not quite that simple when we're dealing with sponsorships."

Stew speaks up for the first time, addressing me directly. "We do have concerns about how far you're planning to go with this. TekTech tends to generally put support behind family brands."

Before I can think up a defense, Claude steps in again. "Zyah wasn't ever pitched as a family brand in the first place. She's broken none of her commitments to TekTech."

To his credit, Hunter has been patient until now. "The short of it is, Claude, that Zyah did not work this hard for this long to have all her talent obscured behind a trashy new persona."

I wince. "Trashy?"

Alex leans forward so he can see his brother. "That's real prejudice there, Hunt. Careful. It's a bad look."

It's exactly the thing Hunter needs to hear to be swayed. He wants to clean up his image? Well, it doesn't do any good to replace his bad-boy rep with that of a misogynist.

I'm grateful, but I hate that Alex is the one to point it out.

Especially when the statement is accompanied by his hand on my bare thigh under the table where no one can see.

It takes everything I have not to shiver in response.

"It was a statement made behind closed doors," Hunter says in defense. "And I'm just saying she doesn't need to resort to sex to sell herself. She's talented enough without it."

Alex moves his hand higher. "You make it sound like she's whoring herself out."

The comment hits a nerve. I specifically stopped sleeping with Hunter because I didn't want to feel like a whore, and yet that's still how he chooses to portray me. Still how I so often feel.

Alex being blatantly handsy doesn't help.

Ignoring the buzz in my lower abdomen, I push his palm from my thigh. "I'm not resorting to sex. I'm embracing the message of the music."

Hunter opens his hands to the air. "Maybe you need to come up with a new message."

"Okay. How about my next album's message is that women belong in boxes? I bet I know which demographic will embrace that." It's too harsh and unprofessional, and I immediately regret saying it.

Not that I don't have a point, but I really am trying to win him over, and sarcasm is not the way.

Thankfully, Claude's right there to calm me down. "The music is good, Riah. It's on-trend. It's what listeners want. Jake's contributions are the icing on the cake. There's nothing to change there."

There's a murmur of agreement, which actually does make me feel better. Or as better as a person can feel when they have little power, and their art is under a microscope.

After a beat, Stew adds, "Honestly, we really like the album cover."

"The cover's done?" Hunter turns accusing eyes toward me then slides them to his brother.

"Yeah, I uh…didn't have a chance to show you yet." Truthfully, I just pretended I didn't have to. As soon as Alex convinced me that the photos were perfect, I let Claude make the final choice and turned it in to Jennica.

Guess my manager forgot to include Hunter in that email.

I cast a glance in his direction, and his shrug says that may have been on purpose.

Like I said before—he's on my side.

"Yes, we were really pleased with it as well. Let me share my screen." Jennica's face disappears, and then there I am in black and white with my legs crossed in Hunter's library.

I feel him tense next to me.

I keep my eyes down but once again I feel his eyes on me. "What the fuck? This isn't what we discussed."

Deep down, I think I'd thought that if this was sprung on him in front of a bunch of other people, he couldn't argue it.

But I forgot who I was dealing with.

I open my mouth to explain that the other photos just weren't working, but as promised, Alex jumps in to justify the choice. "It's classy, Hunter. It's art. It's empowering and also highbrow, and you know it."

Hunter scowls, but he swivels his head back to the screen to study it. "Is that my chair?"

"It's a refined piece of furniture," Claude says, pandering. "The picture is stunning, in my opinion. Catches the eye. Art, as Alex said."

I can practically hear the wheels turn in Hunter's head. After a bit, he concedes, "It's tasteful. Yes."

Claude pounces on the concession. "The performance was the same. It was seductive without being crass."

"We completely agree," Stew says. "We aren't opposed to this direction. We would just like assurances that this exploration of sexuality stays within these current boundaries."

"Done." The word is out of my mouth in an instant. If Stew is on board, Jennica will be on board, and that just leaves Hunter.

"Tasteful, classy, empowering," Stew continues, nodding at his assistant. "We can work with that."

"We can," she says.

"Done," I say again.

"Hunter?" Jennica's the one to ask.

I hold my breath, knowing no one will argue if he swoops in with a big fat veto and an order to rebrand.

"Okay, well…" His frustration is obvious. Even though his vote means more than everyone else combined, he doesn't like to be outnumbered. "If we continue down this path, who's going to make sure that it doesn't go too far?"

"Uh…me." Do they think I have no sense of taste? That I can't handle myself?

Apparently so, because everyone looks around the room as if I haven't spoken.

"Claude, you've been overseeing all of this?" It's Jennica's way of volunteering him for the job.

"I wasn't there for the photo shoot, and I'm headed back to L.A. next week, so probably someone else would be a better fit. Alex, you were there yesterday."

My stomach drops.

Oh, fuck no.

"I don't need a babysitter," I say, but what I really mean is that Alex is a bad, bad babysitter.

"Alex is a brand specialist, actually." Hunter says it

more to himself than anyone else, apparently warming up to the idea. "He knows how to stay within the lines."

"*I* know how to stay within the lines." Seriously, am I on mute here?

I stare across the table at Claude.

"It's just always good to have someone else monitoring these things," he says. "So you can concentrate on the music. It's why you have a team."

"But Alex doesn't know anything about this business." My voice sounds more panicked than I mean it to. More belittling.

I try softening it. "No offense to you, Alex."

"No offense taken. But, Riah?" He waits until I look at him to go on. "This is exactly my field of expertise."

Oh my God…is he actually vying for the position?

"Your field is in brands," I refute.

"And Zyah is a brand. I had the vision for the cover, didn't I? And I think my coaching yesterday helped you deliver, if I'm not mistaken."

Heat spreads down my body. I'm sure if I looked in a mirror, I'd be red from head to toe. How could he actually bring that up in front of everyone? And just stay so calm and collected about it.

I have a strong desire to reach out and grab Claude's pen from the table and stab it into Alex's thigh. I have to sit on my hands to stop the temptation.

Hunter doesn't seem to notice my reaction. "You coached her?"

Alex makes an affirming gesture that comes off as no-big-deal, and I genuinely want to crawl under the table and die.

To make matters worse, Claude has to pipe in on the matter. "It was night and day from the sound check to the final performance."

"Night and day is an exaggeration," I manage to say, but my case is weak.

"I didn't realize." Hunter sounds...touched? Or perhaps just surprised that his brother would do something nice like that without being asked.

If only he knew...

"You should do more of that," he continues. "Coaching. We'd pay you, obviously."

"*We* will?" I don't know whose money he's volunteering here because I'm certainly not hiring Alex for...for...well, for anything, but especially not *that*.

Hunter ignores me. "Temporary gig. Until the album is out and the tour is staged and underway. You have time right now in your schedule. It would be a great transitional project."

"Probably not what I would be expecting salary-wise," Alex says, thankfully, because that's a really great way to bow out.

"Right. We couldn't pay you what you're worth," I say.

At the same time, Hunter says, "We'll make it worth it. I owe you anyway."

"And your way of paying me back is to ask me to set aside my life and focus on containing yours?" There's a tension in Alex's tone, the first indication that he has any beef with his brother.

The first indication today, that is. The sex words he's said have felt too earnest to be just kink.

Ah, criminy. I can't believe I've ever heard Alex Sebastian say sex words. And that we're now discussing him possibly being in a position to say more of them.

Obviously, it can't happen. "That really is asking a lot of him, Hunter."

Again, I'm ignored. "You know what this means for me, Alex. You're the only person I trust."

"You trust me?"

Yeah, Alex, I'm as surprised as you are. Considering what you've done behind his back with his supposed girlfriend.

"Of course I do."

I try once more to stop this nightmare from becoming reality. "There have to be other options. It isn't fair to ask Alex to put his life on pause for something he has no interest in."

"I didn't say I wasn't interested." This time he presses his thigh against mine.

I shift my hips away from him and tell myself I didn't like the way my skin lit up from his touch. "Really, this isn't necessary."

Stew doesn't agree. "We'd feel better having someone around to keep boundaries in place."

"It seems like the perfect concession," Jennica says.

"It's settled then?" Claude looks around the table, while I silently plead for someone to speak up with a reasonable objection.

When no one does, I turn to stare at Alex. Say no. *Say. No.*

His lip curls into a half-grin. "It's settled."

Claude stands to stretch his hand across the table. "Welcome to the team."

I BARELY SAY a word the rest of the meeting. It's depressing that no one seems to realize. They're too busy making arrangements and familiarizing Alex with my schedule and congratulating themselves on creating a winning package that will make everyone a whole shitload of money.

Yay, all of us.

When the meeting is adjourned and Jennica's purple hair disappears from the screen, Stew and his assistant rush off for another appointment, and Claude excuses himself to take a phone call. (The man is always taking phone calls.)

I storm out ahead of Alex and Hunter, wanting nothing to do with either of them for the rest of the day, if I can help it. All of it is frustrating. Every bit. From the part where my art has to be micromanaged to the part where I have to lie about my non-relationship to the part where the hot guy who I shouldn't be attracted to, but very much am, seems to think that my life is just a game.

I just can't imagine what else he's thinking.

I'm still fuming about it when Alex joins me by the elevator. Glancing around, I don't see Hunter anywhere.

"He'll catch up in a minute," he says, realizing who I'm looking for.

And I have my chance.

Grabbing him by the suit jacket, I tug him around the corner where I can confront him with a bit of privacy. "What the hell?"

"He had to visit the little boys' room," Alex says, as if Hunter's what I'm talking about.

"That's not what I'm asking."

His square jawline shifts with his smirk. "Looks like I'm your new branding coach. Congratulations."

Even though we're alone, I lower my voice. "Did you forget exactly what you did to coach me?"

"This alcove is a little deeper, if you'd like to sneak back there and remind me."

"Oh, fuck you, not happening." The stupid thing is that my pulse quickened at the suggestion.

Not that I'd take him up on it. Because nothing should have ever happened between us at all, and definitely shouldn't happen again and more importantly, my pretend boyfriend—his brother—is going to show up any minute.

Alex appears to find the whole thing amusing.

He leans his shoulder against the wall, his eyes glinting. "Get ready to have your career explode. Among other things."

"This isn't a joke."

"Oh, I'm taking this very seriously. I have your calendar now. I'll make sure to skip my morning whack on the days of your scheduled appearances. Wouldn't want you to waste energy having to work too hard. I realize you have to be able to open your mouth to sing."

I'm so flustered by his nonchalance that I can't get a thought out. "This is not…we're not…don't even think—"

He shifts and traps me against the wall, cutting me off. "Don't think…what, sweetheart? That you need me? That I help you be the bad little girl you don't know how to be on your own?"

I'm immediately overwhelmed by the intoxicating scent of him. It's all I can do not to lean forward and inhale. "I don't believe for one minute this is about helping me."

He cocks his head. "You have your reasons, I have mine. All that matters is the end result."

"What happened to '*he's my brother*?' He *trusts* you."

"I guess you're not the only one with slippery morals."

"So you expect me to just be a pawn in whatever fucked up rivalry you've got going on with Hunter at the sacrifice of my best interests?"

"Has anything I've presented hurt your career so far?"

I hate that the answer is no.

And I hate that I actually want him around. Want his advice.

Need his support.

And I hate this fucked up arrangement with Hunter that prevents me from being open with Alex and maybe getting to explore this attraction for real, but mostly I hate that I'm pretty sure he's only into me because he thinks it would piss Hunter off.

It's only a suspicion, but it seems to line up, and for all those reasons, fooling around with Alex again in any way has to be off the table.

It's the one thing I can control, anyway. The rest is out of my hands.

"You can coach me," I tell him. "You can monitor my brand. That's all. I don't need anything else from you."

I try to push out from under his arm, but he lowers his shoulder, blocking me. "You know what? I think you almost believe that. But here's the thing, Riah—your music relies on authenticity, and you can't sing about being used without actually feeling it, can you?"

"That's not what my music is about." It comes out as a whisper because I'm not exactly sure he's wrong.

"Are you sure about that?"

Refusing to answer, I try to escape under his other arm, only to be blocked in by that shoulder. He holds me captive like that for long seconds, then at the sound of approaching footsteps, he finally backs up.

Just in time for Hunter to arrive.

For the first time in weeks, I reach for Hunter's hand, though I have no idea what I'm trying to prove by the gesture and hope he doesn't notice how much I'm shaking when his fingers wrap around mine.

CHAPTER
FOURTEEN
RIAH

T wo days later, I'm on Hunter's arm again at the Sebastian family's annual Spring Fling. I'm pretty sure the sole purpose of this afternoon event is to dress up in pretty clothes and hang out with other rich people and be photographed by lifestyle magazines, but it's under the guise of networking.

It's the perfect place for Hunter to remind the media that he's a good boy now in a steady relationship with a good girl.

Sometimes I wonder if there's any part of his life that isn't an act.

After we finish our press walk and picture posing, I scan the yard looking for familiar faces. "Is your whole family here?"

What I really want to know is, will Alex be here.

Besides some email exchanges regarding my future schedule, I haven't seen or spoken to him since the team meeting. If he's planning to derail my day, I need to be prepared.

As if I could be prepared for the man and his severe gaze and broad chest and…

Hunter interrupts my thoughts before I get too carried away in my hate/lust spiral. Thankfully. "It is a *family* thing, so…."

Not helpful and more than a little bit condescending.

I'm not sure if he was always like this or if he's just been more of an asshole since our breakup. If it's the former, I really don't know what I was thinking when I thought we might be something real someday.

"Right. A family thing."

THIS YEAR, the Spring Fling is at Adeline Estates, Holt's country house in Greenwich. The veranda, which is large enough to be the size of a generous ballroom, has been devoted to the press. Tents, tables, and chairs are set up on the grounds below for mingling. Farther down the lawn, there's a stage with a small swing band playing. There's room on the lawn for dancing, but no one's taken the opportunity to do so. Most of the guests seem to be happy with their cocktails and hors d'oeuvres and society gossip.

In true Hunter style, we arrived late, so if Alex is coming, he's likely already here. But if he is, I haven't yet spotted him.

Hunter grabs two glasses of champagne off a passing tray and hands one to me. "Is there someone in particular you're looking for?"

"No," I lie.

Then mentally chastise myself for being so obvious before going back to telling myself that Alex does not have to be a problem.

It's true, too. Two days has given me time to really think about the situation, and I've realized there really is a benefit to having someone like him helping me out with this rebrand. The stupid physical thing going on between us is just that—stupid and physical. Stress can do a lot of strange things to hormones, and there is nothing wrong with blowing off the stress of this transition with someone like him.

Except that he thinks I'm with Hunter still, which means I'm practically cheating, and either Alex doesn't care and just wants to fool around or—more likely—he's planning to use my "indiscretion" for his own benefit. Whether that's to try to break up Hunter and me—*too late for that, buddy*—or something else, I don't know.

Point is, any nefarious motives of his can be cleared up by just telling him the truth.

"I've been thinking," I say as we make our way down toward the crowd, my arm laced loosely through his. "We should explain things to Alex."

"He's slow, I know, but I already had the talk about the birds and the bees with him when he was ten."

I glare at him.

Then quickly change it to a smile because there are people watching and it's important to look like we're a happy couple. "I mean about us. That we're not…you know…"

"Fucking?"

Seriously, were the Sebastian men raised to be irritating? "That we aren't really together."

And yes, that we aren't fucking. He definitely should know that.

This is a conversation that I'd planned to have during the two-and-a-half-hour ride out here, but Hunter and I had shared the limo with Ax and his date, a dark-haired buxom sorority girl with a fake beauty mark (it smeared during their make out session) and a high-pitched laugh. I never did catch her name, but his women come and go through a revolving door, so it won't matter in a day or two.

Talking about Alex right now when he could pop up at any moment isn't ideal, and especially not with other people around, but I take my chances when I get them.

Hunter takes a swallow from his glass before he pinches his brows together. "Why would we tell Alex?"

"He's on the team. He should know."

The confused expression doesn't leave Hunter's face. "But what does it matter?"

"I don't know." I hadn't expected that I'd have to make a case for it. "It's just weird, isn't it? That he's your brother and you're keeping him in the dark."

He shrugs as if lying to siblings is a normal part of life. "It shouldn't change anything he's doing for you. He should advise you as though we're together."

"Well, yeah, but…"

"Claude doesn't know, and he's on the team. Why would you specifically want Alex to know?"

I don't know how I forgot that Hunter was a born inter-rogator. It wouldn't be an issue if I was transparent about my reasons for bringing Alex into the fold. For half a second, I consider telling him some version of the truth. He might not even care.

But at the last second, I chicken out and make up something that feels plausible. "He asks me things that I should know about you."

He stops walking and throws me a suspicious stare. "Why is he even talking to you about me? Is he trying to get into your pants?"

Despite the fact that I was just about to admit this, I'm immediately defensive. "Who tries to get into my pants isn't your business anymore."

"If it's my brother, like hell it isn't."

"Doesn't matter who, Hunter. You lost the right to have a say when you dicked around on me with Kelsey Kline."

"Kelsey is not the same. You don't see me trying to fuck Whitney."

My entire body goes rigid. "Don't even joke about it."

"Then don't joke about Alex." His glare is unnerving. It's the kind of glare that ends things. The kind that, once delivered, shuts people up. Closes the subject for good.

After several seconds without a response from me, Hunter seems to think that's what he's done—put an end to the discussion—and he starts walking again down the path to the lower grounds.

But I'm too mad to let it drop.

"Whitney isn't the same, either. She's barely eighteen. You're almost forty." Actually, that's probably the same age gap as Ax and his date, so maybe not the best argument where these men are concerned, and not surprisingly, Hunter shrugs like *what's your point*.

I let out a frustrated grumble. "I don't even know how

the conversation ended up here. I'm not talking about getting in anyone's…" I stop myself before I outright lie. "All I'm talking about is business. It would be easier to make sure that I deliver what you need, as well as what I need, if Alex was in on all the ins and outs."

"Well, he's going to have to figure it out without the whole puzzle. He's a big boy. He managed SIC's brand, and that's a whole corporation. I think he's qualified to handle one pop star without being spoon-fed."

I let the belittling dig slide because the reason for his resistance suddenly hits me. "Oh." We're only a few yards from the crowd now, and this time it's me who stops walking. "You don't trust him."

It feels like a monumental discovery. Alex is always around. He has free rein of Hunter's properties. They seem so close.

But when Hunter turns to face me, he doesn't refute it. "I don't trust anyone."

I don't miss the subtext. He doesn't trust me either.

I'm offended until I remember that I have fooled around with his brother behind his back, and even though I really do believe it isn't his business, it's also kind of shady on my part.

But Alex and I aren't the only people in his inner circle. "You trust Ax."

"Ax is different."

"How? Alex is just as loyal to you. He's constantly jumping to help you out, even when there's no benefit to him. Ax isn't even blood related."

"Exactly. I know what Sebastians are capable of."

Cold realization flows through my veins. "Because you'd stab Alex in the back if you had the chance." He doesn't trust his brother because he knows his brother shouldn't trust him.

If Alex really has a vendetta against Hunter, I'm starting to understand why.

"That's really sad," I say.

He gives another dismissive shrug. "Some things are more important than blood, baby."

What things?

I can't imagine anything more important to me than Whitney. The only thing that came close after my mother died was my career, and Whit won out over that, hands down.

And sure, my family life was different than Hunter's. I know his father is toxic as all get out, but that doesn't seem like the case with Alex. In Hunter's own words, Alex has always looked up to his older brother. Leaned on him. Followed him around. That has to translate to love, and if there are things more important than love, I really fucking want to know.

But before I can figure out how to articulate the question, Hunter is attacked by his cousin, Adly.

Perhaps attacked is too strong a word, but she does run past me, barrels into him, and grabs onto the lapels of his tux in a dramatic fashion, very nearly spilling the rest of his champagne. "You must, must, must do something about your asshole henchman."

Hunter arches a brow. "Alex?"

"I am not your henchman."

A shiver runs through me at the sound of Alex's voice.

I turn to find him behind me as Adly answers Hunter. "Your other henchman."

Alex bristles at Adly's phrasing but doesn't correct her. Instead, he pours some of his Coke into my champagne, which makes me feel some sort of way, then gives his attention to my outfit, his eyes scanning down my body, taking me in. My sleeveless dress is long with a train, yet his gaze makes me feel like I'm wearing nothing at all.

Especially when he keeps staring.

I take a swallow of my now drinkable champagne to try to settle my nerves, knowing he's studying each aspect of my look. The dress is such a busy floral print that it takes a minute to realize the black background is sheer. The distinct shape of my breasts is visible if someone stares long enough, my nipples only covered by strategically placed roses.

And Alex is staring long enough.

I wonder if he can tell that my barely-covered nipples are suddenly standing very erect.

And then his eyes move upward. My hair is down with the front pulled back, my makeup natural with a nude lip, and though I spent a long time trying to decide how to dress for today, I suddenly realize he probably wanted a chance to give input.

"Well?" I say when several seconds pass without any comment.

"It walks the classy/sensual line that we're after. I approve. Well done."

It's not exactly an A+ but my insides soar as though they're high remarks. I'm mostly happy because ultimately the deciding factor for me on what to wear was that the dress has pockets.

But then, of course, he has more to say. "The eyeshadow is a bit subtle, but it works because this is a day event. The lip, though, is too muted."

"I always worry a dark color will show up where it's not wanted." It's a poke at Hunter and his purple Kelsey lip stain, and even though I'm not facing him I feel him glaring at the back of my head.

"Start wearing smudge-proof," Alex says, clearly not understanding. Or maybe understanding a little too well.

Ax—who I assume is the actual henchman Adly is hiding from based on the scowl she delivers—steps around Alex. Apparently, he's been there the whole time, and I hadn't noticed. "Why is Little Al giving commentary on your girl's outfit, Hunt?"

Adly lets go of Hunter and claps her hands. "Ooo, will you do Axel's date next? Her dress is hideous."

It wasn't hideous, but I'm pretty sure the jab is meant for Ax, who flips her off with a smirk.

I'm also pretty sure that he really doesn't care about why Alex is critiquing my look, but after Hunter's reaction at the idea that there might be something more between me and his brother, I feel pressed to explain. "He's managing my brand."

It's the first time I've said it without animosity.

Ax might not be interested, but Adly is. "Your brand? That's cool. I didn't know you were doing consultation work, Alex."

"It's his practice job before he sets off into the real world." Hunter chuckles. "His training wheels, if you will."

Ax laughs, and I can feel Alex tense.

I tense up right along with him. Hunter's comments are shitty and degrading, and yeah, maybe it's just guy talk and all in fun, but after the conversation I just had with him, there's a harsh subtext that hits me squarely in the chest, adding context to their brotherly relationship that I didn't have before.

And the context says toxic all the way.

Then there's what his remarks reveal about his opinion of me. *Practice job*. As if my brand and my career are insignificant.

"You're not funny," I say, with as much calm as I can muster, which is hard when I really want to throw the rest of my champagne over his head.

"Ax seems to think so." Hunter chuckles again.

I swear they're mentally giving each other a high five, and for the first time, I realize I've entrusted my career into the hands of a man who is not only immature, but also mean.

Alex's gaze hits mine, hard and unreadable. The usual crackle of tension transpires between us. The animosity too, because I can't forget all the asshole things he's said and done, but now I wonder if he might have legitimate reasons for his behavior.

Doesn't excuse him for being an asshole, but I have stupid goosebumps from the way he looks at me despite the fact, so half the problem is definitely me.

"Of course, Ax is laughing," Adly says, apparently oblivious or too distracted to feel the impact of Hunter's little joke. "This is Ax's third scotch of the afternoon."

"You're counting my drinks, Ad? Ah. How sweet that you care."

"You wish. I'm notating it in your employee file."

"I'm off the clock."

"You're here representing the Sebastians, aren't you? That's not off the clock. We're never off the clock."

Alex abandons us during their banter. I stare after him as he heads to the lower grounds on the far side of the house, away from the crowd. He looks back once as if he knows I'm watching.

As if he's already sure that—the first chance I get to slip away—I'll follow.

CHAPTER
FIFTEEN
RIAH

few minutes later, I'm able to sneak away. It's not even really sneaking, since Irving Sebastian shows up—Hunter and Alex's grandfather—and when he's around, no one pays attention to anyone else.

Alex is several yards ahead of me, but I can still make out his figure as it takes the path south toward the lower grounds. I hurry and chug down the rest of my coke-champagne, maybe so I can pretend alcohol is the reason for whatever it is I'm doing, and deposit it on an empty table before pulling away from the designated party area to follow after the tall tux-clad figure.

Adeline's grounds are extensive, parts reminding me of Central Park with walking areas that tunnel under pathways above. Besides the one glance he cast in my direction when he first left, Alex never looks back as he takes the dirt path up the hill. I lose sight of him when he descends the other side, so I quicken my step to the top.

But once there, I still can't see him.

I shade my eyes and scan the horizon. Either he went to the nearby stables, or he turned into the tunnel at the bottom of the hill. The tunnel seems more likely, I think, but it's dark from my vantage point. I grew up being warned about being a woman alone in poorly lit areas, so I hesitate.

We're on private property, which means there probably aren't any strangers lurking down there, but Alex isn't necessarily safe. In fact, he's often very dangerous.

I'm not a hundred percent sure that isn't the reason I'm following after.

No, you're making sure he's okay.

I curse quietly to myself because I can't even make myself believe the lie.

Then, with my pulse racing, I scale down the hill—carefully, since three-inch stilettos aren't the best shoes for hiking.

Once I'm level with the tunnel, the sun bleeds in from the other side, and though the dark clings to the walls, I can make out more of the trail. Still no Alex, but I can see the pathway bends out of view over there, and he's probably just that far ahead now.

Taking a deep breath, I hurry myself forward into the passageway.

A few steps in, two strong arms circle around me from behind—one around my waist, the other over my collarbone—and I yelp as I'm pulled into the shadows.

"Quiet now or people will come running," Alex's voice rumbles near my ear. "Unless you *want* company…"

My stomach flips like it always does when we're alone. "I don't…think so."

"Then what do you want? Because I can't imagine a single *good* reason that you came after me."

There's no missing the innuendo in his tone. The implication that my motives must be bad—as in *bad girl* bad. As in *oh so wrong* bad. As in *your panties better already be wet* bad.

My heart pounds in my chest like a bass drum.

This was what you wanted, wasn't it?

Everything that's happened between Alex and me has been unplanned and spur-of-the-moment. Choosing to follow him, on the other hand, is so obviously intentional, and my nerves suddenly get to me. "I was just…um. I wanted to be sure you were…"

He finishes for me. "Okay?" He laughs as though insulted, and maybe he is. I can't imagine he would want anyone to think he had his feelings hurt by a bit of sparring from his brother. "And…what? You were planning to make it better?"

Fuck, I don't know. I didn't think. I just followed. As if there was an invisible lure pulling me toward him. Whatever happened after that, I guess I sort of thought that was up to him.

Sort of hoped, actually.

What is wrong with me?

"Never mind."

I try to pull away, but he tightens his clasp on me and chuckles again, a deep and throaty laugh that vibrates through me. "I can handle my brother just fine, Riah. I have ways to make things even."

Goosebumps push up from my skin, and the hairs stand erect down my arms. Any questions I had about Alex's methods of dealing with Hunter and motives for screwing with me are answered when the arm he has wrapped around my collarbone loosens its grip and starts to sweep downward over my breasts.

The method is me. I'm how he gets even. By fucking around with me.

It's not like I need more reasons to pull away and run as fast as I can, but this clarity is sure a damn good one.

But instead of making a move to do so, I sink back into him and let it happen.

Because he's mad at Hunter. And when it comes down to it, I am too. Mad that he's such a dick. Mad that I didn't realize sooner. Mad that he still has so much influence over my life. Mad that he's keeping me from being honest with Alex. The only thing I'm not mad at Hunter about is that he cheated because then I might still be living with the wool over my eyes.

And sure, I'm not the biggest fan of Alex, but the more angry I get with his brother, the more that doesn't seem to matter.

My body sure doesn't seem to care. My nipples stretch toward Alex like flowers turning their head to catch the sun, and one is rewarded when his finger swirls lightly over the tip.

And fuck it. I moan.

He responds by poking a big fat erection into my backside.

"You're not even going to fight me, are you?" He pinches my nipple between his fingers through my dress. "Such a dirty...dirty...girl."

My breath catches in a gasp.

He nudges his nose up the curve of my neck then bites at my lobe. "Leave it to Hunter to have a nasty one."

There's so much wrong with that statement. So much I want to correct. First and foremost, that Hunter does not *have* me, followed closely with the fact that I've been pretty freaking vanilla until Alex.

But Hunter's explicit command to keep quiet is still ringing in my ears, and I don't want to talk about him right now anyway. Or think about him.

Or think, period.

So *without* thinking, I rub my ass up and down along Alex's cock, encouraging whatever it is that he's doing. Attempting to live up to the label he's given me, despite knowing how out of my league I am with him.

"Fuck," he hisses. He bucks against me. "So nasty."

With one hand still fondling my breast, he drops the other to the region of my pussy, and even through my clothing, he manages to find exactly the spot that's begging for the pressure of his touch.

And maybe I am a dirty, dirty girl because I push my hips forward, searching for more friction, humping the pad of his thumb like a dog in heat.

"Greedy, too. You want more, don't you?"

My breath is uneven. "Mm-hmm."

But with my acknowledgment, his hand abruptly stops. "You know there is something that would make me feel better."

"Okay." I swallow, both frightened and excited about his possible demand. "What is it?"

He tugs on the skirt of my dress, gathering it at my waist. "Your cunt. I want to see it."

"...it would? You just want to...look?"

"Need to see what sort of god-level pussy has my manwhore of a brother dumping all his other snatch."

"It's not because of my..." I trail off, not sure I can say the word.

The conversation has me frazzled. This is a step beyond what we've done before. A natural progression, perhaps, except that we're together on false pretenses and wrong pretenses and not even really together. We're leftovers. Two people who happened to be discarded in the same place. So full of poison that we can't share anything that isn't toxic.

But then shouldn't these moments with Alex be miserable and shameful?

Why do I like it so very, very much?

Alex has my panties completely revealed to the empty tunnel in front of us. "Mm. I don't think you're qualified to judge the quality of your cunt. I need to see, and then I'll know."

He could just defile me, and I'd let him. He has to know —I haven't fought, I haven't screamed—and yet like before, he makes me ask for it.

"Please, Alex." I feel my face heat before the word is even on my tongue. "Please, look at my pussy."

"So I can appraise it. So I can form an opinion of my own."

"Yes. So you can form an opinion of your own."

"You want to be so bad, but you can't let go of needing good girl approval, can you?" His words are caustic and belittling, but his subtext is all pleasure as he maneuvers to face me.

Then he walks me backward until I meet the wall.

With his dark eyes glued to mine, he tucks the bottom of my skirt into my corset top, his fingers brushing my breasts as he does. "That gets that out of the way."

It feels like a cue, so I start to bend down to take off my panties, but Alex puts a hand on my sternum and pushes me back to a stand.

Then he wraps his fingers around the band of my panties and wriggles them past my hips and down my thighs, stooping as he does. When they're bunched at my ankles, he lifts one of my legs and maneuvers my panties around my shoe before doing the same with the other leg and then bringing the damp silk fabric to his face.

He inhales deeply, and I both cringe and get wetter at the same time.

"I'm keeping these." He opens his tux jacket and shoves them into a hidden pocket.

"Uh…"

"Will he notice they're gone?"

Hunter? I almost laugh. "No. Definitely not."

It's not completely dark in the shadows, but dark enough to have a difficult time reading Alex's expression. He's either dubious or disappointed. Or both. "You never know. They're mine now."

He pats the pocket which happens to lay over his heart, and I can't help feeling some kind of way about that. It's tricky to try to analyze when I'm drowning in adrenaline and lust, and anyway, I was trying not to think at all.

Still in a squat, Alex squints to study the sight before him. I'm bare, having lasered off my hair when I first started dating Hunter—courtesy of his spa funds—and I find myself wondering if the brothers share their taste in women's grooming and holding my breath until Alex gives me his declaration.

"It's a pretty pussy." He leans in to inhale directly from the source this time. "Smells incredible. Do you know how hard I am just looking at this kitty?"

He brushes two fingers lightly down my slit, gathering my wetness, and hussy that I am, I spread my legs further apart, giving him better access. "How hard are you?"

"Too hard to ignore." He moves to his knees and opens his pants to free his cock.

My pussy pulses when he takes it in his hand and then lazily strokes himself, using my moisture as lube.

I'm captivated watching him. As captivated as he seems to be staring at my pussy. "Did you get your answer?"

"To why Hunter dumped his puss pool for you? Honestly, all I have is more questions. Does he treat this pretty thing like he should? Does he let you ride his face? Does he get you this wet just from staring?" He circles a finger around my opening with his free hand and brings it up to his mouth to suck. "God almighty."

I practically groan with him.

And then he leans forward and licks along my seam and this time I really do groan.

"Ah, fuck. Lean back."

I do and he lifts one of my legs to his shoulder, opening me up to him. It's an unsteady position, even with the wall behind me, especially when he licks me again, now that my lips are spread, and my sensitive spots are open to him. Especially when the tip of his tongue burrows under my hooded skin and finds the swollen bundle of nerves underneath.

"Oh my God." My hands fly to his hair for support. For encouragement.

Holy shit, this man can lick pussy.

He takes my clit into his mouth, sucking gently at first and then with more pressure. Only a minute in, and I'm already seeing stars.

"Someone needs to make Riah-flavored candy. You could make a billion dollars." He keeps his face close when he speaks, so I can feel his breath across my skin, teasing me, whether he means to or not.

I attempt to direct his head to the place I want it. "Stop talking. Keep licking."

"Don't you dare get bossy with me." He pets me with a finger as he speaks—so light that it's torture—his other hand still jerking his cock. "I'm not doing this for you, remember."

"Right. This is to get even." I need the reminder, in case I start thinking there might be more behind this.

"Why else would I be on my knees in my best clothes?"

I have to joke, or I might cry from the way he's edging me. "Because it's Sunday?"

"I don't worship, baby." His tongue takes the place of his finger, and he swirls it around my clit, tracing every delicate fold and crevice. As he continues to explore my folds with his skilled tongue, I can feel myself getting lost in the pleasure of his touch. Every flick and lick sends sparks of electricity through my body, and a climax starts to build.

"Sure feels like worship to me."

"Maybe it feels like worship because you don't get eaten often enough."

I really need to stop saying things that provoke him into

responding because, first of all, I can't stand the teasing when he pulls away to talk, and second of all, I don't have the brain capacity to give thoughtful replies.

My unthought-out reply this time? "I don't, uh…okay."

Alex pulls completely back to stare up at me. "Are you telling me he doesn't?"

His expression is smug, even before I've confirmed, and of course, the truth is more complex than just a simple one-word answer, but that's what I give. "No."

"Say it."

When I don't respond, he sucks my labia so hard, I gasp. I'm sure there will be a bruise, and fuck if that doesn't make me hotter.

He repeats the command. "Say it."

This time, I answer. "He doesn't."

"Say he doesn't eat me to orgasm."

"At this moment, neither have you."

He flicks my clit with his forefinger and thumb, and I jump. "You'll come if and when I want you to, you little slut. Tell me he doesn't lick you like I do."

It's messed up, kinky sex talk. It turns me on and apparently turns Alex on, too. No one expects complete honesty in moments like this.

But the thing is, it's true. Hunter is good in bed, but we never had the chemistry that I have with Alex. Maybe because from the very beginning he kept me at a distance, let me know I wasn't special, told me there would be others in his bed. He was transparent, and it made me hold myself back.

Alex and I have barely talked, let alone talked about what we're doing with each other, and here I am showing him parts of me I've never shown anyone. The dirty girl inside who I never felt comfortable to explore. My desire to be degraded and used. My true feelings about Hunter and oral sex.

"He doesn't lick me like you—" I'm cut off from speech when, all of a sudden, I feel a wet thumb inserted into the tight opening of my ass, sending tingles of pleasure shooting through my body. "Oh my God."

Hunter definitely never did *that.*

My words turn into moans as Alex continues to lick and kiss me, his tongue dancing over my sensitive skin, his thumb thrusting in and out of my other hole until I can't take it anymore. Conversation is definitely over. The only sounds are my heavy breaths, the wet rhythm of his tongue lapping, and the rapid stroke of his hand on his cock. I brace myself against the tunnel wall, and I'm pretty sure my dress snags on the rock behind me and possibly tears, but I am too consumed with pleasure to care.

Finally, when my eyes are streaming tears of pleasure, and the tension has built up to nuclear level, Alex brings me to a powerful climax.

Waves of pleasure ripple through me. My vision blurs and my knees weaken and buckle. Euphoria courses through my body, and though I've never been a screamer, I let out a loud and uninhibited cry of pure bliss.

Aftershocks are still reverberating through me when Alex stands, places a hand on the wall by my head, then strokes himself at a rapid tempo. "If I fucked you right now you wouldn't be able to walk out of here straight. Everyone would know."

"They would."

"Every single person who saw you would say that's a woman who just got properly fucked, and because Hunter's sure to always make his presence known, it would be obvious you weren't walking crooked because of him."

I'm not sure if it's just talk or a threat or if he's asking, and the worst part is that I don't know which I want it to be, so I just nod.

"Should I do that?" His hand moves quickly up and down, his fingers wrapped tightly around his cock as it glistens with pre-cum. "Should I shove my cock so far inside your tight little cunt that you leave here hobbling like a well-used whore?"

"Yes." It falls out of my mouth. A gut response.

Alex's words come through gritted teeth. "Say it again."

"Yes."

His body tenses and his face contorts, and he comes with a ragged, guttural cry, his release spilling onto my bare pussy in hot spurts. The sensation of warm, sticky cum sliding down my leg sends shivers through my body. A faint musky scent lingers in the air as we both catch our breaths.

Though I've had longer to recover, he's the one who collects himself first. "Don't you fucking dare clean this up," he says, nodding to the mess on my pussy and thigh.

As if I even had the means to, out here in my formal gown. It's not like I even have my purse, let alone a spare cloth. He knows I'll have to traipse through crowds of people to get to a bathroom.

Which is when I realize he means don't clean it up at all. He wants me to go home like this. With Hunter.

"Okay," I say.

"Okay." Satisfaction settles in his eyes. He draws his finger in a tiny bit of the cum dripping down my leg and brings it to my mouth. Automatically, I part my lips, and he drags the liquid on my tongue.

He smirks.

Then his smile disappears, and he leans in toward me, as though he's going to kiss me but stops when his lips are hovering just above mine. "Do you think he'll recognize the scent of your cunt on my face?"

The smell of my pussy floods my nostrils, and now in the aftermath, with my hormones settled, reality crashes in.

I put my hand to his chest and nudge him just far enough away that I can look at him with some objection. *What are we doing?*

What the fuck am I doing?

"Alex…we need to discuss this."

He pushes off the tunnel wall and takes a step back. "I'm returning you to my brother with my cum dripping down your leg. I think I've said what I need to say."

I see it now, when I haven't before—this asshole bravado he puts on is just a mask. A front to cover any vulnerability.

A pang of compassion shoots through my chest, and I feel like I understand something about him that he didn't mean for me to understand.

Reaching out, I put my palm to his cheek. "What he says doesn't matter. *He* doesn't matter."

His expression tenses, but he lets my hand stay there. "Hunter? Strange words coming from his girlfriend."

"It's…complicated." I cringe at the ambiguity of my

statement and am on the verge of saying to hell with it and explaining everything when Alex jumps in.

"Complicated as in loyalty doesn't matter when you're only using him for personal gains? Complicated as in the only thing better than one billionaire wrapped around your panties is two? Complicated as in I should have met you first?"

I swear my heart skips a beat.

He turns his face into my palm. "Why couldn't I have met you first?"

"Alex—"

"Shh." He cuts me off with a finger to my lips, his jaw suddenly tense. He cocks his head, as though he's listening, and sure enough, I hear it too—voices somewhere above us. People walking over the tunnel, maybe, or on the trail that will lead them down to us. They're too far away to catch any specific phrases, but they're obviously close.

Alex drops his hand, so he can put his cock away and straighten out his clothing. "I'll go out first. Wait at least five minutes before you follow."

He doesn't wait for my response. Just leaves me with the mixed scent of fresh mown grass and sex and the uncomfortable feeling of an unresolved conversation.

With a sigh, I straighten my dress and lean back against the wall, my head spinning with Alex's last words. It's a couple of minutes later when I'm struck with curiosity.

I dig my phone out of my pocket and turn on the camera then stick it under my dress and click.

It takes me a couple of tries to get a good photo, but when I do, it's there clear as day, just as I suspected—a hickey on my pussy lip. If I were still sleeping with Hunter, there's no way he'd miss it.

Alex took my panties, left me dripping in his cum, and then put a mark on me—I might technically be Hunter's girlfriend, but Alex Sebastian just claimed me as his.

CHAPTER
SIXTEEN
ALEX

When I return to the festivities, I immediately go in search of Grandpa Irving. There's already been too much…too much…in this day, and I'm ready to get out of here, but there's no way I can escape without at least putting in a hello to the patriarch of this mess of a family.

It takes longer than it should to find him. Everywhere I turn I see Riah, even though I know she's somewhere behind me. I see a flash of her dress or the swing of her hair or the slope of her shoulder only to discover upon closer look that the person I'm staring at doesn't resemble her at all.

When I close my eyes to clear her from my brain, she's there too. The image of her is seared into my mind— flushed face, head thrown back, mouth parted as she screamed out her pleasure. I feel her palm against my cheek

—soft and warm and surprising—and my ribs start to cave in, and I can't catch a breath.

It's fucked up, and I don't understand. Don't want to understand. I just need to get the hell out of her shared space, and I don't know, fuck someone else probably. Get Riah fucking Watson out of my goddamn bloodstream.

I'm so distracted that it's purely by accident that I come upon the crowd encircling Grandpa at a table under one of the tents. As usually is the way at these events, he's seated at a center spot, motionless as friends and family rotate around him. His assistant, Elias, stands nearby to make sure no one monopolizes his time. It always reminds me of the lines I've seen of people visiting the pope in Vatican City, though the advice that gets passed on from Grandpa is far from angelic, and instead of blessings, he gives out criticism.

Fortunately, Grandpa has a soft spot for his grandchildren, and his critiques are laced with fondness. While his sons—my father and uncles—avoid these encounters as long as they can, knowing they'll walk away battered, my generation tends to flock to him eagerly.

My cousin Scott and his wife Tess are showing Grandpa their baby when I arrive, so I grab another champagne flute from a tray and quickly down it while I wait my turn, wishing it was something harder, but not wishing it so much to make it happen.

A shoulder nudges mine. "Where've you been? There was a bunny asking about you."

I pivot to see Ax, and before I can answer, he goes on, "Ah, never mind. You smell like pussy. Guess you already got some bunny on your own."

"Bastian Bunny" is the arguably offensive term given to the groupies. The women—and occasionally men—who hang around the family hoping to enjoy the fruits of the billionaire lifestyle in exchange for…well, in exchange for whatever we might want. Usually sex acts, though sometimes just company, and I've heard rumors that Uncle Arthur just likes to paint women's toenails.

Involuntarily, I lick my lips. The taste of Prosecco is fresh on my tongue, but underneath that Riah's poignant flavor lingers, too divine to be compared to a mere bunny.

Thankfully, I don't have to respond because Scott and Tess finish up with Grandpa, and I'm able to sidle up closer.

"Alex, my boy," Grandpa says when he sees me.

"Good to see you, Grandpa." I bend down to hug him then take the seat next to him.

He squints at me. "You're looking rested. The break from the daily grind must be treating you well. Don't let it get you lazy, now. You know that trust—"

I cut him off before he breaks into a lecture I've heard plenty of times over the course of my life about responsibility and integrity and work ethic. "I already have a new gig. I'm—"

Hunter interrupts me. "Here she is, Grandpa. I found her."

When I glance up, I already know who will be by his side.

I look straight at her, but Riah avoids my eyes. Her face is still flushed, though this time I'm sure it's from being tugged through the crowd by her overeager boyfriend. Her shoulders are tense and her breathing shallow, possibly for the same reason, but I like attributing those reactions to the fact that she's now been forced into a conversation on Hunter's arm while her thighs are still sticky with my cum.

Uncomfortable for her, maybe. Gratifying for me.

"Sorry, Alex, are we interrupting?" Hunter actually looks like he cares—he knows how to perform when he needs to. "Grandpa asked about my girl, and I had to track her down."

The words *my girl* hit me in the ballsack, but I take the lump, enjoying the situation too much to let it derail my satisfaction. "No problem. Go ahead."

"Ah, yes, this talented lady." Grandpa takes Riah's hand in his. "I'd hoped to spend time getting to know you over Christmas, but it wasn't to be."

It's a dig at Hunter, who abandoned the holiday plans with Grandpa when he found out Holt would be there as well. Thirty-nine years old and my brother can be such a fucking child.

His arm goes to the small of Riah's back—just above the small tear in her dress that I'm pretty sure snagged on the tunnel wall when she was writhing against it in ecstasy—and from where I'm seated, I see him give her a subtle tap. A sort of nudge, it seems.

She clears her throat. "I'm so sorry about that, Mr. Sebastian. I—"

"Irving," Grandpa corrects.

To which Hunter corrects again with, "Grandpa."

Riah pauses, her eyes darting from Grandpa to Hunter.

"Oh, well, yes. If you're that serious. Grandpa it is." Grandpa's enthusiasm over their potential future makes the champagne in my stomach want to come right back up.

She hesitates but goes with it. "Uh, okay. Grandpa, then."

I won't lie—something primal kicks in when I hear her refer to my grandfather in such a familiar way, and I have to remind myself that the person linking her to the fold is not me—it's my brother.

And when I remember that, a dark apprehension falls over me. What if this *is* serious? What if Hunter marries her? Is this what my future holds? Me watching on as she clings to him? It doesn't matter how I've defiled her if she's wearing his ring. She'll be his in every way that counts.

Though, shouldn't it be even more satisfying to fuck around with Hunter's *wife*?

My stomach knots, and I shift in my seat, trying to ease the discomfort with no success.

"Anyway," Riah continues, "it was my fault we left early at Christmas. I had a last-minute music opportunity that I couldn't pass up, and I didn't want to steal Hunter from you, but he was too sweet to let me spend the holiday alone."

The muscles in my jaw tense.

Fuck that bullshit. It was definitely Hunter who ditched Christmas. Why is she taking the fall for that asshole? Just so he can look good and save face?

"Is that so?" Grandpa sounds pleasantly surprised. "You just might be the girl to turn this kid around, Zyah."

"Riah," I say before I can help myself.

Grandpa's gaze shifts over to me and lingers. "Riah, yes. That's right. The other's a stage name or something."

"Yes," Hunter, Riah, and I say in unison.

Riah chuckles awkwardly. "But I'll answer to both, so whatever you prefer."

"A girl should be called by her right name," Grandpa says.

Hunter never calls her by her right name. I should be gloating, but something's off. It doesn't feel as satisfying as I'd like it to. It doesn't feel like enough.

Maybe it's because Hunter's hand has settled possessively on her hip.

Or maybe it's because she hasn't looked my way since she walked up with him.

Or maybe it's because that potential future is so vivid in my head that I can even picture her in a wedding dress. Walking down an aisle toward me, except I'm standing next to Hunter as his best man, and fuck, it makes me want to flip the goddamn table over.

It's gone too far.

All of this—whatever it was. It was supposed to make me feel better. It was supposed to make me feel *good*. I can't articulate how I feel at the moment, but it's definitely not good.

This has to end.

Not now, obviously. Not here. But I can't be here anymore.

"Sorry to cut the visit short, Grandpa," I say, standing up. "I have something I have to attend to."

"Shame. I was just going to brag about all the great shit you're doing for Zy—" Hunter catches himself. "For *Riah*."

More of the performance.

"You're going to have to brag without me."

I start to move past him, close enough that he must

catch a whiff of my earlier escapade. "Ooo, man. You smell like sex."

I can feel Riah's flush without looking at her.

This couldn't have unfolded any better if I'd planned it. To have him call me out while she's standing right next to him? I should be thrilled. I should be goddamned over the moon.

I'm not. Not at all.

What I feel, to be honest, is alone. And inexplicably betrayed.

Grandpa may be an old man, but he can be as crass as a teenager in a locker room, so the comment doesn't shock him. In front of a lady, though, so he keeps it clean. "Well, well, Alex. Love is in the air all around, it seems. Are you going to be towing a woman up to meet me today, too? Who is the lucky gal?"

Maybe Riah can feel how badly tempted I am to come clean—throw her under the bus right here, right now, and end this whole thing once and for all—because she finally flicks her eyes to me.

I almost do it. I come real damn close.

But at the last minute, with my gaze locked on hers, I say words I wish were true instead. "Literally no one important at all."

———

THE LIMO RIDE back to New York is long enough to both get drunk and sober up again. I swear Reid and Lina talk about their cat the whole two and a half hours and don't notice. Neither do Steele and Simone, who seem to be playing some type of game that involves lists and intense scowling.

I've never been more grateful to be single.

I've never been more aware that that statement's a lie.

Back in the city, I try to sleep off my mood with an early evening nap, but I wake up more sour than when I hit the mattress.

One thing is abundantly clear—this situation cannot continue as is. As I see it, I have two choices. Either I resign as Zyah's brand specialist and stay clear of Riah and my brother for the foreseeable future. Or I tell him that his girlfriend is a cheating ladder-climber and hope that my proof doesn't lodge a wedge between us forever.

Though, if it did, would I even care? It's not like Hunter's my favorite person these days. On the other hand, I have thirty-six years of history with the man, and shitty as he's been to me of late, he was by my side in darker days.

It all comes down to what I think Riah deserves.

In one scenario, her career trajectory continues without alteration. I was hired to help the brand because it was convenient. I'm not egotistical enough to think I'm irreplaceable.

In the other scenario, she's potentially fucked. Depending on how hard Hunter wants to come down on her, he could dismantle her entire future.

I'm a shit person because the latter option has strong appeal. A very deep part of me wants her ruined. Wants her wrecked and angry and…

And what?

Crawling to me?

That's fucking fantasy right there. A plot line in one of

Adly's romance books. I refuse to give the idea any more credence, shove it from my mind, and reach for my phone.

> Need to chat.

I still haven't decided what I'm planning to say when I send Hunter the text, but he replies instantly.

> I'm at Grand Havana. Come by.

After a quick shower, I call a car and head to the member's only cigar club, realizing only after I arrive that I didn't specify that I wanted to see him *without Riah*. I've never seen her there before, and considering how conscientious she is about vocal care, I doubt it would be her scene, but I'm still heedful as I walk through the main room to the private lounge in the back that is permanently reserved under my father, Reynard Sebastian's, name.

Dad rarely shows at the club these days, but it's one of Hunter's frequent haunts, and I enter to a couple of his usual buddies along with a handful of skimpily dressed women. Hunter's seated behind a table on a velvet upholstered bench, head thrown back, eyes closed. Cigar in one hand, scotch in the other. Typical scenario. Nothing of real interest, except the woman's head bobbing up and down over his lap.

A woman who is most definitely not his girlfriend.

Then the most unusual, fucked up thing happens—I'm hit with self-righteous indignancy on Riah's behalf. Never mind that she's been screwing around on him too. Never mind that I have zero right to anger, but I'm outraged. "What the actual fuck?"

Hunter opens his eyes. "Hey, brother."

"Don't." My voice is strained with tension. "Don't try to *brother* me right now. You have a girlfriend. A woman you're introducing to Grandpa like she's about to become part of the fold. Did you forget?"

All attention goes to me. The woman in Hunter's lap lifts her head, but he pushes her back down. "You're good, baby. Keep that up."

Then he throws a puzzled look toward me. "Where's this coming from? Am I missing something?"

His confusion is warranted. I've never raised a brow about his manwhore behavior in the past, and rationally, I know I'm on the verge of showing cards I don't mean to show—cards I haven't looked at too closely myself—but I'm too mad to backpedal.

Besides, this is different. This situation is different. *Riah* is different.

"What you're missing is a fucking clue." I have to work to bring my volume down. "You made a big show of going monogamous. And now this? In a public setting, no less?"

"Oh, fuck. You're taking the branding job seriously. Which I appreciate, but Alex, we're good if this is all on the down-low. Everyone in this room is cool. Right?"

There's a murmur of agreement, and I swear I want to rip every one of their heads clean from their bodies. "This isn't about the media, asshole. You want to convince the world that you're a decent man? Fine. You want to lie to them? Fine. Don't lie to Riah. She doesn't deserve it."

"So this is about Riah. Alright. I see." Hunter bends forward to ash his cigar—as well as he can while getting his dick sucked, anyway—then waves his hand. "Everybody out. I need to talk to my brother for a minute."

Without question, his buddies gather their drinks and start to file out.

"You too, baby." He nudges the woman off his cock. "This isn't happening right now anyway."

Once everyone's out of the room, he stands and fastens his pants. "Taking the team loyalty a bit far, aren't you?"

I'm vibrating with rage. My body is practically shaking. "Yeah, loyalty being a term you know nothing about. After Riah covered your ass today with Grandpa, made you look—"

He cuts me off. "She already knows."

It takes me a beat to process. "She knows, and she has no problem with it?"

But what I really want to know is, *She knows and that's why she's been fucking around with me? Am I her version of revenge?*

"No, she had a big problem with it." He throws back the last of his drink. "Which is why she basically told me to go fuck myself."

Uh… "What?"

He pours another finger of scotch into his glass before answering. He must have asked for the whole bottle when he ordered. Not the policy of the club to allow it, but no one expects Sebastians to play by the rules, least of all Hunter.

Finally, he responds. "She broke up with me back in L.A."

"But…" L.A. was over two months ago now, and the two of them have definitely been coupled up since then.

"Everything since then has been for PR." He says it like

I'm a dummy. As if I should have figured it out myself, and maybe I should have.

But more importantly, why did I have to?

I sink into one of the oversized armchairs, trying to look at everything that's happened with Riah from this new perspective. "Why didn't you say something?"

But what I mean is, why didn't *she* say something?

"Because it wasn't your business," he snaps.

"Since when?" It's a legit question. Hunter loves boasting about his schemes to me. When did that stop?

It's like what he did to me with the investment stock. Once upon a time, he would have brought me into that from the very beginning. We would have worked out a strategy. "When did I end up on the outside of your trust circle?"

He shrugs. "And it's not that big of a deal, anyway. Half of our family relationships are for PR. Uncle Henry and his wife. They tried to arrange a marriage for Scott, too. Did you know? Holt tried to boost ratings for his show by flaunting Brystin like they were together when they weren't. It's a thing we do. You can't be that naïve."

"Fuck you, I'm not. I just don't understand why you didn't tell me."

Another shrug for a response, but his jaw sets, and I realize that whatever this is—whatever bug's gotten in his head—it isn't about me. It probably stems from Sebastian trauma. Not like any of us are in short supply of that.

This is shit I can't help him with.

This is shit I can't waste my time spinning over.

But Hunter's only one half of the equation, and I'm back

to thinking about the question that has me even more boggled—*why didn't Riah tell me?*

It doesn't sit right.

Which is absurd because it shouldn't matter. We're playing a kinky game. That's all. We're not serious. There's no way I should feel more betrayed by her lack of disclosure than I do about Hunter's.

It's a credit to her, too, isn't it? She didn't cheat on him. She's using him, sure, but apparently, they're using each other. On purpose. Consensually.

But what really fucks with my head is that her transparency has only extended to him. With how many times I've mouthed off about her relationship with him, she's had plenty of opportunities to come clean. Why wouldn't she?

The most logical reason I can think of is that she was pissed at Hunter for cheating and wanted her own revenge. Fucking around with his little brother would do the trick. Even if she never admitted it to him, she'd feel the satisfaction.

It's a strategy I know well.

At the same time, she got to explore her new dirty persona. Win-win for her all around, without any regard for anyone else involved.

It's betrayal in its basest form. She acted as though she wanted to be used—so I used her.

But in the end, it was really her using me this whole time.

CHAPTER
SEVENTEEN
RIAH

T he doorman greets me as soon as I get out of the Lyft.

The sight of the door open wide before me makes this all too real, and I panic. What was I thinking coming here? It's not like I can slip in unseen. There are people who could identify me. Granted, this is the kind of apartment building that practices discretion, but that's not a guarantee.

Or am I letting Hunter's the-world-is-always-watching paranoia get to me?

"Coming in, miss?"

Standing here trying to decide is the best way to attract unwanted attention, so I shake my head and hurry around the corner and down the sidewalk to think it out.

It's not like coming to Alex's apartment was entirely impulsive. I've been thinking about it since he left the Spring Fling earlier. The way he looked at me with such pure disdain when he called me nothing—it was enough to never want to see him again.

But then just before he turned to go, his mask dropped, for just a fraction of a second, and I swear I saw something else. Something raw and broken, and right then and there I knew that whatever was going on between us had crossed from mere debauchery to more significant territory. What that territory is—or what it could be—I don't know, but I know that it has to be addressed.

I didn't expect to address it tonight, necessarily.

But eventually.

So I finagled his address from Adly under some bullshit pretense and rehearsed various monologues on the ride back to the city, varying between speeches where I walked carefully around the truth and others where I spilled everything. Even when the others dragged me into conversation, part of me was still focused on him. Still focused on finding the best solution for our precarious situation.

Then there were the long expanses of time where I did nothing but replay our encounter under the bridge, pressing my thighs together against the memory of his teeth on my skin. Humming silently under my breath as I recalled his threadbare admission. *Why couldn't I have met you first?*

By the time I walked into my apartment, the only thing I'd settled on was that Alex had completely and thoroughly wheedled his way into my head.

Even the fact that Whitney was home and awake and in our shared living space for the first time in days wasn't enough to push Alex from my thoughts. Especially when all she had for me were terse, judgmental words about the pictures she'd seen from the day's event and how well I played the lie.

A microwave meal of leftover Chinese and a shower later, I laid in my bed and stared at the ceiling, wondering if any of my current relationships weren't somehow tangled in deceit. Hating myself a little for all of it. Shaming myself a lot.

And then Alex would come roaring into the foreground, and despite all the depravity between us, instead of hate or shame, all I felt was want.

Almost without choosing to do so, I was throwing on a pair of yoga pants and a hoodie and opening my app for a car, and next thing I know, I'm in Chelsea, pacing the street like a lunatic stalker.

What the hell am I doing?

I pull my phone from my hoodie pocket with the intention of ordering another car, when the worst thing possible happens—I get noticed.

"Oh my God, it's Zyah!"

"Holy shit!"

"No way!"

There are five of them overall. All around my age, if I had to guess. Hipsters, coming home from a night at the bar, based on the general smell of alcohol clinging to them.

It's the first time in a long time that I've been unprepared for fans.

Since dating Hunter, almost all my events and outings have been so carefully arranged that I'm usually out of the car and into whatever location with minimal interaction with passersby. Occasionally, there will be a fan or two who manages to snap a pic while I'm at dinner or thrusts a napkin in my direction with a leaky pen, but by and large, fan engagement has been purposeful and carefully planned.

Rarely am I caught dressed down, let alone with my hair in a bad pony and no makeup on. But that's not the really concerning part, which is that I'm outside, alone, on a street that I have no good reason for being on. In the middle of the night, no less. It's not just a PR issue—it's a safety issue. Even the best-intentioned fans can quickly turn danger-ously overzealous.

I'm not sure who is going to kill me first for this— Claude, Hunter, or Whitney—but I'm definitely getting murdered when the pics go live.

And there are never not pics.

"Hey," I say, accepting the inevitable and turning myself on as if I'm walking a red carpet. "What's up? Having a great night? Are you all together?"

I'm not the best at addressing fans. I never know what to say. Everything feels contrived and inauthentic, espe-cially when I'm not expecting the run-in. But in a lot of ways, this is my favorite sort of fan interaction. As unpre-pared as I am, they're unprepared as well. Everything they say is unrehearsed, and they're pretty much always just so thrilled to have had a celebrity sighting that they tend to be more effusive with the praise, even if they barely know who I am.

This group definitely does know who I am though. At least a couple of them are true fans.

"That single you dropped is so good," a light-haired girl says. "I mean, it's so different, and just…"

"Empowering," says her dark-skinned companion. "Not like anything I've heard before."

"Sort of Florence and the Machine vibes," the first says.

"But even more feminist," says the second.

I manage to keep the whole exchange to less than five minutes, posing with them for selfies and scribbling my name on one of the girl's hands (she swears she'll wash it eventually, but not until she takes a thousand pics, so she can have one printed and hung on her wall), and use the question of what I'm doing in their neighborhood as my excuse to depart.

"Ah, I, uh, I'm at a friend's down the street. Just came out for some air. Should probably get back before…" I catch myself before dropping any male pronouns, not wanting to specify what gender of friend I'm visiting.

"Oh, shit. Does Hunter Sebastian live around here?" This from one of the ones who has been quiet until now. "He's so fucking hot, girl. You snatched yourself a dreamboat."

It's barely fifty degrees outside, and I swear I can feel a trickle of sweat down the back of my neck. "He is, isn't he? Not with him tonight, unfortunately. But nice meeting you all. I have to get going."

I turn around and truck it back to Alex's building as fast as I can, cursing under my breath the whole way. This time when the doorman opens the door for me, I rush inside without hesitation. Even if the plan is to just order a car, I can't be waiting on the street for it to arrive.

And ordering a car might not be the best idea. I made it around the corner and into the building before the fans could see where I disappeared to, fortunately, but depending on how fast they post their pictures and whether or not they tag the location, there could be paparazzi looking for me within minutes.

Then it's only a matter of time before they start guessing who I might be visiting. The media might not think twice about a visit to my boyfriend's brother this late at night—for all they know, Hunter could be there as well—but Hunter will find it very suspicious. Especially after our conversation earlier, when he outright asked if Alex was trying to get in my pants.

So it's almost as though I have no choice but to talk to my branding specialist. He's not exactly in charge of my public relations, but he'll know the best way to handle it.

Besides, all that's just an excuse.

I came here tonight because I wanted to see him. *Needing* to see him as well gives me the courage that I need to approach the second doorman, the one inside behind the desk. "Hi, I'm here to see Alex Sebastian."

"Is he expecting you?" he asks, typing as he talks, likely pulling up the list of people allowed to be sent up without permission. "It's late to be coming unannounced."

"He's not." I already know I'm not on that list, but I can't help but wonder if there are women who are. For the first time, it occurs to me that he might have someone with him now.

Shit.

I should have texted first.

I shouldn't be here.

Too late now. "I'd really appreciate it if you could call him anyway."

He looks me over. "Name?"

I pause, trying to decide if this is a situation where my

stage name might get me further than my real name, but if it's at the cost of exposure, it might not be worth it. "Um, Riah. Watson."

Whoever's names are on the list, there must not be many to check against because the doorman has the phone in his hand immediately.

My stomach twists as he dials. The receiver is loud enough that I can hear the phone ringing on the other end, and I hold my breath, straining to listen.

"Mr. Sebastian," the doorman says when he answers. "Sorry to bother you at this time of night. You have a guest in the lobby. Riah Watson."

"Riah?" The surprise is evident in his voice, even muffled. "Uh…what does she want?"

"To come up," I prompt.

"To be buzzed up, sir." The doorman holds the phone from his ear so that I can better hear the reply. Probably more for ease of communication than anything else, but it's still nice.

There's a beat of silence before Alex responds, and the twisting in my stomach turns to wrenching. If he's with someone else just hours after he was with me…

Alex's voice comes through harsh and clear. "Tell her that whatever she needs can be addressed during business hours. I'm off the clock."

"Yes, sir. Goodnight, sir."

But before the doorman can put the phone down, I grab it from his hand. "Let me up, Alex."

The doorman grabs for the phone, but I take a step back, stretching the cord so that the receiver is out of reach, and put a hand up in a stop gesture as if that will prevent him from doing his job.

Meanwhile, Alex sounds more than a little irritated. "Zyah, what the fuck? No. Go home."

I try not to let the use of my stage name sting, but it feels like a deliberate attempt to hold me at arm's length, and now I'm even more determined to see him.

Even more determined to know if he's alone. "Is someone with you?"

God, I sound jealous and desperate.

"Is someone with me like you're with Hunter? Is that what you mean?"

Somehow, I know from his answer that he's alone. His tone is too cruel. If he had company, he should be too preoccupied to waste that much emotion on me.

"Let me up, Alex." The doorman comes around the desk, and I spin away from him. "I'm not leaving this lobby until you let me up, and as I may or may not already have paps outside, career-wise, you should care, even if you don't on a personal—"

The doorman manages to wrangle the phone out of my palm, cutting me off. He glares as he puts the receiver to his ear. "I apologize for that, Mr. Sebastian, I—" This time I can't hear what Alex says in response. "Yes, sir. No problem. Will do."

He hangs up the phone, and pretty sure that I'm about to be tossed on the street, I open my mouth to beg to stay long enough to order a car.

But to my surprise, the doorman scowls and says, "You can head on up."

I spend the elevator ride up to Alex's floor trying to

calm my nerves. None of my practice versions of this encounter considered I might have a hard time even getting him to let me up, which has definitely affected my game.

I also forgot to consider that every time I'm alone with Alex, things…happen. He demands, and my body reacts, and the idea of being with him in his apartment should terrify me more than it does. Should definitely not have me this aroused.

Or maybe I didn't forget to consider that at all.

Maybe I'm lying to myself about the real reason I'm here. Maybe that's why I came out at an inappropriate time of night. Why I didn't text first. Why I didn't call. Because the intention was never just to talk.

By the time I knock on his door, my heart is pounding, and my skin feels hot.

And when he opens his door—just wide enough to frame his form—butterflies take off in my pussy.

My eyes slide down his body, taking in his shirtless chest and bare feet. I've seen him in swim trunks plenty of times but seeing him in just his boxer briefs is a whole different level of eye candy. The outline of his cock is unmistakable and seems to grow hard under my inspection.

When I manage to pull my gaze back to his face, I find his eyes are dark and hooded, though his expression is mean. "You're at my door in the middle of the night, Riah. I'm going to assume you have bad things on your mind."

I start to protest, like I did earlier in the tunnel, but who am I fooling? Certainly not him. Talking can come later. After.

So I close my mouth, running my teeth along my bottom lip and nod.

"I'm warning you now—you cross this threshold, and you're agreeing to whatever happens after that."

Alarms sound in the back of my head, but I dismiss them as easily as I push snooze on a Sunday morning. I swallow; my decision already made.

It's only out of curiosity I ask, "And what exactly will you do to me?"

"Anything I want." He backs up to open the door wider for me.

Like a lamb entering a lion's den, I walk in.

CHAPTER
EIGHTEEN
RIAH

A s soon as I'm inside his apartment with the door closed, Alex spins me around and pushes me against it with the length of his body.

Instantly, I'm wet and wanting. Since when did mere touch turn me on like a faucet?

Though it's more than that. He's rough and unexpected, and when I spend so much time trying to win people by staying inside the lines, he says to hell with boundaries and erases them altogether.

It's embarrassing how fast I turn slut for Alex Sebastian.

Hoping to downplay the intensity of my libido, I try for a casual tone. "Uh…hi."

It doesn't have quite the effect I'm going for when my cheek is molded against the door, and he laughs. "No. We aren't doing foreplay."

Oh.

Should that be a turn-off? Because I'm still very much aroused.

Alex is as well. I can feel his cock get harder as he rubs it up and down along the crease of my ass. It's nowhere near the nerve endings that would most appreciate the stimulation, but he might as well be stroking his dick on my clit for how ramped up it makes me.

Then there's his mouth near my ear, hot and goading as he slides his hands under my hoodie to fondle my breasts. "No bra. Did you come directly from his bed? Were you that sure you would end up in mine?"

As always, Hunter's here with us. His name doesn't need to be mentioned, and it's still very evidently him.

I offer my denial. "I didn't—"

I'm cut off when Alex twists my nipple so hard that my vision goes spotted. "No lies, now. Not here."

No lies.

It's too hard to keep track of what I'm supposed to say and what I'm not when I'm in the throes, and it's not really the time for any big reveals, so I don't answer.

Besides, the rough treatment of my breasts has me too busy moaning. His fingers dig and pinch into my skin, the unique blend of pain and pleasure one I've never experienced. There will be bruises on my body when he's done with me. Nothing that anyone will see, but in places he thinks Hunter will see. Definitely calculated and purposeful.

What is wrong with me that I find that so hot?

It's not just bruises he leaves.

Abruptly, he lifts my hoodie up my torso and over my head, but he traps my arms in the sleeves, and when he turns me to face him, he continues the assault on my breasts with his mouth, sucking my nipples into tight, templed beads before leaving hickeys along my sensitive skin.

"God, you're so depraved." But I'm in no way sinless myself, and my hands coil in his hair, urging him to carry on.

"Because I want him to see what I've done to you?" He peers up at me, his eyes locked with mine as he bites down hard on the inside of my right breast. "Or because I want him to see what you *let* me do to you?"

"Because you get off on both." I reach out and stroke the now very thick bulge in his boxer briefs, demonstrating the proof in point.

"But so do you. Don't you?" He leans back and smacks his palm against the side of my breast, causing me to let out a squeal. "Or is this just part of the act?"

I shake my head because when he says *act*, I think of the ruse with his brother, and he said no lies. But he doesn't know about that, and I'm sure he means my bad girl persona instead, which is less of an act than he seems to realize.

He responds with another slap of my breast. "I wonder if you even know the difference anymore."

Then he's on his knees for the second time in one day, finding my clit with no effort and sucking at it through the spandex fabric of my leggings.

"Fuck, I can taste you through your clothes. And no panties?" He tsks and follows it up with a nip that feels as much reward as it does punishment. "Should I even assume this is for me or is this cum you made for him?"

My confession is breathless. "All of it for you."

With a growl, he tugs my pants down, pulling off a sneaker at the same time as he frees one leg. Then he tosses that leg over his shoulder before licking up my inner thigh. He stops at my pussy to bury his nose in between my lips. When he discovers the hickey he left earlier, he smirks. "You'll have to fuck him in the dark until this heals. Is that your plan, Riah?"

He's smug, and there's also more of that meanness in his tone, the cruelty that I usually suspect is meant for Hunter.

At the moment, it feels very directed at me—the way he says my name like it's a callous taunt—and I'm fascinated to find that, along with scaring me, it sends a thrill down my spine.

He flicks my clit with his thumb and middle finger, then while it's still vibrating with the sting, he lavishes it with soothing licks of his tongue. "Your clit is so fucking swollen right now. Does he do this to you, too? Turn your little bud into a fat juicy berry?"

His face is so close that the sound of his laugh reverberates across my pussy. "But then you said he doesn't put his face between your legs. Ever? Or just recently?"

He knows.

The thought leaves my mind as fast as it enters. Wishful thinking on my part, that Hunter would tell Alex the truth, and this game of ours could evolve to something else.

I can't think about it, though, because Alex lifts my other leg over his other shoulder—my pants still dangling at my ankle—so I'm perched on his shoulders and against the door, and then he incites an assault against my pussy that has me gasping and moaning and grasping at his hair for dear life.

"Ohmygod, ohmygod, ohmygod." My words rush together as an orgasm builds, higher, higher, higher. It's so close that I can feel euphoria already leaking into my bloodstream like the early streaks in a dark sky that foretell the coming sun.

Just as I'm about to explode, Alex pulls back, leaving me wound up and bereft. "Not God, baby. That might work for my brother, but when *I* make you come, you better damn well be giving the credit to me."

Then he stands, his hands under my ass to slide me up the door along with him. When he's completely upright he darts the tip of his tongue along my clit, sending another rush of adrenaline through my veins only to once again back away.

"Fuck you," I say, frustrated.

"Anything I want," he reminds me. Then he grins up at me like the devil he is, before wrapping his arms tight around me and carrying me from the foyer, around a corner, and down a hallway to a bedroom. *His* bedroom.

My stomach erupts in excitement.

He's going to fuck me. In this room. On that bed.

He roughly plops me down on said bed then quickly works to remove my remaining shoe and the pants dangling from my ankle. He doesn't remove my hoodie, though, leaving my arms somewhat trapped in the sleeves. I still have use of my hands, but my elbows are pinched back, thrusting my breasts forward. Judging from the dark glances he keeps throwing in the direction of my chest, Alex appreciates the effect.

When he catches me noticing, his gaze only intensifies,

and I feel a flush run up my décolletage and neck and face until I'm thoroughly heated, and I have to look away.

Which gives me a chance to scan the bedroom.

It has his style all over it. Mocha walls and mixed browns for the bedding. Gray accent rugs cover charcoal flooring. The few furniture pieces are stately and obtrusive. The drawn curtains reveal gorgeous skyline views that are reflected in the oversized framed mirror that covers almost one whole wall.

Out of place in the otherwise spotless room are the shirt and tie he wore earlier, thrown over an upholstered accent chair.

Following my sightline, he picks up the tie and absent-mindedly wraps it and unwraps it around his hand as he appraises me on his bed. "You shouldn't be here, Riah. Shouldn't know this much about your boyfriend's brother's private space."

"He's not…" I shake my head. I'm going to tell him. I know this now. It's decided—Hunter be damned—but I'm struggling over the best way and moment.

Also, I'm sidetracked by the annoyance of how fucking attractive he is with most of his clothes off. Like I said, I've seen him in swimming trunks, but we've always been in public, and any glances I've managed were stolen. This is the first time I've been able to get away with ogling. So you better believe I do. The man is cut. With broad shoulders and a firm chest, he's more muscular than his brother, and easily the hottest man I've ever seen.

And the diagonal lines at the bottom of his torso that disappear underneath his boxer briefs are so hypnotic that I quickly forget what I was saying.

Alex isn't listening anyway. "You shouldn't be staring at me like that."

"I think that's why you like it so much. Because I shouldn't."

"You definitely shouldn't know what my dick tastes like. Do you swallow for him too?"

I hesitate, not sure if I should answer the question honestly or at all.

In my silence, Alex steps closer and dangles the tie over my pussy. The sensation is too light for the already stimulated area and it sends a shiver through my limbs that brings a knowing grin to his lips. "You want to know if my cock will fill you up like his can. Will you feel more or less victorious if it does?"

Another shiver, this one with accompanying goosebumps down my arms. "I'm not thinking about him, Alex."

His eyes narrow, as though he both suspected that's what I'd say and also as though he hates me a little bit for it.

Or a lot.

Hates me for what he thinks is cheating on his brother, even though he's betraying him too. Enjoying it, at the same time.

I'm confused like that myself. Hating Alex for being so angry at me, and also very much enjoying it, but kinky as the confusion is, it's starting to feel like we can't go any further without some clarification.

I prop myself on my pinned elbows. "Alex..."

Then I get distracted again because that's when he steps out of his boxer briefs, unleashing that fantastic Sebastian cock.

I swear, that thing had to be genetically arranged

because it's utter perfection. My pussy clenches at the sight of it, and all my blood runs south.

"Uh…" I force myself to look back at his face, so I can remember that important thing I was trying to say. "I need to explain something."

"Hm. The thing is, Riah, I don't need to hear it." He takes his underwear and balls it up in his hands then bends over me. "In fact, I'd like to not hear anything from you at all. Now open up."

That's all the warning I get before he shoves the briefs into my waiting mouth. "Anything I want," he says again, and I realize now that he truly wants me at his mercy. That if I'm going to be here, I need to be here all the way. Anything that needs saying will come after he's decided I've earned it.

He stares at me, as though waiting to be sure I understand.

And maybe it's stupid to place my trust in him—a guy who has a history of being somewhat of a bully and seems to be using me to relieve whatever pent-up resentment he has toward his brother—okay; it's definitely stupid.

But it's satisfying too.

Choosing to be used. Deciding to be manipulated. Considering how often men do both to me on a daily basis, particularly in my chosen career, it's a nice change to know I have the option to say no.

I mean, it's a little difficult to say anything with his boxer briefs practically down my throat. But even that's still a choice because there's nothing stopping me from taking them out.

So I nod.

And when he holds up his tie, suggesting his plans to keep the gag in place, I nod again.

"Good girl." He grabs me by my ankle and drags me to the end of the bed. "Or do you prefer bad girl? Whoops. Guess you can't answer that."

He gives me another biting smile as he wraps the tie around my head. When the gag is secured with a knot, he flips me to my stomach and props me into child's pose.

Then his hand comes down fast and firm on my ass with a sharp smack, and I cry out behind the gag. "Bad girls get treated bad."

The sting intensifies with each subsequent strike, building until I can feel tears spring to my eyes. I'm desperate for some sign of tenderness or pleasure, wondering if I've made a mistake in trusting him so completely.

Just when I think I can't take any more, his palms return to gently massage away the pain. As he soothes me, he spreads my cheeks apart and slides his cock along my crevice, teasing and taunting me with words now. "Do you have any idea how satisfying it is to see you like this?" He digs his fingertips into my skin with a hiss. "What would he think if he saw you? Or were you always a bedroom slut? I don't want to assume it's just for me."

The anger in his tone becomes palpable and my pulse quickens at the threat of danger, but excitement overwhelms any real fear. Even when his hand comes down again, repeatedly slapping my sensitive pussy this time until it feels like it's on fire.

But then his mouth descends, lapping generously at my swollen flesh until I'm once more near orgasm. Just as quickly as he builds me up, he pulls back, edging me. Denying release. Torturing me until I'm wailing and writhing, desperate with frustration.

I'm drenched and dripping by the time he replaces his tongue with his fingers and moves his mouth to my other hole—the forbidden hole. The one he already breached earlier with his thumb. I've never had a mouth on me there, and it's obscene and debased, and a twisted pleasure-shame starts to sing through my body, and within short minutes, whether he plans to allow it or not, an orgasm sneaks out and takes me by surprise.

The taste of Alex hints on my tongue as I gasp around his balled-up boxers. My skin is electric, and even though I just came, my pussy throbs with emptiness.

And then I feel him—his cock poised at my entrance, his generous tip igniting nerve endings that have felt decidedly ignored.

Without pushing further inside me, Alex stretches over my body, wraps his hand loosely around my throat, and brings his lips to my ear. "Do you know why I ate your ass?"

I kind of assumed it was because he wanted me to feel good, but I can't respond with more than a grunt, and honestly, I'm more interested in having that big boy inside me than the answer.

"Because I've been eating the shit you've been feeding me for weeks. Why stop now?"

Admittedly, my head is spinning, and I'm not thinking

the clearest, but I'm pretty sure there's an accusation there that sounds more spiked than his usual jabs.

I try to lift my torso to peer at him over my shoulder, but he pushes me back down with his chest. "You want to use me, Riah? Go ahead and use me. But you better expect that you're going to get fucked."

Then before I have the chance to dissect anything he's just said, he shoves inside me, and fuck.

That's all there is.

This invasion.

This complete domination of both my body's and mind's attention, and I can barely make sense of...anything.

I'm stunned by the force of his thrusts, by the depth of his penetration, by the blissful friction of his cock against that secret spot, by the just-right squeeze of his hand around my neck. My breaths come shallow and quick, and I feel like I might be falling or flying or maybe it's just the overwhelming reality of being so entirely filled that has me off balance, but I am both so beside myself and *inside* myself that I'm not sure I'll ever truly recover.

It's a dramatic reaction because it's just sex. It's just hormones.

I know that, and still I'm caught in this moment, fully present to just this. Just him.

Alex pervades. He is all I'm aware of. He's bare inside me—how long since I've had sex without a condom?—hot and urgent and demanding. His groans echo mine. His bitter sentence fragments make me squirm and writhe and flush.

"Take what you deserve."

"Can't use me without paying a price."

"Your cunt will ache with my memory."

"Squeeze that tight slut pussy around my cock, and I might just let you have my cum."

When I orgasm this time, it's a tsunami making landfall. I know it's coming, can tell it's capable of utter wreckage, and there's nothing I can do to lessen the blow. It drowns me in pleasure. Spits me up and has me gulping for air while every muscle in my body stutters with its violent strength.

I'm still convulsing with aftershocks when Alex flips me over, crawls up my body, removes my gag, and replaces it with his cock. With his body flush on the bed above me, he bucks his hips, fucking my mouth until I taste the salty tang of cum.

Instantly, he pulls out and sits back on his knees. His eyes hit mine, and there's cruelty—but something else too. Something soft and fragile, and I want to reach out to it. Want to reach my hand to cup his face and tell him I'm here and that I want to be and that he doesn't have to fight so hard to make me hate him because I know he doesn't really want that at all.

But I can't stretch that far with the hoodie around my elbows, and besides, the glimpse of something other is lost as his gaze clouds, and he very purposefully changes his aim and instead of coming on me, he spurts hot white ropes on the bed *next* to me with a gritted roar. Then he collapses at my side.

It's full minutes before my heart settles. It feels like hours before my vision clears. Before my breathing normalizes and my head can function.

The first coherent thought I have is that I was just

fucked within an inch of my life, and it was easily the best sex I've ever had.

Followed by the sobering realization that whatever vulnerability he's hiding inside him, Alex Sebastian wasn't just being mean for the kink of it—the guy is legitimately a fucking asshole.

CHAPTER
NINETEEN
RIAH

As soon as I have bodily function, I wrestle free from the hoodie, lean over Alex, and with as much strength as I possess, slap him across the face. "Fuck you!"

His jaw drop is even more satisfying than the actual smack, especially considering that I think it hurt me as much—or more—than it hurt him.

As I wave my hand, he brings his own palm up to soothe his cheek. "You kind of just did. What the fuck was that for?"

Trying to ignore the pain, I scramble to my feet. "Don't pretend like I have to explain."

I'm too pissed to put in the effort. Hell hath no fury like a woman not covered in come that she rightfully deserves.

It's not just that, of course. That's only the symptom of the greater issue, which is that Alex obviously has some real issues with me that extend beyond just talk. I'm all for a bit of hate-fueled release of steam, but I'm not going to be the target for animosity that I haven't earned.

If that's all Alex has to give me, he's not worth my time.

While I struggle with the sleeves of my sweatshirt, trying to turn them right side out, he rolls off the bed and crosses to the mirror to examine his precious face. "You might have left a bruise. Fuck, that really hurt."

"You're lucky I didn't go for your balls." I eye his now half-hard dick and pretend it doesn't make my pussy clench. "I still could."

I pull the hoodie over my head in time to see him spin toward me. "What's your fucking problem?"

"I should be asking you the same thing." I survey the room and spot my pants on the other side of the bed.

"That was what you came for. Don't even try to deny it. You get off on the degradation."

"Yeah, I do," I say, shaking my shoe from my pants then putting them on. It's the first time I've admitted it out loud, and despite my current mood, it feels good. "Degradation for sex's sake gets me hot. There. I said it. But there's a difference between that and outright cruelty."

Alex opens a drawer of his dresser and pulls out a pair of sweatpants. "What are you talking about? It was all sex."

"Then tell me you didn't mean any of the things that you said."

He hesitates too long.

"Yeah, that's what I thought." I pick my shoe up off the floor and head back to the foyer.

He raises his voice to call after me. "I think I have a right to be pissed. You've been using me—using both of us—for your own gains."

"Using *you*?" *Well, isn't that the pot calling out the kettle.*

I stop to grab my phone from the hallway floor—it must have fallen from my hoodie pocket on the way to the bedroom—and throw a glare back in his direction. "Fine then. I was using you. Just like you've both been using me. Just like every other Bastian Bunny who fucks one of you rich douchebags for something in return. Why am I the one you have a problem with?"

"Because at least they're upfront about their aims." He has his sweats on now and pauses to pull a white T-shirt on before following me out into the hall. "You've been lying to me for...how long has it been since you dumped Hunter's ass?"

"I've been lying to *everyone*. You aren't special." My whole body is vibrating. I haven't even told my sister. I wanted to tell him. How dare he assume he knows what's what?

I'm too angry to say it all. And why should I have to?

Why isn't Hunter the one who has to answer to this shit?

That last thought pushes me to swivel back. "I wasn't supposed to fucking tell, okay? If you want to be mad at anyone about it, be mad at your brother. One more thing to add to whatever shit list he's on of yours."

"As if I'm the only one who has beef with him. You going to try to convince me now that you weren't fucking around with me to get back at him for cheating?"

"What? That's what you really think?" It might be the worst thing he's said so far. "God, you fuckers really think the worst of everyone, don't you?"

I can't imagine being so incapable of trust.

Maybe they're the better for it. Quite possibly there's a lesson to be learned. At least as far as Sebastian men are concerned, anyway.

Deciding there isn't any point in hashing this out with the likes of him, I start once more toward the door, only to spin back again, pointing my shoe at him. "*You* were the one using *me* to work out your anger issues. Not the other way around."

I was just there for the debauchery, which doesn't feel a whole lot better because…stigma…but honestly? I didn't do anything wrong.

"And also," I continue, my volume rising, "how dare you think you have the moral high ground here? I knew I wasn't cheating. You didn't, and yet I didn't see you try to stop it from happening. *He's your brother.*"

His eyes narrow into tiny slits. "Fuck you. Don't begin to think you possibly understand."

"Maybe take your own advice there, buddy." I turn the corner, and I'm in the foyer.

Placing my hand on the wall for support, I lift my foot and slip my shoe on. Then wriggle the other one on. I don't have to look behind me to know he's there. "Whatever. Doesn't matter. This shit between us isn't happening again."

Too bad, too, because I was really starting to own my sexuality without shame and uncertainty. This whole encounter will probably set me a step backward, but I can't think about that right now. If I'm going to explore these debased desires, it has to be with someone who—at least outside the bedroom—treats me with respect.

"Yeah, well we'll see how soon before you're back to

begging me to make your brand believable. 'Dirty me up, Alex.' 'What do you need me to do, Alex?'" His pitch rises as he mocks me, and he might as well have been the one to slap me for how bad it hurts.

I thought we'd been in those moments together.

I'd been vulnerable in front of him. I'd let him see something real and private, and just like that, he shreds everything meaningful about them to pieces.

Lifting my chin, I meet his eyes. "I truly thought no one could be a bigger bastard than Hunter, but congratulations, Alex—you take the cake. It must be such a relief to finally be better than him at something."

It's low, and my lip quivers because I hate that this is what I've been turned into—someone who says things so mean and hurtful—but I don't take it back.

The sting is as plain on Alex's face as my handprint. "Get out of my fucking apartment."

I swing his door open. "Oh, I'm already gone."

But as soon as I slam the door behind me, I remember.

Fuck.

I have to count to ten before, swallowing every ounce of pride, I turn around and knock.

Alex opens the door immediately. "What?"

I almost think I see a glimmer of hope in his expression, but I'm sure it's just my imagination, and I dismiss it without giving it too much thought. "There…um, might be paparazzi waiting for me downstairs."

It takes a second to register.

Then a whole new wave of anger rolls over his features. "Goddammit, Riah. What did you expect coming out at this time of night?"

"Believe me, I'm full of regret." I bring my hand to pinch my forehead, realizing that more caustic words aren't helpful.

I exhale carefully. "But there's nothing I can do about that right now. Can you…?" I'm painfully aware that he just accused me of needing him, and it's like moving bricks to get my jaw to mouth the next words. "Can you…help me, please?"

He also lets out a breath.

He flips the deadbolt, so it won't lock behind him and steps out of his apartment. "Only because it's my literal job, not because I actually care."

"I would never have assumed otherwise."

Without any word of explanation, he walks down the hall to a neighbor's. I follow after him, lowering my head to stare at his bare feet when he knocks on the door, cringing about how late it is to be disturbing people.

It's not long, though, before the door opens to reveal an absolutely gorgeous woman with Asian features and straight dark hair dressed in pajama shorts and a tight T-shirt.

Her entire face turns on at the sight of Alex, and I'm immediately sure that they've fucked. "Hey, babe. You haven't knocked in a while. Thought you had yourself a situationship or something."

I hate myself for hating her. For wondering whether he talks nice to her when he's inside her. For hoping he hasn't visited her lately because of me.

Alex leans against the doorframe like he's a fucking book boyfriend. "Just been busy. Missed you, though." His eyes flick toward me as if that jab was specifically on my behalf.

Fuck him. Fuck him. Fuck him.

"But as much as I wish that was why I'm here now, I actually have quite a different issue." He steps back to reveal me. "Lulu, this is my brother's girlfriend—"

"Zyah! Wow. I'm such a fan. And you're in my hallway!"

Maybe I don't hate her after all.

She gushes on. "Love, love, love the latest single. It's so anti-man—sorry, Alex, honey—which is exactly what our culture is asking for right now. So current. I play it on repeat while I kickbox my bag."

"Whoa. Thank you. I'm—"

Alex cuts me off. "That's just lovely…really…and sorry to move this along, but as I was saying, Ri—" He stops to correct himself. "Zyah and Hunter came over to my place to discuss some branding decisions—I'm doing them a favor, helping out with this transition—"

"You're so generous with your time. That's not all you're generous with, if I remember correctly…" Apparently, Lulu will gush about anyone given the chance.

It was fine when it was for me. When it's for Alex, I'm not into it. "Anyway, the point is…"

But I'm not exactly sure how Alex was setting this up to be spun, so I peter out, forced to look at him to finish.

"The point is that Hunter had to leave early for an emergency business thing and now Zyah's ready to go, but we just noticed how late it is, and we've been informed there might be some media downstairs waiting to catch her in a scandalous situation."

She rolls her eyes as if she's witnessed the spectacle plenty of times. "They're such bloodhounds, I swear. I don't know how you live with it."

He shrugs like he's a goddamned hero. "You know. You get used to it. But Zyah's not quite accustomed to the diligence required to maintain a PR-friendly image—"

I knee him in the shin for the uncalled-for dig.

He goes on as if he hasn't been interrupted. "And I sort of hoped you might walk her downstairs, give her a hug at the door, put her in her car. Make it seem like the two of you have been spending the evening together so that the scoundrels don't try to place her coming from someone else's apartment in the middle of the night. It's an inconvenience, I know, but I'd really appreciate it."

His tone is thick with sin, as if he's promising a fuck instead of asking for a favor, and if I weren't so irritated by how good he is at flirting, I'd admire his plan.

I mean, it is a good plan. Should work like a charm.

"Play the part of Zyah's new bestie? You bet. Let me get some shoes on." Lulu disappears from the door frame.

"You're welcome," Alex says quietly.

"You're a fuckface," I whisper back.

He considers. "Actually, I think that was you who had her face fucked…"

I raise a finger to say something witty and final that I haven't exactly come up with yet, but I'm forced to let the last word go to him when Lulu returns with slippers on her feet and her key in hand. "Ready to go?"

I force a grin. "So ready."

Alex walks us to the elevator, as if he were a gentleman, which he most certainly is not. As the doors close, my new bestie Lulu is too busy flirtatiously waving to Alex to notice me lift both of my hands and flip that goddamn sonofabitch off.

———

LYRICS ARE SWIRLING in my head by the time I get back to my apartment, but instead of going down the hall to my makeshift music room, I knock on Whitney's door. "I know it's late, but I have to talk to you."

Her light is on, so I know she's awake, and as estranged as we've been, she doesn't hesitate to tell me to come in.

I slip in and find her sitting on her bed with her headphones around her neck and a sketchbook in hand. She was likely listening to something before I interrupted, and I'm aching to ask what. She might not have picked up performing like I did, but she's very much into music, and it seems like so long since we just sat around talking about all the artists we love.

But that's talk for people who don't have gulfs between them.

I'm here to build the bridge.

"I should have told you when it happened—I don't know why I didn't, really. Because I thought you might be ashamed of me or because I didn't think you'd understand —but I broke up with Hunter in L.A. when I caught him cheating. We've only been pretending to still be together because I'm good for his image, and he's good for my career.

"I know you might not respect me for lying to everyone about it, and I get it because I'm not sure I respect me either.

But this business is hard, and it takes more than talent and luck, and Mom always said that when you find an opportunity, you have to take it, and that's what this looked like—an opportunity.

"So yeah, he pays our bills, and he did even before we broke up, but it's not without a price. There are rules to the world, Whit, and they aren't pretty, and they aren't nice, especially for women, and we all have to navigate them the best way we know how, and I'm sorry for not trusting you with the truth earlier. I don't want to be someone who doesn't trust people, and I don't ever want to give you a reason not to trust me."

As soon as I'm done speaking, she flies off the bed and tackles me with a hug. "I'm sorry, too. I love you."

I wrap my arms around her. "I love you so much."

This is where I should have gone in the first place—not to see Alex. This is the only relationship that matters. I don't need anybody else.

That's what I tell myself.

Someday, long after Hunter's gone from my life and Alex's bruises and hickeys have healed, I might even find I mean it.

CHAPTER
TWENTY
ALEX

"Gigi's been asking about you," Reid says as he passes me the raita.

We were raised on five-star menus for every meal, but at least once a month, my brothers and I order takeout from a local dive and eat it at Spice when the club is closed and there are no witnesses. It's one of my greatest guilty pleasures. My father would disown us if he knew we regularly partook in something so base.

It's a thousand percent more about the food and dissing our father than it is about brotherly bonding, but there's something of that too. Reid and I meet up most often by ourselves and rotate through several good local spots. When Hunter joins us, it's always biryani.

I pour some of the sauce onto my rice dish and try to picture who he's talking about. "...Gigi?"

"From your *lovelorn* group."

He says it like he's baiting me, and it works—I cringe.

First off, Unrequited Love Support Group is the official title, but no way am I correcting him because, second, Reid never should have found out about it in the first place, and if Hunter starts chiming in about it now as well, I'm going to have to murder the first one for the mention.

"Would you..." I glance at my older brother to make sure he's still sucked into his phone and not paying attention, then lower my voice. "It's not a real group, okay? And fuck off about it, all right?"

Reid does not fuck off about it. "If it's not a real group then what is it?"

I glare at him. If I stare hard enough, maybe he'll read my mind telling him that he can't possibly be this big of an idiot. *Read the room, buddy. I don't want to talk about it.*

But that's probably exactly the reason he's poking me.

"Look, it was a one-time thing. A drunken pity party. Something stupid you say to get the hot girls doting over you." I shove a forkful of biryani in my mouth, hoping that ends the conversation.

"You told a bunch of hot girls you were secretly in love with someone who didn't love you back to get them interested?" Hunter peers at me over the screen of his phone.

And this was exactly what I was hoping to avoid.

"No judging. Just want to get it straight." He almost sounds sincere.

"Like hell you're not judging."

Hunter exchanges a smirk with Reid, then says, "I just haven't ever had to resort to such tactics to get laid, so I'm not sure how it works."

I flip him off. Then flip Reid off too because fuck them both.

Reid throws a piece of naan at me in response. "Anyway, you haven't been to Spice for a while, and she noticed. Thought you'd be in here more now that you aren't at the nine-to-five. Not less. The new job keeping you that busy?"

This topic isn't any better than the last because both of them involve Hunter's not-girlfriend. I don't like admitting to myself that no one else has caught my dick's attention in weeks. No way am I admitting it to these assholes. Reid would razz me for days. Hunter would outright murder me for playing with his things. He isn't the type to relinquish claim, and he'd be pissed that I had ever touched her, let alone been inside her.

Which is why fucking around with Riah is so satisfying.

Or that was why in the beginning, at least.

Lately, it seems there's more to my attraction than just the Hunter aspect. Some of it was there all along, if I'm honest. Like that night I introduced the Unrequited Love Club to the girls because it was New Year's Eve, and I'd had too much to drink, and every time I closed my eyes and tried to decide which Bastian Bunny was going to be in my bed that night, all I saw was Riah. She was a hot piece of ass who was always around, and maybe that was why she was in my head, but also, she was always too good for Hunter. He'd treat her like an afterthought, and she stayed true, and that was enough to be jealous of right there.

With a few too many shots, *what if I had a girl like my brother's* turned into *what if I had my brother's girl,* and after that it didn't matter who I took home with me—they all looked like the girl on Hunter's arm. I hated her for that. For being something I might want.

Then for being something that I wanted.

Now the thought of things really being over, as she claimed they are the other night, doesn't sit well.

Fortunately, I don't have to figure out how to dodge the question because Hunter interrupts with a question of his own. "Alex, isn't this your place?"

He turns his phone toward me and shows me a pic of Lulu hugging Riah outside of, yes, my apartment building. I've already seen this image, as well as seven others caught that night. They were trending the next morning, which was three days ago now. Hunter isn't as on top of managing Riah as he usually is, and I wonder if that's in part because he trusts me to be looking after her instead.

I wish I felt guilty, but I don't.

"Sure looks like it," I say, after pretending to study the image.

"You didn't know about this?" When I shake my head, he turns the phone back to look at it again himself. "Who was she visiting? When was this?"

"Cyber stalking your girlfriend?" Reid asks, and I can't help but feel smug at the discovery that he still thinks the relationship is real.

Hunter looks at him like he's an idiot. "Are you not stalking yours?"

"No, because I actually trust Lina."

Hunter pushes the Styrofoam container of food away from him, as if there will be a waiter cleaning up after us instead of just Reid. "Hope that works out for you, kid."

"Thanks." Reid scowls, but he collects Hunter's leftovers and dumps them in a giant trash can behind the bar.

Hunter seems to think the thanks is for his statement. "You're a Sebastian. Anyone and everyone will fuck you over if you give them a chance." He stands and buttons his suit jacket. "Which is why I'm going to walk next door and ask Zyah what this is about in person."

It's unnerving how my pulse speeds up at the mention of her stage name. "She's in the building?"

Hunter straightens his tie in the mirror behind the bar. "I arranged for her to use the concert hall to go over choreography for her music video."

"I didn't see that on the schedule." After she got herself stuck at my apartment on Sunday, I've been more attentive to her daily agenda. Because it's my job, but also because I like knowing where she is, which I'm sure is also about the job.

I definitely would have noticed a choreography slot on the schedule. She's already learning it? As her brand specialist, I should have approved the routine.

"Last minute thing." Hunter shrugs dismissively. "I ran into Damia Torrence at the Spring Fling and managed to convince her to come up with something quick. The choreographer Zyah's label had hired is a no-name nothing. Damia will come up with something no one will forget."

I wonder if Hunter's interference in her career is something Riah appreciates or if she's as irritated by it as I am just hearing about it. Though, to his credit, Damia Torrence is both world-renowned and incredibly talented. It's a partnership that I fully support. I only wish I'd thought of it.

"I should see what they're working on. I'll come with you." I start to clean up my food, but Reid shoos me away. I thank him then jog to catch up with Hunter, who is already walking out the club door.

Multi-tasking as always, Hunter takes a phone call as

we walk over to the concert hall. I tune him out, too busy thinking about Riah. It's irrational how much I want to see her again, even after what happened last time. The hand-print on my face was gone within the hour, but I still feel marked, as though she'd been the one to nip and bite and bruise up my skin and not the other way around.

She's always with me. If I close my eyes, I can smell her scent clinging to my body like a second skin. I see her face on the back of my eyelids. The memory of her cunt clenched around my cock is so frequent and so vivid that I'm constantly walking around with a semi. I have to think about hugging my deceased grandmother in order to keep myself presentable.

I haven't thought about Grandma Adeline this much in years.

I'm pleasurably jolted into the present when we walk onto the concert hall stage and there Riah is, in the flesh, wearing a leotard and shorts, sweat trickling from her fore-head as she performs a backbend under Damia's watchful eye.

She's more flexible than I realized, and damn, that doesn't help with the hard-on situation.

When she sees us, Damia cuts the music from her phone. Riah collapses on the ground and blows out an exhale.

Hunter doesn't acknowledge Riah. "Hi, Damia. Great to see you. Hate to interrupt, but mind if we have a few minutes with her?"

It's a surprisingly polite dismissal coming from him, and Damia practically falls over herself to comply. "Yeah, of course! Sure. I'll, um, just head next door and refill my coffee."

Her footsteps echo as she crosses the stage. Riah sits up, pulls her knees into her chest, and watches Damia go. "So. What's up?"

She's flushed from activity, like she is after sex, and fuck, it's hard to concentrate, but I do my damndest. "We were in the building, and—"

Hunter interrupts me and cuts right to the chase. "What the hell were you doing out in Chelsea looking so roughed up, Zy?"

He doesn't bother to show her the image, which somehow makes the interrogation feel more about control than actual answers.

Riah obviously knows what he's referring to without visual aid. She tries not to look at me and mostly manages. "Visiting someone."

"You look like you just rolled out of bed." Hunter's downplaying it. The truth is that, although I made sure she was seen with a woman so that the gossip hounds wouldn't come looking at me, I didn't make sure she put herself together. In other words, Riah looks very much like she was just fucked. Her hair is mussed, and her cheeks pink, and I'm almost sure her leggings are on inside out.

Or maybe that's just what I see because I know what I'm looking for.

Riah takes a sip from her water bottle before she responds, and I swear her face gets redder. I'm supremely gratified to know she's likely thinking about that night, about what she was doing. About what I was doing to her.

"Yeah, well. I couldn't sleep, so I *rolled out of bed* and went out instead. Obviously, you've never picked up a copy of People magazine or you'd know stars look like normal people sometimes because—surprise, surprise—they're people too."

"No, they're not. That's what makes them stars." It's dry, but I'm pretty sure it's Hunter's idea of a joke.

When Riah doesn't laugh, I second guess that assumption. "The general public does like to see the uber rich dressed down on occasion. Makes them seem more authentic and relatable."

"Yes, I know, asshole." He turns back to Riah. "If casual is your thing, fine. The real issue is that this wasn't a scheduled outing."

The muscle in her cheek twitches. "I had the whim to see a friend. I didn't realize I was supposed to report all my interactions to you. Are you reporting yours to me?"

"I think you'd rather not hear most of mine."

"Because I don't care."

"Well, none of my trysts got me spotted by the media."

Her eyes bump into mine as she quickly responds. "It wasn't a tryst."

"The point is it could have been seen as one. No bodyguards? A car ordered from an app? In the middle of the night?"

I enjoy watching them argue more than I should. It makes whatever they had together really seem over, and I like that. A lot.

Not that we don't argue just as much.

It's not even about us. Because there is no *us*. It's just nice to see Hunter *not* have the woman for once.

At a certain point, though, he starts to sound belligerent, and before I can stop myself, I jump in. "She gets it."

They both look at me, and I'm forced to say more. "I'm sure Riah understands the situation. And Hunter, you know as well as I do that you can only control so much when it comes to the paps."

"We also know that most shit can be kept under wraps if we're careful enough."

He's calmer, at least, and I take advantage of that. "Get her a full security detail. She practically had one when she was dating you. It will alleviate future problems and will help keep up the facade. Plus, it will make her appear important, which is what you're both going for in terms of brand."

"Appear important?" she says, but it's under her breath, so I ignore it.

"Right." Hunter pulls out his phone and texts as he talks, probably arranging security on the spot. "That was an oversight. Thank you for pointing it out."

He's still texting when Riah stands up and wipes stage dust from her ass. "So…Alex knows about our arrangement now?"

Oh, yeah. I wondered if Hunter was aware she knew that I knew.

Apparently not.

Hunter waits to finish his text before answering. "Thought it might be useful to have him on board," he says, slipping his cell into his pocket.

"What a great idea. Wish I'd thought of it." Her tone is thick with sarcasm, and if she hadn't outright said it the other night, I'd know now that she must have suggested bringing me into the secret first.

It's not like I'm just figuring out that my brother is a narcissistic ass, but it is a bit irritating every time I learn it anew.

"Your reasoning—" Whatever prick thing he's about to say in response, he changes his mind when Damia reappears at the other end of the stage.

She hesitates before crossing over to us. "Did I come back too soon?"

"Perfect timing. All wrapped up."

I'm not exactly sure what Hunter feels was wrapped up or what this whole encounter was for him other than an opportunity to exert authority, but my business here has yet to get started. "Actually, I came by to see the routine. Is that a possibility?"

Riah seems suddenly nervous. "Uh, it's real rough still. I haven't mastered most of the transitions."

"That's fine. I just need to understand the vision."

"You have it down well enough," Damia says. "That last run-through looked solid enough to get the idea."

"I'd really feel better if I could work on it a little more first." Riah locks eyes on mine, her expression pleading.

I'm not an idiot. There's a reason she doesn't want us to see the routine yet. Okay, it's possible that she's just a perfectionist, but since she's looking at me like I might understand, I have to think she might be worried about showing Hunter.

Of course, that makes me all the more curious.

And Hunter isn't the only ass in the family.

"You shouldn't even be at the learning stage without me

approving the concept," I say. "Brand extends to everything you're involved in that's public-facing."

"If you're not comfortable," Damia offers, "I could run it for them."

"No." Riah's glare is set on me. "I'll do it. Thank you, though. Could you start the music from the beginning?"

I pull out my phone as well and turn on the video recorder. "I'm guessing Claude hasn't seen it either," I explain when Riah raises a questioning brow.

I'll have to remember to actually send the file over to him.

With a reluctant nod, Riah takes her place, and then the music begins. It pulses, a deep and low beat that reverberates through the room. Riah's vocals, filled with passion and desire, swirl as she begins to move to the seductive rhythm.

I recognize the music immediately. I've listened to the raw tracks a hundred times now—for branding purposes—and every time through the album, "Finger Painting" always stands out as a stunning piece. It's poetry, really. It could literally be about a tormented artist struggling with the ability to create great art, sure, but a more intent listener will realize it's really about female masturbation.

It's a great choice for a single, and the choreography is perfection.

But also, I see immediately why Hunter won't like it— it's erotic as fuck. Beautiful and refined, but pure sensuality. With each provocative sway of Riah's body, an electric charge is sent through the air. Every movement of hers is controlled and effortlessly sexy, and even if I hadn't ever heard of Zyah, I'd still be drawn in by this. I'd still know this is career gold.

Even without looking at him, I can feel Hunter grow more tense beside me as the song progresses. The music isn't even a third of the way through when, after a particularly seductive move, he steps forward. "Hell no. Not happening. Cut. Cut. Cut."

Though I'm tempted to keep it running, I cut the video on my phone and put it in my pocket.

Riah stops as well, and I'm sure she expected this, but still, she seems surprised. "Why? What's wrong with it?"

"It's inappropriate," Hunter says, like it's obvious.

"Well, you'd be the one to know what inappropriate looks like." It's under her breath, and yet clear as day.

I can't help feeling bad for Damia, who both has to witness this exchange and also is responsible for the so-called offensive routine. Hunter's the one who hired her. The one who paid her, I suspect. The one she really wants to please. She has to be mortified.

"I'm so sorry it's not what you wanted," she says. "I can—"

Hunter ignores her and lays into Riah. "It's not choreography. It's masturbation."

"You do know what the song is about…." She's snarky with the comment, as if he might not have paid enough attention to her music to know the meaning.

Hunter's too attentive to details for that. "The lyrics are vague. It leaves room for ambiguity. This is obvious. It's not happening."

Riah balls her hands up at her sides and plants her feet defiantly. "You don't get to decide that."

"I don't?"

Authoritative and controlling are Hunter's dominant character traits. He gets it from our dad, who is all that times ten. It's genetic maybe, or maybe Hunter just took to social conditioning better than Reid and I did. Regardless, Hunter gets his way, and that's that. No sane person dares to argue.

I must be feeling out of my mind because not only have I never seen him be more wrong, but I've also never been more inclined to tell him. "Come on, Hunter. Be reasonable."

"*Reasonable*?" he repeats, as if there's no way he could have heard correctly. "You know what I'm up against. What kind of image I have to present."

Yeah, but... "At the cost of her career?"

"This..." He points at Riah to indicate the routine. "Is potentially *career-ruining*."

"Hers or yours?"

It takes him a second to answer. "Hers. I'm talking about her career."

No, he's not. He's talking about himself and couching it in concern for her. I know him too well to not see it.

I shouldn't be surprised, and I'm not really. But I've spent a lot of months pointing fingers at Riah for using Hunter, and this is the first time since I've heard about this arrangement that I'm seeing how much it only benefits him.

Once upon a time, I wouldn't have cared. A happy Hunter is good for the Sebastians in general, and I'm a man who was raised to understand the loyalty of blood.

But for some reason, I can't let this one go. "You're being fucking ridiculous. This is tasteful."

Not just tasteful, but important. It's not male-gaze Britney Spears happening here. This is Beyoncé. This is empowering. I wouldn't consider myself much of a feminist, but I'm not blind to what's going on in current culture. Women are having a moment, and this piece is relevant. Why wouldn't he want to capitalize on it?

Hunter stares down at me like I'm an imbecile. "She licks her fingers and then swipes her crotch. This is flat–out porn. I can't endorse this."

"Says the man who—"

I'm cut off by Riah waving her arms in the air like two white flags. "No, no. He's right. Hunter's right."

I'm flabbergasted. "What?"

"It's too far. Too on the nose." She turns her attention to Damia, who is already nodding in agreement. "We need to walk it back a bit. More metaphorical. Can you…? I'm sorry. I know you rushed this."

"It's really not a problem. Totally understand. I worried it was a bit edgy and went with it anyway. Give me a day to rework?"

"Sure. Yeah. We still have two weeks to filming."

"And you picked it up so quick."

I watch the two women rationalize changing the piece with stunned disbelief. They can't seriously think it's too far. The piece is perfection. Yes, it's provocative, but it's fire. It's a statement. Is this what Riah does all the time? Sacrifices vision to get the backing of deep pockets? Is this par for the course in her arrangement with Hunter?

I'm mad with frustration. "Are you all stupid or just cowardly? There is absolutely no reason why any of this has to change."

"Uh, yes, there is every reason." Hunter stares at me like he doesn't understand what I'm doing, and in truth, neither do I.

Why do I care so much? Why am I wasting my energy? If Riah's willing to tone it back, I should let her.

"It's fine," Riah says, seeming to be convincing herself as much as anyone else. "I can tamp it down and still be on brand. As it is, it will get slapped with censorship on some platforms. Both Topaz and TekTech would have a fit. This is good."

"We can still work on both versions if you want," Damia suggests. "Keep the naughtier one for the tour? You can get away with more there."

"That might be an idea." Riah looks to Hunter for his opinion, and I so badly want her to turn her head, so she's looking at me instead that it's all I can do not to grab her face and make her do it.

Hunter shakes his head. "It fucking gets toned down for the tour too. PG-13."

The women exchange a look that I think is probably steeped in code that I don't have the equipment to understand. Then Damia reaches out to squeeze Riah's shoulder. "I'll tone it down and get back to you. Shouldn't be too hard. I'll keep the spirit of the song, too, don't worry."

Phone and purse in hand, she rushes off to get working on a revision.

"Crisis averted," Hunter says when she's gone. Then points at me. "Isn't that supposed to be your job? Should take it out of your paycheck."

Another one of those dry humor jokes. This time, Riah isn't the only one who doesn't think it's funny.

"And while we're on the subject of appropriate—I saw the dress you picked out for the Met Gala next week. It's not going to work. Chains for the torso, Zyah? Maybe if the bottoms of both breasts weren't exposed, but..."

"It's a themed event," Riah protests. "Outfits are supposed to be extreme at the Met Gala."'

"The theme is deity not sexpot," Hunter says.

"Another brand related element no one mentioned to me?" I'm starting to think no one actually wants me to do more than occasionally babysit.

"She chose it on her own. I only just saw it yesterday." Hunter's a pro at pointing fingers.

Full palm on her forehead, she groans. "Where the hell am I going to get something else at this late notice?"

It's purely out of frustration with both of them that I step in. "I'll take care of it."

I'm a fool to volunteer. A gown worthy of the Met Gala at this late date is impossible. Holt knows the woman who owns Mirabelle's, a high-end boutique in the Village, though, and I'm hoping she'll be able to pull through. Hunter would be none too pleased to find me turning to Holt, so I'll keep that on the downlow.

"Thank you," Riah says with gritted gratitude. Either she doesn't want me to be the one to save her, or she doesn't want to be in this position in the first place. Possibly both.

I try not to take offense.

"White," Hunter adds as his phone starts to ring. "I want her in virginal white."

It takes everything in me not to roll my eyes. "I'll see what I can do."

"I have to take this." He waves to us as he puts his cell to his ear and turns and walks away.

Then I'm alone with Riah.

She stares at me for long seconds. The air is charged between us, but I'm not sure if she wants to kiss me or slap me.

Or maybe it's me who's confused because she does neither, and when she finally moves, it's to pick up her water bottle and her bag. "I have a lot of other things I need to be working on, so see you later."

I grab her arm as she walks past me, and while I'm tempted to pull her close and do nasty things to her mouth, I'm also still confused and pissed about what just transpired. "Why do you let him rule you like that?"

"Why do you let him rule *you*?"

I pretend her comeback doesn't sting. "We aren't talking about me right now. We're talking about you."

"Well, I'm none of your business."

She pulls her arm away, but when she takes a step, I quickly jump in front of her. "You're literally my business, Riah. You should have kept pushing back. The three of us could have overruled him."

"Right. Because you like him pissed off."

My eye twitches. "No. Because it's good material. It's strong and is one hundred percent what you're going for."

"Except, he said no."

When she steps around me, I shout after her. "Fuck him. He's not God."

She spins back to face me. "Might as well be, Alex. Who do you think is paying for all this? The three-hundred-thou-sand-dollar donation to Damia's dance foundation? The million-dollar price tag for the award-winning director he hired for the video? Hint, it's not my record label. It might seem like a drop in the bucket to you, but to me and my career, it's everything."

"He's not the only guy with money." It's out before I have time to think it. Before I have time to figure out what I mean.

But she's quicker than me. "You're offering yourself now?"

I only hesitate for a split second. "Sure. Why the fuck not? I have the money, and like you said, I like him pissed." And boy would he be pissed, but if I'm honest, that's not why I'd do it.

But I'm not interested in being honest, so fuck the why. The point is that I'm in. I volunteer. I'll take his goddamn place. I don't need a reason why.

I take a step toward her, embracing this impulsive decision and offering it as a gift. "More importantly, Riah, the video would be what it should be. Your career would be what it should be. You'd have the say."

"No. *You'd* have the say." Her tone is sharp, her eyes bullets shot in my direction. "And why would you suddenly be interested in shoving your resentment in his face? You've seemed pretty content getting your anger out behind his back. Suddenly your gameplan's changed? What's that about?"

"This is about your vision. That's all. Nothing more. About doing the job right. Yours and mine."

"And I'm just supposed to trust you? Because...why? Your dick's been inside me? Spoiler, but so has his."

I manage not to flinch, but she might as well have

slapped me again. Admittedly, I've been fairly preoccupied with the fact that he had her first for some time, but somewhere along the way, it became just a game. I taunted her about him without remembering that it was real. That he'd actually been inside her. That he'd been the first one to make her come. That she'd probably screamed his name before she ever knew mine.

It makes my stomach curl, and I want to punch the wall or cut off his balls or throw Riah on the ground and fuck her until she doesn't remember a goddamn thing about Hunter Sebastian, but while all those options sound satisfying, I'm sure none are very productive.

I take a breath then step close to her and force my voice to stay calm. "He doesn't care about you, Riah. I know you have an arrangement, but it's supposed to benefit you both. Not just him. He's using you."

She looks at me like I'm clueless. "He uses me in public, and you use me in private, but you both use me, Alex. At least with him, I know exactly where I stand."

There are a million things I could say in response. I'd like to argue that Hunter is a lying sack of shit, for one, and that what transpired between us is completely different, and above all, that she can trust that I would do right by her career when he's only in it for what will help him.

But when she turns to leave, I let her go.

Because there are quite a few lessons I've learned from watching my brother over the years, not the least of which being that trust is more than just lip service.

If I expect Riah to really believe I have her best interests in mind, I have to put my money where my mouth is and show her.

CHAPTER
TWENTY-ONE
RIAH

When I wake up the next morning, Alex is immediately on my mind.

He was frustrated and in the moment, but I can't stop thinking about his offer, if that's what it can be called. Would my career be better under his direction? Would I lose momentum "breaking up" with Hunter? Could I count on Alex to work on my behalf?

There's that saying that the devil you know is better than the devil you don't. Which should give Hunter the edge, but does that remain true if I *know* that Hunter won't let me be what I need to be to move forward?

But then is Alex any better?

It's stupid how my body reacts to him. I had more of a relationship with Hunter, and I never yearned for him with a physical longing the way I do with his brother. It's a part of me that I've tamped down for years. Even the instinct to reach for the vibrator in my nightstand drawer is one I've practiced dismissing. My priorities have been Whit and my career, and any other desires were distractions.

But now Whit doesn't need me like she used to, and my career feels out of my hands, and I'm tired of feeling *half-of* all the time—half of a woman, half of a performer, half of a sister. And no, I don't think that the missing part is all based in sexual identity, but it's a start.

Which is where Alex comes in.

He's so bad to me. And I don't trust him.

But he's also good *for* me. Not only does he seem to see the hidden parts of me, but he also draws them out. Validates them.

For his own benefit, of course.

Both of them for their own benefit, which is why I should stop overthinking it and stay with the devil I've already made a deal with. At least there won't be any surprises.

As for what my body needs…

I reach toward my nightstand only to jerk away when my bedroom door flings open. "Geez, Whit. Knock first."

"Sorry!" With the door still open and a wide grin on her face, she knocks on it. "I was too excited. Did I wake you up? Have you seen yet?"

"Seen what?" I rub my hand over my face as I sit up against the headboard.

"Oh my God, you haven't seen it! Wake up! Look at your phone! You're viral!"

I reach for my cell from the charger on the nightstand, which is admittedly harder to do than it should be since there's an eighteen-year-old jostling the bed as she crawls up next to me to peek over my shoulder. "How is it possible you don't have any notifications?" she asks.

"I have everything muted." It's the only way to deal with celebrity status. Let someone else jump every time someone posts my name. It's a full-time job just to manage all the mentions that pair me with Hunter.

Besides, she's wrong—I do have a notification from Claude. I open it up to find he's posted a link and a bunch of emoji exclamation marks. When I click on the link, it takes me to a YouTube video with over a million views. It's me on the frozen thumbnail—my hip cocked, my gaze drawn to the floor of the stage that I was just on yesterday afternoon.

"No, no, no." I'm already panicking when I push play.

Whitney bounces next to me. "There are just as many views on TikTok! Brilliant idea to leak the video footage. They're going insane for it!"

I shake my head emphatically as I watch myself perform the first several bars of "Finger Painting." I look more confident than I felt at the time, and I can see what Alex saw in it. Damia's choreography hits every note perfectly, expressing the layers that I hoped the song would convey. Without knowing the words, any viewer could tell this song is about a woman who needs to feel good in her own body, so instead of depending on others for that care, she takes care of herself.

Like Alex said, it's empowering.

It's also very, very sexy. Sexier than I'd realized while performing it. And while the video stops before Hunter shut me down, I can see why he was having a fit about it. It's not just a dance to an erotic song—it's a statement. One he didn't want me making, and yet here it is with over a million views.

"Fuck."

"What's wrong?" Whitney grabs the phone out of my hand and starts scrolling through the comments. "Is it the reactions? Most of them are good. Ignore the ones that call you a ho."

"They call me a ho?" I grab the phone back from her and scan the comments, seeing all the triggering words that Hunter likely feared—*slut, whore, bitch, cunt.* "No, no, no, no, no."

"There's always going to be haters. Especially when the material is so strong. You just—"

I cut her off. "It wasn't supposed to be leaked. This isn't even the dance anymore. Oh, God, Hunter's going to be furious." I dial him while I'm talking and put the phone to my ear, but it just rings. Considering that it's only seven-thirty in the morning, he could either be out at one of his breakfast meetings or still asleep.

"It wasn't supposed to be leaked? Then how did *Deux Moi* get it?"

I hit END before I get sent to voicemail and stare at my sister because she's right. That should have been my first question. Alex had mentioned taking the footage for Claude, so I suppose it's possible that my manager is the one who sent it out, but there isn't a doubt in my mind who's responsible. "Alex."

I find his number and dial it. This time when it goes to voicemail, I leave a heated message. "What the actual fuck, Alex? You don't get your way, so you pull off some bullshit like this? Are you *trying* to ruin me? This is so absolutely unprofessional, I can't even…" I can't even word, is what it is. I'm too pissed to express myself properly. "This is fucked up," I say again. "And, and, and…you're fired!"

I click END and hurl the phone onto the bed.

"You just fired Alex?" Whit asks as I throw the covers off and slip into the bathroom.

"It has to be him," I call through the cracked open door while I pee. "We decided to change the choreography to make it less provocative, and he wanted to keep it like this."

I'm not even sure I have the authority to fire Alex. There was a contract, and it involved the label and Hunter. Most people don't realize how little authority performers have unless they're deep into their career and topping all the charts. The frustration about all the ways my hands are tied is the same frustration that had me making the arrangement with Hunter in the first place—I have no power.

A thought strikes me as I brush my teeth. "Shit! What if Hunter thinks I had something to do with this?" It comes out garbled though, since I still have toothpaste in my mouth.

"What if what?"

I spit out the toothpaste and come out of the bathroom and find Whitney scrolling through the comments on my phone again. "I have to talk to Hunter," I say, bending down to look for a slipper under the bed. "If he thinks I had something to do with leaking it, he's going to go ballistic."

"But Riah—this isn't a bad thing. This is, like, actually really amazing. The feedback is incredible. You can't change it now. People are dying for the real thing."

I pause with a slipper in hand and try to process what she's saying. "They like it?"

"They *love* it. You should read some of this shit."

I'm tempted, but then I shake my head. "People like scandal."

"That's not what they're saying. They get it, Riah. They're calling it *feminist* and *important*."

Admittedly, a bubble of elation starts to form in my chest.

But then I remember Hunter and how he needs to adopt a more traditional reputation.

"Important and feminist are probably the worst ways the media can describe me right now." I stand and slide my feet one by one into the slippers. It has to be why Alex leaked it in the first place. Not for my benefit, but because he knew his brother would be pissed. "I've got to find Hunter and talk about damage control."

I'm halfway down the hall when Whit stops me, waving my phone overhead. "*Forbes* posted a blog post this morning stating that Hunter Sebastian is more in touch with the youth than any of his relatives because he's dating you, so make sure there's actual damage before you go about controlling it."

My brows knit together. Is it possible that what's good for my career could actually be good for Hunter's as well? "I'll...uh, keep that in mind."

But when I get upstairs, I find Ax watching porn in the theater room—fortunately, with all his bits tucked away—and he informs me that Hunter went out for a run.

Instantly, I'm back to feeling frantic. "He never exercises outside." Hunter hates people with cameras following him around while he sweats. He has to be pretty in need to blow off steam to change that routine.

"He thought it was a good idea to try to draw attention in whatever way possible."

Attention away from me, he means.

My stomach drops. "He's pissed, isn't he?"

"I was still half asleep when Hunter and Alex were yapping about it."

I'm curious about what time they all got up to have this so-called conversation already, and what Ax was doing here so early, but I'm more interested in the conversation itself. "Alex was here? What did he say? Does Hunter know that I had nothing to do with this?"

Ax glares at me like I'm a pesky fly. "Fuck, so many questions. If I cared, I would have paid attention. You'll have to wait for Hunt or go ask Alex. He's lifting right now."

"He's here?" I don't wait for Ax's answer.

Leaving him to rub one out, I head for Hunter's home gym. It's on the other side of the apartment, which ends up being a far enough walk to get me riled up again. It doesn't matter what the response was to this video, either from the public or Hunter. The point is that Alex went behind my back and made bold decisions about my career without my permission.

By the time I walk into the workout room, I'm furious. "How dare you? How *dare* you?"

Alex is lying flat on a bench, shirtless, sweat dripping down his temple as he presses two hundred pounds of weighted barbell from his chest. The fucker not only waits to finish his set before responding, but also has the audacity to look really outrageously hot while doing so.

And aren't you supposed to have a spotter when lifting? Not that I care if Alex gets crushed because of his inflated male ego...

After he returns the barbell to its rack, Alex sits up and wipes the sweat from his brow with his forearm. "Phone was stolen," he says in such an unbelievably nonchalant tone that there's no doubt that it's a lie. "Already had it unlinked from the cloud, but not before the video was discovered. Whoever took it must have looked at my most recent images, recognized you, and saw the opportunity. Terribly unfortunate."

"Does Hunter buy that bullshit?"

He grabs a water bottle and throws back a swig. "Why wouldn't he? It's the truth."

But then he smirks, and I wonder if there's a way I could make that barbell-crushing possibility a reality because I think I legit want him dead. "You're a sociopath."

"Oh, come on, Riah. Have you read what people are saying? They love it. Just like I knew they would." He stands up and crosses to the all-in-one machine where he casually rests his hands above his head on the pull-up bar.

"It doesn't matter if they love it. You didn't have any right!" I refuse to let myself notice how toned his pecs are or how his waist indents with those sexy little vee lines that run underneath his shorts, but if he starts doing chin-ups, I might have to sit down.

"I didn't have a right? It's my *job* to protect your brand."

"Fuck off. This wasn't about your job. This wasn't about me at all. This was about your brother."

He has the nerve to look offended. "This was *in spite* of my brother."

"Yeah, right. Because you don't enjoy pissing him off."

He takes a step toward me, which puts us pretty close because apparently, I wanted to get up in his face with my accusations. "Have I once done anything that he would find out about?"

Well, no. Unless I was going to say something, everything he's done to fuck with his brother has been behind Hunter's back. Like the fuck-you was always more about making Alex feel good rather than bringing Hunter down. Admittedly, leaking the video is not Alex's general MO.

"Exactly," he says, reading my thoughts. "I've never purposefully done something that might interfere with my brother's objectives. Until now. Because he was wrong, and I knew it, and because his mistake came at a price that only you had to pay. That choreography was on point. Leaking it was the right move for your career. You should be thanking me."

"*Thanking* you?" He almost had me agreeing with him, but then that ego of his had to beg for recognition. "You're incredible, you know that?"

"Yeah. Incredibly insightful. I bet you money when that song is released, you have a top ten single on your hands after this. And the two of you were just going to throw that gold away." He rubs his lip with his thumb. "So you want to pay that back on your knees or would you rather lie on the bench, so I can fuck your face?"

"Oh my God, you're insane!" I turn toward the door, mostly because I'm starting to feel very unsafe in his proximity, which probably has more to do with my own willpower around him than it does with him actually being a threat, but then I spin back toward him when I realize I have more to say. "The only reason you don't want anything bad to happen to Hunter is that you're a coward. Because you definitely resent him. You probably would have blown up in his face already if you didn't have a way to work out that resentment—aka: *me*. So actually, the way I see it, *you* owe *me*."

"I owe you?" He laughs. "That's real funny."

"Why? Because you didn't sex talk me into coming on his chair so you could feel smug?"

"No, that was just hot."

I ignore him. "Because you didn't steal my panties and leave your jizz running down my leg, so you'd feel holier-than-thou when you saw him later?"

"Again—"

I don't let him speak. "You keep saying what I'm good for is being used. So when are you going to admit that's exactly what you've done?"

"Okay, sure. Fine." Now *he's* in *my* face. "You think I owe you? Sure. I owe you." Every time he steps toward me, I take a step back. When my back hits the workout machine, I realize he walked me in a circle, and now I'm essentially trapped between him and the machine. "How about I pay up right now?"

"No. I don't think—" I try to duck under his arm, but he brings it around my waist and pulls my backside flush against him. "Alex. Let me go."

"Really? That's what you want?" His mouth is next to my ear, his voice husky, and I swear his sweat put some extra pheromones in the air—or maybe being mad at him is just a really big turn-on—because I'm feeling weak in the knees and moist between the thighs and the correct answer to his question has disappeared from my mind.

"No, you don't want me to let you go." His arm tightens around my waist and when he brings his other arm around me, he lets his hand slip underneath the drawstring waist of my pajama shorts and into my very damp panties. "Because if I let you go, I couldn't show you all my gratitude, could I? That's what you wanted, wasn't it? Paybacks? Because I owe you?"

The tip of his finger brushes against my clit, and I shiver. "Alex."

This time his name comes out more of a plea than a warning, and I officially hate myself.

"All you have to do is take it back. Tell me I don't owe you, and I'll stop."

He starts to pull his hand away, but I'm a glutton, and my arm comes down to hold his in place. "No."

"No, I don't owe you? Or no, don't—?"

"Don't stop." And that's it. I'm officially complicit to whatever happens after this moment. Which means I have no one to blame but myself.

He sounds far too pleased when he replies. "I couldn't possibly stop now. Not when you're dripping wet and begging—"

"I'm not begging." I mean, maybe I'm begging.

"And when I am so egregiously indebted to you."

I moan as his finger slides over my clit, the pressure building and then easing off again. "Yes. Egregiously." Especially if egregiously means I get a big fat orgasm out of this.

My hips push against his hand, trying to get more of that delicious friction, but he pulls back just enough to keep me on edge. "Hold on, now. I need to make sure we have the situation clear."

"You owe me," I reply without hesitation.

"I owe you." His words send goosebumps down my arms as his fingers continue their teasing dance over my clit. "I owe you for putting your career first."

"Well…"

"For knowing what you need. Not Hunter."

Even distracted, it feels like a trap, so I don't respond.

And then his fingers are gone from between my legs and before I can protest, he's maneuvering me so I'm under the exercise machine. "Reach your hands up and hold the bar."

"But you'll come back?"

"Am I the one who knows what you need?"

I answer by lifting my arms to hold onto the bar. My pajama tank rises to expose my stomach, but I'm pretty sure my trembling is due to anticipation. Behind me, I hear Alex rummaging through a cupboard. When he returns, he spreads my cheeks, with my shorts still on, and presses a fat cylinder-shaped object against my asshole.

I realize that it's a massage wand when it starts vibrating.

I gasp as he begins to move it in slow circles over my sensitive back entrance. The sensation is nice enough— okay, more than nice—but the real thrill comes when he returns his other hand to my front side and flicks my clit.

I jolt and let out a moan, unable to stop myself from pushing back against the wand.

"See?" he says as the vibrations become more intense. "I know what you need. I take care of you."

My body tenses as he stretches his hand so he can finger fuck me and continue the ministrations on my clit at the same time. All without letting up on the vibration at my ass.

"Please, Alex. I need to come." The triple stimulation has my head spinning, and I can already feel myself spiraling toward climax.

"Do you admit that you need me? That I'm the one who will take you where you need to go? The only one."

"Stop trying to prove a point." All I want is for him to make me come.

"Say it," he whispers in my ear before biting down on the lobe. "Say I'm the one who knows what you need. Say I'm the one who takes care of you."

God, I'm so close… If I just hold out another…few…

But just when I think I'm about to explode with pleasure, he stops, and the wand drops to the floor at my feet. My body protests at the sudden loss of stimulation, and I turn my head to see what happened, hoping he's only paused so he could strip down and fuck me properly.

But instead, he's backed up several feet, arms crossed, smug expression on his face.

I let go of the bar and turn around to face him. "Alex." I'm not begging. I'm bossing.

"Thought you didn't need me."

"You sadistic son of a bitch." He's the cruelest person I know. It's decided now. Mean. Terrible. Antagonistic. A bully. A bully with a massive tent in his shorts that makes my pussy weep, but a bully all the same.

And I'm stubborn and refuse to give in—not on this—and the wand is still vibrating on the floor, and I'm a self-sufficient modern kind of woman, goddammit.

So I pick it up and press the head against my crotch. "Ha!"

His smirk disappears.

Even through my panties and shorts, the pulse is strong for my swollen clit. Too strong, actually, and I have to adjust the placement, but instantly, I'm right back where he left me. "I don't. Need you," I pant.

"Put it down, Riah."

"Uh uh. I'm going. To come. All. On my. Own." Spectacularly, too. It's right there. Right…fucking…there…

But then Alex is in front of me, reaching for the wand. "I said put it down."

"You're so egotistical. I don't need you to make me come." I twist, trying to keep the object out of his reach.

But he is too quick, and his arms wrap around me in a tight embrace, his strength overwhelming as he wrestles the object from my grasp and holds it over his head.

I spin back to face him and reach for it on tiptoes for a full five seconds before remembering manual ministrations work just as well. So I shove my hand down my panties and furiously start rubbing.

Alex isn't amused. "Don't."

"Mm. Right there." I'm not close anymore, but I close my eyes and pretend. "Yes. Yes."

"Riah. Stop." I hear the wand drop to the floor, and then he's tugging at my arm, trying to take my hand from my shorts. "Stop."

"No. I won't. It's *my* body. It's *my* career. It's mine, and I have to give so much of it away. I'm tired of other people always deciding what's in my best interest and questioning their motives and finding out that they're always selfish and self-centered and never actually about what's best for me. I hate it, Alex. I hate it."

It's resentment that I've held for some time. Much more than he deserves on his own, but he gets all of it, because this isn't just one incident for me. It's one in a long line of decisions made on my behalf. Opportunities taken without my input, many of them that I'm so grateful for, but all of them outside of reach on my own. It's a strange kind of servitude, to have the talent but still lack the power, so I have to tie myself to someone else to get anywhere.

Tie myself so tight I end up in knots.

I don't know when Alex stopped struggling—or when I did—but when I'm done ranting, he's holding me, one arm wrapped around my torso, his mouth buried in my hair.

"Shh." The sound tickles my ear, but the sensation demanding more attention is his thumb on top of mine, gently rubbing my clit. "Let me."

I moan and surrender the task to him. I'm probably too in my head now for orgasm, but it still feels good to be held and stroked, and I let it happen.

Without pausing his massage, he moves so his forehead is pressed against mine. "It was for you, Riah. I did it for you."

His voice is soft, and it pulls at something inside me, asking me to trust. Can I trust him? It's strange how much I want to.

But trust is still a sacrifice when what I long for is freedom.

Just as I open my mouth to explain, a wave of pleasure begins to build inside me. It starts as a tingling sensation at the base of my spine, spreading through every nerve in my body. My breath catches in my throat and my heart races as my body responds to the growing intensity, building, building, building…

Then there's a noise from the hall, and we both freeze.

Alex realizes it's someone coming before I do, and he pulls his hand out of my panties and steps away from me. I don't even try to tie the drawstring, but I pull down my tank to cover it just in time for Hunter to walk in, phone in hand, sweaty from his run.

"I think this might end up okay. *Forbes* is calling me *in touch* and…" Hunter pauses when he looks up from his screen and sees me. "You come to scream at him too?"

I'm so weary from my mini breakdown and the argument and the (several) missed orgasms that I feel more like crying now, so I just nod.

"Either he's a fucking idiot for misplacing his phone, or he's an obstinate asshole genius for forcing this to get leaked." Hunter holds up his own cell, indicating the viral video. "Take your guess which I believe. He's smart to never admit it."

With Hunter watching me, I glance over at his brother. I'm pretty sure I already look red-faced and distracted from our prior activity, but I feel a whole new flush wash down my body when Alex brings his thumb to his mouth and sucks.

"Look, she's so mad, she's red," Hunter says. "I was too, Zy, but I think it's going to work out okay." He walks over to Alex, who fortunately has removed his thumb from his mouth, and pats him on the shoulder. "You're one lucky motherfucker."

It occurs to me finally what Alex risked for this. It's the first time he's openly opposed his brother, and I can hear in Hunter's tone that there will be consequences in their relationship, despite the reception the leak has received. He really did do it for me. In spite of Hunter.

It makes me feel some kind of way that I don't want to think about at the moment.

Can't think about.

"Social media is calling you the number one star to watch, babe. You're not going to hold a grudge, are you?"

I think I hate Hunter's approval as much as I hated Alex taking matters into his own hands. It's patronizing being told how to feel about something so important to me. It's all just more of the "everyone has power here but me" dynamic, and I can't bring myself to respond.

Alex doesn't have the same problem. "No. She knows who's got her back."

His eyes pierce into me, and even though I thought we'd made some breakthrough in our battle, I realize that I'm trapped again. That *no* will be a lie because I'm actually glad about the outcome. That *yes* will mean he wins after all.

And letting him win means trusting him.

Without saying a word, I turn and leave.

CHAPTER
TWENTY-TWO

RIAH

I stare at my reflection in the mirror, stunned.

The gorgeous white dress that Alex selected for me is the epitome of elegance and sensuality. The bride trope that I'm sure Hunter wanted for the piece has been reversed, a nod to Madonna's iconic style from the 80's, but with a modern and classy twist. The open back and plunging neckline exude confidence and sexiness, while the ruffle cascading down the skirt opens up to reveal my hip, adding a touch of daring to this otherwise sophisticated ensemble.

It's a masterpiece of design, perfectly fitting my new personal brand, and I know that even though I won't be haute couture like so many are at the Met Gala, I still fit the theme and will be a highlight on the red carpet. Without pissing off Hunter, which is a bonus.

"I've never seen you look more beautiful," Whit says, watching from the doorframe.

Zully finishes separating the curls that hang down my back and nods. "I'm a transformation genius. What can I say?" When Whit gapes, Zully laughs. "Oh, you mean the dress. Yes. It's chef's kiss." She pinches her fingers and thumb together with one hand and tosses them dramatically in the air.

"You're chef's kiss, Zully." I don't lean in to hug her because I know she'll freak out about messing us up. She's doing triple duty today. Not only did she do my hair and makeup, but now she has to run off to do Brystin's and her own since they're going to the gala as well. "You going to make it?"

"Right. I forgot I was on my way out. See you there!" She already has her suitcase of supplies packed up, and after profuse thanks on my part, she leaves, insisting I don't walk her to the door.

Once she's gone, Whit ventures into the room. She's rarely gushy, so when she circles her arms around me from behind in a hug, and rests her head on my shoulder, I don't let myself worry about messing up my hair. "It's not the dress or the hair and makeup. It's you."

I place my hands on Whit's at my waist. "Mm. It's the dress."

"Yeah, it's the dress." I can see her smug smile in the mirror. "And you fired this guy."

I roll my eyes. "Oh, whatever."

In the week and a half since Alex leaked my music video, neither of us have mentioned the voicemail. I also haven't seen him in person, but he's definitely been working. Several times a day, he's in my inbox, copying me as he discusses PR strategy with my publicist and Claude and the record label and the tour sponsors. He's constantly in contact with me and my social media manager regarding posts and comments. My followers have exploded on all platforms, and frankly, I'd be overwhelmed without his insight.

At every chance possible, Alex seems to be trying to prove that he knows what I need. That he's the one helping me make waves with my career.

It would be hard to quantify who has done more overall at this point, him or Hunter. I've been ignoring the inkling to try to add it up and compare.

But then Alex sent this dress, and I'm like, Hunter who?

Whit meets my eyes in the mirror. "I'm glad you have someone on your team who gets you. You should make sure you tell him he's good."

I nod, half thinking that the guy doesn't need the ego boost, half thinking I should probably tell him a lot more than that. Right now, though, I'm more focused on the other person who gets me. Whitney and I have been closer since I explained about Hunter. A lot of tension was relieved when she got a job at a trendy new modern art gallery a couple of blocks down, but I think there's still something she's working through that she hasn't shared with me. She's often quiet. Stays in more than she used to. Spends more time in her head.

I squeeze her hands. "You sure you don't want to come tonight?"

We're close enough in size that Whit could wear the dress that Hunter axed for me, and Alex says we have a ticket available. We'd have to hustle to make it happen at this point, but since I had to get ready so early in order to book Zully, there'd be time.

As expected, Whit shakes her head. Then she pulls away, as if just by asking, I've sent her back into retreat. "Thank you, but heels. No." She makes an exaggerated shudder. "I like hearing the fashion commentary in real time, anyway. I already have leftover Chinese heating in the microwave. Probably done by now."

She uses the excuse to lead her out of the room, but she stops again at the door. "Can I live text you the internet's impressions, though?"

I can imagine how annoyed Hunter will be if I'm constantly checking my phone all night, but it's my sister. "Uh, do you even have to ask?"

An hour later, I'm about to go upstairs to meet Hunter when he sends a text.

Car arriving in five.

I take it as a cue to go straight downstairs instead.

When I don't find Hunter in the lobby, I step outside into the late May afternoon, and sure enough, a car is already waiting. I'm surprised it isn't a limo, since that's what I'd been told we'd be driving in, but rather a Bentley.

"Ms. Watson?" the driver asks.

"That's me."

He stands aside to open the door for me. I slide into the backseat, expecting to see Hunter already seated on the other side, but instead, it's another Sebastian. The one who sends my pulse rising and my stomach swirling. He's dressed in a classic double-breasted tux, black undershirt, no tie, hair trimmed and sculpted to perfection.

"Alex. What are you...?" I trail off when I notice how he's looking at me. His eyes skate appreciatively across the skin exposed at my neckline, and just like that, my nipples stand up to salute him, as if he's the man who owns them.

I'm suddenly very aware that being this close to the man, for even a short amount of time, is a dangerous idea. To punctuate the thought, the driver gets in behind the wheel and all the locks click, sealing my fate.

"Hunter got tied up across town." Alex intuits my unasked question and answers smoothly, clearly unaffected by our close proximity to each other. "We're timed to meet him there."

I swallow the lump in my throat, which I'm pretty sure is my heart, and try to figure out how that led to me being alone in the backseat of a car with Alex. "He took the limo. And this car is...?"

"Mine."

He's talking about the vehicle, an inanimate object that he clearly bought and owns, but I swear it feels like he's talking about me. Feels like he's claiming me.

The heat that sweeps over me is so overwhelming, I have to look away.

Without my eyes on him, rational thought returns, and then I'm confused because the driver is one that I've seen before, even though I've never been in one of Alex's cars. "But—"

As if he can read my mind, Alex explains. "We share our team of drivers."

"Oh." It means that anything that happens on this car

ride could get back to Hunter since there's no window between the front and the back, so we'll have to behave.

I don't know whether that makes me feel relieved or disappointed. It should, at least, make this trip feel less dangerous, but experience has taught me that Alex manages to take what he wants when he wants it.

It's an unfair thought. I'm as much to blame for everything that's transpired between us, and as inappropriate as we've been, Alex has never put us at risk of being caught.

Once again, I feel that urge to trust him.

The thought gets pushed away with the realization that Alex wouldn't have picked me up if Hunter hadn't told him to. Another command doled out from older brother to younger, probably couched as a favor.

And for whatever reason, Alex jumped, as always.

"Thank you for the ride. I'm sorry you had to go out of your way."

"Why? Because you think you'll have to owe me?" he asks.

If I wasn't red before, I am now. For a myriad of reasons. Obviously, I'm thinking of the last time we played the owe-me game, and while it ended with a serious case of blue clit, my girl parts must not remember because they're suddenly buzzing.

The reminder fires me up in other ways too. Because I'm still mad at him. For edging me, which is maybe a bit petty, but also for leaking the damn video. And for reminding me how little control I have in my career and how much I have to rely on deep pockets like his and his brother's. And especially for proving that, as much as I don't want to be a person who uses my body for negotiation, I somehow can't keep sex out of the equation with Alex.

"Oh, you can't still be pissed. Surely by now, you see it's all worked out to your benefit." Apparently, anger is the only one of my emotions that registers to him. Which is probably for the best.

"Yeah, well, you got lucky."

"I didn't get lucky. I knew."

The video's only now settling after the viral wave. A slew of PR opportunities came out of it, and my sponsors added several dates to the tour schedule. It's honestly been one of the best things to have ever happened to my career, and as much as I want to believe it could just have easily gone the other way, my gut says that Alex wouldn't have let that happen.

Still. "It's the principle."

"You have those?"

I swing my head to glare at him so fast that I won't be surprised if I get whiplash.

"I'm kidding," he says, already smiling when I turn his way.

Even joking, I'm not amused. "Fuck you."

"I'm trying."

It's low, so only I can hear, and the soft rumble of his voice sends a delicious shiver down my spine. Or possibly it's the words themselves. It's the first time he's outright declared he has any interest in a repeat of the past, and I really wish I wasn't as thrilled by it as I am.

I close my eyes for a beat, hoping to calm the desire in my blood, and a thought pops into my head. "Wait. Was that why you leaked the video? Because you thought that…?" I glance at the driver, and even though he doesn't seem to be listening, I don't finish the sentence.

Alex gets my meaning, anyway.

Hand on the bench between us, so close his fingertips brush the open slit of my dress, he leans in and practically whispers. "Do you really think I'd have to *earn* my way back into your bed?"

I try to pretend like I'm not already damp at the core. "I said it would never happen again."

"You didn't mean it."

"I did."

"So tell me, that day in the gym, if it had been more than my fingers that I'd offered, you would have said no?" As he talks, he draws the tip of his index finger along my exposed thigh. Higher, higher, higher until he reaches my hipbone. The glint in his eyes when he realizes I'm not wearing underwear—impossible with this dress—is predatory and mesmerizing.

I swallow.

Again.

Obviously, his insinuation is correct. I would have spread my legs as fast as liquid is pooling in a spot beneath me. Thank God the ruffle wraps around to bunch behind my ass to hide any stains on my dress, otherwise, I'd have a whole other PR crisis as well as possibly ruining another Sebastian leather seat.

It would be his fault. Not mine.

I try to hold onto that mindset. "The point is…"

All thought suspends when his hand reaches farther

under my dress and finds the bitch pussy that's responsible for the mess. "The point is that I know what you need." He teases my clit like it's his own personal fidget toy. "I know what will move you forward. Just like I knew that choreography would be a magnet for your audience. Just like I knew that you would look stunning in this dress."

I blink and try to force myself to concentrate on his words. Hard when I'm currently fighting with my thighs— should they open or close? Especially hard with Alex's brute expression and skilled fingers.

The sound of the turn signal breaks the spell, fortunately. I remember the driver. Remember our circumstances and nudge Alex's hand away, praying that the rearview mirror isn't tilted to see the backseat.

Then I latch onto his last statement and steer the conversation to safety. "The dress is incredible, Alex. I don't know how you did it. I can't thank you—"

Hand safely back in his lap, he cuts me off. "You can't thank me because you don't need to. It's my job. I'm committed to making sure you have what you need to be successful."

"And he isn't." I purposefully avoid Hunter's name. There's no question who I mean.

For a second, I think he's going to go through the spiel again of all the reasons his brother is wrong for my career, but he surprises me. "You tell me."

I don't have to think about it. Bringing on Jake Dunham and getting *Rolling Stone* and then Damia to choreograph. Plus, all the money and PR. "He's brought a lot to the table, Alex. He leveled me up big time. That's irrefutable."

"When it benefitted him as well."

"That's sort of the reason for the whole arrangement."

"But what has he done for you lately?"

I let myself think about this in earnest. Because now that the most important connections have been made, Hunter's focus has admittedly been elsewhere. He rarely contributes to team conversations except to tell me where he needs me to be and when. He doesn't try to collaborate with me like he used to. Doesn't ask for my thoughts or ideas.

But maybe that's just because my career is at a different point now.

And even though it wasn't the direction he wanted to go, he's certainly embraced the success that's come from the video leak. "Okay, he was wrong about the choreography," I concede. "But he gets that now. And with the dress for tonight…he wanted something that only worked for him, but you found a way to meet both our needs. You pivoted."

"What are you saying?"

"I'm saying there's no reason to disrupt the status quo. This works."

"This works." He repeats my words dully, as though those couldn't possibly be the ones I've just said.

"There are bumps sometimes, but we're managing. Aren't we? Thanks, in part, to you." That's not giving credit where credit is due, though it kills me to admit. "*All* thanks to you, I suppose."

"So don't rock the boat. You want to ride it out as it is and hope I can put out the next fire as easily as I did these because good old Alex knows how to pivot."

It sounds like a thin strategy when he says it like that, so I merely shrug.

He looks like he wants to throw something. Me, possibly.

The thing is, don't rock the boat is exactly the opposite of what I'm trying to do with my new persona. I *want* to rock the boat. I want to be disruptive. I want to be a voice in the social conversation about women's rights to own their sexuality.

So if Hunter equals the status quo, why am I fighting so hard to keep him?

I angle myself to face Alex. "What do you suggest instead?"

This time he's the one to glance at the driver. "I told you already."

He means on the stage when we were fighting about Damia changing the choreography. When I reminded him that Hunter provides the checkbook, and Alex volunteered himself to bankroll instead.

But words said in the heat of an argument are like words said during sex—they don't count. "That was impulse-driven."

"You're right. But I've thought about it more, and I stand by it."

It's tempting. So, so tempting.

Because he has proven himself where my brand is concerned. Over and over. He gets my vision. But he's also more often an asshole than he's not. Plus, there's the whole, we can't be in a room together without touching each other's genitals thing. Which I'm not sure isn't just part of his agenda, and oh yeah, what exactly are his motives, anyway?

"Why are you so eager for me to...?" I lower my voice

and lean toward him, bracing my hand on the seat. "Break things off with him. This is about sticking it to him, isn't it?"

"No." Alex is emphatic then seems to remember himself. "No," he says again. Quieter. "You think this arrangement is in his best interest? You aren't hurting him, but you aren't helping him in the way someone else could. At this point, breaking things off with you would do more for him than not. There are some truly conservative people on the board. And it would grant you freedom to express yourself authentically."

"And...what? You'd step in with the money? Because it's your job?"

"You'd be more an investment, in this scenario."

"An investment." I practically shudder. "I know you don't believe me, but I don't exchange sex for favors. I won't do it. I draw the line." Probably wouldn't have to say it so much if it didn't feel so close to being a lie.

Alex's hand is back on the seat between us, the tips of his fingers nearly touching mine. "I'm not asking for anything in exchange, Riah." His sincerity is palpable. "An investment means I get paid on the back end. I don't expect you to fuck me for the funds."

It's almost a relief to have it said outright.

But then that smirk appears, and his voice goes low. "I expect you to fuck me for *fun*."

My skin prickles, and I bite back a smile.

I shouldn't even be considering this. It's got bad idea written all over it.

And I still don't know his motives. "Why?" I ask, point blank.

"If I need to explain the fun in fucking, then I've seriously been doing something wrong."

I exaggerate a roll of my eyes. "Why do you want to invest in me?"

He ticks off the reasons without having to pause and think about it. "Because I have the money. Because you're an investment I believe in. Because Hunter stole my last investment project from under my feet."

"There!" I literally clap my hands together. "I knew it. You want some sort of payback."

"No, I don't." He leans in even closer. "Contrary to what you seem to think, I'm not *after* him. Does he piss me off? Yes. Do I resent him? Yes. It doesn't mean I want to actually hurt him. I just meant that I had a plan, and now because of him, I need a new one. And I think you could be a good plan."

"A good plan." I don't know how I feel about that terminology. It's logical, which is what's needed for business deals, but does it diminish what I'm trying to do? What I'm trying to be?

"Don't overthink it, Riah. It's not supposed to be patronizing. It's good business. For both of us. He's good at bringing people together, yes. That's a strength of his. I'm a thousand times better at building a brand, and that's the stage you're at right now. *That's* what you need. You need *me*."

He sits up straighter. Then, almost as an afterthought, he goes on, "And like I said earlier, he needs something that isn't you. He's going to figure that out soon, too, and wouldn't it just be easier for everyone to take care of it now?"

Is that true? It might be. Or he's just trying to convince me that this isn't about bringing Hunter down.

Fuck, I don't know. "Why *don't* you want to hurt him? And don't give me any of this because we're blood crap because I've seen what blood means in your family, and it's not a lot."

He lets out an exhale, and while he's quiet, it doesn't feel like he's calculating but rather deciding what he wants to reveal.

"No matter what happens with Hunter, I know I'm going to land on my feet," he says finally. "He makes sure of it. Ever since I was a kid when my mother left... He didn't just let me tag along all these years. He made a place for me at every table. Because I'm *his people*, and that's what he does for his own.

"You've noticed that about him too, I bet. It's why you trusted him to help you out in the first place. Because sure. He looks out for himself, and yeah, his priorities take precedence, but he genuinely wants to take his people with him. He needs you to have a certain image, but he truly wants you to succeed for you too. He took my investment, but as soon as he finds something else for me, he's going to throw it my way. He's going to make sure he gets what he's after, but it's not going to matter if he can't bring us all there with him."

"You really believe that?"

"I know it. I've seen it. You don't?"

I do, actually.

Or I did. I mean, I get exactly what he's talking about. It's definitely what's attractive about his brother. He has charm for days when he wants to. He talks big talk, but he also makes it happen. He's inspiring. He makes you feel like he believes in you, and then it's impossible not to believe in yourself too. And so what if he's sometimes distant or self-centered because look at everything he's done. Look at everything he's made you do.

But hearing it from Alex, when I'm listening as an outsider instead of being clouded with the emotions he inspires, I wonder if Hunter's real skill isn't enthusiastic support, but rather, manipulation. "It seems like a really good way to make everyone around him think they need him, even when they don't."

Alex's eye twitches. The only indication that I might have hit the nail on the head and struck a nerve at the same time.

But it's only a second before he pivots. "Even more reason to ditch him then, don't you think?"

We ride for the next few minutes in silence. There's been a lot said, and there's a lot to think about, but really the only thing I'm thinking about is how it doesn't feel lonely in Alex's quiet the way it does in Hunter's. And how Hunter doles out cash on my behalf, but Alex makes me feel cared for. He bought us groceries before he left us in L.A.

He remembers what I like to drink.

He calls me by my birth name, and I know he sees the boundary between my onstage persona and my real life and understands that, even when that line blurs, I'm still just Mariah Watson at the end of the day.

When we arrive at the Met Gala, Hunter is already there, standing on the red carpet ahead of us, looking very groom-like, dressed in a traditional designer black tuxedo.

Ax and his unfamiliar date are off to the side, blending into the background as Hunter engages in a lively conversation with a well-known entertainment host. I can see Hunter animatedly gesturing, but the noise and commotion around me make it impossible to hear what he's saying.

Something bold, probably. Something that will be quoted in tomorrow's news.

A line manager gestures for Alex and me to wait until the interview is finished before joining them on the carpet, and it's only now, with the heat of his body so close at my back and the cold of Hunter's personality waiting for me ahead, that I realize. "You don't have a date?"

"Zyah!" Someone shouts from the crowd of observers, and I smile in that direction, posing for the cell phone pic that is surely being snapped.

The sound of my name seems to catch Hunter's attention, and he points to me. His eyes narrow as he takes in the dress, and then he smiles approvingly before waving me over.

Alex really did know how to straddle the line with this design, didn't he?

I feel his hand press at the small of my back, nudging me toward Hunter, but Alex bends close first to answer my question before sending me off. "Only woman I wanted to bring keeps trying to cling to someone else's arm."

Dozens of cameras flash as the words hit me. Though I start toward Hunter—my boyfriend as far as all these people are concerned—I can't help but glance back at Alex. I wonder what the pictures will show when those land on the internet. What my expression gives away.

Once I've joined Hunter, we finish the carpet walk

together, sharing our interview time as a couple. More than once it occurs to me that we cut our individual press time in half like this. Is Alex right? Are Hunter and I hurting each other more than helping?

Though I also notice that more questions are asked directly of me than ever have been before. Will Hunter even let me go?

We lose Alex in the hubbub, and I don't see him again until nearly an hour later. He's at the bar, maybe a dozen feet away, and while Hunter is regaling a young movie starlet (that I'm fairly certain he'll try to sleep with later, if he hasn't already) with an embellished story from the time we met Oprah Winfrey, I take the opportunity to slip over to Alex's side. "Are you going to the after-parties?"

"Wasn't planning on it." He takes his drink from the bartender and thanks him then steps aside for the next person in line.

I lower my voice. "If I came over..." I shake my head. I've learned my lesson. Much easier for Alex to be caught coming out of the building I share with Hunter than the other way around. "If *you* came over, we could discuss this more. Make a plan for the best way to...pivot."

It's as good as saying yes to his proposal without actually saying yes, and my heart pounds in my chest waiting for his response.

He takes a sip of his drink—scotch, I think—and looks out over the crowd, as if this conversation is insignificant. "If I come over, there's no way I'm not fucking you."

I'm sure I fail at my attempt to appear as aloof as he is, but I do manage to keep a straight face. "Okay. I'll keep that in mind."

For the rest of the evening, I feel like Cinderella, anxiously counting down the minutes until it's time to leave. Except in my scenario, I'm running toward one prince and away from another—and instead of princes, they're both wolves.

CHAPTER
TWENTY-THREE
ALEX

Hunter hands a champagne flute to me before lifting up his own. "Shall we toast?"

Riah already has her glass, and she lifts it as well. I'd been the one to choose the bottle, so I know the variety is sweet enough for her taste. "What should we toast to?" she asks.

"The dress, of course. We already hit several of the best-of-the-night lists, and it isn't because of my outfit." His gaze is too possessive as it sweeps down her body, as far as I'm concerned, and he's standing just a little too close for my comfort.

Almost instinctively, I take a step toward her. Balancing out the triangle at least.

"So it's a toast for Alex." Riah shifts her weight in my direction. An iron rod leaning toward a magnet, and I'm already half hard.

I'll be inside her before the night is over.

I can't let myself think about that with Hunter in the room or my intentions will be obvious.

"To Alex, then." There's a hint of animosity in his tone, which is easy to ignore because malice is a patented Sebastian love language. "I knew there was a reason I wanted you working on our team."

Our *team*.

I swear I can feel Riah cringe at my side. It's *her* team. The rest of us should work to serve her since she's the one who's irreplaceable.

Though, if I know my brother, he probably doesn't see it that way.

Coming to Hunter's apartment first wasn't the ideal plan, but it was the easiest, as far as appearances were concerned. Appearances for Hunter, I mean. I come and go from this building all the time, so the press doesn't care, but if I were spotted arriving and didn't pop into his place, he might have questions.

So after Riah invited me over, I canceled my car and caught a ride with the two of them when the night ended. I'd thought I'd come up with Hunter then sneak down to her place after he went to bed. But then, in the elevator, he'd invited her up for a nightcap.

I'm not sure she realized that she looked at me before answering.

"Yes. Come up," I said.

So now we're recapping the evening over prosecco while I pretend that I'm interested in anything other than getting naked with the woman my brother is currently being far too handsy with.

"Damia sure seemed to gloat about the reversal on

'Finger Painting.'" There's no reason for him to need to touch Riah when he says this, but Hunter rests his hand on her waist all the same.

"As she should." She leans her weight on the opposite leg as if she's trying to get distance without being obvious about it.

Perhaps it's just habit now. He's spent all night touching her. He's in the mode. I should give him some slack. That's what my head says. That's what's rational.

But it's taking everything in me not to physically extricate him from her.

I lean on the edge of the couch, my jaw tense as I watch. I'm invested in how this plays out, obviously. Any other woman and I wouldn't care about the outcome. *If this one wants to fuck my brother, so be it. There will be another one.*

There is not another Riah.

It's already infuriating that he was there first. But he let her get away. He doesn't deserve to get her back.

Fortunately for me, she seems as uninterested in that as I am. She fakes a yawn—it doesn't reach her eyes the way a real one would—and brings her empty hand up to cover her mouth. "Excuse me. It's been a long night. I should probably think about going down."

She quickly glances at me. I'm already looking at her— of course I am. I've watched her enough by now to read her silence. *Yes, I see it's him making advances. Yes, I'm still planning to fuck you.*

"Already?" Hunter's grip on her waist tightens, and he pulls her into him.

My muscles tighten, at the ready.

But Riah can take care of herself. She pushes him away, forcefully. "What the fuck are you doing?"

"Inviting you to stay." His innuendo is clear.

"You're inviting me to sleep with you, and not fucking happening."

Bravo, baby. Bravo.

His grin is mocking. "So the new sexually liberated Zyah is just a hoax?"

"The new sexually liberated Zyah has standards."

"Sounds like a fun challenge." He reaches out to her elbow. Tries to tug her back in.

I'm on my feet immediately. "She said no. Leave her alone."

He isn't listening to me, but like I said before, she's good. "Get your hands off me, Hunter, or I swear to God, I'll knee you in the nuts."

The slit in her dress even allows her the movement to do so.

Still holding the flute in one of them, he raises his hands in surrender. "Can't blame a guy for trying." He looks at me, as if I'm going to back him up or bump his fist.

Only place my fist is going is in his face if he tries to pull that shit again.

My face must say something to that effect because his smile quickly fades. "You're right though. Been a long night." He slams back the rest of his drink then sets the glass on the bar. "I'm ready to turn in myself. Goodnight, Zy. Hit the lights before you hit the sack, Alex, will you?"

"Yep," I say.

At the same time, Riah says, "Goodnight."

She's more polite than I would have been; I'll give her that. I would have kneed him anyway. Fucker.

Hunter disappears down the hall; no doubt he'll call one of his girls for phone sex or turn on some porn. Riah and I stare at each other, tension strung taught between us. The sound of Hunter's bedroom door shutting only draws the string tighter.

"So." She swallows.

I take a final sip of my drink then cross to her to retrieve the flute from her hand before setting them both down on the bar behind her. Her breath seems to quicken. I can practically hear her heart, pounding in her chest when I reach over to flick the light switch. My hand lingers on the wall, partially caging her in.

The blinds in the living room are never drawn, so even with the lights out, it isn't dark. The city lights and the moon stream in through the floor-to-ceiling windows, and I can clearly see every crease of her expression. Her thoughts are all over her face, so she doesn't even have to ask, but she does anyway. "Take me downstairs?"

I should.

I planned to.

But fucking Hunter, and his hands where they shouldn't be. It makes me feel like I want to prove a point. Like I want to erase his touch, in whatever way possible. Like I'm a dog in another dog's den, and I have to piss on everything to remove his scent.

"Where in this room has he fucked you?" It's not a whisper, but close.

Hard to tell in the dim light, but I'm pretty sure her

cheeks darken when she realizes what I'm asking. *Why* I'm asking. "Alex...no."

But it's not the no that she gave Hunter.

It's charged and challenging. As though she knows it's a bad idea, but also an appealing idea, and she wouldn't mind being convinced into it.

I place my free hand on her waist and bring my mouth to her ear. "Tell me where in this room he's fucked you, Riah."

I hate that I'm imagining all the places they could have been. In front of the fireplace, on the floor, over the coffee table, against the windows. So many places that need scents covered.

She doesn't answer, but her eyes flick to a spot behind me. I peer over my shoulder, following her gaze. "The sofa. He fucked you on that sofa."

She bites her bottom lip.

"You know what that means, don't you?" I slide my hand under the slit and find her pussy wet and wanting. "It means I have to fuck you on that sofa."

"Alex..." It comes out breathy. A song played with the stroke of my finger across that plump nub. "He's right down the hall."

"So you'll have to be quiet." Her clit fattens as I massage it in circles. She's already gasping with each inhale. Already trembling as she fights a whimper. "Do you think you can do that?"

Her knees buckle, and she has to brace her hand on my arm. "Uh hm."

God, she's so wet. Her pussy scent wafts around me, thick and ripe. I want to lick the air and collect her taste.

Instead, I move my mouth to hers and lick along her bottom lip, the same one she was just biting, and she moans.

"Not convincing, Riah. I need to know you can be quiet before I let you come."

"Please, Alex. I can do it. I can be quiet. Just please. Please, let me come." She begs so pretty, and so quickly this time. Usually, it takes longer to get her to this edge.

To be fair, we've been playing foreplay for more than a week now. I beat myself raw in the days after that fight in the gym and never felt relief. She's earned an orgasm or two.

But I'm also a bit of an asshole, so I pull back on my pressure and decide to make her work for it. "If I let you come—if you're a good girl and keep it quiet, and I let you come right now, are you going to be able to come on my cock, too? Because I'm going to tell you something." I move my hand from the wall to her throat, stroking the soft spot at the base of her neck with my thumb. "I really need to feel your cunt squeezing around my cock. Can you do that for me, baby?"

"Yes. Yes. I promise. Yes." Her eyelids flutter, and then, as if she suddenly has the presence of mind, her eyes open wide, and she brings her hands to clutch at my lapels. "Will you come for me, too?"

It's certainly my intention. I'm a little surprised she thinks she has to ask until I remember last time I fucked her, how I pulled out and came on the bed.

I brush my lips against hers. "On you or in you?"

Her pussy spasms, as though she's thrilled just to be asked. "Will you come inside me, Alex?"

"Is that where you want me? You want me inside you?"

"Yes. Yes."

"And when I'm inside you…you want me to fill your tight little pussy up with my cum?"

She nods, but I want to hear the filthy words on her tongue. "Say it. Tell me you want my big, thick cock to fuck your tight, wet hole until we both come."

"Please. Please fuck me with that gorgeous Alex Sebastian cock and then fill me up with your hot cum." She shivers when I reward her with a scrape of my fingernail against her clit. "I really, really need you, Alex, please."

She's desperate and shaking, and even though it would be fun to edge her a while longer, I haven't forgotten that what we're doing is dangerous. That Hunter could decide to come back out here at any time.

The fact that my cock feels like a loaded gun with a hair trigger might also have something to do with my sudden merciful attitude.

I resume the harder pressure, change my stroke to the one I've learned she likes best, and within a minute, she's exploding all over my hand. Her body shakes with pleasure, and her eyes shut tightly while her mouth falls open. She starts to cry out but then, remembering she needs to be quiet, she falls against me and muffles the sound against my shoulder.

I stroke the hair at the base of her neck as she rocks her climax to completion, whispering praise in her ear. Telling her how good she is. How fun she is. How strong.

She's still shaking when I lead her to the couch. I'd carry her if the dress wasn't an obstacle. I practically do with how much weight she leans on my shoulder.

Once there, I push her to take a seat and then stand in front of her. "Take my cock out."

While she fumbles with my fly, I work her tits free from the bodice of her dress. There's not a lot of stretch, but she's braless, and I'm able to adjust enough to shimmy the fabric down below her breasts, which bolsters them up, fat and round. It's an obscene display that makes my cock twitch, and I'm almost disappointed that she asked for me to cum inside her when this canvas is begging to be painted.

But like she said earlier—I know how to pivot.

With my cock in hand, I rub my tip across her nipples, smearing pre-cum on the sharp points. It glistens in the moonlight, and fuck, I don't think I've ever been so hard.

I nudge her backward, so her head is propped on the armrest. Then I arrange her legs—one foot on the floor, the other braced on my shoulder—and push her skirt up, exposing her pussy. The hip-high slit in this dress was practically designed for an easy fuck. I can't even pretend I hadn't thought of that when I picked it out, since that's the main reason I chose it. It's the brand she's settled into so naturally—sophisticated and glaringly sexual. A woman ready to spread her legs, but completely on her terms.

I'm lucky her terms include a fair amount of defiling because seeing her spread out like this in my brother's living room sparks something mean and primitive inside me. I place a knee on the couch near her ass and run a hand down her raised leg. All the way down the inside of her thigh. Then I palm her pussy, coating my hand with her juices. "Are you always this wet, Riah? Or just when another man is about to fuck you on your ex's furniture?"

"Only for you." The fucking perfect thing to say, as if I wrote her a script.

I use my wet hand to lubricate my cock and then notch my crown at her opening. I don't know what position she was in with Hunter—whether it was one time on this couch or several—and while there's a part of me that could get caught up on the details of recreating her past, the only thing that really matters it that she sees my face. I need her to know who it is that's inside her. Need her to see me looking down when she peers up toward that ceiling, erasing any other face she may have seen in the past.

I'm so desperate with that want that I'm suddenly unhinged.

Without giving her warning, I push inside. Her cunt is hot and tight and under other circumstances, I might want to savor the feeling of just being still inside her, but this is not that time. I immediately pull back out and thrust back in, adopting a steady tempo.

Riah moans softly, using the back of her hand to cover her mouth as I continue to ride her. Despite her attempts to muffle our sounds, we aren't quiet. The sound of our thighs slapping together blends with the wet sounds of skin on skin.

She doesn't need the help—I can already feel her tightening around my cock—but I reach down to play with her clit, magnifying her pleasure.

"Eyes on me," I snap when her lids close briefly.

Her gaze hits mine, and then something completely wild takes over. I feel a sense of desperation. To pound him out of her. To break down any remnants of Hunter that still lay claim to her. "Is this how he fucked you?" It's a hiss of a whisper. "Is this how good he treated this pussy?"

"No." She's emphatic, even in her state of bliss. "No, Alex."

Maybe it's a lie, but I choose to believe it. I can't not believe it. Not believing it would crush some part of me at the core. An impertinent need to be better than him at this one thing. To be the best for her like I've never been for anyone else. "That's right. He could never fill you up the way I do. Your cunt squeezes me so good, baby. I bet your pussy has never held onto a cock like you hold onto mine. Tell me it's only me, Riah. Tell me this pussy's mine. Tell me."

She nods and squeaks out a "yes" and "only you" and "yours," rotating the response to fit the request until she's hit by another orgasm and unable to say anything coherent as she quakes underneath me.

Her pussy gets even tighter around my cock, but I push through. I fuck her like I'm trying to make an imprint. Fuck her like we're not just in Hunter's apartment, but also like he's standing over my shoulder. Like he's watching me sully his ex-girlfriend on his couch. Like he can tell by watching that he never deserved her. That he'll never be able to live up to this right here, right now.

I've been so close to orgasm for so long, and still, when I finally come, it's almost a surprise. My body tenses and trembles. Pleasure spreads like wildfire, starting at the base of my spine and exploding to the tips of my toes and the top of my head. It's by far the most intense climax I have ever experienced. With a guttural moan, I call out her name and continue to thrust into her, making sure she receives every last drop of my cum.

I'm still inside her when I hear something.

"Shh," I say, and she goes still.

This time we both hear it—movement. The sound of a door opening.

I'm not sure how I manage to react so quickly when my brain is so drained of blood, but I pull her with me from the couch and out the balcony door at lightning speed. Outside, we hide behind one of the concrete support panels and peer inside the window. Not a second too soon, because Hunter appears wearing nothing but boxer briefs.

Did he hear us?

Part of me hopes he did. Part of me wishes we hadn't run. That he'd truly caught us in the act.

But though there are appealing bits to that scenario, it's not a mess I want to clean up, and in the end, I'm relieved when he simply goes to the bar and pours himself a drink, which he then takes back with him to his room.

It strikes me how alone he is. How pathetic. And for the first time in my life, instead of envy and resentment where Hunter is concerned, I kind of feel sorry for the guy.

It's a fleeting emotion.

As soon as he's gone, it's just me and her again. We let out a relieved breath in unison that turns into adrenaline-filled laughter.

Riah wipes tears from her eyes. "I swear I nearly peed myself."

"I wouldn't have known. You already made a pretty big mess."

"Uh...kind of think you were responsible for the mess."

She grins up at me, and I'm sure I've never seen a woman more beautiful in all my life.

I pull her into me and kiss her. For so long that time loses meaning. My hands cup her face. Her mouth tastes like champagne, and my tongue wants to gather every bit of her. I can't remember the last time I kissed a girl this long and it wasn't part of foreplay—though every moment is foreplay with Riah, even immediately after sex.

I don't think I've ever kissed a girl and never wanted it to stop.

We do stop, eventually.

Hair tangled and face aglow, she gathers her dress around her and crosses to the balcony wall. She leans her arms on it and looks out over the city. "I feel like I own the world when I'm up here. Is that how you feel all the time?"

I move behind her and wrap my arms around her waist, only partly to ease my anxiety about her leaning over a ledge at this height. I kiss her temple instead of answering. What would I say?

I've never felt like I owned anything of value until this moment.

I've never wished more that I owned the world, only so that I could give it to her.

CHAPTER
TWENTY-FOUR
RIAH

Alex strokes his fingers through my hair. Pressure hard, like he's combing it, which he somehow seems to know I love. "Tell me about your mother," he says, as though it's the most casual thing to say in the world.

"Oh. Wow. That's just out of nowhere." There's been chitchat through the night, but this is the first time either of us has initiated real talk. We've yet to mention Hunter, which feels liberating somehow, and we haven't left the bedroom once. Whitney probably doesn't even know for sure that I'm home since she'd already gone to bed when we got in.

"It's post-coital conversation," Alex says. "Don't women get off on that stuff?"

"Generally, there's a bit of warmup before going for the deep wounds, in my experience."

"Hmm. Wouldn't know. If they talk after, I usually kick them out."

"You do not." But his expression looks sincere. "You really do?" I think back to the past. Times we stayed under the same roof when I was dating Hunter. It does explain why his dates were rarely around for breakfast. "Huh. You're kind of an asshole."

He shrugs, and my head bobs with the motion.

I don't know how we ended up in this position—him stretched long over my bed, my body curled perpendicular to his with my head on his chest—but it's strangely comfortable.

Not just physically comfortable, but emotionally. I can't remember the last time I felt this relaxed. There's absolutely no tension between us, probably because we spent most of the night fucking. The clock on my bedside table says it's just after eight, and I don't think we got more than a couple of hours sleep between us.

I should be more tired, but here he is, looking in my eyes, and I'm wide awake. "Even…um…what was her name? That model you took to *The Nutcracker* last December." We'd double dated that night—me and Hunter, Alex and… "Aria. That was her name. You kicked her out of your bed too?"

"I didn't even let her take her clothes off."

Naked and wrapped around him, I'm way too pleased with this knowledge. "That's surprising. You really seemed like you were having a good night."

"She wasn't the only person I was with that evening." He doesn't give me a chance to react before going on. "Tell me about your mother."

It's not that I'm opposed to talking about her. In fact, I kind of want to tell Alex about her, but some self-preserving part of myself worries it's too serious a subject for a man who doesn't like to engage with his partners once they're done sexing. "Are you going to tell me about yours after?"

"Probably not."

"That doesn't seem fair."

"Do I seem like the kind of guy who plays fair?"

I sit up, wrapping the sheet around my body. Unconsciously, I move closer to him, so my thigh presses against his torso, almost as if my body is drawn to make contact with his skin. "How about this: I'll tell you five things about my mother, and then you can tell me five things about your mother."

"Do the five things have to be true?"

"That's the general idea."

"Well, that's less fun." He tugs the sheet from my grip, exposing my breasts.

I resist the temptation to cover myself back up and instead savor his heated gaze. "Should I wait to go, or can you concentrate while you stare?"

"What's that?" He smiles, drawing a lazy finger around one of my nipples. "I'm kidding. I'm listening." He raises his gaze to mine to prove his point.

I'm not sure how much of his attention my words will hold at this moment, but he's the one who asked, so I oblige. With my hand lifted, I tick off my list on my fingers as I speak. "Her name was Eileen Renee Ward. She was sort of an artsy, hippie, free-soul sort of type—always starting some new hobby or craft. She loved playing the guitar and wished she could sing, but she couldn't carry a tune to save her life. She encouraged my singing and songwriting every day of her life."

I still have one finger up, but that last one feels like it needs explaining. "Like, she used to let me play perform using the coffee table as a stage. She'd turn the lights off and shine a flashlight on me and everything. Real fun lady. And, number five, it's been six years since she died, and I still miss her all the time like it was yesterday." Not wanting to dwell in sadness, I rush to add, "Your turn."

"How did she die?" He's avoiding his turn, but he also seems genuinely interested.

"Brain aneurysm. Out of the blue. I was on tour, and she was watching from backstage—she and Whit toured with me when she was out of school—and when the show was over, I came off the stage and there were all these EMTs and policemen. They took her to the hospital, and she died later that night. Absolute worst day of my life."

He reaches to cup my neck. "I'm sorry that happened to you."

It's been a while since I've let someone feel bad for me about my mom, and with Alex, it doesn't feel like pity. It feels like comfort, and I linger in it for a beat before saying, "Your turn."

"And then you put your career on hiatus to raise Whitney?" He keeps his hand on my neck, massaging his fingers into my skin. "What about her dad? *Your* dad? Do you have the same dad?"

"Same dad, yes. Not in the picture. He left when she was a baby. I don't remember a lot about him except that he yelled all the time and sometimes got rough with my mother. Even if I knew where to find him, there was no way I was leaving Whit to him."

"But your career was going well at the time. You could have hired people to help."

I nod, slowly. He's getting dangerously close to revealing a truth I don't generally share.

"Your mother was so invested in your career. It seems the last thing she would have wanted was for you to stop performing because of her."

"Ouch. You really are bad at this post-coital stuff." It only stings because it's on the nose. I'm used to these kinds of comments from the Barbara Walters types—reporters trying to bring on the tears to help ratings—but not from the people in my personal life.

I'm not sure that's a good thing. Maybe I need to let down some walls and start trusting.

Alex seems to be asking me to do just that. "I'm just trying to get inside you. In every way you'll let me."

It's surprisingly tender coming from him, and my chest tightens with emotion until the cheesiness of it hits me. With a grin, I roll my eyes and nudge his hand from my neck. "Sure."

He smiles back, but it fades quickly. "I really do want to know."

Taking a beat, I gather the sheet around me again, feeling too exposed, and stare at a mole on Alex's chest. "The truth is, without my mother, I didn't think I could do it. I love singing and writing—don't get me wrong. And I love performing, too, but I always feel like I don't deserve to be there. Like I somehow cashed in someone else's lottery ticket. Mom, though…she believed in me enough for the both of us. Without her…"

I trail off, not because I don't want to share, but because it feels too big of a thing to explain. Too selfish of a thing. The most wonderful woman I ever knew left the world, and while I missed her for all sorts of reasons, for a long time, the worst part of her being gone was that I no longer felt brave enough to step on a stage, no matter how much I wanted to.

On top of that, I truly felt relieved. The pressure was gone, without her. I didn't have to worry if I'd fail. I just wouldn't try, and that would be that.

"It was the coward's way. Using Whitney as an excuse. I made myself a bit of a victim about it too, telling everyone how much I wished I could still be working—and part of me did—but really, I was just too scared. It was only when I was out of money and realized I had no other skills that I finally decided I had to make it work."

When I dare to look up at him again, Alex's stare is intense. "You're judging me."

He shakes his head. "I'm understanding you."

"What are you understanding?" I can imagine what's going through his head, realizing I'm a chickenshit. That I'm pathetic and weak.

But he lazily bends his arm to prop his hand underneath his head and says, "How you let yourself believe you needed someone like Hunter."

The mention of his name pops the imaginary bubble we've been in, and I suddenly feel unreasonably defensive. "It's not that simple. Even if I was the most confident performer in the world, I couldn't have gotten Jake

Dunham to produce me. He wouldn't have even given me the time of day."

"Maybe not. You'll never know since you didn't let yourself find out."

"You *are* judging me." I sit up straighter. "Listen, Mr. Deep Pockets. You take for granted what money can buy a person because you've always had it. Not to mention the fact that you're a man, and that's a whole other level of privilege."

"You're right. You're right." He brings his hand to my waist and coaxes me down to his chest.

Then he rolls to his side so my legs are sort of draped across him and we're facing each other. "I'm not trying to say you made any wrong decisions, Riah. I just don't think Jake Dunham would ever make music with someone he didn't respect, no matter who made the introduction." He traces my jawline with his finger. "Admittedly, I'm biased. I don't know how anyone could listen to one of your songs and not fall completely under your spell."

"Oh, whatever. You heard my music a long time before you ever took notice of me."

"Hm. Okay. Or maybe you were dating my brother, and I wasn't allowed to take notice."

My chest flutters thinking of Alex possibly wanting me from afar, but after a beat, I decide it's just talk. "You still thought I was with him when you finally did."

"I got tired of following the rules. Everyone has a breaking point."

So maybe not just talk then. I don't know. He throws me when he says stuff like this because it makes me feel hopeful. It's proof this thing between us is more than just kinky sex, and while I don't actually need more proof to believe it, I can't help feeling cautious.

Whatever this is that's happening, it's delicate, and I panic and search for safer ground.

"Talk about not following the rules—you still haven't told me about your mother."

"I never agreed to that game."

I throw his own words back at him, drenching them in sarcasm. "I'm just trying to get inside you. In every way you'll let me."

"Fuck. You bitch." He laughs. "I said, that, didn't I? Did I really sound like that?"

"Like you're trying to romance me? Yeah. You did."

"God, how annoying."

"I don't know. I thought it was kind of sweet." So much for safer ground.

"Ugh." He cringes like I've physically hurt him. "Gross."

"You're just trying to avoid the game."

"No, I'm really disappointed in myself right now. You should let me fuck you in the ass so we can take this back to a purely physical connection."

When he says it, it's validation, and I'm suddenly brave. "Too late. You've already proved it's more—you're still here."

"And you've done a lot of talking, too." He smirks.

My responding grin is wide, and I hit him while his guard's down. "Tell me about your mother."

He laugh-groans. "Fuck. Five things? Just five things?"

"Just five things."

Like I did, he holds up a finger for each item. "Her name

was Pavla Bartos. She was born in Czechoslovakia. She divorced my father when I was eight. I haven't seen her since. She lives in Ibiza with her new family and refuses any contact. There. That's five."

I also know their father had paid her off to never see them again, and I waffle for a moment, trying to decide if I should let on that I know. I'd hoped he'd bring it up himself.

In the end, I cup his cheek and go for transparency because I want him to feel like he can trust me, and because, as cheesy as the line was, I really want inside him too. "You must hate her for what she did."

"Hunter told you." He doesn't seem all that surprised, though maybe a little irritated.

"I'm sorry. Maybe, I shouldn't—"

I start to pull my hand away, but he holds it in place. "No. I…" He takes a breath. "I don't hate her. It was an impossible decision. My father left her with nothing. Even if she hadn't chosen the money, he would have found a way to keep us from her. He wanted us fully indoctrinated in his values, and he couldn't do that with shared custody. She didn't have any power in the situation."

I'm impressed that he can recognize that.

I'm also heartbroken that he has to. "It's okay to still feel hurt. Even if you understand her reasons."

He nods and caresses my wrist while I stroke his cheek. Then he nods again and swallows, and I think he might be having trouble finding his voice. "My father is the one who should be hated——and I do hate him—but I'm so comfortable with that hate now that it's weirdly become sort of a form of love."

This time I'm the one who has to take a breath.

"Heavy, right? Are you happy now? Digging up child-hood trauma, what do you expect?" His levity helps lighten the mood.

"I'm not happy that you've lived like this. But I'm understanding."

"You're going to turn everything back at me, aren't you? Fine. Tell me. What is it you understand?"

"Why your feelings about Hunter are complicated." I'm serious, and it's true, but also the throwback is somewhat humorous, and I can't help grinning.

Abruptly, he's above me, arms braced at either side of my head. "You know what isn't complicated? The way I feel about this pussy of—"

Just then, my bedroom door flings open, cutting him off. "Hey, I... Whoa." As soon as Whitney realizes what she's seeing, she brings her hand to cover her eyes. "Sorry! Sorry!"

"Geez, Whitney. Do you *ever* knock?" I really should get in the habit of locking the door since she always does this.

"Sorry! Sorry!" She repeats the word over and over as she quickly leaves, pulling the door closed behind her.

I peer up at Alex, who's trying not to laugh. "Whoops," he says.

"Well, that happened." I cover my face with my hands and try not to die.

"Is she going to be traumatized?"

"Confused, probably." I don't even want to imagine what she's thinking about me. The Hunter situation was already such a weird thing. Now his brother?

Sister-turned-mother instinct kicks in, and I start to roll out from under Alex. "I should…"

"Yeah, yeah. Go." He moves to his back and adjusts the hard-on that I'm pretty sure was about to give me some action before we were interrupted.

Sighing, I remind myself that there will be other hard-ons and reach for the first thing I can find to cover myself, which ends up being the black shirt Alex wore last night with his tux.

He hisses as I button it up. "You're killing me."

Other hard-ons, Riah.

A minute later, I find my sister putting on her backpack at the front door. "Whit. Sorry. I shouldn't have snapped."

She looks as embarrassed as I feel. "I should have knocked."

"It's weird. I know. I was going to tell you."

She shakes her head, her twin braids swinging. "Hey, no explanation needed. I like Alex."

"Oh. Okay. Good. I do too." I barely manage not to giggle.

Whit smiles as though she's ready to giggle with me. "I was just coming in to tell you I'm leaving for work, and I ate all the bacon." She glances toward my bedroom. "But looks like you got sausage so…"

I raise my hand to cut her off, definitely about to laugh now. "Don't."

"Bye, sis," she says, opening the door. "Have fun. Be safe. Use protection."

Well, that could have gone a whole lot worse. And now the cat's out of the bag, and I don't have to worry about how to tell her.

But now reality has kicked in and as I return to my bedroom, I'm very aware of the thing Alex and I need to talk about—or person, rather.

He's still in bed when I get there, sitting up now, back braced against the headboard. He raises an eyebrow in question.

"She's cool. She likes you."

"And she doesn't like Hunter?"

"No. Not really. Don't look so smug." I don't bother taking his shirt off when I crawl across the bed to join him.

And now that he's brought up Hunter... "We should talk about him," I say.

Alex lets out a groan.

"We have to talk about him eventually."

"Fine." He pulls the sheet down, exposing his still very present hard-on. Then he reaches for me. "Sit on my cock while we do. It will make the conversation bearable."

"It will make you distracted."

"You're projecting. I can focus just fine."

I let him pull me so I'm straddling him because it's been almost an hour since he's been inside me, and after how much sex we had last night, an hour feels like a lifetime.

He holds his cock while I hover above it.

"My album is out in two weeks." I sit back, slowly, feeling every delicious inch of him as I slide down. "A public breakup right now." *Damn, he feels good.* "Is going to pull focus." *So good.* "In the wrong way for both of us." *So, so good.*

"You were right. I'm distracted. Talk later. Fuck now." He grips my hips and rocks me back and forth, establishing a tempo he likes, never mind that I'm the one on top, not that I'm complaining.

I don't even bother trying to resist.

A HALF HOUR LATER, sweat-drenched and panting, I'm stretched out beside Alex, head once again on his chest as he rubs my back.

Exhaustion is creeping in on me, finally, and my lids feel heavier with each breath. I'm on the brink of sleep when he speaks. "No public breakup. Just stop attending events together. If it's never specifically mentioned, and if you aren't seen out with anyone else, people will assume you're just preoccupied with your tour. We can let the breakup leak when things are calmer."

Just like that, I'm awake again.

I consider his plan before I respond. It's good. The best way to proceed, for everyone involved, though it also means that being with Alex will mean continuing to sneak around, and as hot as that's been to do so far, it feels like our relationship is ready for another level.

Then there's Hunter…

"You think he'll be cool with it?" I ask.

I want to ask if Alex is cool with it, but I don't—because the truth is, if he said that he doesn't care about what's best and that he wants to claim me as his, I don't know if I'd be strong enough to put my career first.

And it's much too early in our relationship to make that sort of sacrifice. Hormone-and-emotion dazed as I am right now, I'm smart enough to know that.

"I can show him numbers that support distancing himself from you," Alex says. "Especially, after your album drops. I don't think he's thought that through. He won't want to share that spotlight."

He doesn't sound sure, but his words are convincing, so I decide to believe for the both of us. "Okay."

Now for the worst part.

I lift my head, so I can look at him. "When do we talk to him about it?"

He studies me with his mismatched eyes. "Do you have anything scheduled together before the album release?"

Fortunately, since the drop is in two weeks, my calendar is filled with my own things, events that Hunter won't be attending.

Mostly, anyway. "There's just your grandfather's birthday this weekend."

"Shit. Okay." A second passes. "Fuck." He scrubs a hand over his face. "All the SNC board members will be there. It's his best chance at showing them upfront and personal that he's more settled."

I'm not sure what I *owe* Hunter at this point, but it's not nothing. And I care for him. More importantly, I know Alex cares for him. Is it really that big of a sacrifice to be there for him for this final event?

"I should give him the birthday party," I say.

At the same time, Alex says, "You should give him the birthday party."

It's settled then. "We'll talk to him next Monday."

He nods, slowly, and I can tell he doesn't like it, but at least we're in this together. I stretch my neck up to kiss him.

It's a slow, lingering kind of kiss. The kind of kiss that seals deals.

Then I put my head back on his chest and tell myself that this is temporary, the end is in sight, and that I'm on the brink of a whole new era in my career. This isn't the worst situation to be in. It's silly how hard it is for me to embrace that.

Alex seems to be struggling as well. "Full disclosure—I'm having some complicated feelings about you being on his arm again, even knowing it's the last time."

Once again, I lift my head. "Like what kind of complicated feelings?"

"Like I might have to make sure you're wearing my cum when you show up to meet him."

I grin up at him. "I think that can be arranged."

CHAPTER
TWENTY-FIVE
RIAH

An orgasm starts to hum at my core as Alex jackhammers into me from behind. I'm bent over the counter in his grandfather's pantry, which is literally the size of my kitchen. Each time his pelvis hits my backside, it presses against the jeweled chrome plug that he stuck in my ass only moments before, sending an indescribable jolt of pleasure through my entire body.

It's the first time I've ever had anything in my ass other than a thumb or a tongue, and I'm an instant fan. Particularly of this specific plug, which I'm fairly certain is a pink diamond rather than the cheap pink zirconia versions I've seen online since Alex said he had it custom-made.

"You wore the dress for him," he said when he'd pulled me into the pantry and presented the gift. I didn't have to ask who the "him" was. "This, you're going to wear for me."

So hot and bossy, I lifted my skirt right then, never mind

the fact that there are over a hundred people milling about outside this room for Grandpa Irving's birthday.

Now I'm braced against the counter, vision darkening, as I try not to scream from the intensity of my approaching climax. I have to say, while the sneaking around has been fun, I'm really looking forward to a time when we don't have to worry about being quiet.

Alex seems less concerned about noise, or maybe he has more faith in my ability to control myself than I do.

"Whose cock is inside you right now?" His voice is gritty and low, but above a whisper.

"Yours."

"Who does this pussy belong to?"

"You."

He brings his thumb between us to push the plug, and I jerk in surprise bliss. "Whose ass is this?"

"Yours. I'm all yours. All, all yours." I'm already panting and stuttering when my orgasm washes over me in a tumultuous wave. My legs start to wobble, and my limbs go rigid. My pussy clenches involuntarily, and Alex's rhythm slows as he battles to push back in.

Impatient or tired of fighting, he fucks me shallow for several strokes. "Do you need the taste of my cum in your mouth to make sure you remember when you're out there?"

I don't need any reminding. There's no confusion as far as I'm concerned. Having spent every night with Alex this week and any time we were able to sneak away during the days, I feel thoroughly claimed by the man.

But I'm willing to play the game so I say, "Yes. I do."

Abruptly, he pulls out of me, spins me around, and nudges me to my bare knees.

I'm still recovering from my own release when the tangy taste of my pussy overtakes my senses as he shoves his cock inside my mouth. He instantly takes the tempo he'd used fucking my cunt, and all I can do is relax my throat and take it. My eyes sting. The Italian stone floor is rough on my knees. But it's only a handful of brief minutes before he spills into me with a long grunt.

"Show me," he says, as he always says when I suck him off because he likes to see his cum coated on my tongue.

I open my mouth and feel a drop ooze out onto my bottom lip.

He grins like he's won the lottery. Or like a normal person would grin if they won the lottery, since Alex is so rich, I don't think he'd notice the cash influx, even on that level. "You're a wet dream right now, you know that?"

He pulls out his phone and snaps a pic before telling me to swallow.

Once his cum is sufficiently down my throat, he puts himself away, helps me to my feet, and bends to clean me up with a linen napkin. I'm not even going to ask what he plans to do with it after.

When he's done, I straighten my skirt and nod toward his phone. "Can I see?"

He unlocks the screen and hands it to me, and there I am looking like an old-money porn star. If the mashup didn't exist before, it does now, and I'm surprised how pleased I am with the image. It's obscene as all get out, but the white bejeweled, cap-sleeved, A-line dress I wore for the occasion adds a hint of class. As if a camera had caught a prep school Audrey Hepburn on her knees after prom.

Alex might have chosen the dress with Hunter's needs in mind (though the short skirt and easy access to my pussy arguably serve the former), but there was no way I was going to be allowed to attend this party without Alex first dirtying me up.

And dirty me up he did. Complete with pictorial proof.

I'm tempted to delete the image. As satisfied as I am with it, nothing good ever comes of sexy pics.

On the other hand, I'm the only one in the shot, and I'm completely clothed. And considering how much time Hunter will be with me today—introducing me as his, touching me with familiarity—I know Alex needs something to help him feel like I belong to him.

If this does the job, I'll let him have it.

I hand the device back, image still on the screen, but not without a warning. "You better not lose this phone, or people will assume that's Hunter's cum in my mouth."

"Are you trying to ruin this for me?" He pockets the phone then pulls me to him and wipes at a spot by my mouth. "I think you left most of your lipstick on my dick."

I pull a tube out of my pocket—score for a dress with pockets—and my own phone. "I'll freshen up before I go out there." Using the camera app as a mirror, I reapply my lipstick. "What about the…um…" It's silly how I can do nasty things with Alex but still stumble over words like butt plug.

Fortunately, I don't have to spell it out for him to understand. "I told you—you're wearing it for me."

My head swings toward him. I thought he'd just meant

while we banged. "You want me to wear it...out *there*? With your family and everyone?"

The gleam in his eyes is possessive. "Be glad it doesn't vibrate."

I can just imagine him turning up the speed anytime Hunter laid a hand on me. Yeah, that would be a disaster.

He leans in to kiss me, which means I'll have to fix my lips again, and take the opportunity to snag my panties from inside his jacket pocket. "No way am I wearing that in my ass without these."

The asshole has the nerve to look like I've spoiled his fun.

I put them on anyway.

Then his expression grows serious. He looks me over from head to toe, as though he wants to mark every inch of me with his eyes.

It dislodges something in my chest. A pin of sorts that I stuck in my heart after my mother died. If no one new got in, then there would be far less there to lose. Now this warm, tingling emotion is seeping into the space created with the pin's loss. Immense already, it grows with every second that he stands here staring. Stretching me. Changing me.

By the time Alex tears his gaze away, my throat is so tight I can barely swallow. "Wait a few before you follow."

He leaves the pantry, and I have to reach my hand out to the counter to steady myself for several breaths before I'm composed enough to make a second attempt on my lips.

Some say falling in love is weightless, but to me it feels heavy. Not so heavy it can't be carried, but there's a heft to it, like an anchor. A pull that doesn't go unnoticed.

I tuck the thoughts away for a future song and force myself to buck the fuck up.

One more day playing Hunter's girl, and then even though it will be a while before Alex and I announce ourselves as a couple, at least there won't be any more tug-of-war.

Several minutes have passed when I push out of the pantry, my knees red and my ass pleasantly full. The raucous sounds of partygoers drift in from elsewhere in the apartment, but the kitchen is pretty quiet since all the food for the event has been brought in by a caterer.

Or it is until Ax abruptly arrives.

He enters through a door that I think leads to the laundry room. Which is kind of funny since, before this moment, I would have said Ax had never seen a washing machine in his life.

But it's also really not funny because it feels like I've been caught. Why else would he be hanging out in the laundry room? Is he spying? Did he see Alex leave, too?

Immediately, I look for an excuse to be here. "I was just coming in to get…" My brain freezes, and I can't think of what I might be looking for.

Ax just nods like he doesn't give a shit. "Good luck with that."

Then he straightens his tie and jacket and exits out into the dining room.

I stand there for what has to be a full minute watching after him, overthinking. I'm almost certain he's chasing Hunter down right now to tell him what he just saw. Or getting ready to announce it to the entire party. Or sending a text out to a local news source.

Or…wait.

He works for Sebastian News Corp. All he has to do is text the entertainment desk to give them the scoop, and they'll run whatever he says because he's the head of programming. He probably even knows about the butt plug. Maybe not the worst thing for my brand, but oh my God, Hunter's going to kill me.

Or am I being ridiculous?

The answer comes when the door from the laundry room flies open again. This time Adly emerges, cheeks flushed, lipstick smeared, dress rumpled. A state of being I'm all too familiar with.

Not me who was caught, then, but *them*. Ax and Adly.

Together.

Holy shit.

Her gaze hits mine, and she freezes like a deer in head-lights. Though her face is stoic, I know she's trying to come up with an excuse, just like I was only a minute before. Knowing how quick she is with her wit, I'm sure she'll manage better than I did.

I shift my weight onto my hip and lift my chin, waiting to hear it.

But then she sighs and crosses to the microwave, where she straightens herself up in the reflection. "Ever accidentally fall on a dick attached to a man you don't even like? And then somehow keep falling on his dick over and over and over again because you're some kind of masochist or are into some sort of hate-kink or have Daddy issues or a rich-girl complex or whatever term the latest *Cosmo* is using to label chronic bad decisions? No? Just me then?"

She doesn't leave me room to respond between her

questions, and as soon as she asks the last, she turns and walks out of the room the same way Ax did.

Okay then.

It's validating to know I'm not the only woman around here keeping secrets. When I follow out a second later, I feel a whole lot less anxious about Alex and his brother and the butt plug in my ass.

Hunter finds me almost immediately. "Where have you been?" He sounds more excited than terse, thank God. "Everyone's asking for you. I even sent Ax looking."

Maybe Ax thought I might be inside Adly's panties.

I hide my smile with a cough and my hand. "Bathroom. Sorry. I think the shrimp cocktail must not have sat right."

"I'm sorry to hear that. You look ravishing, though."

Freshly-fucked glow does wonders for a complexion.

"Thank you. I'm feeling better now, so I'm all yours." I give him my hand and try not to think about Alex while feeling very much like a traitor.

Hunter takes it and starts to tug me toward the heart of the party, then stops suddenly. "I really appreciate you being here today, Mariah. I probably don't deserve it, and it truly means a lot to me."

It's not only his use of my real name that surprises me, but his tone. Hunter's gift is charm, and yet I think he's actually being sincere.

"It's no problem. I'm glad to be here."

He holds my stare a beat too long, which should maybe be a red flag because right after that he leans in to kiss me.

It's for show, I'm sure. There are people everywhere around us. Paparazzi met us outside the apartment building, but none were let in the doors so it's only family and close friends, fortunately. Still, these are the people who Hunter needs to believe he's a changed man, and it likely requires more staged intimacy from us.

Nevertheless, I can't bring myself to let his lips touch mine, and just like at his apartment the night of the Met Gala, I turn my head. His mouth lands on the side of mine, and when he straightens, his expression appears more rejected than anything else.

"I just reapplied my lipstick." I tell myself it's a valid excuse.

He nods several times before donning a smile. "Good call since lipstick has been my downfall in the past."

I'm not sure what he wants me to say in acknowledging the reason for our breakup. It feels a little like he's looking for some sympathy. What I want to say is that it wasn't the lipstick that was his downfall so much as his inability to keep his dick in his pants, but it's not a day for fighting, and I do think he's trying.

"Come on." It's me tugging on him now. "Let's go find your family. We have a show to put on."

The sooner we get to performing, the sooner this will all be done.

Outside the dining room where Hunter met me, the place is packed. It's surprising how many people can fit in one apartment. Granted, the place is ten thousand square feet with another two thousand feet of terrace, and nearly every space of common area is occupied.

Crowded as the place is, I don't spot Alex. I'm sure it's purposeful and for the best, but out of sight does not mean out of mind. Every step I take is accompanied by a subtle pressure, the constant reminder of the smooth, rounded object filling me from behind. Its presence adds an electrifying edge to every movement, and I have to concentrate to zone out the sensation.

There's enough else going on to preoccupy my thoughts, at least. Though I've been in Hunter's life for quite some time now, there are still so many Sebastians I've never met. It takes us almost forty-five minutes just to get through the living room, with all the introductions along the way, and by the time we have, my brain is at max capacity for new names.

Finally, we reach the library where the key family members have camped out. Grandpa Irving has a central spot in a large leather armchair. Footrest up, beer in hand, one eye on the muted television where a Formula 1 race is streaming, the man looks like he might be just as happy celebrating his ninety-seventh birthday alone, but he does a good job engaging with those around him all the same.

Here, I recognize far more people, though Alex still isn't among them. All of Irving's children are present with their spouses. Henry and Margo. Samuel and Giulia. August and Arthur both seem to be date-free for the occasion. Hunter and Alex's father, Reynard, is here with his wife Nelani, who is just starting to really look pregnant at six months along.

There are other familiar faces as well. Reid and Holt and a bunch of Hunter's cousins who I've met but can't name.

While Hunter is drawn into conversation with one such cousin, Adly pops up at my side. Without acknowledging our earlier run-in, she surveys the room. "So many men."

Then she sighs, takes a glass of champagne off a tray, and slips out onto the terrace.

The prominence of men in the room is almost over-whelming. If I didn't have a role here to play, I'd probably follow after Adly. As it is, these are the people who matter most to Hunter's quest for the CEO position at SNC. Though Irving designated each of his children to work either at the News Corp or the Industrial Corp, they are all on both boards. Additional board spots are occupied by some of the grandchildren, though I'm not entirely sure how those were distributed.

Point being, I'm stuck with the abundance of testos-terone, whether I like it or not.

To Hunter's benefit, being with one of the few women in the room helps draw the attention to us.

"Good to see you again, Mariah." Even with a pregnant wife at his side, Reynard's gaze lingers on my legs before lifting to my eyes. "You have an album releasing soon, I hear. How wonderful that your hobby has been so successful for you."

"Hunter's been so supportive." It takes remarkable restraint not to lash back. I already hate the man for what he did to Alex's mother. His misogynistic viewpoints shouldn't be surprising.

Hunter sweeps in with his signature charm. "She's incredibly talented, Dad. You're not giving her enough credit. I'm lucky to have caught her eye."

It's disgusting how smooth he is.

"You won't still tour when you have children, will you?" This from Uncle Arthur. They're all cut from the same cloth.

Literally, though Grandpa Irving is somehow the most

progressive of them all. "Leave her alone, boys," he snaps. "And stop staring at her tits. You'll scare her away."

To me he says, "You have to ignore the boys. I raised them terribly and they'd already been molded by the time I realized."

I open my mouth to respond, but he starts shouting at the TV, and so I decide not to bother.

Besides, it's Uncle Henry's turn to size me up. "You've really helped this boy clean up his act. Honestly, I didn't think it was possible. I mean, your taste in what you think is entertainment could be improved, but at least he isn't being photographed in a different woman's bed every week anymore."

"He might have just gotten better at hiding it." Uncle Samuel is probably as terrible as all of them, but if I have to choose a favorite, right now he's it.

"Hiding it's all that matters," Reynard says. His wife doesn't even flinch. Either she's oblivious or knew exactly what she was getting into when she married him.

Both options sound like a miserable life.

"He'd be an incredible asset to the News Corp," Hunter's father continues. "It should be a no-brainer, but since he's been required to jump through hoops, he's proved he can do so. With a strong woman at his side, he's an obvious replacement for Samuel."

Samuel bites back. "Don't begin to think he can fill my shoes."

"On paper, he's practically the same thing," Reynard insists.

No one wants to hear what I have to say, but I don't want anyone too hung up on me being part of the package.

"Hunter is so qualified for this position. Even without me. He's the perfect candidate all on his own."

As expected, I'm ignored. "I was faithful every day I was married to Sonya." Samuel's voice rises. "Even before her, I never acted like the slut your son is."

"*Reformed* slut," Holt says, which makes me want to giggle because I don't think he's trying to give a compliment. Especially, when he adds, "Presumably."

Reynard glares. "Your opinion isn't welcome in this room. You had your shot, now shut the fuck up."

Grandpa Irving perks up at this. "His opinion is welcome in any space I own. And as of right now, I still own everything, so keep that in mind when you go tearing each other down, son." Without pausing, he's once again interested in the race. "Did you put money on this, Elias?"

His assistant nods. "Placed the bet this morning."

"We're winning. Happy birthday to me." Grandpa lifts his beer with a grin.

"It would be an easier reformation to buy if there were rings exchanged." Henry, I'm told, is into arranged marriages. So this statement doesn't come out of nowhere.

What does come out of nowhere is Hunter's response. "We've been talking about it, actually."

I tense at his side. It's just talk, I'm sure. Anything to get the board's approval, but we haven't discussed this as part of the sham and considering the fact that I'm about to break up with him, it's probably not the best direction to go.

Not that I can say that right now.

I dig my fingernails into his palm and hope he gets the interpretation.

"Oh, that's lovely," says Margo. "Have you discussed a date?"

It's too far. I can't allow it, no matter what I owe him. "We honestly haven't discussed it." I add, "That seriously," so it doesn't sound like Hunter was just out and out lying, like he was.

"So which is it?" Henry asks. "You've discussed it, or you haven't?"

Fuck.

"Well. We...uh...you know...it's personal." I stutter trying to find an easy exit from the conversation. "But the point is that—"

Hunter interrupts my attempt to steer the talk back to his merits. "To be honest, Uncle Henry, it's been very vague discussions, but I think we're on the same page."

There's a finality to his statement that makes me breathe a sigh of relief.

Until he says, "Which is why I thought today, with all of my family here to witness, it's time for a more definite commitment."

Everything after that happens too fast.

Like someone accidentally hit the fast forward button, and I can see the action occurring before I have time to quite catch up.

One minute Hunter's holding my hand. The next it's in his pocket. Then there's a box in his palm, and he's getting down on his knee, and somebody's gasping—maybe me— and someone else is prematurely clapping, and someone says, "Well, I'll be damned," and then the room hushes, and when I look around wide-eyed for someone to rescue me, there's Alex standing in the doorway from the terrace, coming in just in time to see his brother pop open the box, and say…

"Mariah Rebecca Watson, please do me the honor of becoming my bride."

Thank God for the panties, because I'm pretty sure I just shit a jewel-studded butt plug out my ass.

CHAPTER
TWENTY-SIX
RIAH

I thought I was used to having all eyes in a room on me, but I've never felt more on the spot than I do right at this moment. My skin is hot, and I can feel beads of sweat rolling down my back. Seconds roll by like they're pushing through cement, and it feels like I'm stammering forever, everyone around me hushed, waiting for a reply.

A reply?

What the fuck am I supposed to say?

What in the hell made Hunter think this was a good idea? Is he really this desperate?

His expression is what I'd call smug hope. Does he think I'm going to say yes?

I can't even look at the ring. I can't stop glancing at Alex —for help, for comfort, to let him know this wasn't my idea, I don't know—whose jaw looks so tense I think it could crack nuts. My guess is that he'd love to crack

Hunter's about now. All that to say he's as anxious as I am, and certainly no help.

Fortunately, no crowd can handle silence for too long.

"Look. She's too moved for words," someone whispers, which is when I realize that stress tears are running down my cheeks. And then it's like the seal is broken and several people start murmuring at once.

"She's thinking about it."

"What does she need to think about? That boy practically bought her her career."

"I think silence means no."

"For the best. She's an embarrassment to her craft."

That's only what I can make out. I'm sure there are far worse things being said in whispers too low for me to hear. The thought almost tempts me into saying yes, just to spite the uppity bitches, but even if I didn't have the sense to know that would only make things worse, I can't seem to find my voice.

I swear five minutes have gone by, though the grandfather clock in the corner says it's only been one, when Grandpa Irving stands up and roars. "What in God's name are you doing, boy?"

He's instantly at Hunter's side—a surprising feat for someone his age—urging him off his knees. "Didn't your fool of a father teach you anything? You never surprise propose to a woman. And you especially don't do it at an event meant to celebrate somebody else. You look like an idiot. Get on your feet and put that obscene show of wealth away, you moron."

Then he turns to the rest of the room. "As for all of you —stop your gawking." He waves his arms like he's shooing away a bunch of pigeons in the park. "A relationship isn't a spectacle. Give them some privacy, you fucknuts."

Sufficiently chastised, all eyes leave me as fast as they came. Phones are brought out of pockets as people pretend to catch up on texts. New conversations are started amongst small groups. There's an awful lot of commentary on the weather, all of a sudden, as well as an interest in the onscreen car race that hadn't been there before.

Then Grandpa Irving turns to me. "If you're interested in talking to this turd, you can use the cigar room." That's all he says before heading back to his seat, muttering. "If Adeline was still here, she'd be disappointed in the lot of you. God bless her soul."

A few more tears splash down my cheeks—relief tears this time, until I realize Alex is no longer standing at the door, at which point they stop dead in their tracks as panic starts to set in. Alex is the only person I care about right now. The only person I feel obligated to.

But Hunter's the one in front of me, ring tucked away, at least. He opens the door to the cigar room. "Shall we?"

Do we have to?

That's what I want to say, but despite his grandfather's speech, I'm keenly aware that everyone's still watching us in their periphery, and I do have some rather choice words I'd like to share with Hunter.

"Yes. Let's." My voice is back, thank God. And I don't try to soften my tone.

Hunter isn't fazed by any of it. "After you."

Fists balled at my sides, I enter the small room, trying not to walk like I have a butt plug half sticking out of my ass, and wondering if the walls are soundproofed. The fact that the distinct smell of cigars has been confined to just this space leads me to believe the door is thick and probably well-sealed, which is a good thing, because I'm not sure I can be alone with this man without yelling.

But I decide to try.

As soon as the door is shut behind him, I whisper-hiss at him, "What the fuck was that?"

Casually, as though he hadn't just proposed and been rejected in front of his entire family, Hunter plops in a chair and props his feet up on the ottoman. "It was a calculated move that benefitted my position."

His relaxed temperament only infuriates me more. "*Your* position? We're supposed to be in an arrangement that suits us both. You didn't think you should run a freaking proposal by me?"

"Did you think you should run it by me when you decided to pose half naked in my library for your album cover? Or when you sexed up your performance on SHE? It doesn't seem that we're obligated to discuss every decision with each other, does it?"

My hands spread into claws, and it takes everything in me not to scratch up his pretty-boy face. "You had the opportunity to push back against the cover, and those are minor—*minor!*—decisions in comparison to a goddamn engagement extravaganza."

"It's family only. You're blowing this out of proportion."

"Oh, right. Like it won't be leaked." Something about this whole encounter is throwing me off, but I can't settle my brain enough to figure it out. Like, why did he think this would benefit him? "Are you expecting me to say yes?"

"You could. I still think we have a lot to gain from a

union. You know how this culture loves to celebrate a super couple."

I've become so entrenched in the benefits of us splitting up, it's hard to believe that he can find merits to double down together. "Are you nuts?" I pace the room as I talk. I've given up on whispering but wouldn't say I'm all-out shouting. "Your base is already pushing back against my brand. They think I'm a slut and a whore. Even your family out there—did you hear them? I'm beneath you, as far as they're concerned.

"And that's just how our relationship is hindering you. Having to consider how everything I do will affect you has stifled me incredibly. That video was the best thing I could have done. I wouldn't have nearly the momentum going into this release as I do without that, and we were going to nix it because of you. We aren't benefiting each other anymore, Hunter. And you think the best idea is to propose?"

He opens his arms in a shrug-like motion. "Then turn me down."

It hits me now, what I couldn't figure out. Why he'd think this move was the right one. Because he's not a dummy. He would have thought out everything that Alex has, which means Hunter already realized that we're not good for each other anymore. He expects me to turn him down. This is his way of initiating a breakup.

The question still is, why didn't he involve me in planning it?

I hear the door open behind me just as I land on the answer. "You know, don't you?"

He stands up, his eyes moving from mine to the person

behind me, who I'm sure is Alex, without having to turn around and look. I'm especially sure when Hunter's expression loses the indifference and fills with rage. "About the two of you fucking right behind my back? Yeah, I fucking know. Next time you're going to spread your legs in someone's living room, you should remember that sex smells and rich people have security cameras. So who's the idiot now?"

Everything falls into place.

If Hunter knew about me and Alex, he had to assume a breakup was going to happen down the line, and rather than try to come up with an amenable plan of how to orchestrate it, he decided to play the situation in his favor. Rejected in front of his whole family by the woman he wanted to marry? Great grab at the sympathy card, and he gets to distance himself from the scandal of my brand at the same time.

I might have even agreed to that scenario except for the timing. Now instead of people focusing on my release, all they're going to be talking about is how I broke the heart of one of America's hottest billionaire bachelors.

While I'm figuring all that out, Alex skips directly to retaliation. He rushes past me and lands a solid punch to his brother's jaw. "You're a fucking egotistical bastard."

Alex is already winding up for a second punch by the time it occurs to me to try to stop him.

I grab for his arm. "He's not worth it, Alex."

Hunter rubs his hand over his reddening skin. "Like you haven't been strategizing in her favor. For how long now? The whole time? Pretending to support me and secretly planning to bring me down. What options did you leave me?"

"Planning to *bring you down*?" Alex is so worked up, I have to put myself between the brothers, afraid he'll strike again. "I've been by your side for years, you asshole. Years of you treating me like I deserved to be in your shadow, and I still made sure you were always seen in a good light. Even when I wanted to fuck you over, I looked out for you instead."

"Looked out for me by fucking my girlfriend." Hunter turns his glare on me. "Though I guess I can't blame you, considering how easily Zyah's legs fall open if she thinks she's going to get something out of it."

This time when Alex starts for Hunter, I almost get out of the way.

But I have enough sense to remember that we have to walk out of this room eventually, and Hunter already has the sympathy card playing in his favor, so I force myself to pull Alex back again. "He's just looking for a reaction. Don't let him get to you. And to be fair, he should have heard it from us. That was a shitty way for him to find out."

To Hunter, I add, "We were planning on telling you."

"Are you defending him? What he did out there?" Alex's eyes are wide, the brown streak in his left darkening the blue more than usual.

"No, no. God, no." I shudder. Hurt or not, Hunter went too far. "Just trying to take control of the optics."

Alex is too far in the mad zone to let it go easily. "We thought about him. We were trying for a win-win situation all the way around."

Preaching to the choir, boy.

"It's a win-win situation now." Hunter's tone is crisp with taunting. "I win a clean reputation, and you win the whore."

Alex lurches, but I wrap my arms around him before he can make any progress. "Don't give him what he wants."

Admittedly, I'll probably replay all Hunter's shit words later in my head and have some intense feelings about them myself. Though it does help that Alex is at least trying to stand up for my dignity.

Alex growls in response, and for half a second, I think he's going to ignore me and beat his brother to a pulp anyway. Not that Hunter doesn't deserve it.

But then he closes his eyes, takes a deep breath, and when he opens them again, he's a tad bit calmer. "I can't be around him without fucking his face up."

"Better leave then because you showed how little self-control you had when you couldn't stop yourself from fucking my girl."

Seriously, *I'm* going to fuck up Hunter's face if he doesn't shut up.

Hard as I imagine it is for him, Alex takes the high ground. He backs up, hands in the air, until he reaches the door. Then he bursts out of the room like he might just go looking for something else to beat up.

It only takes me two seconds to know I'm going after him, no matter what people will say when I follow.

First, I have some of those choice words to deliver. "You're going to look around you one day, Hunter, and find you're very much alone." It's surprisingly softer than the kinds of things I'd originally wanted to say, but I have a feeling they have an impact when Hunter doesn't have a quick reply.

I start for the door only to be reminded about the object that's preventing me from walking like a normal human. With my backside turned away from Hunter, I reach under my dress and pull the loose plug from my panties.

"Oh, for fuck's sake," he says, when he realizes what's in my hand.

Snatching a tissue from a side table, I wrap the plug inside it. "Be glad I didn't shove it up your nose." The thought crossed my mind.

Then I remembered it was custom made and couldn't bear the thought of Hunter throwing it in the trash. Or over the side of the building. Or using it to further degrade my image—publicly or privately—as I have a feeling, he might be intent on doing.

So into my pocket it goes, and out the door *I* go.

There's an immediate lowering of voices once I'm in the library. Followed by a rush of overly loud talking, as though everyone's afraid of another bashing from the patriarch.

I care fuck all what anyone's saying. I'm only interested in Alex, and a quick scan of the room tells me he's not here.

I start for the living room, only to be stopped by Adly. "Alex took off. If you hurry, you can catch him."

"Thank you." Before I head to the elevators myself, I pause, wondering if I should say something about why I want to follow him or why he came into the cigar room in the first place. Not that I have any idea what that would be.

But then Adly settles a reassuring hand on my arm. "No explanation needed."

I decide right then and there that I'm going to make it my mission to be better friends. We're both smart women trying to exist in a world run by conceited, controlling men. So many of the other Sebastian wives seem to have bought into the idea that we should all be at each other's throats, but I'm pretty sure Adly hasn't, and even if she actually has, I refuse to do so myself.

As if she's three steps ahead of me, she says, "We'll do coffee. Now go."

I don't need any more prodding.

I think luck is on my side when I find an elevator open and waiting in the foyer. I know it is when I find Alex still in the lobby.

He's pacing like a tiger in a cage, constantly looking from his phone to the doors outside. Waiting for a car to arrive, presumably. It's obvious he's in pain, and the ache to comfort him runs deeper than any of my personal wounds. Hunter's just an investor for me at this point, but he's still Alex's brother.

Of course I go to him.

He starts talking when I'm still several feet away. "After everything we've done to protect his image…"

"I know."

"He has the nerve to say we're trying to bring him down?" He runs a hand through his hair, leaving it spiky and untamed and yet he still looks so unfairly put together.

I don't even want to know how I look right now.

When I reach him, I take his free hand in both of mine. "Hunter's just hurt. What he said…what he did…it doesn't matter."

"He's not hurt. He's self-serving. He's oppressive. Always has to make sure he lands on top."

"But that doesn't mean we have to land at the bottom. There can be more than one top."

This is about more than just me; I know. Alex is dealing with years of resentment. A lifetime of feeling second best. As big of a mess as this feels right now, this blow up might be the best thing to happen for him. Maybe he can finally cut himself free from Hunter's shadow.

It doesn't mean I'm not thinking about my own situation as well. "I think we can still figure out how to spin this if we work together."

"Work together? You're kidding me, right?" He pulls his hand from mine, and I try not to take it personally. "There is no working with him after this. I want him destroyed."

"No, you don't. Not really."

"No, really. I really fucking do." He points his finger in the air. "He doesn't even deserve that job. Holt deserved it, and even he couldn't hold onto it. And Hunter thinks he should have it?"

"If he really doesn't deserve it, he won't get it." Realizing that might be a little too karma oriented for Alex to buy into, I amend. "Or he won't keep it. We don't have to do anything to make that happen. Let's not waste energy on him."

It already feels like so much of my energy has been wasted on Hunter and his agenda. Maybe Alex was right. Maybe I could have "gotten here" without his brother. There's sure a lot I could have done for myself with the time I spent on him.

Since that's something I can't get back, all I can do is focus on the future.

More specifically, I need to figure out how to turn this engagement—which Hunter will surely leak if someone else doesn't do it for him—into something that doesn't distract from the release of my album. As savvy as my team is, it's Alex who has the best brain for this.

"I'll tell you what we do." His tone is laced with new excitement, and my hopes lift. "We let it out that this whole thing between you was a fake relationship. It will ruin him with the board."

As easily as they lifted, my hope is dashed. "It will also put me in a bad light."

He goes back to pacing. The only indication he gives that he's heard me is that his suggestion changes. "You could tell the world you're with me."

"I don't see how that helps."

It's clear to me now that this conversation needs to be tabled. He's not in the right headspace to think about my needs, and it's not fair that I try to put that on him when he's dealing with this much repressed anger.

I try to get his attention, so I can tell him that. "Alex…"

He spins to face me, but he beats me to speaking. "Why didn't you say no?"

I shake my head, thrown. "What?"

"Upstairs. You could have said no."

The horror of that moment returns in a flash. Hunter on his knees. The room waiting for my response. Alex, watching, his expression tense.

"I couldn't think." It's the truth. "I was too surprised."

"Is that really it? Or were you still thinking about him? About making sure he didn't look bad?"

"I didn't see the point in stirring drama." My tone is sharp, like his, and I force myself to take a breath. I know his beef is with Hunter, but I'm starting to think he's too angry to remember that. "What's going through your head, Alex?"

He also takes a beat, so I know he's really thought about it when he says, "You just always choose him."

"Oh my God. I don't."

"You do." He's surprisingly calm for this accusation. "You stayed with him when he cheated on you. You agreed with him when he nixed the choreography. You let him tell you what clothes to wear."

"I'm wearing clothes *you* told me to wear right now."

His phone dings, and he checks the screen, which gives me a second to regroup and remind myself what matters. "Look, I get where this is coming from, Alex, and maybe this is the wrong time, or maybe it's the exact right time. I don't know. But you need to understand, you're the only Sebastian I care about."

I swear at myself because it's a chickenshit declaration, and if I learned anything from Hunter, it's go bold or go home. "I'm in love with you, Alex."

It does the trick. One second he's distracted, the next he's very present, his expression optimistic and intense. "You are?"

I'm too raw to do anything but nod.

He closes the space between us so that we're only a breath apart. "Then tell the world you're mine."

It's the most important thing I've said to anyone in

years, and it isn't enough. He wants proof. And on the one hand, can I blame him? Who wants to be somebody's secret? Why would he think that's love?

But there's more at stake for me than he can understand with his money-lined pockets and rich-boy privilege, and does love really have to mean giving up what's important to me to be believed?

I pinch the inside corners of my eyes to stop the threatening tears. "Can we please talk about this when there aren't so many high emotions on the table?"

He takes a single step back, and nods.

But it doesn't seem like the kind of nod that says, *Yes, that would be fine*. It seems like the nod that says, *I see, so that's how it is*.

Then, without saying a word, he turns and leaves the building.

Each step he takes away from me feels like an entirely new loss, and impulsively, I run after him. Pushing through the glass doors, I call his name. "Alex!"

He turns back immediately and instantly I'm in his arms, swept into a knee-knocking, mind-numbing, breath-stealing kiss.

It's epic and fierce and impassioned.

It's a wordless pronouncement of emotion that makes it impossible to believe that he doesn't feel for me the way I feel for him. A kiss like this is not for foreplay. A kiss like this is the main course. The whole fucking point. It's I-love-you-too-so-what-the-fuck-are-you-going-to-do- about-it?

As it turns out, I don't have to do anything.

Because Alex always takes matters into his own hands when he doesn't get his way, and when the kiss is finally broken, and I return to the world, I realize there are a lot of people watching us. Cameras are going off. There's applause and catcalls and curious chatter.

The paparazzi who had been here when we'd arrived, are still here waiting to catch a few good shots as we left.

And boy did they catch a good one.

I'd forgotten about them, but there's no doubt in my mind that Alex hadn't. The smug look on his face says it all as he walks backward to the waiting car.

He holds his hand out in my direction. "Come with me, Riah."

There's a movie version in my head where I do. Where I can run away from every real part of my life and love is enough to exist on. A version where I see this as the ultimate grand gesture instead of what I know it truly is—a deep and gutting betrayal.

For the second time today, I'm frozen in place with too many eyes on me.

But this crowd doesn't have a savior in the form of Grandpa Irving, and when I don't move to go with Alex, the several feet between us become a continent filled with photographers and reporter-wannabes holding out their phones for my comment.

"The world was under the impression you were dating Hunter Sebastian, is this not true?"

"Is this whole thing today a publicity stunt?"

"Is Hunter's rumored infidelity the reason you're kissing his younger brother?"

"Which Sebastian are you actually seeing?"

These are the kinds of questions I've learned not to respond to. At least that's what my team always tells me.

But both of my top advisors have managed to piss me off today, and I'm feeling a bit spiteful.

If the answer to dealing with celebrityism is to only look out for yourself, then why am I concerned about either of the Sebastian brothers? Maybe it's time to think about what's good just for me for once. How long did Hunter date multiple women without anyone blinking an eye? Isn't the brand-new Zyah all about owning her sexuality, loud and proud? If I'm already going to be painted as promiscuous, I might as well claim it all on my own.

So I surprise everyone and give an answer. "Obviously, I'm seeing both of them. I'm a modern woman. Why should I have to choose?"

Take that for a spin on the narrative, motherfuckers. As of now, the only person Zyah belongs to is herself.

CHAPTER
TWENTY-SEVEN
RIAH

The thing about saying Zyah belongs to me is that she still very much doesn't.

Over coffee in a private room at Panache, Claude's the one who delivers the bad news. "Topaz is cutting the promotions budget for the album."

At least he's telling me face-to-face, which makes it a little more bearable than hearing it over email or even a phone call. He'd already planned to fly in from L.A. for the album release, but after the weekend's drama, he decided to make the trip a few days earlier to help me deal with the aftermath.

Mostly, I wanted him to be with me when I negotiate with Hunter about our official breakup so that I don't get railroaded into something that only serves Hunter's agenda and not mine. Not that Claude has any more say than I do, but I'm clinging to the idea of power in numbers.

Point being, when I woke up this morning, I'd figured that upcoming encounter would be the worst thing I had to deal with today, but Claude's statement about my label is perhaps even worse.

"Why would they do that? It doesn't make any sense." In the four days since my Why Choose video went viral, my album preorder numbers have gone up in droves. My social media account followers have ballooned to an all-time high, and my single, "Speak," is being played on more radio stations than ever. "People are here for this, Claude. Doesn't Jennica get that?"

"*Women* are here for this, you mean. And Topaz is owned by men. It's out of Jennica's hands."

"What exactly is their excuse? Loyalty to Hunter, or…?"

"I'm sure that has a lot to do with it, though I wouldn't go so far as to say he's behind this."

"There's some relief to that, I suppose." I honestly don't think anything he could do would surprise me anymore.

"Their exact verbiage for the decision, though, is…" Claude stretches his arms out to read from his phone, like the man too vain for readers that he is. "'Improper display of morals in opposition to the guiding principles at Topaz Entertainment.'"

"So they'd rather keep repressing women's sexual rights than make money, is what you're saying. Because if a male artist was caught fucking around with two sisters, that would just be another Tuesday on tour."

I instantly regret the sharpness of my tone. "Sorry. It's not your fault that our culture is old fashioned and repressed."

"Well, that's only the half of it, I'm afraid."

"Oh, fuck me with a chainsaw, what now?"

"While TekTech is fully supportive of your rights to live your life however you choose, they aren't able to accommodate the request for bigger venues for the tour. They just can't guarantee the fans will show up if the marketing isn't behind the album."

I rub my hands over my face and start to wish I'd asked for whiskey in my coffee.

It's not like I don't understand TekTech's position, but this is a big blow. A lot of people don't realize that the bulk of an artist's money is made on tour, specifically from merchandise. Everything else earned is divided by so many people—the label, producers, other artists, PR, manager, agent, etc.—that big ticket sales don't necessarily add up to big bucks for the talent.

I'm really trying not to spiral, but I can't help looking down the road. "Topaz has me contracted for the next two albums. What does this mean for those?"

Claude sighs. "It's possible they won't even let those go into production."

"In other words, they have my career in a chokehold." And not the good kind.

And all because I made some impulsive, flippant remark about my love life that wasn't even true, which is beside the point, because even if it was true, it shouldn't be anyone's business.

"Is there anything I can do? Walk back the statement? Promise to keep my legs together or whatever it is that these macho assholes want to hear?"

"I don't think you can walk back something that was caught on video."

"But I could admit I wasn't with Hunter." Though that would contradict the rumor that he proposed. Thankfully, Hunter hasn't yet acknowledged it as of yet, but I'm sure that's only a matter of time. "Or say that Alex kissed me out of the blue."

It needed voicing, but I wouldn't really do that. After I told the world I was dating both men, we decided as a team to take the stance of not commenting at all on my love life— or lack thereof—but also, I wouldn't betray someone I had real feelings for like that.

Not that Alex cares what I'd do or wouldn't do for him since he hasn't bothered to speak to me about anything other than work since Sunday. Or maybe it's me who hasn't tried to speak to him. We're both obviously hurt/mad and playing stubborn. I don't even know what I'd say to him if he reached out right now, if that would make things better or worse.

Whichever, it's not something I can focus on at the moment, so I force my attention back to Claude.

"Addressing it at all just invites more opportunity for criticism and wouldn't be in your personal best interest. As far as Topaz is concerned, my impression is that their decision is final."

That's because of Hunter, I'm sure. He might not be besties with the owners, but they all run in the same circle, and there is a loyalty amongst their kind that cannot be explained or reasoned with.

I refuse to cry at a Sebastian-owned restaurant. "So what are our options?"

"You could buy out the company," Claude jokes. "I believe they're only valued at a couple of billion."

"Only that much." Alex couldn't even save me if he wanted to with figures that high. "It's hopeless, then."

"No, of course not." He takes a sip of his latte before he expounds, as though gearing up for a speech. "We can do our own marketing. Find sponsors to invest in larger campaigns. Drive up the sales organically. Push the tour ourselves. Take advantage of any connections you might have. If we work hard enough, you could potentially earn enough on this album to buy out your contract later on."

It's a lot of work, but not more than most artists have to put in. I've been spoiled, honestly. I wanted my early success to be a predictor of my future, and when it wasn't, I latched onto someone who could help lighten the load. I really don't have any place to complain.

Still, it's daunting. Especially when I don't even know where I'm going to be living after this breakup. New York apartments don't come cheap. Plus, I'm in full-time training for the tour now. Two hours on the treadmill, every day, singing while I run, plus weightlifting. Next week my album launches with a show at Spice, and then I start learning choreography for the tour. It's exciting and over-whelming all at once.

It feels like a moment where I have to decide how much this means to me, how much I'm willing to work now and in the future. If I didn't have my contract to worry about, I could produce my songs myself and go totally indie. It would mean hustling all the time, but I'd be my own boss, and after dealing with so many figureheads with different agendas, I'm very motivated by that possibility.

But I have the contract. I don't know if I can stomach two more albums of this shit, so if there's even a chance I could do a buyout, I want to go for it. "Okay, then," I say. "If that's what it takes, I'm here for it."

"Glad to hear it." Claude goes serious. "I wish you'd told me about the arrangement with Hunter."

My insides twist with guilt. "I should have."

"And Alex."

The mention of this Sebastian cuts much deeper, and I have to look away. "Well, I'll tell you now—I'm in love with him. But we've both fucked things up, and I don't even know if he's interested in trying to work things out."

Claude voices the painful truth that I already know. "It's probably best that you concentrate on your career right now."

"Yeah." So Alex becomes nothing but fodder for some new songs, I suppose. As is the way with all my heartbreak. With all the emotions I have to unpack, I'll have another album ready in no time.

Hunter shows up shortly after. I expect it to be a terse encounter—which it is—but either Claude's presence helps diminish the tension or the situation has just worked out so well for Hunter that he doesn't have a lot to bitch about.

Either way, he's reasonable, and I do my best to take advantage.

"How about this?" he says when I ask him not to deny the engagement rumors circling the gossip sites. "I'll agree not to address them at all, but I get to tell my family that I broke things off because of your blatant infidelity."

I let out a sarcastic laugh. "Isn't that ironic. You're the

one who cheats, and I'm the one who gets labeled the charlatan."

To his credit, he doesn't act smug. "Only within my family, and they're all pretty tightlipped when it comes to speaking out about private drama."

It's true. Knowing Hunter, I've learned more than one deep dark Sebastian secret that has never made it to the public. His own mother's death, for one. I'd tried to bond with him about it once when we were dating, since I'd read that she'd died of a brain aneurysm like my mother. He'd admitted then that she'd really committed suicide.

He refused to share more, but it sure proved the ability for the Sebastians to stick to a cover story.

Still. "I actually like some of your family members."

"Who? Adly? Brystin? Reid?" He seems to purposefully skip Alex's name. "Tell them your own version of events then. They aren't who I care about, and I doubt anyone who believes you would be talking to the board members anyway."

God their family is so fucked up.

"Geez. I feel so much better." I mean, I really don't care what his snooty old uncles think about me, but I was really hoping for a public denial.

On the other hand, it might be best if he doesn't comment about any of this at all.

Claude seems to think so. "So neither party addresses any engagement or breakup rumors, we let the public speculate at their will. Are we in agreement?"

"I won't be openly dating anyone. That should keep some ambiguity." Hunter will probably earn more sympathy from his family if he doesn't jump right into another relationship, but I can't help but wonder if he's trying to feel out my intentions.

I decide not to give him more information than he needs. "Fine. I agree." Nothing gained from that on my end, but nothing lost. "What about the apartment?"

I hold my breath, ready to argue for a below-cost rental agreement if necessary because I really don't have time to move at the moment, and if I need to purchase my own marketing for this album, I'm going to have to penny-pinch.

"I actually sold the apartment this morning." It's so nonchalant I could scream.

Somehow, I manage to keep my voice steady. "To who?"

"A private investor. It doesn't matter." Hunter flags the waiter for a refill on his drink. "But the terms stipulate that the current tenant remain in the unit until the lease is up, which is in exactly twelve months. You're welcome."

It feels gross. I don't like the idea of owing Hunter anything, but it's a relief to know that Whitney will have a place for the year, and it gives me time to figure out what's next. "Thank you."

He chuckles. "Don't sound too put out. I bought low and the market's high. I made a more than decent profit."

This time when I say thank you, it sounds—and is—more sincere.

"I think that's everything then." I'm eager to be done with this whole thing.

But Claude holds up a finger. "Actually, Hunter. Would you consider talking to Topaz? They've decided to cut off all the marketing for Zyah's album other than campaigns they've already contracted to pay."

Hunter's eye twitches, and I get the distinct feeling this isn't news to him, but that he was hoping it wouldn't be brought up.

"I wish I could," he says, and sounds almost genuine. "The guys who own it are in tight with my father."

Any hope I had crumbles. Reynard Sebastian is ten times the bastard his son is. He wants Hunter to have the CEO position at SNC more than anyone and would do anything to make it happen. Apparently, that includes publicly fucking over the woman who supposedly broke his son's heart.

"He wanted to halt the release all together," Hunter continues, "which I managed to talk him out of. Convinced him it was bad PR to go after a 'feminist icon.'" He makes the quote gesture around the phrase feminist icon, and I have to refrain from rolling my eyes. "But get me the invoices for a few million in marketing spots, and I'll cover it."

My stomach feels queasy.

Claude, however, looks like a kid in a candy store. "Do you have an exact number you'll commit to?"

I interrupt before Hunter can answer. "I really don't want to feel indebted to you."

"Let's say five mil," he says to Claude. "And you aren't indebted, Riah. This was an arrangement that was supposed to suit both of us, remember? I come out okay. You should too."

I'm sure there's a personal motive to his benevolence. He's still a silent tour sponsor, and full auditoriums help him there, so that could be it. But instead of trying to figure out what that might be, I decide to appreciate the gesture. I did my part, after all, and he was an asshole. I should be rewarded.

Then I go a step further because if I really want this behind me, I need there to be closure. "I should have told you about..." I can't bring myself to say Alex's name. I'm afraid of what emotion will be conveyed. That I'll give myself away. But I'm sure he knows what I'm talking about. "Not that my relationships are any of your business, but I didn't have to be so in-your-face behind-your-back about it."

He's silent for a beat, his stoic expression giving nothing away.

"Look." He glances toward Claude, as if trying to decide if he wants to say what he's going to say in front of him, then goes on. "My list of wrongs is probably as long as yours, if not longer, and I'm not planning on saying I'm sorry about anything. So it's...whatever."

It might be the closest thing to an apology that Hunter's ever given.

After that, there doesn't seem to be anything else worth saying.

Claude and I thank him for the meeting. Hunter says he's staying for lunch and will take care of the bill. He wishes me luck on the album release, and I tell him that I hope the job he's after is everything he's looking for.

When I stand up to leave, against my better instincts, I give in to impulsivity. "Have you talked to your brother?"

He takes a sip of his drink and stares at the menu that I'm sure he has memorized. "Reid? Not in a few days."

"The other brother."

He blinks, then meets my gaze. "I don't know what you're talking about. I don't have any other brothers."

It's Alex who has earned the brunt of Hunter's wrath, then. After everything Alex has done for him? *What a fucker.*

"You're a real piece of work, Hunter Sebastian." I'm not even careful with my tone this time.

"I appreciate that."

"It's not a compliment."

"Didn't think for a minute that it was." He grins that smarmy grin of his that once-upon-a-time convinced me to hand over my panties.

Now, I see nothing but red flags. Heaven help the next girl who falls for it.

THAT NIGHT, I find the balls to call Alex.

I've wanted to. Fought the urge every time I've picked up the phone.

Having things cleared up with Hunter makes it easier, I think. He's always been the third party in my relationship with Alex, and if we have any hope of pursuing anything in the future, then it needs to be without that extra weight.

It also doesn't hurt knowing that the two of them haven't teamed up to make me the villain, which was only a fleeting concern I'd had, but a valid one. They're blood relatives. They've known each other all their lives. I've only been part of the picture for a year now. The fact that Alex and Hunter are still on the outs doesn't make me happy—

for Alex's sake—but it certainly gives me hope that whatever is between us can be salvaged.

All that said, I'm somewhat surprised when he answers on the second ring. "Claude emailed me," he says instead of hello. "I'm up to speed."

As if that would be the only reason I'm calling.

It's the kind of thing someone says when they're trying to prevent a conversation, but I don't let it get me disappointed. If he really didn't want to talk, then why did he answer? He could have sent me to voicemail and delivered a text.

He has to want to hear my voice as much as I wanted to hear his. "Good, good," I say. Then, "Alex…"

I've thought about what to say to him for days and prepared a speech for at least an hour before I dialed, and now that he's on the line, I go blank.

It doesn't matter. He doesn't need more to understand where I'm going. "Riah, don't."

His voice is gravel, and maybe there's validation in that. In knowing this isn't easy for him. That he's hurting.

I know that already, though. I get his fucked-up impulse to draw the media into our drama just so he could feel better about our shitty situation. I've spent days reminding myself that he had reasons for behaving badly, and that it doesn't mean he doesn't feel something for me. Or everything, even.

But I've had to put blinders on to be that understanding. I've had to ignore how much it hurt me, and he can't even give me a conversation in return? I told him I loved him, and he responded with selfishness.

I told him I loved him, and he didn't say it back.

I've spent days distracting myself with work, just barely keeping my insides from spilling out, and all of a sudden, I can't anymore.

So here I am, heart on the table, begging for a morsel like a desperate street urchin. "Is that all you have to say? Is this just over for you?"

"Fuck, Riah." It's under his breath, but clear. Then louder, "I'm trying *really hard* to put your career first for a minute, okay? Trying to put *you* first. And when I'm with you…when I let myself think about me and you…" I can practically hear the shake of his head, throwing the thoughts of us off. "I don't want to be distracted. This is important."

It's the wise thing. Noble, even.

But I'm tired of being that strong. "*We're* important."

My name slips off his lips again, low and anguished.

"Isn't that what you wanted? For me to prove that I meant what I said?" I won't say it again. Not when he hasn't, but he knows.

"I shoul—…" He doesn't let himself finish, and God, that's a killer.

I'll spend hours wondering what he would have said, if I let myself. He should have…*said he loved me back*?

Should have stayed?

Shouldn't have fucked me over for his own ego?

Whatever he regrets, he won't let me have it. "The album release first," he says instead. "Okay? And then… And then we talk."

There's a lump in my throat that won't let me respond.

After a beat of silence, he doubles down. "Your team

advisors would agree the album should be your main focus."

It's all true. It's basically what Claude said. My days are filled from the time I wake up until I crawl into bed for the next week. I need sleep, not sex-filled nights. I need to focus. I don't have room for thoughts to stray to relationship woes. This is for the best.

"Okay, Riah?"

I swallow hard. "Okay."

"Okay." There's relief in his tone. Exhaustion too, and I can sense he's about to hang up, and that will be the last we talk in this way until...?

When...exactly?

I need to know. "Wait...Alex? Will you be at the release concert?"

His smile carries through the cellular lines. "Wild horses couldn't drag me away."

I hold the phone by my ear long after he's gone and think about crying while I overanalyze every word of our conversation, looking for hints about his feelings. I was already looking forward to release day with nervous excitement, knowing it might be the start of something new career-wise. But now it could be the start of even more.

Or the conclusion of something I'm not ready to be over.

In the end, I don't allow myself more than a few tears. There are too many photo shoots scheduled this week for puffy eyes, and if Alex is going to play the need-to-be-focused card about *my* career, then I should really try to do the same.

But sleep won't come when my heart is full, so I let

myself wallow and write a song before I put my emotions away.

> "I'm breaking.
> I'm ready to fall from the weight that I carry
>   inside.
> I'm breaking.
> Do you hear me? I'm breaking."

CHAPTER
TWENTY-EIGHT
ALEX

"Do you love her?"

I swivel on my stool to see if anyone else around us might have heard Reid. Fortunately, Spice is buzzing with the typical nightclub din, excited and hyped for Zyah's show, and no one is paying attention to the club owner chatting up the agitated suit sitting at the bar. It probably helps that Reid had enough tact not to use Zyah's name.

Still, I seriously consider slugging him in the nuts for the audacity. "What the fuck kind of question is that?"

"Fucking straightforward question. Only four words. Which one of them do I need to define?"

There's a reason little brothers have a reputation for being annoying, and this is a perfect example.

I'm tempted to ignore him, but I'm too nervous to keep my mouth from spouting off. "Fuck you, I understood the question. I don't understand why you're asking it. We don't ask each other shit like that. I haven't answered the shithead media peeps who keep asking, why the fuck would I tell you?"

He's unusually tolerant of my crisp tone. "Will it help if I tell you that I love Lina?"

"Any creature with a brain knows that, you dipwit. She has you wrapped so tight around her pussy, you can hear meowing any time you're within twenty feet of each other."

Reid falls into silence, and I let out a silent sigh of relief.

It's not like I don't know the answer. It's like there has been this second pulse inside me for weeks now. A heartbeat other than my own, with me every moment of every day, fed from my veins, straining my blood flow and increasing it all at once. For a long time, all it did was make me ache.

Then one night I was lying in bed in Riah's arms, my head pressed against her chest, and I realized the rhythm of her heartbeat matched that phantom thing inside me, and I thought, *This must be love.* Attached in some invisible, indescribable way to someone who exists both inside and outside of myself.

What else could it be?

I should have told her right then. Should have told her a million times. Especially should have told her when she said it to me, but I was so focused on winning and Hunter losing, that I forgot what the real prize was.

The worst part is that I didn't realize what a shitty thing I'd done to her until she'd gone viral for her response, and even then, I had to go through a whole day of feeling pissed and wounded before I calmed down enough to just miss her.

When it did finally hit me, I wanted to run to her and fix it. Wanted her to tell me it could be fixed, which was just more of me being selfish. But I'd already told her we wouldn't talk until after her album release, and it feels like one bad deed on top of another to go back and say I've changed my mind.

So now everyday I'm kicking myself. Every day is torture because everything that's up in the air is my fault, and I had to be a fucking grandstander and act like she isn't the most important thing in the world to me and put her off. I'm an asshole and an idiot. There's nothing else to it.

The only comfort is knowing that she's able to devote everything to her career right now. Her daily schedule pops up on my phone first thing every day, so I'm aware that she's busy and probably doesn't have time to think about me at all. I remind myself constantly that she's at the finish line, and I'll be there for whatever she can give when she's on the other side, yet still I'm wondering if I'm really what she needs or just Hunter 2.0, stepping in to rescue a woman who wished she didn't have to be saved. She told me she loved me, but she's also been clear that her career is her focus. Is there room for me at all on her priority list?

I can't let myself think like that.

I love her. That's all I'm sure of.

I love her, and she should be the first one to know, so I'm glad Reid gets the hint and lets the subject drop.

Except, after several beats, he pipes up again. "It's just that the kiss in that video seemed pretty hard to refute. You want to talk about obvious? I've seen you with women before. You've nev—"

I pivot toward him and get in his face. "What is it you're

trying to get at, Reid? You suddenly into the gossip circuit, or are you gathering info to use against me?"

"You are fucking paranoid as shit, man. Back off." When I don't move, he takes a step back himself. "I'm just wondering why the hell you're out here, biting your thumbnail, and jostling your knee like you've just had a line of coke, when you clearly want to be back in the artists' lounge with her, and the only answer I can come up with is that you must not really love her."

My face contorts like he's just served me a raw onion. "What the fuck kind of reasoning is that? Maybe I'm out here instead of back there because I love her. Don't talk about what you don't know."

"I'm *trying* to know." He's clearly irritated now. I'm honestly impressed it took so long. "Fine. It's none of my business. But since Zyah is *your* business, you should probably know that the few times I've been back to check on her, she's seemed disappointed when I walk through the door, like she was hoping it was someone else instead. My guess is, that someone is you. Take that information or leave it. I've got a club to run, so fuck you."

I immediately feel a pang of guilt. About Riah looking for me, not about Reid getting his panties twisted, but I suppose he has good intentions, so when he starts to walk away, I grab his arm and stop him. "Fuck you, too."

He seems to understand what I'm really saying. "You're welcome."

I wait another ten minutes after Reid leaves trying to make up my mind about whether or not to go to see her. I sent flowers this morning for release day, and sent a text that she hasn't responded to, which is understandable considering all the interviews she had lined up for the day. I'm here for the show, like I said I'd be, and I'm vibrating with the need to see her, but if I go back now will I just derail her focus?

After the show, there's a whole party planned on the roof of the Sebastian Center. Her attention will be split in a million different directions. If I see her at all, it will surely be brief. I promised we'd talk after the album came out, but I'm not holding my breath for that to happen soon. The best thing I can do for her might be to give her space.

Then again, if she's looking for me...

There are twenty minutes until showtime when I finish off my drink and make my way back to the artists' lounge. Since the club isn't a typical performance venue, Reid decided not to put a green room into the architectural plans. Then he opened and discovered he needed a space for DJs to chill between sets, so he transformed an unused storage space into a seating area that he generously labeled the artists' lounge—generous since some of the DJs are fucking hacks, if you ask me. Zyah is definitely the most talented person to make use of the room.

The door to the lounge is cracked open when I get there. I pause to read the sign posted outside, prohibiting photos and recordings of any kind beyond this point. Voices filter from inside, and I can tell there are several people with her, so instead of knocking, I slip in quietly.

The room is more crowded than I'd expected, but I spot Riah immediately. She's sitting in front of the mirror, wearing a robe, while Zully powders her face.

"I can't believe you agreed to go on tour with me. No one makes me look as good as you do," Riah says, and it hits me that she's thinking ahead to a whole period of her life that has nothing to do with me.

Zully glances at Adly, for a reason I can't imagine. "I'm not committing to the whole thing—"

Riah cuts her off. "I know, I know. Of course, you have other things cooking. You're too talented not to. I'll take what I can get."

Since she's preoccupied, I get a chance to look around. I recognize most everyone in the room—Claude, Whitney (Reid must have looked the other way when she showed up since she's underage), Brystin, Holt, Adly, Lina, plus a handful of people who I take for a mix of team assistants, casual friends, some influencers, and super fans.

While I'm glad to see she has a ton of support, I also feel very unneeded. The mention of the tour doesn't help. I suppose there could be a place for a brand manager to travel with her, but it would be a stretch, unjustified unless the artist wants me around for personal reasons as well.

Has she thought about that possibility at all or did our fling always have an end date?

It's petty and self-centered to worry about right now, but it's clear I'm superfluous, and I start to wonder if I shouldn't have come.

But then Riah looks in the mirror and instantly meets my gaze. "Alex!"

The exclamation catches the room's attention, and the chatter dies down as all eyes swivel from her to me and back again.

Fuck.

I somehow forgot that we've been one of the top-trending

items on social media this past week. Everyone's interested in *what's going on with those two.* It's exactly the kind of attention she was hoping to avoid since it detracts from her album.

I shouldn't have come.

But it's like there's a cable tied between us, and every second that she holds my stare, it's like she's turning a crank, drawing me another centimeter in.

There's nothing in the world that could make me leave, not courtesy nor propriety nor common sense. I'm here for the fallout, whatever it may be.

Claude is the one who breaks the spell. "Well." He stands, taking on managerial responsibility. "It's about time to get Zyah to the alcove." There's a rustle as the others react, thinking they're being dismissed. "No need to leave. Whitney, at the very least, will be watching from back here on the monitor. Anyone is welcome to stay."

He turns to my girl—is that what she is? "Riah? I'm happy to walk you down, or…?"

It's a clever way to throw the ball in her court. Gives her a perfect chance to choose differently, but she doesn't hesitate. "Alex, will you walk me down?"

"Sure." *Did you even have to ask?*

She puts on a few finishing touches—glitter on her eyebrows, another round of hairspray. I spot her black heels and grab them while she disrobes. Underneath she's wearing the Ermanno Scervino beaded dress that I chose for the occasion. It's inappropriate for a regular show where she's dancing and moving around, but for this intimate setting, the spaghetti-strap, floor length dress is sultry and stunning. Not only does it hug every curve, but her black bra and nude panties can be seen through the sheer fabric, making her look near naked.

It's nothing she could have worn while dating Hunter and fits her brand perfectly.

I have to blink and breathe for fear of an ill-timed hard-on.

When she reaches for her heels, I squat and wait for her to lift her foot. Then I slip the shoe on, my fingers grazing her ankle, wishing it was bare skin instead of the three layers of tights that are the industry's secret weapon against "jiggle."

Still, I feel the warmth of her through the material, and all my blood goes south. Instantly, I'm back to that day of her photo shoot, in Hunter's bathroom, when I thought I only coveted her because I thought she was his, instead of the truth, which was that I was drawn to her despite the farce.

She must be thinking the same thing. "We've been here before."

She says it quietly, but not so quietly that Claude doesn't hear. "Every time with the jitters," he says, assuming she's talking about her performance. "It's good energy. Don't let it fuck with your head."

I only realize she's trembling as I slip on the other shoe. This time I take more liberties, running my hand up her calf, lingering. I don't think it's my imagination that my touch steadies her.

Down on my knees, peering up at her, I wonder if the onlookers would recognize this as worship.

They wouldn't be wrong.

But she doesn't need me to elevate her to deity. There's a

whole world waiting to make her their god. The first of her would-be apostles are just down the hall now, eager for her to take the stage.

I rise to my feet, resigned to deliver her to them.

Much as I wish we were, we aren't alone in the hall. Employees pass by now and then on their way to the break room, and a few members of her entourage begin the walk with us since the path that heads toward the stage also leads to the part of the club designated for audience members.

With my hand at the small of her back, I guide her in front of me, as happy to remain silent as not, but I'm greedy and fear I'll lose her attention to anyone else who decides she's free for conversation.

I bend my mouth near her ear, so she can hear me as the club music gets louder. "You're ravishing."

Her breath stutters. "I'm nervous."

"You're going to blow them away."

She peers up at me, and I swear I drown in her eyes. "You really think so, or is that what you think you're supposed to say? Because I think you're *supposed* to say something like break a leg."

"Do I ever say what I'm supposed to say?"

She giggles, and then we're at the door to the alcove. Originally, it was a storage room behind the DJ stage, but as Spice grew in popularity and prestige, more and more artists booked the club for premieres and special performances, which meant Reid needed a spot to serve as a sort of backstage area.

So the storage room became an alcove with two doors— one leading to the hall, the other to the stage. Inside there's a small couch, a mini fridge, a coffee station, and a monitor to view the performance. The light is muted so it doesn't bleed under the door or through the shutters on the inset window. All in all, it's the size of my bathroom but serves as a decent holding area.

When we walk in, there's a pink-haired techie waiting to fit Riah with her microphone and earpiece, but it only takes a minute to do since levels and everything were set earlier during sound check.

"Break a leg," the techie tells her when she's finished.

Then she leaves, and when the door shuts behind her, Riah and I are alone in a five-by-seven, dimly lit space.

I'd like to say that kissing her isn't the first thing that comes to mind. That I'm not overcome with an insatiable hunger. That I have a modicum of self-control. Perhaps it's even true, but as soon as she starts moving toward me, all restraint goes out the window, and we come together like a mediocre writer and an overused cliché.

Sense hits me when she's in my arms, my lips hovering just above hers. "Your lipstick."

She's shaking her head before I've finished speaking. "It's kiss-proof."

And so I claim her mouth with mine and kiss her like she's the oxygen that has refused to flow freely through my lungs since the last time I kissed her. That kiss that was "heard" around the world, captured in a video that's been viewed more times now than Porn Hub's top play of the month. It had been a kiss to prove something, and while I meant everything that I'd put into it, I can't deny it was more of a performance than it was anything else.

This one is different.

This one is for her.

It's fervent and intense but also tender and lingering. We pull back periodically—both of us at turns—to find each other's eyes. I can only imagine what she's looking for when she does. For me, it's to see if she knows. If my kiss is enough to expose my deepest emotions. If she can glean that what I feel for her is solid and real and anchored.

I love you, this kiss says.

The words try to tempt my tongue to speak them out loud, but the thudding bass from the club music reminds me where we are and where her head needs to be, and I don't think it's fair to put something so big on her when this moment shouldn't be about me at all.

With that thought, I force my mouth to break from hers. Then I rest my forehead against her temple, my arms tight around her waist.

"Alex." Her voice is soft and still the sound of my name from her lips hits every vertebra along my spine. "I need…"

She trails off, and I'm thrown back to the dressing room before her performance at SHE. She was a baby starling with new wings, and I helped her get centered. I used her and dirtied her up so she could access the emotion she didn't trust to reach her on her own.

But she's not that same woman anymore.

Only a month later, and she knows who she is now. She's not afraid to turn siren and seduce her audience with her sultry song.

It occurs to me that maybe she doesn't know that. "You don't need anything, Riah."

"But I…" She swallows.

I turn her around and nudge her toward the door.

Reaching past her, I open a slat on the shutters, so she can peek outside. Club goers are already pressed up against the stage, waiting for the show. Many are dressed in outfits reminiscent of Zyah's recent looks. Several have adorned merch that they purchased on the way in. When the DJ asks if the crowd is ready, they explode in cheers.

"You already have them." I push up against her, self-ishly seeking friction for my aching erection. "They're already in your hand."

She says nothing but her back straightens, and her chin lifts.

"You've already got their cocks stiff and their pussies wet, and they're here because they want you to give them relief."

I buck my hips, rubbing my hard-on along her ass.

She makes an *mm* sound in the back of her throat, and that's all the encouragement I need to go on. "All the other singers they could show up for, and they're here for *you*, baby. They don't want to be fucked by just anyone, they want to be fucked by Zyah."

"Am I their whore?" Her voice is thick and sultry. When she rocks her pelvis back against my dick, I curse myself for not coming back earlier, so I could edge her properly before she had three layers of tights on and five minutes until showtime.

Tugging her dress up until I have enough slack, I push my knee between her legs and hold it up, rested against the door, inviting her to ride my thigh. "You're their favorite little plaything. They paid good money to be fucked by you. They'll wish they paid more when they see how good a slut you'll be for them."

She pushes back, sliding her pussy along my leg. It can't be nearly enough friction to get her anywhere, but that's not the point. The point is to remind her how sexy she is. That she's a goddamn goddess. So she can own it when she walks out there and turns their whole world upside down.

"So you go out there, Zyah, and you lick their swollen clits with your melodies and you suck their tiny dicks like the whore they paid for, and when you're done—"

When you're done…come back to me.

But before I can say it, the red lightbulb on the wall illuminates—the signal that it's time to go on—and the chords of her first song begin, and the audience goes wild, and anything I might have said gets lost in the ruckus.

She looks back at me once, then takes a deep breath.

"Break a leg," I tell her, then step out of the way as she pushes through the door to take the stage, and my final words are swallowed down my throat.

I watch her from the lifted slat as she lights the place on fire with her first song.

"I wanna be
I wanna be yours
But I can't give you what I don't own
Can't be your woman
Can't be your savior
Cuz I sold my soul to a devil"

I've heard it a million times before, but the words strike a chord this time. It was one of the last songs she'd recorded for the album, as I understand. Written after she and Hunter broke up and they'd made their arrangement, and I hear it now for the prison it means to depict.

Even without him in the picture, she's still not free to fly as high as she can. Her wings are clipped by the men who actually own her work, and that makes her a prisoner, unable to truly choose what she wants without concern about financial backing. I know she said she loved me, and I do believe that she does, but can she even legitimately make that claim when she could benefit from my wallet the same way she once benefitted from Hunter's?

All I really want from her is to feel chosen. Not second best or the backup prize or the dirty secret or the new sugar daddy, and I know I owe her a grand gesture for the shit I've put her through, but I don't want money to be the reason she chooses me. I don't want to be the lesser of two evils. I don't want her to one day feel tied to me with no escape because it's best for her career.

I don't want to be my brother, holding her hostage in a relationship she's long outgrown.

There's only way I can think of that makes sure that doesn't happen—I have to man up and give Riah her freedom.

CHAPTER
TWENTY-NINE
RIAH

I walk into my apartment, toss the key in the bowl next to the door, and drop my heels—I'd taken them off in the limo—to the floor. The temptation to plop down right here on the floor is overwhelming, but I manage to hobble to the living room and fling myself across the sofa.

It's quite possible I've never been this exhausted in my life.

I even caught myself snoozing on my bodyguard as we drove home from the taping of whatever late show I filmed tonight. I mix them all up since it's been a different one every night this week. Show, not bodyguard, though the company rarely sends the same guy more than once as well. Thank God, since the drool I left on this guard's shoulder was embarrassing.

Times like these, I'm really glad to know they all sign NDAs.

It's not even that late. Ten thirty, maybe? I'm too tired to look at my phone.

Then it starts ringing with the tone that says it's Claude. He's back in L.A. now, and every time he calls it's with some important update about a new offer he's received or chart numbers, so I force myself to roll over and dig my phone out of my pocket and try not to think about how grateful I am for Alex making sure that all my interview outfits *have* pockets since I've banned all thoughts of him in general.

Oh, it's ten forty-two, I think before I answer.

"What's up?" I'm too tired for formalities like *hello.*

Claude, on the other hand, sounds irritatingly wide awake. "Three words for you—S.N.L."

I don't bother to tell him that those are initials, not words, because most everyone knows they stand for Saturday Night Live, which is every musician's dream.

Suddenly I have the energy to sit up. "What?"

"They want you for their musical guest on the next season premiere. We'll have to reschedule the tour dates in Salt Lake City to make it happen. I'm assuming you're good with that?"

"Do you even need to ask?" I'd reschedule an even bigger city for a chance just to walk onto the set of SNL, let alone be a musical guest.

Even when I was in the throes of the Hunter Arrangement, as Claude and I now refer to it on the downlow, landing such a gig wasn't on my radar. I'd let Hunter decide what was within the realm of possibility. I realize now that, while he talked big and delivered big, he didn't dream big. He only promised what he knew was within reach, and this past week the universe has shown me over and over again that it is capable of giving more than he imagined.

Needless to say, I'm learning to dream bigger.

Honestly, though, it's so incredible that if I weren't so busy everyday with interviews, appearances, and tour rehearsals, I'd spend the whole day pinching myself.

"Glad you said that because I already accepted. Stew is arranging the reschedule first thing tomorrow morning." There's a sound of a car honk in the distance, and I suspect he's talking to me from his car. "At this rate, I'm going to have to dump all my other clients and make you my full-time job."

"You have other clients?" It's a joke. I've been small fish for Claude for years. This change in hierarchy is just another detail of success I couldn't have fathomed.

Just like when he called this morning to tell me that my album had debuted in the top one hundred on the Billboard charts.

And yesterday when he sent over a contract to play at next year's Coachella.

And this afternoon when he texted to tell me that Vera Wang had reached out to Alex to talk about designing me a custom dress for the Teen Choice Awards in August.

Of course, rather than saying his name, Claude said BM, meaning Brand Manager, since he knows better than to say Alex's name to me right now. I'm not sure if Claude realizes that BM also stands for bowel movement, but I'm moderately delighted every time I see the initials and think of a giant piece of shit.

It's a far healthier attitude than being miserable over the

man. Fortunately, my schedule is keeping me too busy to even consider wallowing.

"*SNL*," I repeat, just to erase the flash of Alex's name from my mind. "How is this even happening?" When Topaz pulled out of their marketing, I truly thought the album was doomed.

"The people are resonating with what you're putting out there. TikTok loves you. You've reached the SpicyBookTok community, I hear. Those women love your willingness to express yourself sexually. I really don't think there would have been such an amazing response if you hadn't gone there with your work. It took guts, and it's paid off."

I hadn't thought of myself as brave in the way he's suggesting. I'd been more scared of the people who "owned me" being pissed off and suppressing me than I had been worried about how listeners would react, though there was a bit of that too. The music and the themes I talk about in my songs came from a place of honesty, and I did have to be vulnerable to perform the music authentically, which was daunting at first.

I really don't think I would have been able to do it if it hadn't been for one person.

Every night when I'm in bed, I allow myself five minutes to think about him—I literally set an alarm. Since I'm hitting the sack soon, I let myself say it now. "Alex helped encourage me."

More accurately, Alex got dirty with me, but I'm not going to say that to a man who could practically be my father.

"I'm sure he might have been a vehicle to facilitate your expression, but Riah? You wrote those songs on your own before he came into the picture. Those viewpoints are all you."

I hear what he's saying. I remind myself that it's true.

It doesn't erase that underneath the excited busyness of my current life, I'm heartsick. "I miss him," I admit.

"I know, honey." While I haven't told Claude much, he knows the bare bones—that after he showed up to the concert on my release night, Alex pretty much ghosted me. "He still hasn't reached out again?"

Except for professional communication that I'm mostly only copied on and one lone text… "Nope."

"Well, he's working harder than ever to make sure everything that goes out to the public about you fits the parameters of your brand. He wouldn't do that if he didn't feel something for you."

"Sure." Or he just has serious work ethic, and he's finishing out the contract he originally signed that expires when I set out on tour.

Because if he really felt something for me, he would have been there when the show was over. He would have answered the phone any of the times I tried to call. He would have reached out, so we could have that talk he promised once the album was released.

"Have you considered reaching out again?" Claude prods gently.

"I'm not doing that."

"No risk, no reward."

"Claude, please. It's okay." I know he means well, but I don't need him to pep talk me through this. I've risked and risked, and there has been no reward.

First, I told Alex how I felt, and he barely acknowledged it.

Then, I was the one who reached out to him when he went into head-down mode after he kissed me in front of the paps—something he still hasn't apologized for.

And I tried to call him a few times after the show, after the text he sent where he finally declared feeling something for me, and each time, he sent me to voicemail.

How many times am I supposed to keep trying? "I have other things to focus on, Claude. I don't have the time or the energy to chase him down."

"That's the right attitude." Claude actually sounds relieved to not have to fix this. "You don't need him. You never needed anyone."

It's eerily similar to what Alex said in the alcove before the show.

Not for the first time, I wonder if that's what caused him to run. Does he think I don't have room for him in my life now? Always playing second best to Hunter, I know Alex has issues with feeling like he's enough—just another version of Imposter Syndrome, which I understand all too well. Is he worried he doesn't have enough to offer me?

After Claude hangs up, I open my messages and scroll to the one Alex sent me the night of the show. It was waiting for me when I came off the stage, in place of him. With the album's release, all sorts of acquaintances have crawled out of the woodwork to send congrats and try to reengage, so I have to scroll through a ton of texts before I find his.

I saw the whole show. You were 🔥 🔥 🔥.

> Your performance made me realize what I
> need to do, and I have to leave town.
>
> Whatever happens next, I hope you know
> you're a ⭐.
>
> I love you.

I've read it so many times I have it memorized, but reading it again tonight, all the emotions return from the first time I read it. Exhilaration and hope and butterflies and over-the-moon joy.

Of course, a lot of that was adrenaline from the show, and it propelled me through the after-party, despite his absence. But that night when I tried to call, he didn't answer, and I started to worry.

When every call the next day was also sent straight to voicemail and none of my calls or messages got returned, I recognized his text for what it is—a goodbye. For what reason, I'll never know for sure. Because he thought it was the best way to patch things up with Hunter? Because he was too intimidated by the media scrutiny on my life? Because he's an asshole who likes to mess with women's emotions?

Or, as I'm wondering now, because he's afraid he can't be what I need?

I could hold onto some romantic hope that he'll show up again whenever he's dealt with his shit, but that requires energy I can't afford to spend.

In the end, it doesn't matter.

He's not here, and my life goes on.

Whit sneaks up on me so quietly, I don't notice her until

she's propped on the arm of the couch. "Thinking about Alex?"

I shrug and put my phone back in my pocket. "Not anymore."

Usually, that's enough to change the subject, but she nods at the corset-topped, sheer beaded jumpsuit I'm wearing. "This one of his picks?"

"Yep."

"You wore it on television?"

I nod. "Do you not like it?"

"No, I like it."

There's something there that she's holding back, though. The same thing that she's been secreting away for weeks now, and maybe I'm too tired to exercise patience, or maybe I'm just too annoyed by Alex's lack of communication to let Whit continue pulling the same shit, so instead of dropping it, I push her. "...but?"

She twists her lips as she considers. "No but. Just...does it make you uncomfortable dressing like that in front of millions of people?"

It's a strange question coming from the girl who, only six weeks ago, dressed in skimpier clothing for a job interview.

Considering that's how long this tension has been running quietly between us, I wonder if there's a connection.

"Does it make you uncomfortable?" I ask, suddenly afraid my worst fears have come true and that my exploration of self has put her in an awkward position. "Are people saying things to you about me?"

She makes a face like I'm an idiot. "No. And if they did,

like I'd fucking care what anyone else thought. That's so high school."

As if she didn't only graduate last year.

"Okay." I'm relieved, but also lost. If she's not bothered by my persona, then what is it?

It's a lack of knowing what to say that keeps me silent, and miracle of miracles, that's what does the trick.

"It's just…" She slides from the arm to the couch next to me. "Someone else picked it out for you. A guy. Like…is that because your team decided that you have to add sex to sell your music? I mean, once upon a time they were trying to make you all goody-two-shoes, and next thing you know, you're wearing sheer dresses and dancing really provocatively. Did you even get a say in it?"

It's funny how I took for granted that she knew all of this, but I guess she was only there for the first conversations about my new brand. It hadn't occurred to me that she might think I'd been coerced into it.

It hadn't occurred to me how important that information could be, particularly considering the direction I ultimately decided to go.

"Oh, no, honey." I shake my head, realizing that's the wrong answer. "I mean, yes. I had a say. I chose this look. This was what I wanted."

"It was?"

"Yeah. You know, I feel really comfortable in my body. Sometimes I have anxiety about it, of course, like anyone, but it fits what I'm trying to say with my songs."

Her eyes are narrow, like she's thinking. Processing.

I'm so intrigued by what's going on behind those dark eyes that I can't keep myself from pushing. "Does it bother you that I'm expressing myself this way? I know the media said a lot of shit about me with the Alex/Hunter thing…"

She's quick to stop that line of thinking. "No. God, no. I really don't care about what the media thinks, Ri. Fuck other people's opinions. If this is who you want to be, I'm all for it."

There's still a *but* there that I can't uncover. "What's going on, Whitney? Can you talk about it?"

"Yeah. I guess." Her eyes move to her hands, folded in her lap. "It's not a big deal, really. Just there was this guy. A couple of months ago now. He was in one of my fan art Discord groups. This was when I was looking for a job, and I said something about it, and he private messaged me and said that he worked at a tattoo shop in Brooklyn, and he was willing to maybe train me, but he wanted me to send a picture first."

"Oh no." My stomach sinks, sure this is going in an all-too-familiar direction. The details might be different, but most women I know have a story that starts similarly. The best endings leave a bad taste in the mouth. The worst leave permanent mental and emotional scars.

I'm scared to death that Whit's is one of the latter.

Thankfully, she seems to guess what I'm thinking. "He didn't want nudes, or anything." She waves her hand like an eraser on a blackboard. "Actually, I think he did want nudes. But I sent him a selfie of what I was wearing that day, which was real baggy overalls and a long-sleeve shirt, and he asked me if that's the way I always dressed, and I said yes because…" She gestures to the outfit she's currently wearing, almost identical to the one she's describing.

"Except when you're going to job interviews, your clothes are as shapeless as Billie Eilish, and I love you for it."

Her cheeks turn pink, and she looks back at her thumbs. "He told me he didn't think I was a good fit after all. I thought maybe he'd looked closer at my art and decided it wasn't his type, but I got curious and followed his Instagram account for his shop, and all the women that work there dress really skimpy. Tits out. Skin showing. Which is fine, if that's what they want, but…"

The puzzle pieces come together, finally. "So the message you got was that you need to dress a certain way if you want to get a job. And it probably didn't help that at the same time, without talking to you about it, I started dressing like this and being more provocative with my performances."

"Yeah."

"Well, that sucks." I want to put my arm around her, but I know she's probably feeling too fragile for that right now. "Our culture sucks, Whit. A lot of the time. *Most* of the time. The expectations on women… We're expected to be pure and chaste, and yet, when men are in charge, they often exploit us sexually, however they can. It isn't right, and you should never do something that makes you uncomfortable for any reason, even to get a job. *Especially* to get a job."

I think about what I've said only after I've said it. "I wish someone had told me that a few months ago. Dressing like this doesn't make me uncomfortable, but pretending to date Hunter did."

"It did? I thought it was kind of fun fooling everyone."

"The pretending didn't really bother me, I suppose, and

maybe that makes me a bit of a sociopath." I pause to let her laugh. "But I had to suppress who I wanted to be when I was with him, and *that* made me uncomfortable."

"Because he didn't like the new you?"

"He preferred the goody-two-shoes."

She looks at me, searching. "But this is really who you want to be now?"

"Yeah, it is." I have to pause because I've never put this in words, and I'm not exactly sure how to articulate it. "I think that women have been made to be ashamed of their bodies for a long time. Too long. And we've been made to be ashamed about our sexuality, and I have insecurities about it sometimes, but, um. I know I'm your older sister and this might be weird to think about, but I'm a sexual person, and I should be able to express that. Women should be able to express that. If they want to. Or not. If they'd rather. We should normalize the whole spectrum of sexuality in women—and men, for that matter—from prude to extremely kinky. There isn't a one-size-fits-all, and there shouldn't be."

Unable to hold myself back any longer, I wrap my arm around her and pull her in tight. I'm happily surprised when she doesn't wriggle out of the hug. "I should have talked to you about this earlier."

"About your sex life? Um, I'm good thanks."

I throw my other hand around her, trapping her good now, and snuggle my head against hers. "You don't want to hear the details? The day my album cover was shot—"

"LA LA LA LA LA!"

She puts her fingers in her ears, too, and tries to pull

away, but I tighten my grasp. "Then there was this one time, at this fancy party out in Connecticut…"

This time she manages to escape. "That's it. I'm out."

I'm having too much fun. "I was thinking about getting my clit pierced—"

"Mariah! Ew. Be you all you want but please, I don't need to know."

She's already heading toward her bedroom, but I call after her. "I love you, you prude!"

"I love you too, you slut."

I've never been prouder to be called the *s* word in my life.

CHAPTER
THIRTY
ALEX

I squint after the woman as she crosses the lobby of Hunter's apartment building and exits onto the street. *Was that…?*

While my head is still cocked in the direction of the doors, someone thumps me on my shoulder.

"Hey," Ax says, when I turn toward him. "We doing this?"

"Yeah, yeah. We are. Is he here?"

Ax looks at me like I'm crazy. "No way. He'll be back anytime though, so if you want to do this…?"

"I do. Just thought I saw Adly leaving, and I wondered why she'd be here if Hunter isn't."

Even if Hunter was here, a visit from her would be weird. They're complicated cousins—partly because they're really half-siblings, but that's one of those Sebastian super secrets no one talks about—and they do not tolerate each other's presence.

"Weird." Ax suddenly is interested in straightening his shirt, which is actually what's weird since he's in sweats and a T-shirt and barefoot, suggesting he doesn't give a fuck about his current appearance. "Maybe she was visiting Riah or something."

Except she left this morning for her tour. Trust me, I'm aware of her every movement, and not being able to get things wrapped up so I could be back before she set out is a minor regret.

Out of my hands, though. Better late than never.

"Or it wasn't her," I say.

"I'd say it probably wasn't." Ax's tone sounds strangely like a gangster's, convincing someone they didn't see what they definitely saw.

I might be curious under other circumstances, but I'm not really interested in speculating on Adly's *why*-abouts and Axle's weird behavior when I have a full day's agenda. "Anyway. Ready when you are."

He nods then heads toward the elevator.

I follow after him.

Ax gets me past the guard, claiming me as his guest. I'd suspected that I'd been removed from the approved list, but now I'm sure of it. I hadn't wanted to rouse Hunter's attention by attempting to get through myself. If I wasn't on the list, the guard would have called up and that call would be forwarded to Hunter wherever he was, and there's a good chance I would have been banned from the building entirely after that.

Which is why I'd texted Ax and asked for a one-time-only favor.

It was a fifty-fifty chance he'd come through, and for once, the gods are shining on me.

Not wanting to take advantage of him, I don't even peek over his shoulder in the elevator to see the new code that Ax enters that will take us to Hunter's floor.

But I ask anyway, just to know. "He changed the code then?"

This time Ax looks at me like I'm crazy and also like he doesn't like being the bearer of bad news. "Yeah, he did."

"Figured."

The elevator starts to lift. I'd be happy enough riding in silence, but Ax is fidgety and unusually chatty. Perhaps his conscience is getting to him. For all intents and purposes, letting me up is a betrayal. "You were out of town?"

"Yeah. For almost a month. Landed and came straight here."

"You look it."

"Yeah, well." He's being kind. I look worse than that. These weeks away from Riah have been miserable. It's no fault but my own, and I have no right to complain, but I can't hide the toll it's taken.

I pray to God it ends up worth it.

Ax doesn't even let a beat pass. "Heard your dad saying he was helping you work out a deal of some kind?"

Of course, my father would make it sound like he'd been cooperative instead of one of my main obstacles. It took a lot of half-truths and misrepresentations to get him on my side—which to his credit, I learned how to do from him and Hunter—but once he was, I managed to pull every string I needed pulled.

"Signed everything this morning." Then I spent the

plane ride closing my other deal. If my father had known about that one, he would never have stepped in with the first, so I'd left it for last. Plus, I needed to make sure I had funds left over before I committed.

That second deal's the reason I'm here.

I expect Ax to ask more about it, and I'm already trying to work out how I'll politely evade, but it's a needless concern because he seems to lose all interest when we arrive in Hunter's foyer. "Okay, well. Here you go. I'll be in the gym."

He seems eager to distance himself from this deed and yet there's no way that Hunter won't know who let me in.

I probably shouldn't care about the details, but I can't help myself and call after him. "What are you going to say when he asks about you letting me up?"

He stops and shrugs. "I don't know. Figure it out then."

It begs another question. "Why are you doing this?"

He gives me a *come on* type of expression. "You think you're the only one who gets tired of Hunter's shit now and then?"

I'm fleetingly grateful for the camaraderie, and also feel a tinge of pity for my brother who can't seem to manage a decent relationship with anyone.

If I have to guess, Ax understands that dichotomy better than anyone. "So do whatever you need to do and be done," he says. "Just remember. The worse you stir a turd, the more it stinks."

I get what he's saying. "I'll do my best to leave him intact."

"That's all you can do." He gives me a wave then disappears down the hall.

Alone, I wander through the empty rooms and decide to settle in the den. Hunter's desk chair tempts me to sit. I'm surprised he hasn't gotten rid of it. After discovering Riah and I in his living room, I'm sure he went back through other security videos, looking for more proof of our "deceit." Only thing I can figure is that the tapes must not go back that far.

I'm still gratified to have that secret, but it's less satisfying now than it once was. I enjoyed the game with her when I didn't think Hunter would get hurt. Knowing that he feels wounded has tainted the prize. Dethroning him now when he's already lost his power over me feels like insult added to injury, so I hunker down in an armchair instead.

Feet up on the ottoman in front of me, I wait.

Almost an hour passes before I hear the ding of the elevator arrive. In that time, I catch up on all the news on my phone and replay every video ever posted on Riah's TikTok and Instagram accounts.

Hunter would say I'm pussy-whipped. In another lifetime, if she were another girl—if I had met her first—he'd razz me to no end.

I want to grieve for that alternate life, but truth be told, I think this one could actually work out to be the better outcome, despite the cost.

I'll know for sure after the day is done.

First, this confrontation, and it's not even the hardest on my task list.

As predicted, Hunter doesn't take long to make it to the den. He's dressed down, for him, wearing a tailored suit with no tie, and I'm inclined to be curious about where he's been, but he's a habit I'm breaking, so I push the curiosity away.

He's so engrossed in his phone—furiously texting, as he often does—that it takes him a minute to notice me. When he does, he freezes in his tracks. If he's mad, his features are schooled not to show it.

His tone, on the other hand, is bitter as brussels sprouts. "Must have had something big on Ax to convince him to let you in."

The asshole in me wants to tell him that Ax didn't need any persuasion at all, but this isn't meant to be a combative interaction, so I just shrug.

"Do I need to review my security tapes to see who you fucked in my apartment this time?"

"I've fucked lots of girls in this apartment over the years and you never batted an eye."

"How many of them were mine?"

"She wasn't yours."

He doesn't have a leg to stand on if he wants to argue. He must know that, and instead tries to take the upper hand by circling around his desk and taking a seat on his throne. It's subtle, but a power move all the same.

Once he's seated, he throws his phone on the desk, crosses one leg over the other at the ankle, and leans back. "You and I both know this was never about the girl."

"I'm surprised you realize that."

While his perception is refreshing, it doesn't lead to productive commentary on his part.

"Doesn't sound like the beginning of an apology. I'm guessing that's not why you're here, then. If it's to explain yourself, I'm not interested."

The impulse to squabble is strong. I have to take a deep breath and remind myself what I'm here for. "Actually, it's a courtesy call. I have some news that I thought you deserved to hear directly from me."

It's the one real regret I have about Riah where he's concerned. We knew he'd have feelings about it. We should have been upfront. I figure the adult thing is to grow from that mistake and not repeat it.

He looks confounded. As though he can't for the life of him imagine why I would think he would want to hear anything I have to say, but since it isn't worth it to him to waste the energy on explaining that he simply gives a disinterested, "Go for it."

I expected his ambivalence and don't let it deter me. "Holt and Adly are attempting a buyout of SHE network. They invited me to be part of it, and I said yes."

"Mm." His features harden. "You're investing in one of SNC's rival companies. With a man who despises me."

"I honestly don't think Holt cares enough about you to say that he despises you." That's a low blow. Hunter treats the animosity between them like a trophy. It doesn't have any value if it's one-sided.

That might be half the impetus behind his next statement alone. "Sticking the knife right in my chest this time. That *is* courteous."

"Don't pretend like you haven't done your share of backstabbing."

"When I'm CEO of SNC, first thing I'm doing is putting you out of business." He's so sure of himself. So entitled. He doesn't even seem angry, just matter of fact.

"Go ahead." I've learned my lesson. Hunter will fuck

over every deal that doesn't suit him, so this time we got insurance. "I wouldn't advise it, though. Grandpa's given us his full support, and you know going against that is akin to double-crossing the godfather."

He'd be a fool to go against anything Grandpa Irving has blessed, and Hunter knows it. Grandpa has always welcomed healthy rivalry between businesses, and if his grandkids are on both sides, all the better.

His jaw flexes, and his cheek quivers below his eye. I've finally hit a nerve, which was more of a prediction than a goal.

He uncrosses his leg and leans forward, forearms braced on his desk. "What is it, Alex, if it's not the girl? You still pissed about me swooping in on your investment? Is it jealousy? Tired of being in my shadow?"

"Probably a bit of all of that. Nothing that couldn't be forgiven if you were just a decent human being. If you'd just treated me like your brother instead of your personal assistant. That would have gone a long way."

"You're such an ungrateful little fuckface, aren't you? Do you have any idea what I...?" He shakes his head, too angry to finish his sentence. "You have no clue. No goddamn clue."

It's rare to see Hunter truly pissed, and I'll be honest, I struggle not to flinch. His self-important attitude is typical, but I actually have no idea what he thinks I don't understand.

For better or worse, he gathers himself enough to explain it to me. "When we were young, you know what Dad would do if I didn't come home with the best grades in the school? It didn't matter if they were straight A's. If I wasn't first in class, he'd bring me into his study, fill a glass with water, and make me balance it on my head while he lectured me about *our legacy*. Made sure I understood that it was all on me because if I didn't rise up to the top, if I didn't make him proud, he was leaving everything to charity. All of it. Yours and Reid's inheritance as well. That's gone if *I* don't succeed.

"He'd go on and on. Seemed like hours, sometimes. In detail about all the ways I'd already let him down. Tell me how I was the reason my mother killed herself. My failures. If I'd only done better…

"And if the glass was still on my head when he was done, then that was that, but if it had fallen—and more often than not, it had because that's a long time for a kid to stand up straight, especially when he's shaking in his shoes —then he made me clean up the mess *with my tongue*."

My stomach is in a knot. I've never heard any of this before. "Hunter, I—"

But he isn't interested in my feelings. "The worst was when the glass would break. Trying to navigate the shards of glass. Is that what you're jealous of, Alex? You wish that was you instead? Rather have that than the shadow?

"So yeah, I took your fucking investment because that helped *me*, and the only way I help you is by winning. *Me.* So don't fucking talk to me about how you've been treated. You play the role you're assigned, just like I do. Just like all of us do."

It's a too-long held secret, meant to explain a lifetime of bad behavior. Too big to process in the span of just a few minutes. Too ugly to look at without the impulse to turn away.

It's hard to find words. There isn't anything sufficient, and I'm horrified and ashamed that this went on in my house, and I didn't have any clue. It tears me up that he didn't think he could talk to me about it. "I wish you'd told me about that a lot sooner than now."

He lets out a cruel laugh. "Because you feeling sorry for me helps…how?"

"I don't feel…" I mean, I do feel sorry for him, but not any more than I did before this reveal.

I move from where I'm sitting to the chair directly in front of his desk. "Dad did a number on all of us, Hunter. I'm not going to say that your shit is as bad as mine or worse —I don't know if pain is something people can compare. But we probably could have survived it a whole lot better if we'd leaned on each other. Dad knows that. He made *sure* we kept our shit to ourselves because together, he might have had less power over us. He won a lot of rounds before we were even mature enough to know we were playing. *He* was head of the class when it comes to terrible. There wasn't any choice but to survive the best way we knew how."

"Great speech. I'm fucking moved."

His monotone only incites my fervor, and I lean forward. "See, the thing is, though, Hunter, you're almost forty years old. If you're still drinking the poison now, that's on you. Look at Holt—he got out. And Reid got out. Adly and me? We're getting out too, and if you want to stay here and chase after what Dad thinks you're entitled to, then you're on your own. I can't feel sorry for someone who has the freedom to make different choices but won't."

It's harsh, and I mean it.

At the same time, I recognize this is as close to vulnerable as my brother gets.

And I might not have another chance to give him credit where it's due. "Thank you, though. For trying to protect us when we were kids. I'm sorry there wasn't someone around to protect you, too."

He studies me, his jaw twitching now and again.

His chest expands as he takes in a deep breath and releases it, then he leans back slightly. Not relaxed or resigned, but like a temporary halt. He glances toward one of his bookshelves, where a rare picture of the three of us brothers sits in a frame. "Think this next kid's going to make him worse or better?"

"I'm too scared to wonder about it." I think so rarely about our stepmother's pregnancy that it always surprises me when the subject comes up. I'm sure I'm blocking it out on purpose. Reynard Sebastian bringing another child into the world? There must be a hell, and that child is about to live it. "And Nalini? How long will he let her stick around?"

"Maybe they'll have a girl, and everything will be different."

"Do you think that rumor's true that she was pregnant before, and he made her get rid of it when they discovered it was a girl?"

"I hadn't heard that one. Who told you that?"

"Reid. Who heard it from Adly."

He considers, and for a minute it's like the old days. Like the lunches at Reid's club, shooting the shit about our fucked-up family.

Then he laughs. "We're going to fucking dance on his grave, aren't we?"

"If we're still capable of dancing. Our luck, he'll inherit Grandpa's long-life gene."

"Fuck. That's..." He shakes his head. It's too awful to think about. Too long of a prison sentence to endure in any way other than one day at a time.

With that dreadful thought let loose in the world, the mood once again shifts. The pause is over.

"Zyah's tour started today," he says, his voice once again hard. "I heard what you did. Are you going to—?" He changes his mind mid-sentence. "Actually, I don't want to know."

For the best, since the last thing I want to talk about with him is Riah.

Besides, I've delivered my message. I don't have any reason to be here anymore, and I stand. "I do need to get going, though. I'm hoping to catch her show."

I *will* catch her show. It'll take a miracle to make it there before she takes the stage, but I'll catch most of it if it kills me.

Hunter stands as well. Then he offers his hand to shake, like we've just completed a business transaction, and I suppose in a way we have, so I accept the offer.

"Thank you, Alex, for coming by and telling me about SHE. That took balls." Then he drops my hand. "And now I never want to see you anywhere near my apartment again."

It's the knife to the chest that he'd accused me of. I can't lie and say it doesn't smart like a motherfucker, but I didn't suppose this talk would change anything. I've chosen my side—which, from his point of view, is against him—and there's no convincing him otherwise.

"I can do that," I say. "I'll let myself out."

I had crying shamed out of me before I was eight years old. I remember sobbing once in secret after my mother left, hiding in a storage cubby under the back stairs of our country home. Never have I shed a tear since then.

But on the elevator ride down from his apartment, I think about the brother who comforted me in the years that followed. Who let me tag alone and shared his friends and gave me free rein of his property and possessions. I think about how I wasn't given the chance to be there for him and how it's too late to ever fix that, and this full-grown man cries.

When I reach the lobby, I wipe my eyes, and then I step out of the shadow into the sun.

CHAPTER
THIRTY-ONE
RIAH

I run off the stage, drenched with sweat, my veins coursing with adrenaline as the crowd cheers behind me.

God, I feel incredible.

Like I could lift a car or reach the moon or never want for anything else ever again.

That's the magic of a solid performance, and opening night was just that. All the energy it takes is given back tenfold from an engaged audience, and even though I will eventually crash from this high, at this moment I'm invincible.

Nothing can bring me down.

Not Topaz's continued disregard of my strong sales.

Not the interviewers who want to only talk about my relationship with the Sebastian brothers instead of my music.

Not the empty space in my heart that Alex has left with his vanishing act.

Well, okay. That last one still hurts like a bitch, but other than that, I'm fucking on top of the moon as I fly into Whitney's waiting arms.

She hugs me tight, despite my sweaty physical state, and smothers me with praise. "You were ah-mazing! Who are you, even? I can't believe we're related. That was insane!"

There's no time to linger in her out-of-the-ordinary affection because Claude's here as well, and Stew, who rarely shows up for the first night of a tour but came out to Boston to see mine, and Jake Dunham, who flew in to perform on one of the numbers with me.

Plus, there are crew members and venue managers and team assistants and local photographers and high-profile media personalities. Someone's removing my mic pack. Someone else is helping me with my headset. Everyone wants my attention, and that's more than cool, but I'm painfully aware of my need of a shower.

Claude's a pro at his job, though, and he tugs me along toward the dressing room so that I don't have to make my own awkward withdrawal from the throng of people who want to snap pictures and shower me with congratulations and complimentary commentary.

Despite Claude directing most of them to wait for me in the green room, a good deal of them follow after us. I'm the pied piper with an entourage of rats parading down the hall until we reach the security guard stationed midway down the hall.

"Only first-level security beyond this point," Claude

instructs. "She'll be out in thirty minutes or so."

Claude flashes my badge—yes, even I have to have one —and I pass the guard then stop in my tracks because Alex Sebastian is waiting in front of my dressing room.

His smile is unsure, but his eyes are steady. "Saw the show. You were magnificent, baby."

Admittedly, my heart flutters.

Thank God no one can see inside me because that is not a reaction I would like to share with anyone.

On the heels of that, however, is the reaction he deserves. "Oh, hell no." Being so energized means all my emotions are magnified, and Alex showing up after weeks of silence—wearing a tailored gray three-piece suit with a black dress shirt and no tie, scruffy-faced and looking better than any asshole deserves to look—brings me instantly to peak rage. "No, no, no, no, no."

"Careful, now," Claude warns me.

There's still a pack of people on the other side of the checkpoint. They can't exactly see beyond the guard, but they can hear, which means I should cool my shit unless I want the social media blasts tonight to once again skip over my music to focus on my men.

But I am who I am, and I'm already stomping toward the fucker.

"How dare you?" For the second time since I've known Alex, I slap him across the face. "How dare you turn up tonight, of all nights. This is *my* night!"

Then—because I'm hopelessly mad about the man and can't help wanting what I want—I grab him by the lapels and pull him in for a kiss.

The nasty kind.

The brutal kind.

He reciprocates in kind, and I love it and hate it all at once. Mostly hate that I love it.

When his arm snakes around my waist, I jerk away. He does not get to claim me. No goddamn way.

I kind of want to slap him again for trying, but I think the last one hurt my hand as much as it hurt him, so instead I grasp his jaw and squeeze. "You have some fucking nerve. I don't want you here. You hear me? You need to go."

He tries to say something, but I clutch his jaw tighter. "Don't. Whatever you have to say, it doesn't matter."

There's a murmuring of spectators wondering what's going on as I push past Alex into my dressing room, letting the door shut behind me, and when he doesn't immediately follow, I open it back up. "Are you fucking coming in here or what?"

Claude and Whitney, the only members of my entourage who had clearance past the guard, exchange a look.

"I think she has this," Claude says.

Whit shrugs, which must mean she agrees enough not to worry about it because she goes with him when he turns and walks away.

I make a mental note to ream them both for deserting me in my time of need while simultaneously feeling very validated that I do actually have this.

Alex, meanwhile, looks both frightened and self-satisfied as he brushes by me and enters my dressing room, massaging his slapped cheek with his palm.

"Oh, don't you dare look smug." I follow after him and

prop my hand on the wall while I bend to unzip my thigh–high black vinyl boots. "I knew you had balls. Why wouldn't you? You Sebastians get everything you want, don't you? Every time. No reason to ever have to feel contrite or regretful, or heaven forbid, give an apology because you can just do whatever you want with no care to consequences."

"To the contrary, I have a lot of regrets, and I'm—"

"Did I say I was finished speaking?" I've lost my height advantage with my boots off, but I refuse to let that weaken my wrath.

Because this wrath is valid.

This wrath is deserved.

This wrath multiplies irrationally when he gestures in surrender and says, "By all means, go ahead."

"Thank you for assuming I need permission to speak in my own goddamn dressing room." I twist back and forth as I talk—yell, rather—trying to reach the zipper on the back of my dress. It's a black asymmetrical mini skirt with cut outs at the waist and a sparkly strap that wraps around my neck and waist, making it more complicated to get out of than I'd like. "Can you fucking help me?"

"My pleasure."

He's too grateful to just unzip me, which is frustrating for all sorts of reasons, and when his fingers graze my bare skin, my knees buckle, and I start to lean into him before remembering I hate him.

"Don't touch me! Did I say you could fucking touch me?" I jolt away from him and let the dress shimmy to the floor.

"An accident; I promise." He does a fairly good job of

keeping his attention on my eyes rather than my now bare breasts, his gaze only flickering down a couple of times.

Honestly, I'm here for it. All that training I've been doing has put me in the best physical shape of my life, and Alex Sebastian can stare all he wants as long as he's eating his fucking heart out at the same time.

"An accident. Sure." Next, I wrestle with the fishnets which are layered on top of two other pairs of tights. The secret is to take them off one by one, but I'm pissy and impatient, so I stupidly try to wriggle out of all of them at once while I deliver the next volume of my rant. "I don't even know where you've been. Who those hands have touched. Whose bed you've been in—or who's been in yours—and there you go, *accidentally* brushing my skin like I'm okay with getting cooties. Oh my God, you're so... so...so..."

It's hard to concentrate on insults while performing the most angry/awkward strip routine of all time.

"I was in Los Angeles." Alex leans a shoulder against the doorframe to the bathroom and watches me struggle. "And the answer is no one. Touched absolutely no one. Shared my bed with no one. Completely devoted to you. Do you need some more help?"

I pause my battle to point a finger at him. "Don't you even dare. I do not need your help." It's less impactful than I'd like because just then I manage to pull the tangle of tights off one foot with such force that I stumble forward.

Before he can catch me—which to his credit, he tries to do—I put my hand out to stop him. "I said, don't!"

"Okay. Got it." He folds his arms across his chest, and I

have a feeling the gesture is akin to sitting on his hands, so he won't be tempted to come to my rescue.

With one foot free, the other is much easier to remove, and I stand up tall and proud, as though I haven't just made a fool of myself and am not now completely naked. "Excuse me, I need to get into my bathroom, and you're in the way."

He takes one small step to the side, so I still have to brush against him when I walk in. Or maybe I don't *have to*, but I pretend like I do with a "hmmph."

Inside the bathroom, I reach into the shower to turn on the water and adjust the temperature. "Completely devoted to me, my ass," I mutter. "So devoted you disappeared when we were supposed to talk."

"I didn't disappear, exactly. I left a text." His tone says he recognizes the argument's weak. "Anyway, it's true. I *am* devoted to you."

I spin to find he's returned to his entirely too sexy lean-in-the-doorframe pose, facing into the bathroom now instead of out.

"Wasn't talking to you, you asshole." I throw him my best scowl. "Why are you even here?"

"I…well, I'm here in Boston to see you. And your show. To talk to you, mostly. And I'm in your bathroom because that's where you are."

"Talk? *Now?* On the opening night of my tour? Only a month late. And you've barely said anything since you got here."

"Not like you've given me a chance."

"Sure. Blame it on me." I step into the stall and under

the shower head, wincing when the water is hotter than I'd expected.

"I'm not blaming anything on you. I was explaining."

I stick my head out and find he's moved from the doorway to lean against the vanity. "While you're explaining, how about you explain why you thought I'd want to hear anything you had to say after you blew me off—again —with a motherfucking text?"

I draw back into the shower to squirt shampoo into my palm, but also because my emotions are becoming tangled, and if I don't actively stay angry, I might end up crying.

"Okay, in fairness. I might not have gone about that the right way. Leaving like that."

"You think?" When I stick my head out of the shower this time, he has the audacity to look remorseful, and that almost makes me madder than when he looked smug.

So I point the showerhead at him, spraying him good in the face.

That makes me feel pretty fandamntastic. Momentarily, anyway.

"All right. I deserve that. I deserve worse. But I really do have things to say."

"I can't hear you in here." It's a lie. I heard him just fine.

Just my stomach is knotted, and I'm starting to fear that he won't have a good reason for his absence—what good reason could he possibly have?—and that I'll still take him back.

Or worse, that in the name of being true to what I deserve, I'll kick him to the curb, and I'll be miserable and alone and missing him for the rest of my life, and damnit. It's so much easier just being mad. "Said *I love you* in a fucking text. Like it was just no big deal. Who the fuck does that?"

All of a sudden, Alex is inside the shower with me, fully clothed, pushing me against the back wall until I'm trapped beneath him. "*I* do. I *did*. I did because I fucking love you, Mariah Watson, and it is the *biggest* deal. It's such a big deal that I wanted to lasso the stars and give them to you so that you wouldn't get stuck in anyone else's orbit ever again."

I open my mouth, but nothing comes out, so I promptly shut it again.

"Now." His gaze trails down my body. "I promised a conversation, not a fuck, and it's really hard to remember that when you're naked and wet and toned like a rock star. So finish your shower and come to me with clothes on, and we'll talk." His lip curls into a smirk. "And then I'll fuck you."

"That's awfully optimistic." It comes out weak. Not surprising since I'm literally only still standing because he has me pressed against the wall.

"Well. Like you said, we Sebastians have balls."

He glances at my mouth. Traces his thumb against my bottom lip, but doesn't kiss me, which is probably a good thing or else I'm pretty sure we'd end up fucking first, and after this speech, I really, really, really want him to prove he deserves me.

When he lingers, I pretend to be the strong one. "Would you get the fuck out of here already?"

"I'm going."

Once he's left me in the shower, I can breathe.

And cry, but just a little, and it mixes with the water, so it doesn't really count.

His disappearance—I'll never call it anything different—has given me a lot of time to doubt. Was there anything even real between us or were we just two people saddled with the same thorn in our side by the name of Hunter?

For me, it was definitely real.

I was stuck and Alex got me unstuck, and maybe that was his only purpose in my life, and I should move on now, but I don't want to. My life is bigger when he's in it, and not because he has money or connections or even because he gives good orgasms, but because he lets me be who I really am. He doesn't worry whether I'll outshine him or eclipse him. He lets me be me, and he still fits at my side.

That's hard to find. Especially for a woman who wants to do big things with her life.

But what was I for Alex?

I thought he realized that I see him, too. He gives to and supports the people who he loves, and I thought he recognized me as the lone person in his life who wouldn't take advantage of that.

Then he disappeared, and I thought he must not have realized that after all. Maybe I was always just a vehicle for his resentment toward his brother, and once I couldn't play that part anymore, his fierce attraction was gone.

So what does it mean that he's here now? Will I take whatever he has to offer, even if it's not the everything I deserve?

I've done that before. I guess it worked.

But I'm not the same person I was when I met the Sebastian brothers, and I can't settle for the same kinds of arrangements now. In the beginning, I didn't think I was good enough for the world Hunter propelled me into. I wasted a lot of time making myself smaller, so I'd fit into it. Now I see that it's a world I don't even want to be part of.

I want to make my own world.

I would love for Alex to make that world with me, but he can't straddle that and the Sebastian world, playing by their misogynistic rules and trusting no one while trying to live in ours. Nothing meaningful can be built with scraps. If he wants to make that world with me, he has to give me everything.

And realistically, that's probably too much to expect from most people, let alone a Sebastian.

By the time I turn the water off, my anger has faded, but my high has too. I towel off and don one of the robes left for me, a fluffy white one rather than the silk which makes me feel like I'm being hugged.

When I come out of the bathroom, Alex is in nothing but black boxer briefs, and my resolve wanes. I'm not the only one who's been hitting the gym a lot recently.

If I have to be dressed, shouldn't he? Why, oh why did he have to soak his suit in the shower?

My fault for spraying him in the first place.

After I get over the pornographic display of tight ass, I realize that he's bent over an open suitcase. It's such a banal sight. So out of the billionaire typical lifestyle. It's Louis Vuitton, at least. He hasn't completely shattered my image of him.

But doesn't he usually have people to port his luggage for him? What is he doing with it here? And it's not just an overnight bag. "That's um, a rather large suitcase."

He glances over his shoulder at me as he pulls out a pair of dark slacks. "I'm hoping you'll let me stick around."

"For how long?"

"The whole tour?"

His hope pokes at me, looking for an opening that I want too badly to give.

But no.

No.

"Alex…" It's harder to be strong than it should be.

He drops the slacks on the couch and turns his back to me to grab something else.

Without him looking at me, it's easier. "I don't know if —" I'm interrupted by a thick manila envelope flying in my direction. "What's this?"

"Open it up."

I'm curious, but more than that I'm grateful for a reason to procrastinate the hard words that have to transpire between us. The envelope isn't sealed or labeled, signaling it's just a mode of transportation.

Inside, I find two separate bunches of papers held together with paperclips. I scan the documents. They're confusing. Contracts and legalese. Topaz's parent company is listed and Alex's name, but the rest is over my head. "I don't know what I'm looking at."

But then I spot a bullet-itemed section that lists out **Zyah Untitled album 1** and **Zyah Untitled album 2** as well as the album I just released, **Transactional**.

"I wanted to buy the whole imprint," Alex explains, which doesn't really explain anything. "Figured you'd be more comfortable if I wasn't just purchasing your music, but they laughed in my face. I didn't have enough collateral for that, even if they wanted to sell. So I had to settle for just your albums."

My head flicks to look at him, searching for an indication that he's joking.

There isn't any.

He's more timid than I've ever seen him, though. He brings a hand up to rub the back of his neck, nervously. "I couldn't get all of them—sorry about that. For a company that doesn't want to back you, they recognize your earning potential. I mean, I think they're under the impression that they overpriced, but I actually think I got them for a bargain."

"What…so *you* own my music?"

"No. No. *You* own your music." He clears his throat. "Or you will when you sign."

I look back at the papers. It's definitely his name on the first contract, but when I flip to the second stack of documents, I see it's a yet-to-be signed contract between Alex Sebastian and Mariah Watson.

My stomach does a weird thing where it feels like it's both light and dropping at the same time. This is…fuck. It's too much. The dollar amounts noted don't take up all of his trust fund, but it's a decent portion.

It might as well be all of it.

"Oh, Alex. I can't accept this."

"It's not a gift," he says quickly. "Think of me as a bank. A bank who's giving you an unbeatable interest rate of zero percent."

I narrow my eyes. That's akin to losing money, and that feels too much like being bought.

"An interest rate of one percent, then, if that makes you feel better." He waves a hand dismissively. "We can work out the details later. Small businesses get money loaned to them all the time and the CEO gets to own whatever they create. Essentially, you're a small business, and I believe in your product, and I think you should own what you create too.

"But don't worry—I know it's not helpful if you don't have distribution, so Topaz is still handling that. Basically, you're now your own imprint. You get to manage your music however you like. You get a bigger piece of the pie, and you still have a big, established company backing you. For the next two albums, anyway. After that, you can go somewhere else if you want."

My hands are shaking, and I have to sit down on the sofa arm. "I don't understand."

That's not what I mean, exactly. Part of it, I understand very clearly—Alex Sebastian just gave me everything.

What I don't understand is, why?

Alex gets what I'm asking. "I finally recognized how little power you have with your music, and how being with Hunter helped you, and I wanted you to...." He lets out a breath. "I want you to want me, but I don't want you to want me for your career. So I thought if I removed the reason for needing help..."

His head tilts, and his expression falls. "You know, I really thought I was doing this as some big noble thing for you, but now that I hear myself try to explain it...I think I'm selfish. Insecure, definitely. I just...I didn't want you to have to make impossible decisions like my mother. I wanted you to want me for me."

I drop the contracts on the sofa next to me. "But I already wanted you for you, you idiot. I already chose *you*." It might have been confusing because I didn't go with him that day that Hunter proposed. Because of what I said to the press. "If you'd stayed to talk…"

"So I fucked up? So I fucked up." He runs both hands over his face and through his damp hair. "I don't know. I don't know how people do this, Riah. I'm a thirty-six-year-old man, and all I know about love is that it can be bought and sold. All I know about relationships is that public perception is key. I don't know how to earn you. I don't know how to be enough for you."

He rushes to me. Bracing his hands on my hips, he drops his forehead to mine. "Tell me how. Whatever it is. I'll do it. I'll give it. I'll be it. I can't let another person that I love leave because I didn't know how to make her stay. Tell me, Riah. Tell me what to do. I can't lose you too."

"Hey, hey, hey." I brush a tear from my cheek before bringing my hands to cradle Alex's face, tilting it, so I can look him in the eye. "I'm not the one who left."

He shakes his head. "No, you weren't."

"You didn't have to earn me, Alex. You were always enough. *You.* All you have to do is be here with me. In this relationship."

"So buying your music was—"

I cut him off. "No. That was amazing. No one has ever done anything like that for me, and I am *so* grateful. So grateful that words don't do justice. It changes everything for me, and I'm…I'm…" I have to swallow past the lump of emotion in my throat. "But I would have loved you anyway, you fool. I love you anyway."

He searches my eyes then pushes a wet strand of hair off my face before pressing his lips to mine. He holds them there for a beat, as though clutching onto me with his kiss.

"Will you have me then? Can I be here with you? On the tour and in a relationship?"

I start to say yes and then close my mouth again. I want him. Of course, I do. But I respect myself too much to let him walk back into my life without conditions. "Being here with me means we shut the world out, Alex. It doesn't matter what the public knows or thinks. We trust what's between us. If I tell you I'm yours, then I'm yours."

He closes his eyes then opens them again. "I understand that now. So...*are* you mine?"

"Yes, you fool." I kiss him. "Yes, yes. I'm so very much yours, Alex, that it feels like I'm not whole when you're not around."

"I know that feeling." He kisses me again, longer this time. "I'm sorry for leaving, Riah. I was miserable without you. And I'm sorry for...Hunter. For letting him get between us. I'm sorry—"

I cut him off with another kiss. "Just...never again."

"Never again. I love you. I love you so much."

This time, kissing turns to groping. My hand finds the outline of his cock in his briefs. His hand slips under my robe to find my breast. We're quickly headed toward that fuck he promised me when there's a knock on the door.

We pull away just enough to be decent when my sister comes charging in.

"Oh my God, Whitney." I'm laughing when I say it though.

"Hey, at least I remembered to knock." She winks. "Just wanted to remind you there are people waiting for you. Nice to see you back, Alex."

She goes as quickly as she came, leaving us panting and blue-balled.

"They're here for me," I say, trying to make excuses. "They have to wait, don't they?"

But Alex has already stepped away like a good boy. "We should be responsible. Give them the star they came for. That's what tonight's about. The music, remember?"

He's exactly what I need. A man who puts my career first.

A man who puts *me* first.

"Okay," I groan. "But after this meet and greet, we have reservations for a late late dinner. Maybe in the limo, it could be just you and me, and you let me ride you like I'm your whore?"

The grin he gives me nestles deep into my chest like a secret language only we share. It's more than that, too. A promise of not only a night to come, but of a life to come as well.

"You know, Riah Watson. I think that can be arranged."

EPILOGUE
ALEX

Nine months later

Her back to my chest, Riah bounces her pussy up and down my cock like an athlete. After performing almost nightly on an eight-month tour that included both US and international legs, my woman can hover in a squat like nobody's business, and I'm the luckiest man on earth to be able to receive the benefits.

The *Transactional* tour was by all accounts a success. Owning her own music didn't solve all of Riah's problems, of course. She was still responsible for providing her own marketing. Since brand management wasn't filling all my time, and since I was traveling with the tour anyway, I took it upon myself to arrange additional promotion and sponsorships in each city we stopped in. The Sebastian name goes a long way, even now that I'm not working for the family empire, and we were able to raise enough money to make up for the ad spend she'd lost.

Most of it was due to how firmly Zyah's latest album has resonated with listeners. The music stands for itself, without paid promotion, and the show she put on was hailed one of the best tours of last year.

For my part, I consider the zenith of my genius to be arranging for easy-open snap crotch panels to be added to all of Riah's bodysuits. Of course, that never fixed the issue of layered tights, which more than once were destroyed by overeagerness and a pair of scissors. The sparkling Elie Saab romper that she's wearing right now for tonight's Grammy Awards has a snap panel as well, and she's completely bare-legged.

I assured her wardrobe coordinator it was for ease in bathroom visits, but I wouldn't be surprised to find there's a tabloid post circling around somewhere blaming the outfit requirement on "Zyah's insatiable sex drive."

For once, the media wouldn't have it wrong.

In general, we don't pay attention to what's reported about Zyah these days, unless it comes from a mainstream reputable source, and only then if it's spouting something that needs to be addressed. Sure, the public will scrutinize and speculate and judge no matter what, and that was hard for us to grapple with in the beginning, both of us for different reasons. She was sensitive when derogatory commentary would extend to how she raised her sister, and I would become a possessive alpha primate whenever it was suggested she was dating someone new—which is literally every time she's seen in public with a member of the opposite sex and sometimes the same sex, too.

But we worked through it by being there together. By talking through it. By lots of fucking—for reassurance and for fun. We even make a game of it these days, enjoying how little the world knows about her real love life. Neither she nor her team have made any comments about it since she declared she was dating both me and Hunter, and we've been careful not to be seen alone together. It means no one really knows about us, which has made sex kinky as shit, but it has also helped us build a relationship without the interference of outsiders.

As she says herself, Zyah is only one part of Mariah Watson, and the rest isn't anyone's business. Including and especially how much my little slut loves to be used.

"Squeeze me, good, baby," I tell her now, settling my hands on her hips, so I can control her tempo. We're getting close to the drop-off spot, which means we're moving at a snail's pace, and there are already fans lined up on the sidewalks, trying to see into the windows of the dark-tinted limos and SUVs.

It also means we need to speed this up unless Riah wants to spend the whole night aroused and on edge.

She's already nervous enough about being nominated, and so I'm pushing for her to release. "Put your hand down there and pet your sweet little clit, Riah. I need you to get my dick good and wet with your cum."

She lets out a whimper. "I'm trying."

"That's not good enough." I lean back, adjusting my pelvis, so I hit deeper. Then I peer out the window, deciding it's time for a little verbal stimulation. "See all those people out there, wishing they could see in?"

"Yes."

"They're a bunch of wannabe starfuckers who would give their left tit to be riding someone's cock on the way to perform at the Grammys. You're living out the celebrity-lifestyle dream, and you can't do your part and cover me with your cum?"

"I...I... Oh, God, Alex."

She's close now. Her thighs are creeping closer together, her pussy's getting tighter. Her braless tits are bouncing like a girl on a trampoline, and fuck, if she doesn't hurry up, I'm going to be the one exploding.

I move my hands from her hips to her ass, lifting up the material of her romper, so I can watch my cock disappear over and over again into her hot little cunt. The puckered star of her asshole teases me with its accessibility. I want to lift her ass to my face and fuck that hole with my tongue, but I remember our timeline and don't let myself get distracted.

Instead, I lick my thumb and push it inside her to the knuckle.

That does the trick, and her orgasm rips through her so forcefully that she screams. Loud enough that heads outside the car turn in our direction. It gives me immense satisfaction to know they can't do more than wonder.

With Riah taken care of, I could easily pound out my own release, but I'm enjoying the job of dirtying her up.

I remove my thumb and slap her hard across her ass. "On your knees. I want to watch your eyes water while you suck me off."

She scrambles to the floor of the limo and positions herself between my thighs. It's one of my favorite nasty things—shoving my cock in her mouth when it's dripping with her pussy juice. She's such a dirty girl the way she takes me, too. Playing with my balls and deep-throating, her eyes tearing up from gagging.

"Fuck, you're a goddess." It's true and such a juxtaposition. She should be worshiped—and she is, both by her fans and by me—yet right now she's on her knees in front of me, choking on my cock like a grade-A whore. "Should I coat your throat with my cum or do you want it somewhere else?"

She's obviously not capable of talking at the moment, but she takes a hand and brings it to her throat.

God, I love her kinkery. "Is that why you decided not to wear a choker? Because you wanted to walk in with a pearl necklace instead?"

She smiles around my cock.

Happy to comply, I pull my cock from her throat and fuck my hand to finish, spilling my cum along her delicate collarbone, careful not to drip any on my tux.

After, I grab my phone from my pocket and take a pic. She's both trashed and still red-carpet ready, and I'm definitely saving this photo in my favorites.

Then I tuck my phone away and tug her up so that I can lick my cum off her skin before kissing her. Thank God for the kiss-proof makeup or it would have already been left in a ring around my dick.

"You could have left me decorated," she says when she's cleaned up and back in the passenger seat at my side. She has her own phone in hand, using the camera to check her appearance. "My brand manager would say it fits my image."

"I didn't think they needed to know *everything* about us."

It's an appropriate response only because we're about to have Our Official Reveal. In just a few minutes, we will walk the red carpet together for the first time. The media will jump on this moment. We will be called out as a couple. Fans will start referring to us as Zylex. Every interviewer will ask Riah, "How are things going with Alex?" instead of, "Is there anyone special?"

It's a big night for her already, but this officially makes it a big moment for *us* as well.

We've talked about this at length. I've wanted to claim her as mine since that day she said she loved me. Before that, even, if I'm honest. But when she agreed to be a *we* with me that first night of her tour, I promised myself that would be enough. No other validation was necessary. *No one's business but ours.*

Surprisingly, making it official was her idea.

She suggested it the night she learned she had several Grammy nominations (for both the *Transactional* album and her single, "Speak"), when we were in Paris for the international leg of her tour. It seemed like a good timeline. Nine months together, mostly in secret, would give us a good foundation before inviting others into our relationship.

We presented it to the team, as is typical in high-profile relationships. This I'm already familiar with, having grown up in the limelight. There was worry about our coming out upstaging her night, career-wise, but as Riah pointed out, the Grammys are after the fact. The sales have already happened. The music has already been recognized.

I'm all for it. Hell, if she even hinted at marriage, I'd get down on my knee and present her with a ring on the red carpet if I hadn't already learned the hard way that public proposals are not cool at all. I might have vowed that acknowledgment wasn't important, but I'm still egotistical as fuck. You can't change a tiger's stripes.

It seems like a good next step for us, too. We've spent most of our time together on the road, and haven't had the opportunity for many real dates, but now we're home and entering a new era. It will be hard to hide that we're together. Whitney already has a roommate situation lined up with friends she met at the art gallery she works at, so Riah is moving in with me in the next couple of weeks. The paps are going to catch us eventually.

We'll be settled here for a while, I think. Riah is starting work on her new album. This time she's recording in New York, again with Jake Dunham. Meanwhile, I'll be putting more face-to-face time into the SHE project, which will be easier now that we're in town.

I've never been close to Adly or Holt, but working with them, even long distance, has been a healing experience. I haven't talked to Hunter since that day in his apartment, though I've seen him at a few family affairs. As fucked up as my family is, I'm used to having them around, and Adly and Holt are the best replacements for what I've lost since they're actually family as well.

On every front, a new era.

I'm nervous about what these changes might mean for me and Riah, naturally. I think that's part of the reason why she's letting me decide what to say to interviewers tonight when they ask about us. She's planning on sticking to her customary "no comment" line when anyone asks about anything other than her music, which I stand behind fully. It's not only a smart way to keep the public focus where it should be, but it also keeps a bit of mystery surrounding the Zyah brand.

Alex Sebastian, on the other hand, is not mysterious. Being the less ambitious middle child, the media hasn't been as interested in me as my older brother, and I haven't had as many opportunities with a mic thrust in my face, but when I have, I've always been straightforward and off-the-cuff. I haven't planned a single word, but chances are when I'm asked about Riah tonight, I'm going to be fucking demonstrative.

"I hope you know what you set yourself up for," I tell her as we pull up to the curb.

"Possessive hovering alpha? Oh, I know."

Seems like we have that clear.

A few minutes later, we climb out of the car and enter a free-for-all clusterfuck. I've been to several events like this over my lifetime, but this is the first time at the Grammys for both of us. There's a security line and a maze made of partitions leading to the press arena and stands where fans have purchased tickets to watch stars walk the carpet. Non-ticketed fans are gathered here as well, held back by guardrails and men in black suits who are so fancy they could be mistaken for ticketholders except that they have walkie-talkies on their belts.

Nikki Minaj was just in the car ahead of us and Hozier in the car behind, so there's a lot of attention elsewhere, but when Zyah turns toward the fans, a decent number of them call out her name.

She gives them her realest smile, and she reaches for my hand.

Even when she's shining for them, she's still here with me.

It hits me hard, how this incredible person means so much to so many people. In every way, she's a star. She genuinely lights their worlds with what she creates. Her songs bring people to tears. People live to her music—they dance, they party, they relax, they fuck. She's played on radios and in the background in restaurants and bars and elevators and the dentist's office. Every day when she goes to work, she becomes a role model and an icon and a soul speaker and a best friend.

Then she comes home to me.

In the past, when I said it was enough to know she loved me, I had to convince myself it was true. And I did because I knew we had no chance if I didn't.

Now, though, it actually is enough.

She's blinding as she shines for her fans, but she's only giving them the smallest part of her. What's real between us happens in secret. Everything else is as put on as the arrangement she once had with my brother.

So when we reach the arena and the first interviewer asks her about our relationship— when she shakes her head and looks to me to answer—I lean into the mic and say, "No comment."

Her hand in mine, we walk on together.

WANT MORE SEBASTIANS?

Meet the Sebastians in a world of power, sex, secrets, and brutal billionaires

Check out the Sebastian family tree at www.laurelinpaige.com/sebastian-family-tree

Man in Charge - Scott Sebastian office romance, boss/employee romance, alpha billionaire, arrogant playboy heir, public spice,

Man for Me - Brett Sebastian billionaire romance, friends to lovers, office romance, he fell first, short read/novella

Brutal Billionaire - Holt Sebastian billionaire romance, imagined love triangle, boss/employee, forbidden, morally grey, alphahole, "good girl"

Dirty Filthy Billionaire - Steele Sebastian billionaire romance, kinky, class differences, "you owe me", short read/novella

Brutal Secret - Reid Sebastian billionaire romance, forbidden, age-gap, curvy girl, forced proximity, first time, awkward heroine, obsessed hero, new adult, no third act breakup

Brutal Arrangement - Alex Sebastian billionaire romance, forbidden, brother's girl, good girl to bad girl, obsessed hero, morally grey, pop star, alphahole, imagined love triangle

Brutal Bargain - Adly Sebastian coming soon

Brutal Bastard - Hunter Sebastian coming soon

ALSO BY LAURELIN PAIGE

WONDERING WHAT TO READ NEXT? I CAN HELP!

Visit www.laurelinpaige.com for content warnings and a more detailed reading order.

Brutal Billionaires

Brutal Billionaire - a standalone (Holt Sebastian)

Dirty Filthy Billionaire - a novella (Steele Sebastian)

Brutal Secret - a standalone (Reid Sebastian)

Brutal Arrangement - a standalone (Alex Sebastian)

The Dirty Universe

Dirty Duet (Donovan Kincaid)

Dirty Filthy Rich Men | Dirty Filthy Rich Love

Kincaid

Dirty Games Duet (Weston King)

Dirty Sexy Player | Dirty Sexy Games

Dirty Sweet Duet (Dylan Locke)

Sweet Liar | Sweet Fate

(Nate Sinclair) Dirty Filthy Fix (a spinoff novella)

Dirty Wild Trilogy (Cade Warren)

Wild Rebel | Wild War | Wild Heart

Men in Charge

Man in Charge

Man for Me (a spinoff novella)

The Fixed Universe

Fixed Series (Hudson & Alayna)

Fixed on You ❘ Found in You ❘ Forever with You ❘ Hudson ❘ Fixed Forever

Found Duet (Gwen & JC) Free Me ❘ Find Me

(Chandler & Genevieve) Chandler (a spinoff novel)

(Norma & Boyd) Falling Under You (a spinoff novella)

(Nate & Trish) Dirty Filthy Fix (a spinoff novella)

Slay Series (Celia & Edward)

Rivalry ❘ Ruin ❘ Revenge ❘ Rising

(Gwen & JC) The Open Door (a spinoff novella)

(Camilla & Hendrix) Slash (a spinoff novella)

First and Last

First Touch ❘ Last Kiss

Hollywood Standalones

One More Time

Close

Sex Symbol

Star Struck

Dating Season

Spring Fling | Summer Rebound | Fall Hard

Winter Bloom | Spring Fever | Summer Lovin

Also written with Kayti McGee under the name Laurelin McGee

Miss Match | Love Struck | MisTaken | Holiday for Hire

Written with Sierra Simone

Porn Star | Hot Cop

ABOUT LAURELIN PAIGE

With millions of books sold, Laurelin Paige is the NY Times, Wall Street Journal, and USA Today Bestselling Author of the Fixed Trilogy. She's a sucker for a good romance and gets giddy anytime there's kissing, much to the embarrassment of her three daughters. Her husband doesn't seem to complain, however. When she isn't reading or writing sexy stories, she's probably singing, watching shows like Billions and HGTV design competitions or dreaming of Michael Fassbender. She's also a proud member of Mensa International though she doesn't do anything with the organization except use it as material for her bio.

www.laurelinpaige.com
laurelinpaigeauthor@gmail.com

Printed in Great Britain
by Amazon

39345954R10263